John Hands's *Perestroika Christi* is a wonderful thriller and I could not put it down. It is set in the crisscross world of the KGB and the Vatican, with scenes (extraordinarily prescient, it turns out) of Ukrainian nationalism: an elaborately crafted plot leads to a surprise outcome.

—Norman Stone
Guardian Books of the Year

A most impressive political thriller . . . I cannot think of another which is both so accurate and in many ways so prophetic.

—Sir Rodric Braithwaite
British Ambassador in Moscow

Thriller writing is in deep trouble. The collapse of the Cold War leaves one of the main platforms bare. . . . One novelist who has overcome the problem is John Hands, in his first novel. . . . Genuinely scary, exciting, well plotted and nicely written.

—Harriet Waugh
Sunday Telegraph

John Hands's fast moving first novel explores the penultimate battle, fought with dastardly and Machiavellian brio . . . read this clever and vivid book.

—George Bull
Sunday Times

Devilish cunning . . . ambitions which aspire to the level of Brian Moore rather than Morris West.

—Chris Petit
The Times

John Hands weaves an ambitious tale of intrigue. . . . suspense so well built up.

—Michael Dove
Sunday Express

A first novel and a remarkable one. Remarkable for its insight into the behind-the-scenes goings-on in both Russia and the Vatican. Remarkable for the quality of the writing. Remarkable for the creation of a believable set of highly intelligent characters. Remarkable for a plot that is very complex but which is presented cogently and clearly at every stage. . . . a formidable achievement.

—Graham Jones
Wales on Sunday

A sound piece of plotting that captures a whiff of *Gorky Park* but leaves an aftertaste of *The Omen*.

—Peter Millar
The European

John Hands has his finger on the pulse in his gripping first novel *Perestroika Christi*.

—*Today*

A riveting first novel.

—*Publishing News*

Compelling interest as it reaches its awesome climax.

—*Western Telegraph*

A superb novel, which on one level is a thrilling story of intrigue and suspense, and on another a brilliantly researched and startling exposé of the devious machinations going on in the Kremlin and the Vatican . . . the authenticity of the background to this fascinating drama is so real it is often breathtaking.

—*Rochdale Observer*

Ingenious and taut thriller.

—Manchester Evening News

Moves from one intrigue or deception to another, and on to an ingenious and disturbing conclusion.

—The Tablet

One of the joys of reading is that every so often one comes across a novel which begs the reader to absorb concentrated fact amid first rate fiction. *Perestroika Christi* by John Hands is such a novel. . . . riveting thriller.

—Southern Evening Echo

A gripping and amazing novel.

—Western Morning News

Chillingly prophetic thriller.

—Islington Chronicle

One of the best novels of 1990 . . . remarkable as a novel, let alone as predictive fiction . . . a departure from the recent technothriller school of threatened nuclear war, its conflict between Vatican and Kremlin is no less realistic and, scarily, all the more likely.

—London Student

A thriller which keeps you guessing until the end as to whether the title means the reconstruction of Russia by Christ or the reconstruction of Christ by Russia.

—Sesame

PERESTROIKA
— CHRISTI —

John Hands

HarperPaperbacks
A Division of HarperCollinsPublishers

This is a work of fiction. The characters, incidents, and
dialogues are products of the author's imagination and are
not to be construed as real. Any resemblance to actual
events or persons, living or dead, is entirely coincidental.

HarperPaperbacks   *A Division of* HarperCollins*Publishers*
10 East 53rd Street, New York, N.Y. 10022

A paperback edition of this book was published in Great
Britain in 1992 by Grafton, an Imprint of
HarperCollins*Publishers.*

First HarperPaperbacks printing: July 1994

Printed in the United States of America

HarperPaperbacks and colophon are trademarks of
HarperCollins*Publishers*

10 9 8 7 6 5 4 3 2 1

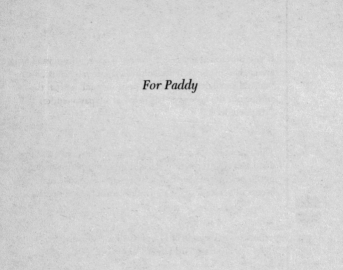

For Paddy

Preface to the Second Edition

After this novel was written in 1989 and first published in 1990, reality took the liberty of copying the book's fictional events in a way that has proved eerie. Reality then continued to follow the plot more faithfully than the last chapter dared. In this second edition, therefore, I have taken the liberty of inserting two real events that invest the last chapter with added authenticity.

I pray that reality does not continue to follow the plot to its conclusion.

John Hands
1 December 1992

Acknowledgments

A large number of people helped with this book. Some contributed wittingly, others were not aware that their knowledge, freely given, would be used for a novel. Some may not be mentioned for their own protection. Of those that may, I wish to thank particularly:

In Moscow: Mykola Muratov and Alexey Mukhin, who took me to places tourists do not go; and Archpriest Alexander Kozha of the Moscow Patriarchate of the Russian Orthodox Church. Books on the Soviet Union by Hedrick Smith, John Barron, and Martin Walker also proved useful.

In the Ukraine: The president, Ivan Hel, and his wife Maria, plus members Stephan Khmara and Father Petro Zeleniuk, of the Committee for the Defense of the Ukrainian Catholic Church, together with the indefatigable Bishop Pavlo Vasylyk (the Ukrainian Catholic Church was then an illegal organization, and three of them had served a total of thirty-seven years in the prison camps); Bohdan Horyn, leader of the Ukrainian Helsinki Union in the Lvov region; and Sergei and Ilona Zabolotny of Kiev.

In Rome: Cardinal Achille Silvestrini, Prefect of the Supreme Tribunal of the Apostolic Signature, former Secretary of the Council for Public Affairs of the Church, and former President of the Pontifical Commission for Russia; Cardinal Joseph Ratzinger, Prefect of the Sacred Congregation for the Doctrine of the Faith; Cardinal Johannes Willebrands, President of the Pontifical Council for Christian Unity; Archbishop Francesco Colasuonno, Apostolic Nuncio "with special charges" in the Secretariat of State; Archbishop Paul Marcinkus, Pro-President of the Pontifical Commission for the Vatican City State and President of the Vatican Bank; Archbishop Jan Schotte, Secretary Gen-

eral of the World Synod of Bishops; Archbishop Jose San-
chez, Secretary of the Sacred Congregation for the Evan-
gelisation of Peoples; Monsignor Peter Coughlan, Under
Secretary of the Pontifical Council for the Laity; Monsignor Brian Chestle of the Secretariat of State; Father Sal-
vatore Scribano, official of the Pontifical Council for
Christian Unity responsible for relationships with the Eastern Churches, plus Father John Long SJ, faculty member
of the Pontifical Oriental Institute and consultor to the
Pontifical Council for Christian Unity, both of whom were
members of the Cardinal Secretary of State's team that visited Moscow in June 1988; Monsignor William Purdy, former official of the Secretariat for Christian Unity; Father
Leonard Boyle OP, Prefect of the Apostolic Library; Father Michael Sharkey, official of the Sacred Congregation
for Catholic Education; Marjorie Weeke, official of the
Pontifical Council for Social Communications; Monsignor
Iwan Dacko, Chancellor of the Archeparchy of Lviv and
Private Secretary to the exiled head of the Ukrainian Byz-
antine Rite Catholic Church; Monsignor Jack Kennedy,
Rector, Monsignor Jeremy Garratt, Vice-Rector, and the
staff and students of the Venerable English College; Fa-
ther Paul Symonds SJ, Under Secretary of the Curia of the
Society of Jesus; Father Gerald O'Collins SJ, Dean of the
Faculty of Theology of the Gregorian University; Father
Giovanni D'Ercole, Vice-Director, and Sister Giovanna, of
the Vatican Press Office; Father Sabino Maffeo SJ, Vice-
Director of the Specola Vaticana at Castel Gandolfo; and
John Broadley CMG, Her Majesty's Ambassador to the
Holy See.

    In Britain: Archbishop Luigi Barbarito, Apostolic Pro-
Nuncio to Great Britain; Father Pat Brown, formerly private secretary to Cardinal Hume; Sister Ann, Mother
Superior of the Canossian Sisters of Charity in Britain; Father Roman Cholij of the Apostolic Exarchate for Ukrainian Catholics in Britain; Father Oliver McTernan and
Peggy Atlee of Pax Christi; Taras Kuzio and Peter Shutak

of the Ukrainian Press Agency; and the Novosti Press Agency. Peter Hebblethwaite and George Bull provided generous help, both personally and through their books on the Vatican.

General Sir John Hackett, Phillip Mitchell of the International Institute for Strategic Studies in London, and David Isky of Virginia, USA, among others, advised on Soviet military deployments. Doctor Iain Dow, Alasdair Dow, Associate Professor of Anaesthesiology at the University of Maryland, USA, and pharmacist John Iles advised on the use of drugs.

Details of the revelations of Fatima were derived from: *Fatima: In Lucia's Own Words* edited by Fr Louis Kondor SVD, Portugal, Postulation Center Fatima, 1976; *Fatima Revealed* by Brother Michael de la Sainte Trinité (translated by Timothy Tindal-Robertson), Devon, Augustine Publishing Company, 1988; and *Fatima: the Great Sign* by Francis Johnston, Devon, Augustine Publishing Company, 1980. Sister Mary Grace of the Ave Maria Institute in New Jersey, USA supplied information on the history of the Kazan Icon of the Mother of God.

Different translations of the Bible have been used to suit particular contexts of the book. Extracts from Mtt 24: 3–5, 10–11, 15; Acts 8: 3; 2 Tim 4: 3–4; Rev 13: 15–17 and 14: 15 were taken from the *Good News Bible* published by the Bible Society and Collins © American Bible Society 1976. Extracts from 2 Thess 2: 3–4 were taken from the *Revised English Bible* © 1989, by permission of the Oxford University Press and the Cambridge University Press. Extracts from Rev 12: 1–3 were taken from the *Holy Bible, the Revised Version*, while Rev 20: 7–8 came from the King James Version.

I'm grateful to Antony Wood, a translator and publisher of Russian literature, for his helpful comments on the manuscript, and I'm especially grateful to Maureen Waller of Simon & Schuster Ltd for her skill, support, and commitment.

Sole responsibility for use of any information supplied and any inaccuracies therein rests with me.

JH
London

PRELUDE

FOR THE FIRST time since he had caused Katie Maguire's death, James Ryan was at peace.

He removed his clerical collar, rolled up the sleeves of his black shirt, and relaxed in the warm sun of this spring afternoon. From his seat on the roof terrace of the Venerable English College, he looked out over Rome's historic quarter. The closely packed jumble of red-tiled Renaissance roofs was broken by the domes of two nearby basilicas, white against the clear blue sky. But Ryan's gaze was drawn by the large dome across the Tiber, which Michelangelo had designed to be seen from every quarter of Rome, the dome of Saint Peter's, tomb of popes and center of Christendom.

Doubts had surfaced when he had begun his studies here for the priesthood. The dozen other first-year seminarians possessed a conviction that he lacked. Was he offering his life to God out of guilt for the recklessness that had killed the woman he adored? Was he choosing a life of celibacy because no other woman could ever take Katie's place? Was the priesthood a way of escaping from bitter despair?

The support of the College community, steeped in the tradition of the English Martyrs, had helped. But most of all, this proximity to the Holy Father, whose rock-like faith was almost tangible, had banished all doubts about submitting himself to the will of God.

"Hanno colpito il Papa!"

The anguished cry came from below.

Stephen Lambton, a postgraduate student, joined Ryan at the iron railing that overlooked the cobbled courtyard four stories beneath them. Sirens wailed from the direction of the Corso Vittorio Emanuele.

"Hanno colpito il Papa!" repeated Nella, the College laundrywoman, before she ran to her apartment on the far side of the courtyard.

"They've shot the Pope," said Lambton. "See if there's any news on television."

Stunned, Ryan could only say, "I think there's a seminar in the television room."

"I'll deal with that. You tell the rector."

When Ryan reached the television room with a breathless rector, the students had been joined by four of the Elizabettine Sisters in their veils and habits, who normally never ventured beyond the kitchen. They were clustered round the television set. It showed the white-cassocked Pope John Paul II slumped in the arms of his private secretary in the back of a jeep that was trying to force its way through a panicking crowd in front of Saint Peter's Basilica.

"What happened?" asked the rector.

"The Pope was shot just after he'd started his audience in Saint Peter's Square," one student replied.

"It was exactly seventeen minutes past the seventeenth hour on the thirteenth day of the month," said old Sister Loreta, who was fingering her rosary beads.

"In Italy, seventeen is also an unlucky number," Lambton said to Ryan.

"It's the Feast of the Virgin of Fatima," said Sister Immaculata.

"Padre Pio prophesied this," sobbed Sister Diomira. "He told Cardinal Wojtyla that one day he would be made Pope, but his reign would be short and end in bloodshed."

"The Antichrist has struck," said Sister Loreta. "The end of the world has begun."

This superstitious babble reflected the televised chaos

and added to Ryan's feeling of unreality. He needed to see for himself, to make sense of the whole thing.

He backed out of the television room, and ran down two flights of marble stairs and along the black and red tiled corridor to the large main door. Outside, he turned right on the narrow Via di Monserrato and hurried toward the Victor Emmanuel Bridge.

The studied expression on Lev Babakin's face did not betray his satisfaction with what he saw on the television screen.

When the sound of gunshots, the cries of the crowd, and the wailing of sirens had prompted the other customers to abandon their *cappuccini* and beers at the bar on the Via di Porta Angelica and head a hundred yards up the road through Bernini's colonnade and into Saint Peter's Square, Babakin had remained at his pavement table. It gave him a strategic view up the street; he could also see the television set, which the barman had switched to the broadcast of the Pope's Wednesday public audience.

The chaos was even better than Babakin had predicted. The crowds surged first away from and then toward the popemobile. A state police car, siren blaring, nearly collided with a Rome traffic police motorcycle. A black *carabinieri* jeep screamed down the Via della Conciliazione and drove straight through a scattering crowd into Saint Peter's Square. Three *carabinieri* brandishing submachine guns leapt out and were confronted by the Vatican's own blue-uniformed *vigilanze*. Italy, after all, had no jurisdiction in Saint Peter's Square, which was part of the sovereign Vatican City State.

Lieutenant-Colonel Babakin, chief of Line PR at the Rome Residency, did not conform to the popular image of a KGB officer. Receding hair accentuated the domed forehead; collar-length hair at the back added to the appearance of an intellectual. The light gray, Italian bara-

thea suit was the kind worn by advertising executives.
The long elegant fingers that rested on the tablecloth
could have been those of a pianist. Only the cold blue
eyes were disturbing.

Babakin saw a short, moustached figure hurrying down
the Via di Porta Angelica from Saint Peter's. In flawless
Italian he ordered two beers.

By the time the man was halfway down the street, Babakin knew something was wrong.

The short man sat down at Babakin's table and started
to speak. Babakin's eyes indicated the glass of beer. The
man took a gulp and then lit a cigarette.

"What's the problem?" Babakin asked quietly in Russian.

"They got Agca," replied the man in heavily accented
Russian.

"Who did?"

"A nun grabbed him and held on until the police arrived." The man looked away from those penetrating
eyes.

"The other Turk?"

"Celik escaped."

"Why didn't he use the stun grenades?"

The man sucked on his cigarette and shrugged helplessly.

"Where is he now?"

"He reached the Alfa. Bayramic drove him off."

"Where was it parked?"

"On the Via della Conciliazione. Outside the Canadian
Embassy."

The cretins, Babakin thought, while displaying no sign
of his anger. The traffic police had almost certainly recorded the license number.

"He'll be at the embassy soon," the man said. "Kolev's
already had the truck cleared for customs in the embassy
grounds. Celik will be across the border into Yugoslavia by
three o'clock tomorrow morning." The short man lit an-

other cigarette from the stub of his first one while he waited for Babakin to speak. "And me?" he prompted.

"Go back to the Via Rubens and wait for instructions," Babakin said.

As the man stood up, Babakin added quietly, "And for God's sake, don't hurry."

Babakin sipped his beer and looked at the television screen. The Pope had been taken by ambulance to the Gemelli Clinic. The crowd remained in Saint Peter's Square, praying for the spiritual leader of one in five of the world's population.

Although the Bulgarian had diplomatic immunity, it was clear he couldn't be allowed to stay in Rome. How best to remove him? Babakin would have liked to have him sent back and shot, but even return followed by demotion was too risky. It could point the finger at the *Darzhavna Sigurnost,* and thence to the KGB. There was only one reason for sending him back to Bulgaria that would deflect suspicion. It went against the grain, but Babakin took out his pocket notebook and wrote in coded shorthand:

1. Petrov to be recalled to Sofia for transfer back to regiment and promotion to colonel.

The next newsflash tested Babakin's powers of self-control to their limit. The program cut to the steps of the Gemelli. Barely visible behind a barrage of microphones, Professor Emilio Tresalti, the Clinic's Health Director, announced: "The Holy Father has not been wounded in any of his vital organs."

Babakin knew that would cost him the Resident's job.

With the applause of the Saint Peter's Square crowd in his ears, Babakin wrote in his notebook:

2. Immediate. Telegram in name of General Secretary. Shock and outrage at assassination attempt, and best wishes for Pope's speedy recovery.

Babakin leaned back in the yellow plastic chair. It shouldn't take even the Italian police long to find the papers planted in Agca's room in the Pensione Isa. He added:

> 3. Discovery of Gray Wolves connection plus 24 hours—
>
> (a) Tass to highlight links with extreme rightist terrorist organizations;
> (b) *Izvestia* to stress membership of banned pro-Fascist party;
> (c) Novosti to conclude plot orchestrated by secret Italian P2 masonic lodge working with CIA because of Pope's opposition to right-wing regime in El Salvador.

He checked that week's code and added the classification "Chairman's eyes only".

The two members of the SID, the Italian secret service, who were supposed to monitor the Soviet Embassy from their room in the Ufficio Centrale per I Beni Archivistici on the other side of the Via Gaeta, were probably reading the sports pages of a newspaper or else playing cards. Babakin, however, never took an unnecessary risk. He decided to send the signal from the Villa Abamelek on the Janiculum, and to go there by an indirect route.

He took out a 500-lire note, placed it under the glass ashtray while tipping the Bulgarian cigarette stubs into the street, and stood up. He strolled to the Borgo Angelico where his black Lancia was parked. He drove unhurriedly through narrow streets lined by ochre-colored buildings until he reached the Castel Sant' Angelo.

Only when he turned right and joined the wide Tiber Embankment, which Roman drivers treated as a racetrack, did he vent his feelings. He slammed his foot hard on the accelerator and forced the car into the outside lane, high above the polluted river. The traffic lights turned red at the intersection with the Victor Emmanuel Bridge. He kept his foot on the accelerator. A young man dressed in

a collarless black shirt and black trousers hurried from
the bridge to cross the Embankment. Too late he saw the
Lancia. The startled face uttered a cry of surprise. The bon-
net of the Lancia sent James Ryan spinning into the gutter.

Part ✤ One

SPRING

Chapter ✥ One

THE BLACK CAR left the road from the top secret compound, turned on to the Shchelkovskoye Highway, and headed southwest toward Moscow.

From the glass front of the yellow concrete-tiled cabin, marked on each side wall with the initials GAI in blue, the speeding black Volga appeared identical to those used by upper-middle ranking Party functionaries and industrial bosses. The two traffic militiamen, under strict instructions to enforce the law without discrimination or favor following a popular Supreme Soviet decree, reluctantly left the cosiness of their watchpost. There would be no ten-rouble note in this driver's license. They climbed into their patrol car, switched on siren and flashing lights, and gave chase.

Lieutenant-General Lev Babakin looked in his rear view mirror and saw the row of flashing red and blue lamps on the roof of the mustard-colored Volga. He pressed his foot on the accelerator and enjoyed the surge of power from the turbocharged Chaika engine as the fast-approaching patrol car seemed to go into reverse. What appeared to be a standard Government Volga had been specially built for Babakin at the Gorky Car Works; the traffic militia

boasted that it could outrace any foreign car. At the next
GAI post no one attempted to stop him. The patrol car
flashed its headlights in recognition; a gray-uniformed arm
waved from the passenger window. Babakin didn't acknowledge; his satisfaction lay in knowing the first car had
radioed through to say that General Babakin was on his
way.

The birch trees that lined the long straight road through
the flat countryside were greening. Babakin was in a good
mood. When the call from the Kremlin had come, he had
been at Balashikha Center, run by Department 8 of Directorate S within his own First Chief Directorate of the
KGB. The center was used for training in sabotage and ter-
rorist techniques, and he had been practising on the pistol
range. He wanted the men to know that he was no desk-
bound bureaucrat, and needed neither driver nor bodyguard. Although the top of his head was now completely
bald and his face was gaunt, the eyes hadn't changed, and
the long elegant fingers resting lightly on the steering
wheel could still shoot a pistol as accurately as the center's
top marksmen.

Intriguingly, the telephone call had been made by
Dmitry Kirillin. The last time Babakin had seen Kirillin
was in 1981 at the Rome embassy. Kirillin had been appointed assistant commercial attaché during the last couple of months of Babakin's stint there.

Kirillin had impressed himself on Babakin for three reasons. First, Kirillin wasn't a KGB officer, which was usual
for that post, but a career bureaucrat from the Ministry of
Foreign Trade. Second, although he dutifully turned up at
the weekly political meetings in the embassy, sardonic re-
marks reported back to Line KR betrayed a skepticism
about the Party. Third, his hard work distinguished him
from the majority of embassy officials, who had obtained
their Rome posting because they were relatives or friends
of one of Brezhnev's cronies. Kirillin worked as though he
constantly had to prove himself.

KGB records showed that, on his return to the Soviet

Union, Kirillin had been appointed deputy manager of the VAZ car factory at Togliatti, where he had increased production to 700,000 Zhigulis per annum under a deal negotiated with the Fiat corporation while he was in Rome. He ought now to be in the vanguard of *perestroika* in the manufacturing sector. Instead, he had been plucked out of the Ministry for Machine Building for Light Industries to take on the newly created post of special assistant to the President. That could mean anything, from messenger boy to something approaching White House chief of staff. Babakin had suspected the latter. His suspicion had been confirmed when his man in the *Upravleniye Delami,* the Administration of Affairs Department of the Central Committee, had informed him that Kirillin had been allocated an apartment in the recently completed luxury block at the junction of Sivtsev Vrazhek and Starokonyushenny Lanes in the Arbat district.

He was also intrigued that Kirillin had asked to meet him in the Alexander Garden rather than inside the Kremlin.

At the end of Kirov Street Babakin swung right into Dzerzhinsky Square. He slowed past the seven-story ochre Italianate *palazzo* that rose from its black granite two-story base. The Lubyanka, Moscow Center of the KGB, looked downhill on the Kremlin from the top of the square. No, Babakin decided, the KGB would not bow to the demands being made in the Supreme Soviet. It was not a new and less prominent headquarters the KGB needed, it was a new and more acceptable image.

He drove on down the busy Marx Prospekt and parked his car where it wouldn't attract attention, next to the line of other black Volgas used by out-of-town Supreme Soviet deputies who stayed at the Hotel Moskva during parliamentary sessions.

A vast area of tarmac, the 50th Anniversary of the October Revolution Square, stretched out beyond the gray bulk of the Hotel Moskva. Babakin walked down the subway steps leading to the Marx Prospekt metro station and emerged among a group of tourists from the subway exit on the other side of the square.

He separated from the crowd milling outside the Central Lenin Museum and walked past the red-brick Historical Museum. Beyond the line of official yellow taxis three men stood idly by their parked cars. The one dressed in a brown leather jacket fell into step with Babakin.

"Excuse me, sir," the man said in English, "you American? *Français?*" he added with an envious glance at Babakin's suit. "You need roubles? I give you twenty roubles per US dollar. Okay, twenty-five roubles."

When Babakin ignored him, the man persisted. "How many you want? I give you best price."

Babakin stopped and stared into the man's eyes. He spoke in Russian, softly, but in a tone that made the man blanch. "The official rate is six roubles forty kopeks to the dollar. I suggest you confirm that with the militia."

The man scurried back to his Moskvich and drove off.

If that brainless thug Grechko had made a public show of cracking down on currency touts and other vermin, the KGB's image would be a damned sight better. Still, Babakin consoled himself, Grechko's days were numbered.

Babakin's good mood returned when he walked through the open wrought-iron gates. The Alexander Garden was a blaze of color in springtime. Breeze-blown beds of red tulips swayed before immaculate lawns. Babakin's path lay between a mass of pink apple blossom and a line of fir trees guarding the high crenellated red-brick Kremlin Wall, which in turn guarded the even higher white-edged yellow Arsenal.

A solidly built man wearing a navy blue suit was already at the Obelisk. He was reading the names of the revolutionary and socialist thinkers carved down the front of the monument.

"There's space for a twentieth name," Babakin said.

Dmitry Kirillin turned round. He had put on weight since his Rome days, but little else had changed. He looked younger than his thirty-four years, his hair was still cut too short to disguise how much his ears stuck out, and he still had an open, honest face, the kind that people trust.

"General, it is good of you to come," Kirillin said genially as he held out his hand. "We last met in Rome many years ago."

"Indeed."

"I have some bad news. You won't be appointed KGB chairman."

The unaccustomed bluntness caught Babakin by surprise. Despite the rage that flared inside, his relaxed expression did not alter.

"The Prime Minister nominated you," Kirillin continued, "but Korolev nominated Sergei Grechko."

"Who would oppose reform of the KGB," Babakin stated.

"Precisely. Grechko is not acceptable to the President, but his nomination was supported by Gubarev and Dobrik. That was enough to block your appointment. Shall we walk?" Kirillin said, gesturing to the path back to the Corner Arsenal Tower. "The President had to accept a compromise candidate."

Babakin forced a laugh. "So Boris Pudovik finally got the job?"

"No. General Blagov."

Babakin stopped. "I don't believe it."

"Blagov was proposed by Ulanov. The President needs Ulanov to deliver a further fifteen percent cut in defense expenditure."

General Vladimir Blagov, an old-style Party member, was head of the *Glavnoye Razvedyvatelnoye Upravleniye,* the Chief Intelligence Directorate of the Soviet General Staff. There was little love lost between the KGB and the GRU which, until the rise of Lawrence Beria, had been the premier Soviet intelligence service. Now, however, the Third Directorate of the KGB was charged with enforcing ideological conformity within every unit of the Soviet armed forces, including the General Staff and the GRU.

"The men will never stand for a takeover by the GRU," Babakin said.

"The 'men' are in no position to choose their own chairman. The reputation of the KGB . . ."

"I appreciate that," Babakin interrupted, "but an Army takeover . . ."

"There'll be no takeover," Kirillin said as he walked on. "When Blagov's appointment has been confirmed by the Supreme Soviet, he will be transferred from the General Staff and become an officer of the KGB."

"With a marshall's gold star?"

"No. He will be promoted to colonel-general."

"Presidential Council?"

"No. He will be elected to the Central Committee, that's all."

To Babakin that was a mixed blessing. He didn't want Blagov in the Presidential Council, but downgrading the Chairman of the State Security Committee to mere membership of the 250-strong Central Committee of the Party was a bad omen; it was one more blow to the KGB's authority. "Blagov's record on *glasnost* is poor. He won't improve our image."

Kirillin stopped. They had reached the Tomb of the Unknown Soldier. A bride in a white wedding dress, watched by her groom, was placing her bouquet on the black granite soldier's cloak and helmet that partly covered the horizontal red porphyry memorial slab in front of the eternal flame. "The Army's popularity may have decreased," Kirillin said, "but most Russians think it's the only body able to stop the Motherland sliding into anarchy."

"Is that what the President thinks?"

Kirillin turned to face him. "In a genuine socialist democracy, the armed forces have no role beyond that of defending the people against external aggressors. It follows that any involvement by army personnel in internal security or political matters can only be a temporary expedient."

Babakin continued staring into the eternal flame, burning brightly even in the spring sun.

"That is why I arranged to see you," Kirillin continued, "before the President has an official meeting with Blagov."

"What are you suggesting?"

Kirillin shrugged. "I've been candid with you. You must act as you see fit."

Babakin thought quickly. The President's position had weakened still further. But he'd already made his play, he couldn't change sides so soon. "I suggest the President needs an independent source of information on KGB activities, including advance notice of key intelligence before it reaches the Presidential Council or the Politburo."

Kirillin nodded. "I was hoping we'd reach the same conclusion. This seems a good place to meet."

Babakin looked around. "As one venue, yes. But it's a mistake always to use the same location. If I telephone to say, 'It'll be fine by a certain time,' then we meet at the Obelisk; 'It'll be dry,' means the imported wines counter of the Central Committee store on Granovsky Street; 'It'll be raining or snowing,' means the steam room of the Sandunovsky Baths; 'It'll be devilishly cold,' means the Cathedral of the Assumption."

Kirillin smiled. "When the defense cuts are in place and things have stabilized, the President will undoubtedly wish to review the leadership of the KGB."

Babakin remained expressionless.

"But," said Kirillin, staring intently into Babakin's eyes, "I must be assured that Blagov's successor has a personal loyalty to the President and his policies."

Babakin returned the stare. "You have my personal assurance of loyalty, Dmitry Sergeyevich."

"Good." Kirillin's genial expression returned. "Then I look forward to meeting you again, Lev Stepanovich, be it fine or devilishly cold."

Babakin watched the thickset figure walk back along the path toward the Obelisk of the Great Revolutionary and Socialist Thinkers. One of the hooded crows that haunt the Alexander Garden hopped after Kirillin. Babakin wondered how soon before spring was overtaken by winter.

Chapter ✤ Two

AMID THE REVVING engines and exhaust fumes on the Victor Emmanuel Bridge, the Ford Escort waited for the traffic lights to change. Cars roared past along the Tiber Embankment heading south.

Monsignor Vincent Henderson, vice-rector of the Venerable English College, turned to his passenger. "The driving hasn't improved since you first came to Rome, James."

Father James Ryan looked toward the junction with the Tiber Embankment where he had nearly met his fate all those years before. When the Escort did move forward, Ryan was oblivious of the overtaking Roman drivers. As the car turned left into the Via della Conciliazione he leaned forward to see once again the view that never ceased to fascinate him. At the end of the long, wide avenue, the pillared façade of the basilica, capped by that majestic dome, rose above Saint Peter's Square.

Henderson pulled into the side of Pius XII Square, by a row of yellow taxis parked in front of a stone office building. "I'm afraid I've only been inside the Apostolic Palace once," he said.

"That's once more than I have," Ryan replied.

"What I mean is, I'm not sure which entrance you need. I went in by the Bronze Door, at the end of the right-hand colonnade."

"That's good enough for me."

Henderson handed Ryan two cheap brown suitcases from the boot. "Good luck with the job, James."

Ryan grinned. "I've always believed that if you have talent you don't need luck."

"Good luck anyway."

Ryan laughed. He picked up his worldly possessions and negotiated a pedestrian crossing, dodging the cars that sped round the Largo del Colannato, the road bordering the two semicircular arms of Bernini's colonnade that partially enclosed Saint Peter's Square.

Although it was only a quarter to nine in the morning, the May sun had already warmed the cobblestones. Tourists and pilgrims and nuns displaying an exotic range of headgear and habits milled around Saint Peter's Square. Laughing students dressed in brightly colored T-shirts and shorts congregated round the Obelisk in the center of the square.

Ryan walked under a high arch and up a flight of shallow stone steps to the tall Bronze Door, which stood open. A young Swiss guard, in large black beret and billowy costume of blue, orange, and red stripes, stood at one side, facing across the door. As Ryan attempted to enter, the guard shouted *"Alt!"* and banged down his halberd diagonally, blocking the door.

"I have an appointment with Archbishop Korchan," Ryan said in Italian. The guard, who looked as though he needed to shave only once a week, stared impassively ahead.

Ryan repeated his explanation to no avail.

An older Swiss guard, with three medals on his costume, strolled down to the door, cast a cursory glance at Ryan's dress, and smiled.

For the third time Ryan explained who he was. The

young guard banged his halberd back to the vertical, allowing Ryan to enter and follow the sergeant to a desk.

The sergeant looked at a logbook and shrugged. "I don't have a Father Ryan on my list."

"My appointment is at nine o'clock with . . ."

The sergeant raised his right hand to silence Ryan, picked up a black telephone, and spoke rapidly to someone called Gino. He put the phone down, looked in amusement at Ryan and his suitcases, and said, "They're expecting you at the Saint Anne Gate. You can drive through there to the Saint Damasus Courtyard and take the lift straight up to the Third Loggia."

Ryan sighed, looked at his watch, and asked how to get to the Saint Anne Gate.

"Use the staircase here if you want," the sergeant offered.

"Thanks," Ryan said. He picked up his suitcases and began to walk up the wide, gently sloping marble corridor that merged into a long straight staircase.

"Not the Royal Staircase," the sergeant laughed. He nodded toward another staircase opposite his desk. "But first you'll need a pass." He pointed to a door next to this second staircase.

Ten minutes later Ryan emerged from the top of the second staircase into a cloister. He put down his suitcases and fished in his pocket for the pass.

"I have an appointment with Archbishop Korchan," Ryan said.

"Sure," the Swiss guard said, without looking at the pass. "I'm afraid you can't use the lift now, Father. The Spanish Prime Minister's due at twenty past nine."

The ochre paint of the stonework enclosing the Saint Damasus Courtyard at the ground floor level was faded and peeling. On the opposite side of the cobbled courtyard, and to Ryan's left and right, a triple-tiered loggia rose above the ground floor. The open side of these arcades, looking on to the courtyard, had been glazed in and hung with discreet full-length white net curtains.

The dowdy appearance of the Apostolic Palace was offset by a dozen Swiss guards of honor, wearing their brightly
colored Renaissance uniforms and sporting red-plumed
helmets, who were standing to attention by a red carpet on
the far side of the courtyard. Several men in black morning
suits with full decorations fussed around. A bishop, wearing a black cassock girdled by a wide purple sash, a purple
skull cap, and a silver pectoral cross, stood on the red carpet that led from the courtyard and through an arch to the
lift.

"Go through the arch to the left of the center one," the
guard said. "You'll find a staircase. Keep going up till you
reach the top. A guard will tell you where to go."

"Thanks."

The clock on the Second Loggia, above the central arch,
showed ten past nine. Feeling conspicuous, Ryan walked
as quickly as he could across the courtyard, looking away
from the reception party and the bunch of waiting photog-
raphers.

At the top of the staircase he pulled open the door to
enter the Third Loggia. The contrast with the shabby exte-
rior of the Apostolic Palace shocked Ryan. Soft light from
the outer wall of white diaphanous curtains fell on the
inner wall of richly colored stuccoes which were reflected
in the shining marble floor. The principal painting opposite
each arch was an early sixteenth-century map of one country in the known world, depicted in gold against an aquamarine sea. The vaults above the corridor boasted ornate
insignia of popes, together with a mixture of Church and
biblical figures in classical poses.

"Father?" the Swiss guard repeated.

Ryan looked down from the ceiling. "I'm sorry. I have
an appointment with Archbishop Korchan."

Before he could unfold the pass he had retrieved from
his pocket, the Swiss guard said, "OK."

Ryan turned left and made for the door at the end of the
corridor.

"Not that way, Father." The Swiss guard grinned.

"That's the door to the Pope's apartment. Turn left at this end and you'll see an entrance hall to the right, halfway down the next section of the loggia. You can't miss it."

"Thanks." Ryan's aching arms picked up the two suitcases yet again.

The large entrance hall of the Secretariat of State was decorated like the loggia. Two men sat behind a mahogany desk to the right. It would be unfair, Ryan thought, to describe these *uscieri* as doormen. Their dress, well-cut lounge suits, and their manner, well-practiced omniscience, were a world removed from the demeanor of their British equivalents. Ryan was instructed to take his suitcases and wait in a small reception room.

For ten minutes Ryan sat on the edge of a gilded Renaissance chair, not wanting the sweat that soaked the back of his jacket to touch the ornately woven padding.

A cleric, whose scarlet-buttoned and scarlet-edged black cassock was held at the waist by a magenta sash, swept in. His chubby face, auburn curls, and disdainful expression gave him the appearance of an overlarge, overage, and overbearing cherub. "Father Ryan? Archbishop Korchan was expecting you at nine o'clock."

Archbishop Korchan sat behind a large desk loaded with piles of papers in front of a crucifix. Three telephones rested on a table to his right. Behind, a picture of the Pope smiled down. To his left, the ubiquitous white net curtains billowed in the breeze from a partly opened window that reached almost to the vaulted ceiling.

The archbishop, a powerfully built man who wore a scarlet-edged caped cassock with a brass pectoral cross tucked in his purple sash, stood up. The broad face below the graying wavy hair smiled. He stretched out his hand to shake and not be kissed. "It is good to see you, Father Ryan," he said in accented English. With a conspiratorial glance toward Monsignor Botone, his secretary who had conducted Ryan to his office, he added, "I trust you have been made welcome."

Ryan liked the man immediately. "Thank you, Excellency."

Korchan chatted for a few minutes about Ryan's new post. He then turned to Botone and spoke in Italian. "Pietro. Please ask Monsignor Grimes to join us."

He put his *zucchetto,* the small purple skull cap, on top of his wavy hair and looked at the clock. "In a few minutes I am afraid I must leave to join the Cardinal Secretary of State and Archbishop Benedetti. We have a meeting with the Prime Minister of Spain after the Holy Father has finished with him."

There was a knock at the door. A monsignor with a pinched face, thinning sandy hair, and pale blue eyes, walked in. Like everyone else in the Secretariat of State, he wore full ecclesiastical dress appropriate to his rank.

"Father Ryan," said Archbishop Korchan, "permit me to introduce a fellow Englishman, Monsignor Grimes."

Grimes coughed into his hand. "I hail from Scotland, Excellency." His Italian was colored by an Aberdonian accent. "That is not the same as England."

"Ah yes," said Korchan. "You too have your nationality problems. Nonetheless, I hope you will show Father Ryan round and then deliver him back here to me at eleven-thirty."

"As Your Excellency wishes."

"No offense meant, Father Ryan," Grimes said once they were alone in the Third Loggia, "but it wouldn't be doing to have these people misunderstand the difference between England and Scotland."

"Don't worry. And the name is James."

"Well, that's a good Scottish name. I'm Andrew. So you're to be the Pope's new private secretary?" He studied Ryan's fresh features and unruly auburn hair. "You look rather young for it."

"I am thirty-four," Ryan confessed.

"You don't look it. Mind you, I've always said that celibacy retards the aging process. Looking forward to your new job?"

"To be honest," Ryan said, "I don't know. I don't even know how I got it."

"There's no mystery there, laddie. The Pope needed an English speaker as his second private secretary. The American hierarchy are hardly flavor of the month in this place. You were trained in Rome, and you have the experience of being Cardinal Harding's secretary in Westminster. Frankly, there wasn't much competition."

"Don't get me wrong," Ryan said. "I didn't apply for the post."

"Nobody applies for any post here. You are chosen. Twenty years ago my bishop said he was seconding me for three years to the Secretariat of State."

"You must like it here."

Grimes stopped in his tracks. "Like it? I hate the place. It's hell on earth." He looked at Ryan's expression. "The city, I mean. It's hot, sticky, dirty, noisy, and full of wops. We should never have joined the Common Market."

"But if you've lived in Rome . . ."

"I do not live in Rome," Grimes interrupted. "I work in the Vatican which, thank God, is rather more cosmopolitan since Paul VI, and I stay at the Casa Internationale del Clero. That's rather like a high class hostel run by a religious order on the Vatican's behalf. You must come and see me there some time. I tell people I live in the attic, but in fact I've the best room in the place, and it doesn't cost me a lira more in rent."

They had reached the end of one section of the Third Loggia. "Now, what do you want to see?"

"A cup of tea?" Ryan ventured.

Grimes beamed. "Splendid man. We'll have a brew in my office. You canna find decent tea in this city. All fancy teabags. Mother sends me over proper tea."

Ryan followed his guide along a bewildering series of stairs and corridors. "Pope Alexander VI lived here," Grimes said as they passed through a suite of rooms containing works of modern art. "He's the Borgia who fathered a dozen bastards. Got the papacy by bribery using the money he'd filched as Cardinal Vice-Chancellor of the Holy See."

They climbed up the Borgia Tower and Grimes showed Ryan the view from his office. "The Belvedere Courtyard. Courtyard of the beautiful view, would you believe? Now they've turned it into a damned car park for Vatican officials. The Italians don't care, of course, as long as they can drive their smelly cars. They're not civilized." He removed a kettle from a cupboard and filled it from the tap above a handbasin in the corner of the room. He unplugged his desk lamp and plugged the kettle in.

"Forgive me for asking," Ryan said, "but if you dislike it so much, why do you stay here?"

Grimes removed two cups and saucers from a filing cabinet. "I stick it because my bishop asked me to be here. You've got to understand, James, people who are here because they *want* to be here are the wrong type entirely. Without people like me no work would ever get done in this place."

"How many people do work in the Apostolic Palace?" Ryan asked.

"About half," said Grimes, heating the teapot before measuring out three spoonfuls of tea and pouring in the boiling water. "What scale did they put you on, James?"

"I think Archbishop Korchan mentioned something about my being one of the *officiali minori.*"

"I'm talking about *salary* scale, laddie. Clerics with a doctorate usually start at Level Five. Have you got a doctorate?"

"Afraid not. Just a master's."

"What in?"

"Business administration."

"That's probably worth more than some of these theology doctorates they hand out here in Rome. Digestive biscuit? You insist on starting at Level Five. Mind you, I don't imagine you're having to pay rent for living with the Pope, are you? I pay half my salary back to the Vatican in rent."

"I don't really know," Ryan said. It was feeling distinctly

like his first day at boarding school. "I could ask Archbishop Korchan, I suppose. But I don't know if he's the right person to ask. I don't even know what he does."

"Korchan is *Sostituto* Secretary of State." Grimes rolled the Italian word round his mouth. "Most people translate that as substitute. That's not really accurate, you understand. The *Sostituto* heads the section of the Secretariat that coordinates all the different departments of the Roman Curia. The other section, headed by Archbishop Benedetti, handles relations with foreign governments and coordinates the papal nuncios abroad." He paused. "Crudely speaking, you can think of Korchan as Internal Affairs Minister and Benedetti as Foreign Minister, with Cardinal Secretary of State Fasolo in overall charge as Prime Minister."

"Where does the Pope fit in?" Ryan asked.

"The Pope?" Grimes raised his eyebrows. "Why, he's God, of course." He poured out the tea. "You canna get decent milk in this place either." Grimes gave Ryan an appraising look. "You'll do well to keep in with Korchan. He's the one who picked you for this job. Mind you, that'll make the Romans suspicious of you. They'll think you're a Slav."

"Why on earth . . . ?"

"In this place you tend to get branded a Roman, a Slav, or a liberal."

Ryan sipped his tea. "I hardly qualify as a Slav."

Grimes tutted. "You don't have to come from the east to be labeled a Slav round here. Cardinal Zingler, who heads the Congregation for the Doctrine of the Faith, what I call the ideology department, is from Austria. Apart from the Pope, there's no one more Slav than Zingler. The Romans can't stand him. They think he's crude and unsophisticated."

"What are you?"

"Me? I keep out of all that business and just get on with my job. Which reminds me, I don't know what I'm doing here talking to you with all this work to do. Can you find your own way back?"

"I think so," Ryan said uncertainly. "Is there any chance of seeing you again? I'm just beginning to realize how much I don't understand."

Grimes thought while he poured himself a second cup of tea. "Well, I suppose so. I do have to come back to the office tomorrow afternoon at five. The Pope has a siesta at three-fifteen. He won't be needing you then. We could meet at, say, four tomorrow."

"That's great, Andrew. You can show me round the Vatican Gardens. I've always wanted to see them."

"If you like. In that case we'll meet in the Saint Damasus Courtyard. But it'll be the blind leading the blind."

"Pardon?"

"I've never been round the gardens. Don't look so surprised. Why should I? I come here to do translations. When work's over, I can't wait to leave the place."

It took Ryan twenty minutes to find his way back. He just made it by eleven-thirty, but Archbishop Korchan hadn't yet returned from his meeting. Ryan smiled politely at the *usciere* and ignored the request to wait in the reception room. He examined the frescoes in the entrance hall. One showed a map of the Americas. North America was marked *Terra Incognita*.

"It still is an unknown land for some people in this building," a dulcet Italian voice said behind him.

Ryan turned round to see a handsome prelate with silver hair in bouffant style below his skull cap.

"You must be Father James Ryan," the prelate said, inspecting Ryan as though he were a prize gelding, from the fresh complexion to the lithe figure, and back to the pale green eyes that hinted at an innocence bordering on vulnerability.

Confused, and unsure whether the color of the prelate's sash was crimson or purple, Ryan said, "That's right, Eminence."

The other smiled appreciatively. "You elevate me. I am

but a humble archbishop." He shook Ryan's hand. "Antonio Benedetti." He held on to Ryan's hand a fraction longer than Ryan would have wished. "Your patron is coming. We shall meet again, Father Ryan." He disappeared into the Secretariat as Archbishop Korchan arrived.

Korchan apologized for being late, and led Ryan to a small chapel. A candle glowed in a red glass case to the left of the altar, showing that the Blessed Sacrament was housed in the tabernacle.

Korchan genuflected and then turned to Ryan. "We have a few formalities to complete, Father. How is your Latin?"

"Rusty, I'm afraid, Excellency."

Korchan handed him a card, together with an ancient illuminated copy of the Gospels. "It is an oath in two parts. Read it before you take the oath."

Ryan managed to translate the first part, which was a profession of faith. It started with the Apostles' Creed and continued to pledge fidelity to everything the Church taught about faith or morals, whether by solemn definition or by the ordinary teaching authority of the Church, especially those things concerning the mystery of the holy Church of Christ, the Sacraments and the Sacrifice of the Mass, and the Primacy of the Roman Pontiff.

Seeing him struggle with the second part, Archbishop Korchan took back the card. "The second part is known as the Pontifical Secret." He cleared his throat before translating for Ryan's benefit: "I, James Ryan, promise in the name of Our Lord and I confirm by vow and oath that I shall be a faithful and obedient servant of our Holy Father the Pope and his lawful successors; that I shall diligently carry out the tasks entrusted to me by my Office; and that I shall keep secret all matters arising from my Office. So help me God and these holy Gospels of God which I touch with my hands."

Korchan looked at him from beneath hooded eyelids. "Say now, Father, if you find any difficulties with taking this oath."

Ryan shook his head. He took back the card, knelt down, and put his hand on the book of the Gospels.

He couldn't imagine any circumstances in which he would have difficulties keeping the oath.

Chapter ❖ Three

TWO DAYS AFTER his meeting with Kirillin, Lev Babakin was waiting with his colleagues in the oak-paneled conference room next to the Chairman's office in Moscow Center. Most of the furniture in the room had been there when the Cheka took over the Lubyanka in 1917. The long oak table, around which seven members of the presidium of the State Security Committee now sat, was the same table around which directors of the Rossiya Insurance Company met before the Revolution to decide how best to protect the security of their capital.

Babakin sat at the end of one long side of the table. To his left, at the head of the table, two high-backed uncomfortable chairs were empty. A squat man sat opposite Babakin. Sergei Grechko, whose counter-nomination had blocked Babakin's appointment as Chairman of the KGB was completely bald. His shiny head and face, double chin and snub nose might, by themselves, have given the impression of a jovial uncle. The pig-like eyes and mean mouth were more in character. Babakin thought him uncouth. Grechko headed the Second Chief Directorate, the domestic security service.

Next to Grechko was the man Babakin had displace as head of the First Chief Directorate, the KGB's foreign intelligence service. Boris Pudovik was now in charge of the Chief Directorate of Border Guards, whose 200,000 troops protected the 40,000 miles of the Soviet Union border, mainly from citizens wanting to escape rather than from foreigners wanting to enter. Pudovik's lined face had the well-worn look of a man who had seen it all. Babakin found him slow and old-fashioned. It irritated him that Pudovik's analyzes often proved right in the long term.

The other First Deputy Chairman of the KGB, Yevgeny Panov, was absent. Panov was in charge of the Eighth Chief Directorate, which handled electronic surveillance using satellites, spy ships disguised as trawlers, and equipment inside Soviet embassies.

Igor Shatalov sat at Babakin's right. Shatalov had been Babakin's deputy at the Fifth Chief Directorate, and had succeeded Babakin when the latter had taken over the First Chief Directorate. The Fifth had been created in 1969 by Yuri Andropov to suppress the dissident movement, and had outstripped the Second Chief Directorate's reputation for brutality. Under Babakin, however, it had adopted more subtle methods. Shatalov was a pale imitation of his mentor; he didn't have an original idea in his head, but he could be relied upon to do as he was told. The Fifth had officially been wound up as a concession to the Supreme Soviet. Its staff had been reconstituted as the Directorate for the Protection of the Soviet Constitutional System.

The three other deputy chairmen headed the Third Directorate, the Seventh Directorate, and the Ninth Directorate, which were responsible for ideological conformity within the armed forces, surveillance of enemy agents inside the Soviet Union, and the physical protection of Party leaders and key Party and State installations. It was typical of the KGB's shambles, Babakin thought, that in its periodic reorganizations, new directorates were created and old ones abolished while continuing ones retained their titles: the numerical designations were as logical and as useful as the KGB's computer system.

Babakin wasn't surprised that Panov was late. He was surprised that Savitsky, who headed the personnel department and who normally attended presidium meetings, was absent.

No agenda or other papers were on the table. The only signs of Blagov's new regime as KGB chief were two large maps on the wall. The map of the world had First Chief Directorate residencies marked by red pins and illegal residents by black pins. The map of the Soviet Union had Second Chief Directorate headquarters at republic, region, territory, district, and city levels in a rainbow of pins. Babakin found it so cluttered by a multicoloured mess of pins as to be useless. At least Blagov hadn't removed the bronze head of Andropov, which held a position of eminence in the room second only to the inevitable Lenin urging on the invisible masses.

Babakin looked at his Rolex watch. Blagov had only one minute left if he was not to be late for his first meeting of the presidium.

Precisely one minute later General Vladimir Blagov entered, followed by a woman Babakin had not seen before. The seven deputy chairmen at the table held the rank of either lieutenant-general or major-general. None wore uniform except on formal State occasions. Babakin observed their expressions when they saw that not only was Blagov in service dress but also that his uniform carried the KGB insignia and that the silver star of a colonel-general was pinned to his tie. Blagov had been a member of the KGB and a colonel-general less than forty-eight hours.

Blagov sat down. Hard eyes stared out from under bushy black eyebrows at each man in turn. Short, slightly wavy, gray hair combed back from his brow emphasized his broad Slav features and heavy jowls. "Good afternoon, gentlemen. There are only two items. First, personnel. Savitsky is no longer head of the Personnel Department. He will be replaced by Colonel Andrei Borisenko from the GRU. This is Comrade Kruglova, my personal secretary."

The woman, who sat at Blagov's right holding a pencil above a shorthand pad, did not smile.

"Second, a situation review . . ."

The door opened and Panov came in. "Sorry I'm late, Chairman. I've been to a meeting at the State Committee on Science and Technology."

Blagov looked as though he had seen a slug crawl into the room. "The presidium of the State Security Committee takes precedence over all other meetings. Is that clear, Panov?"

Babakin was pleased. Blagov had made another mistake. Behind Panov's disheveled appearance was a brain second only to Babakin's own in the KGB. Public humiliation wasn't the best way to solicit Panov's skills in new technology which, heaven knew, were rare enough in any State ministry or department.

"We shall begin," Blagov continued, "by reviewing the Committee's objectives, after which we shall agree a new strategy."

He stood up and began pacing the room, hands clasped behind his back. "This organization was established to be the sword and the shield of the Communist Party of the Soviet Union. In recent times it has lamentably failed in that task. Let us examine the shield."

He took a pointer from below the map of the world. "First, the external threat. The only areas where the borders of the Motherland are secure are north to the Arctic and east to the Pacific. Everywhere else our borders are threatened. The half dozen Muslim soviet republics that protect our southern flank are disintegrating into religious fanaticism . . ."

"I doubt," Babakin said in a calculated provocation, "that Turkey, Iran and Afganistan are poised to invade Moscow."

Panov grinned.

Blagov glared. "The biggest failure of all, General Babakin, for which you bear direct responsibility, lies beyond our western border. The Party's loss of control in Poland, Hungary, Czechoslovakia, and the German Democratic Republic means the Western Outer Rim no longer provides a secure buffer against NATO forces. Worse, for the first time since the Great Patriotic War we face the threat of a reunified Germany dominating Europe."

"I'm not sure what the First Chief Directorate could have done to prevent these changes. It seems to me . . ."

"Precisely!" Blagov slammed his fist on the table. "You weren't sure what to do! What you should have done was provide a thorough intelligence assessment of the economic experiments being planned by the western satellites. Any fool would have realized that they would lead to political instability."

Babakin remained calm. "It was the Party leadership in the satellites who decided on the economic reforms. I believe the idea was to avoid being dragged down into the same mess we are in."

"The KGB failed to anticipate the consequences of those measures and failed to prevent their implementation! Have you lost all control over the satellites' security services?"

"What strategy are you proposing now, Comrade Chairman?" Babakin asked in a voice finely balanced between reasonableness and sarcasm.

The KGB chief placed his knuckles on the table, leaned forward, and said in a low voice, "Now I am chairman the first priority of this committee will be to ensure the Western Inner Rim holds fast, from Estonia through to Armenia. If we fail to take action soon, Russia itself will be an open target."

He stood up straight. "That means cooperation, no competition, between the First, Second, and Seventh Directorates, and the Directorate for the Protection of The Soviet Constitutional System." He looked at Zolotukhin, head of the Seventh. "I look to you to brief us on the foreign subversion behind the unrest in these republics. The subversion that the First Chief Directorate has failed to warn us of."

"May I compliment you on your analysis, Comrade Chairman," Grechko said. "I propose a Western Inner Rim Sub-Committee, chaired by the Second Chief Directorate, to achieve the coordination you want and to prepare specific measures for your consideration."

"Approved."

Ho, ho, Babakin thought. Yet another committee. If committees solved problems, the Soviet Union would be the most advanced nation scientifically, technologically, and economically in the galaxy.

"May we take it that any measures in this area will conform with the directives issued by the Security Commission of the Supreme Soviet?" Panov asked.

Blagov smiled for the first time. It was not a comforting smile. "You will permit me, Comrade Panov, to deal with committees of the Supreme Soviet. Politicians come and politicians go. This committee has permanent responsibility for the security of the State." He turned his attention back to Babakin. "I have been examining the accounts of our foreign residencies. Hard currency appears to be ladled out freely under broad headings of 'operational purposes' or 'necessary expenses,' with no receipts and little or no accounting."

Babakin was unperturbed. "Residencies don't exist to shuffle paper or keep records. They're out there to act. I judge them on their results, not on their accounts."

All eyes turned to Blagov, who only just succeeded in controlling his temper. "As Comrade Panov was so eager to remind us, we are now in an age of accountability. If the Soviet Army has to undergo savage cuts, do not think you may continue as before."

Babakin shrugged. "The value of scientific and technological data stolen each year from the West by my directorate is enough to fund the operating costs of the entire KGB ten times over. May I suggest, Comrade Chairman, you ensure that some of this data is employed in developing a decent computer system for the KGB."

Blagov placed his hands on the table and leaned forward until his face was level with Babakin's. He made a show of taking in every detail of the man in front of him, lingering on the suit that was replaced every six months by the tailor Babakin had patronized during his Rome tour. Blagov didn't speak.

A lesser man would have been intimidated, but Babakin stared back, confident he had the measure of the new KGB chief.

Blagov's lecture resumed with criticisms of each deputy chairman in turn, combined with exhortations to root out the unidentified traitor at the highest levels of the State apparatus who was supplying intelligence to the CIA.

Babakin's attention wandered. The woman Kruglova, who sat next to the chairman, was tight, Babakin decided. Hair swept tightly back into a bun. Tight lips below tight, horn-rimmed spectacles. Tight dress which showed full breasts and a thickening waist. Legs tightly crossed. Tight everywhere, no doubt. Those shapely legs were her best feature, Babakin concluded. An interesting woman.

The meeting ended at five-thirty. The dingy green corridors, lined with frayed red carpet and patroled by armed sentries, were packed with staff jostling to leave the building. Babakin didn't return to the office he used in the Lubyanka, but left by a back staircase that led to an exit into Furkasovsky Lane. He passed the line of parked black KGB Volgas with their telltale registration plates—numbers beginning in 05 or letters beginning in MM—and turned right into Little Lubyanka Street. He merged into the crowd hurrying down the steps to the Dzerzhinskaya metro station. He stopped at one of the public telephone booths just outside the glass doors to the metro, inserted a two-kopeck coin, and dialed.

Chapter ✤ Four

DETERMINED NOT TO be late for his first appointment on his first day, Ryan woke well before his wristwatch alarm began bleeping at 5:45 A.M. He climbed out of bed and ran the water as gently as he could into his washbasin, conscious that his room was above the Pope's bedroom.

He washed, shaved and dressed, and crept down the stairs from the attic to the main floor of the papal apartment. Two of the lights in the corridor were already switched on. He turned right and tiptoed past the main door of the Pope's bedroom, and turned right again at the end of the corridor. The entrance to the private chapel was opposite the door to the office he was to share with Monsignor Kasamir Hoffman, the Pope's other private secretary.

His efforts not to disturb the Pope were unnecessary; the Pope was kneeling at his prie-dieu, directly in front of the altar. Ryan slipped in and kneeled at the back of the small chapel.

He tried to pray himself, but his attention kept wandering. He didn't find the chapel conducive to prayer. Perhaps he had grown accustomed to the warmth of wood, the comforting smell of beeswax polish. Here, austere marble shone coldly. Ryan felt the modern design ought to have been simple, focusing on the altar. But modern bronzes, mosaics, and lighted panels depicting gospel scenes disturbed the clean lines of the chapel.

Ryan's gaze kept returning to the back of the Successor of Saint Peter. His cassock, with its cape and sash, wasn't the pristine white that appeared on television, more a yellowish off-white. The shoulders were hunched, the head bowed, the fingers clutched rosary beads. This stooped figure was motionless apart from the occasional look up to an icon of the Blessed Virgin Mary to the right above the altar.

His first meeting with the Pope the previous day had shocked him. Instead of the vital, charismatic figure who cast his spell over audiences of hundreds of thousands, the Pope who had greeted him in the private dining room was an old man. He spoke and moved slowly. His face was drained. Only his eyes flashed sporadically with an intensity that betrayed an inner passion.

Ryan turned to the sounds behind him. Hoffman was directing a dozen people to take their places in the chapel. He pointed to the chairs at the back for two groups of nuns; he beckoned four elegant ladies dressed in black and wearing mantillas to chairs in the middle; he placed two priests near the front to the left; and he led one gaunt man, with lank blond hair and drooping moustache, to a chair on the front row, within reach of the Pope.

The bells of Saint Peter's struck seven. The motionless Pope stirred. He stood up, and looked round through half shut eyes.

Hoffman signaled Ryan to take his place as altar server while the Pope vested for mass.

After mass, Ryan followed as Hoffman led the privileged congregation along the corridor and indicated where they should stand in a large, bookcase-lined *salone* which had gold curtains, in addition to the usual white net ones, bordering the tall windows.

Monsignor Kasamir Hoffman was a powerful, broad shouldered man who wore a high Roman collar and simple black cassock without the red trim to which he was entitled. His short, iron-gray hair was brushed straight back from a wide forehead. Beady eyes peered suspiciously out from behind steel-framed spectacles. Tight lips and thrust-out chin completed an impression of almost permanent defiance. Only with the Pope did that expression change to solicitude.

When the Pope entered the *salone*, Hoffman guided him, whispering in his ear before the Vicar of Christ approached each of the groups in turn. The Pope spent longest with the solitary moustached man. The Pope spoke little, but listened intently with his head cocked to one side.

Afterwards, in the private dining room, two Sisters of the Maria Bambina Order, covered from head to toe in old-fashioned wimples and traditional black habits with a red heart stitched to their breasts, served breakfast for the Pope, Hoffman, and Ryan. Three other nuns, together with Giuseppe, the Pope's valet and chauffeur, lived in the private apartment. Ryan looked down at the fried potatoes, ham, eggs and sausages, and wondered when it would be diplomatic to inquire about muesli.

By nine o'clock the Pope was in his private study adjoining his bedroom. Hoffman led Ryan to the office they shared. The bare white walls were decorated only with a crucifix, a photograph of the Pope, and an idealized painting of the Virgin Mary wearing a crown of twelve stars on her head and a thorn-pricked red heart on her breast. Hoffman sat down at his desk, which faced the connecting door to the Pope's study, and began writing and making a series of telephone calls. Ryan sat at the other desk, wondering what to do.

Eventually, Ryan stood up and pulled aside the net curtain to look down into Saint Peter's Square.

"What are you doing?" Hoffman demanded.

"Just looking," Ryan replied.

"Even the Holy Father may not be seen at the windows of the Apostolic Palace, except at noon on Sundays and holy days to give the people his blessing."

"I wasn't intending to give a blessing from the window," Ryan tried to joke.

"These windows are not for looking out of," said Hoffman sternly, "but for letting light in."

"The Holy Father looks . . . tired," Ryan ventured.

Hoffman sat back in his chair and stared at Ryan. "So would any man who had to bear the Holy Father's burden."

"If there's anything I can do to help . . ."

Hoffman nodded slowly. "Pray. Like the Holy Father, pray the rosary constantly and dedicate your life to the Immaculate Heart of Mary as the Virgin of Fatima requested."

Ryan frowned. "But wasn't that claimed apparition . . ."

Those beady eyes cut Ryan dead. "Never let the Holy Father hear you speak like that. It would cause him great distress."

"I'm sorry."

"The miracle of Fatima has been authenticated by Holy Mother Church."

"Don't misunderstand, Monsignor, I'm not denying that Our Lady appeared at Fatima. But as to what she actually said, we only have the word of three illiterate children."

"Who else? Didn't Christ repeatedly warn that unless we become like little children we shall not enter the kingdom of heaven? They were the chaste white souls on which the Mother of God wrote her Son's message to mankind."

"But surely any message constitutes what dogmatic theology deems a private revelation, as distinct from the great revelation of Scripture?"

Hoffman shook his head despairingly. "And people wonder why the Holy Father is so concerned about the theological formation of our priests." He leaned forward, his chin thrust out even further. "In this day and age we are witnessing the greatest denial ever of the fundamental truths of the Church, combined with a contempt for the authority of the Pope. There is not a single article of the Creed that so-called liberal theologians have not questioned; but neither is there a single truth of the Faith that Our Lady of Fatima has not confirmed, from the virgin birth of Christ to the evil of sin and the existence of hell. The Blessed Virgin came to reinforce the revelations of Scripture. Make no mistake, Father Ryan. Our Lady's message was addressed not just to three children but to the whole human race. It is a cry for prayer and for penance, to rescue the world from the abyss."

Chapter ✤ Five

THE IMAGE OF the cold and aloof English was a European myth, Ryan decided. For the previous two years as private secretary to Cardinal Harding, Ryan had enjoyed the friendliness and informality of Archbishop's House, Westminster, where Cardinal Harding walked around in an open-necked shirt when he wasn't receiving official guests, and where the small staff had gone out of their way to make Ryan feel at home.

In the Vatican, only the Pope and Archbishop Korchan had made him welcome. It wasn't just the Romans who were haughty; inside the private apartment he felt like an intruder. Monsignor Hoffman's only instructions were to be available in case he were needed. The Polish nuns took their cue from Hoffman, and treated him with a mixture of formality and wariness.

Lunch that first day was a lonely affair for Ryan. The Pope sat at the center of one long side of the rectangular table. Hoffman sat at one short side, to the Pope's right, while Ryan's place was to the Pope's left. On the other long side, facing the Pope across a vase of freshly cut spring flowers at the center of the white tablecloth, was a guest. It was the gaunt man with lank blond hair and drooping moustache who had been at the Pope's private mass earlier that morning.

Hoffman's introduction had been cursory, and Ryan had missed the man's name. As the conversation over lunch was conducted entirely in Polish, Ryan didn't obtain any clue as to the man's identity.

Ryan poked at the mixture of Slav and Italian dishes that the nuns set before them. When Cardinal Harding wasn't on official business, he and Ryan had only a bowl of soup and a slice of toast for lunch.

He watched the guest's vaguely familiar face, talking more animatedly as the meal progressed. The Pope said little. He appeared not to be listening, but every so often he nodded, and the man responded. Hoffman stared down at his plate, but his eyes occasionally darted up from behind his spectacles to watch the Pope or Ryan.

It was gone three o'clock by the time Hoffman had shown the guest to the private lift down to the Courtyard of Sixtus V. The Pope retired to his bedroom.

Ryan intercepted Hoffman in the corridor. "Would you mind if I went out for an hour in the gardens, Monsignor? I could do with a walk."

Hoffman's beady eyes peered at him through his spectacles. "Go if you must. But be back here before four-thirty. Bishop Spiazzi will be bringing the list of tomorrow's audiences, and I won't be here. My mother in Gdansk is unwell and I'm catching the five-thirty plane. I'll be flying from Poland on Thursday direct to Strasbourg for the papal visit."

"I'm sorry to hear about your mother," Ryan said. "I do hope it's nothing serious."

"Remember her in your prayers."

"Certainly. But Monsignor . . . ?"

"Yes?"

"What do you want me to do while you're away?"

"Serve at the Holy Father's private mass in the morning, and then just be available the rest of the day, as I told you, in case he should need anything. The Prefect of the Papal Household arranges all the papal audiences. Cardinal Fasolo comes every evening at six-thirty to discuss matters of State. Don't let him overburden the Holy Father with paperwork. The Holy Father must save his strength for Strasbourg."

Ryan left for the Vatican Gardens wondering how on earth he was meant to prevent the most senior cardinal in the Catholic Church from overburdening the Pope with paperwork.

Chapter ✣ Six

LIKE THE TRINITY, the Vatican is three in one. It is the Holy See, which is the episcopal seat of the Bishop of Rome, uniquely recognized in international law and diplomacy as a sovereign entity distinct from the territorial sovereignty of the Vatican City State; it is the Roman Curia, which is the civil service of the Holy See, consisting of dicasteries, or departments, modeled on the court of Imperial Rome; and it is the Vatican City State, which is the smallest sovereign state in the world.

Behind Saint Peter's Basilica and the adjoining Apostolic Palace—the series of palaces, chapels, halls and galleries that house offices, State and private apartments, and the Vatican Museums—the Vatican Gardens rise up the Vatican Hill, occupying about half the 109 acres of the triangular-shaped walled citadel.

At a plateau near the top of the hill, Grimes stopped and wiped his brow. "That must be the Palazzina of Leo XIII."

A central, circular tower dominated the large, fortified building. Radio masts projected from the top of the tower.

"It was the Vatican Observatory before they moved the Observatory to Castel Gandolfo on account of the pollution," Grimes said. "Now it's the headquarters of Vatican Radio. Just a black hole gobbling up money. These days it's only the poor devils in east Europe who bother to listen." He sighed. "Rumor has it that the Vatican Bank never recovered from the Banco Ambrosiano disaster in '81. You have just joined, James, an organization that, for all practical purposes, is bankrupt."

Ryan wasn't paying attention. His mind had returned to the community bank Katie had set up in Boston. It's your choice, James Ryan, she had told him after they both graduated from the Harvard Business School. Join some big corporation and make yourself lots of money, or else join me in putting the Church's social teaching into practice. There'd been no choice, of course. He would have followed her anywhere. Between them they had helped organize local community and cooperative businesses in Roxbury. Those had been the most rewarding days of his life until . . . until that day he'd taken Katie climbing on Mount Washington.

"I said the Church is bankrupt," Grimes repeated.

Ryan nodded and looked at his watch. "I must get back. Monsignor Hoffman told me that he's leaving for Poland this afternoon, and I'm supposed to hold the fort."

"That is just typical. These people drive me round the bend. They never plan ahead. They're simply not capable of it. Try and fix a meeting next week and they'll say, 'Ring me on Monday and I'll see what my diary's like.' I know what my diary's like three months ahead. But can you get these people to put an engagement in their diaries for next week? They just can't do it."

Grimes continued gossiping while they walked back down the hill. "I suppose you've met all the big white chiefs by now."

"I haven't met Cardinal Fasolo. He's due this evening 'to discuss matters of State,' according to Monsignor Hoffman."

"Fasolo's a deep one," Grimes said. "He never lets you know what his own opinion is. But here's a tip that'll stand

you in good stead. If you want to know what Fasolo really
thinks, listen to Benedetti. They're as thick as thieves. Both
are part of the Pontifical Academy mafia, you understand,
but Benedetti is much more indiscreet."

"Tell me, Andrew. Why did you say Archbishop Korchan is so powerful? He isn't even a cardinal."

"He isn't a cardinal yet, but he wields a lot of influence
around here. The Secretary of State may have a daily meeting with the Pope, but those are formal meetings. You'll
find the Pope often has Korchan round in the evening to
talk things through."

"Is Archbishop Korchan Polish?"

"No, no. He's Ukrainian. Strange man in some ways.
He'll never let on, but he hates the Russians. He was only
freed from a labor camp when international pressure
forced Khrushchev to let the Ukrainian Metropolitan
Slipyj attend the Second Vatican Council. Slipyj was ill and
needed an assistant, so they let him take Korchan. They
both stayed on in Rome after the Council, and Paul VI gave
Korchan a job in the Congregation for Eastern Churches
just to keep Slipyj happy."

"I'm sorry to dash off like this," Ryan said, "but Monsignor Hoffman said it was important I was back before four-
thirty."

"Don't think you're the only one who does important
work around here," Grimes said. "I shouldn't be telling you
this, but the reason I was called back in was to do the official English translation of a secret draft agreement. The
Spanish Prime Minister will present it next week to the
European Community heads of government. Benedetti
wants it before tomorrow morning to brief the British Ambassador to the Holy See."

Chapter ✣ Seven

LIKE THE VATICAN, the Kremlin is a walled citadel within a city, designed during the Renaissance by Italian architects. It is two-thirds the size of the Vatican City State and, like the Vatican, is roughly triangular in shape and rises up the slope of a hill. The base of the triangle is the southern section of the red-brick Kremlin Wall, between the Water Pump Tower and the Beklemishev Tower, which overlooks the Moscow River. The northwestern section overlooks the Alexander Garden. The northeastern section rises steeply up to the Savior Tower and then runs alongside Red Square to meet the northwestern section at the Corner Arsenal Tower.

The most modern building in the Kremlin, the massive white marble and glass Palace of Congresses, was sunk five stories below ground so that its roof was no higher than the nearby neoclassical State Armory and Arsenal buildings. From the back of its main auditorium, Dmitry Kirillin looked down over the heads of the 2,250 delegates to the Congress of People's Deputies to the platform below. This was the moment he had dreaded since his appointment two weeks before.

At the center of the platform, watched over by a monumental Lenin, sat the Soviet President, the man who had asked Kirillin to be his special assistant. At the rostrum, haranguing both Lenin and the President, stood Anatoli Fyodorovich Filipchenko, the man who had been one of Kirillin's closest friends since Moscow University days.

He, Filipchenko, Vitaly Mazunov, and Nina Petrushkova had been students in the economics department. They had formed an exclusive student club called the Eclectic Music Appreciation Society: they collected and played bootleg copies of Western pop music and got drunk whenever they could afford to.

All three men were in love with the vivacious, self-willed Nina from Georgia, with her nymphet figure and her black pageboy bob of hair which she insisted on calling her Mary Quantaya. The year of their graduation she chose Vitaly. Only because he had the best collection of Rolling Stones records, Anatoli lamented. He was inconsolable for a week. He and Kirillin borrowed a dacha at Nikolina Gora from one of their professors. Anatoli stayed sober only enough to place the needle on the Peter Sarstedt record *Where do you go to, my lovely?* which he played non-stop all weekend.

They had all joined the Party. Kirillin because it was the only route to a good job and foreign travel. Nina because she felt women should have as much say as men. Vitaly because Nina had joined. And Anatoli because he wanted to reform the system.

The romantic Anatoli hadn't changed.

Mesmerizing eyes stared out from the rostrum. With expansive gestures of his arms, Filipchenko scorned the President's policies for failing to put meat, sugar, and soap in the shops, for failing to put washing machines in the homes, for failing to build the decent homes the people deserved and, most shameful of all in a self-styled socialist society, for failing to raise forty million people above the official Soviet poverty line.

The President's policies were empty rhetoric, he argued. They led to elements of a market economy being grafted onto the existing system of centralized planning, producing the worst of both worlds. It was hypocritical of the President to praise Lenin while laying the blame at the feet of Stalin and Brezhnev. They had simply carried out Lenin's ideas. Those ideas had failed. They must be rejected in their entirety, as they had been rejected by the peoples of eastern Europe.

He turned to face the President. "If the changes in eastern Europe were inspired by the Soviet Union's policy of *perestroika,* have you thought about applying the policy of *perestroika* to the Soviet Union?"

Amid laughter and applause, Filipchenko turned back to face the deputies and, in a steadily rising voice, he demanded an end to the *nomenklatura* system and its privileges for Party functionaries, the complete conversion to a free market economy, the selling off of land, apartments, and whole industries in order to cut the budget deficit, the total privatization of agriculture, and sovereignty for the republics.

Privately, Kirillin sympathized with many of Filipchenko's ideas. Publicly, millions of Soviet citizens had voted for them.

The President sat there, occasionally interjecting to correct a matter of fact, rather like a benevolent headmaster with a gifted but erratic pupil. The Western media would describe it as a masterly, controlled performance by the President. They little knew what lay behind that genial, authoritative indulgence they so admired. In private he raged against Filipchenko and his allies. Hadn't they learned anything from history? He could not afford to make the same mistakes as Khrushchev. Khrushchev had recognized those same weaknesses in the Soviet system back in the 1950s. His impulsive experiments with the Soviet economy had confused everybody; his slashing of the Soviet Armed Forces by over a million men had wrecked the careers of thousands of middle ranking officers, demoralized the rest, and alienated the General Staff; and finally, his attempts to limit the period that any Party official could serve had created so many enemies within the Party that his downfall was inevitable. Didn't Filipchenko and his politically illiterate friends realize that a leader of the Soviet Union must carry the country, the Army, and the Party with him if his reforms were to stick?

Kirillin wasn't watching the enthusiastic applause from the Baltic, Georgian, Moldavian, Armenian and progressive Moscow deputies. He was watching the reactions of the Politburo members in their reserved section of the auditorium. They sat there, stone-faced, in their red plush seats. When Filipchenko's tirade was over, Leonid Dobrik went to the rostrum. The Chairman of the Party's Central Committee Commission on Agriculture declared that it was Filipchenko's version of *perestroika* that was bringing the country to economic crisis and political chaos. A free market society based on the survival of the fittest brought soaring inflation and massive job losses. It benefited only black marketeers, property speculators, and those nationalists who wanted the Soviet Union to collapse into anarchy.

The unimaginative Dobrik wasn't the one to worry about. Kirillin was studying the man with wavy white hair and a broad face, who peered through gold-rimmed spectacles to see which deputies failed to join in the applause for Dobrik. Nikolei Korolev was Chairman of the Party's Central Committee Commission on Ideology. He had been brought to Moscow at the same time as the President because of his record in cleaning up the Novosibirsk Regional Party Committee and his successful experiments in agricultural reform. He and the President had become colleagues and firm friends in the middle ranks of the Central Committee apparatus. Both shared an abhorrence of the Brezhnev stagnation and corruption. Both believed radical reform was essential. But when Korolev was appointed head of the Party's Ideology Commission, their paths began to diverge. It was as though the view from the fifth floor of the Central Committee building on Staraya Square had altered his vision. The Party's chief ideologist had become its chief defender of Marxist-Leninist orthodoxy.

Kirillin sighed and closed his notebook. The following Wednesday the President was due to wind up the Congress's spring session, and Kirillin had to prepare the first draft of the President's speech that would launch the Government's program for the rest of the year. How on earth was the President to introduce vital economic reforms without tearing the country apart?

He climbed the stairs to reach the soulless marble foyer, and left Khrushchev's legacy to the Kremlin by its main entrance. He turned right, away from the Soviet red star atop the tall spire of the red-brick Trinity Tower, and passed through a line of waiting black Zil and Chaika limousines to cross Ivanovskaya Square, where a solitary gray-uniformed militiaman, armed only with a whistle, protected the government buildings on the other side.

Kirillin entered the yellow and white neoclassical Supreme Soviet Presidium Building by a side door in the southeast wing that faced the tall white tiered Ivan the Great Bell Tower. Inside, a khaki-uniformed trooper with blue KGB insignia asked politely for his pass. Kirillin explained who he was. The guard, who looked barely out of school, was impassive. While Kirillin searched in vain for that damned pass, two more KGB troopers holding Kalashnikov automatic rifles emerged from a door near the entrance to block his way. A sergeant followed them and strolled up to Kirillin, who repeated his explanation. Sure, the sergeant said, and where is your pass?

"He's a friend of mine," a cultured voice from behind said.

"Yes, sir!" the sergeant said as the guards presented arms.

Nikolei Korolev smiled. "Don't worry," he said to Kirillin, "they'll soon come to recognize your face. In the meantime, they like to see paper permits."

Both men took the elevator to the fourth floor and

walked down long, red-carpeted corridors, past yet more KGB guards, to the northeast wing of the building.

"Where are you going, Comrade Korolev?" Kirillin asked.

"To your office. With your permission I shall wait there until the President returns. We need to discuss the speech he is to make next Wednesday to the Congress."

Korolev pulled back the white net curtains and looked out over the top of the Kremlin Wall into Red Square. "What do you think of this afternoon's session?" he asked reflectively.

"Interesting," Kirillin said cautiously.

Korolev continued to look out of the window. "Filipchenko is correct in some respects and wrong in others," he said. He turned to face Kirillin. "The two most successful socialist economies used to be those of the German Democratic Republic and Czechoslovakia, both centrally planned Marxist systems." He sat down in the chair on the other side of Kirillin's mahogany desk. "Look what's happened since they abandoned the leading role of the Party. We don't need to tinker with the system, Comrade Kirillin, we need better discipline and better organization to make it work properly."

Encouraged by Korolev's conversational manner, Kirillin said, "In a democratic socialist society, surely we need to take into account the views of those who want a different approach?"

Korolev's voice became even softer. "We are not like Czechoslovakia or Hungary. Western-style democracy has never been part of Slav culture. An unfettered multiparty system here will create anarchy."

"But we're committed to a multiparty system," Kirillin protested.

Korolev raised his eyebrows. "An *unfettered* multiparty system? We may have given up our constitutional monopoly of power, comrade, and we shall certainly cooperate with all those parties who favor a renewal of socialist society, but the Party must maintain its role in unifying the country. We can have no truck with organizations committed to extreme nationalist policies, to inter-ethnic violence, or to policies that threaten the very fabric of our society, whatever the demagogues in the Congress say."

Kirillin reddened. "The Congress is part of the fabric of our society."

Korolev removed his gold-rimmed spectacles. He peered myopically at Kirillin. "Have you ever been to the United States of America?"

"I spent two years in Italy."

"I'm speaking of the Promised Land of Free Enterprise, that supreme example of Western achievement which right-wing populists would transplant to the Soviet Union. Let me tell you, Comrade Kirillin, that when I took a short walk in one direction from our mission at the United Nations in New York I saw the most disgusting displays of personal wealth. And when I walked in another direction I came across human wretchedness, poverty, and homelessness on a scale which made me weep. Yes! Even me. It was the same in Washington. And are any of these people happy? Rich or poor? No! Because they have all sacrificed their spiritual values to the gods of greed and materialism. Do you want a city, Comrade Kirillin, where it's not safe to walk the streets after dark? Where murder, drug-taking, theft, and organized crime are uncontrollable? Where you're turned away from hospital unless you can prove your private health insurance payments are up to date? Where you have the freedom to starve to death?"

Korolev mopped his brow with a large red handkerchief and replaced his spectacles. He continued in his softer tone. "You were too young to remember the Great Patriotic War and the devastation it left us. Let me tell you, this nation has many achievements to be proud of. Of course mistakes were made. But certain proposals coming out of the Congress of People's Deputies won't put those mistakes right. They will destroy our moral and cultural heritage. It's already happening in Moscow. Organized crime, drugs, and prostitution have flourished since certain people have misapplied the policy of *perestroika.*"

A green light on Kirillin's telephone flashed to indicate that the President had returned to his office.

Korolev looked at the light. "The President and I became friends in the Central Committee. Filipchenko is a friend of yours, isn't he?"

"I met him at university," Kirillin said.

Korolev rose and walked toward the door. He stopped and turned to Kirillin. "It's important to know who are your real friends, the ones you keep rather than the ones you discard."

Chapter ✦ Eight

CARDINAL JOHANN ZINGLER was early for his meeting with the Pope. Giuseppe showed him into the private secretaries' office.

Zingler was one of the few cardinals in the Vatican's equivalent of a civil service who was known, by reputation at least, outside Italy. As Prefect of the Sacred Congregation for the Doctrine of the Faith, he headed the most powerful of the twenty-four dicasteries of the Roman Curia. His Congregation had begun life in 1542 as the Supreme Congregation for the Holy Inquisition of Heretical Error. Over the centuries it had changed its name and its methods but not, according to most of Ryan's colleagues in England, its mentality.

As a young theologian in Austria, Zingler had first attracted attention for his radical views and scathing criticisms of the Vatican. Over the years his position had shifted as he had been promoted. Now responsible for maintaining doctrinal orthodoxy within the Catholic Church, his conversion from poacher to gamekeeper was complete.

Ryan had been led to expect a crude Austrian bully. Instead, the silver haired man who inquired after Ryan's well-being was charm itself. Had he been dressed in ordinary clothes rather than a crimson-trimmed black cassock, he might have been mistaken for a kindly professor. Ryan discovered, however, that first impressions can be deceiving.

Zingler put his folder down on Hoffman's desk and lowered himself into Hoffman's chair. The voice was courteous but the words were blunt. "I trust, Father Ryan, that you do not intend to follow the example of one of your predecessors?"

"I'm afraid I don't know anything about the previous papal secretaries, Eminence."

An enigmatic smile played on Zingler's face. "I'm referring to a previous secretary to the Cardinal Archbishop of Westminster. The one who left the priesthood in order to run a political organization."

"It isn't a political organization, Eminence. The Campaign for Nuclear Disarmament is devoted to bringing about peace in the world."

The voice remained soft, but the smile hardened. "It is a sign of the times that too many Catholics—and that, regrettably, includes a majority of the Catholic hierarchy and priests in the United States—believe that present world problems can be resolved by secular means, such as disarmament, economic aid, and so forth. They fail to recognize that the world's problems derive from a spiritual crisis and can only be resolved by spiritual means." He tapped the folder he had brought in. "This is the message the Holy Father will deliver to the European Parliament at Strasbourg on Friday."

"But surely, Eminence, that doesn't preclude working in the world to bring about peace and reduce poverty?"

Zingler brushed this aside. "It may appear noble to deplore the crushing burden of the arms race. The solution, however, is not to campaign for nuclear disarmament, which would expose us to considerable risk, but to remove the cause of the arms race, which is sin."

Ryan's cheeks burned. "Are you trying to say Communism, Eminence?"

"Let us say Godlessness, Father Ryan, shall we?" He stood up dismissively and looked at his watch.

Ryan accompanied Zingler down the stairs to the Pope's private library. Cardinal Fasolo was just leaving. The courtesies exchanged between the two princes of the Church were civil but entirely lacking in warmth.

Ryan found he could do little to help the Pope prepare for his trip to Strasbourg. The Secretary of State and his staff took overall responsibility for the arrangements; Bishop Spiazzi, Prefect of the Papal Household, coordinated the lists of audiences and meetings; and Giuseppe looked after the Pope's personal needs. He watched the papal party take the private lift down to the car waiting in the Courtyard of Sixtus V.

He returned to his office and sat looking at the Pope's typed schedule; marked in red ink next to each entry was a telephone number to ring in case the Pope needed to be contacted in an emergency.

The green telephone on his desk rang.

"Father Ryan. Antonio Benedetti here. I've arranged a little dinner party this evening for the British Ambassador to the Holy See, among others. I'd be delighted if you'd join us. You might find it a little more amusing than eating alone with the Maria Bambina Sisters."

"That's very kind, Excellency."

"Splendid. Seven-thirty for eight."

"Oh, Excellency . . ."

"Yes?"

"Do I dress for dinner?"

"If you feel you must."

Chapter ✣ Nine

ARCHBISHOP BENEDETTI'S APARTMENT was in the Palazzina della Zecca, across a cobbled square from the Sistine Chapel.

Benedetti's black-suited valet led Ryan to the main reception room. By now, Ryan no longer stared in wonder at Renaissance palaces; they were simply places where people worked and lived. He was, however, surprised to be offered champagne.

Benedetti introduced him with a flourish to "Her Britannic Majesty's Ambassador to the Holy See."

Derek Stapleton resembled an avuncular prep school headmaster. He peered over the top of half-moon spectacles. "Welcome back to Rome, Father Ryan."

Webster Dillon, the United States Ambassador to the Holy See, was a large, loud Texan who wore a boot-lace tie. Ryan mentally added a stetson and hand-tooled, high-heeled boots.

"Real pleased to meet with you, Father. Any friend of Antonio's is a friend of mine."

Benedetti smiled knowingly at the last guest. "Vittorio Agustoni currently languishes as the Republic's foreign minister though, we pray, not for much longer."

Ryan recognized the elegantly dressed man with graying temples and silver moustache as a former Italian prime minister who was rumored to be favorite to head the next coalition government. Other rumors linked him with the secret P2 masonic lodge.

"What qualities do you possess, Father," Agustoni asked, "that you are invited so soon to one of Rome's most exclusive dinner tables?"

"Ad magnas res natus est," Benedetti said.

"He was born for great things," Stapleton translated for Dillon's benefit.

Ryan's embarrassment was relieved by the valet announcing that dinner was ready.

The only women present, Ryan noted, were the nuns who could occasionally be glimpsed handing the valet dishes to serve. The meal was the best he had ever had in Italy. Correction. The best he'd ever had. Here he was offered a choice of vintage wines; in the papal apartment guests were offered a carafe of Frascati as an alternative to mineral water. As the wine bottles emptied, so the talk flowed more freely.

"What we gonna do about the mess Poland's in?" Dillon asked.

Stapleton looked at Benedetti.

Benedetti threw up his hands in mock horror. "When I passed through the Basilica the other day, I heard a Polish priest asking God whether he would ever live to see the day that Poland emerged from its economic crisis. God replied, 'I'm afraid not. And neither will I.'"

The others laughed. The valet cleared away the remains of the *dolci* and began serving cognac.

Dillon said, "You gotta come clean with me, Antonio, about Vatican policy toward the Soviets. They've had a big rethink at the State Department. The President's agreed we prefer fat Russians to thin Russians."

"I confess," said Benedetti, "that most Russians with whom I've been acquainted have seemed a trifle overweight. Personally, I prefer a slim figure, like James's."

"Hell, you know what I mean. A Soviet Union that collapses economically is gonna react like a wounded bear, hitting out at everyone. It'll be back to the old bogey of a foreign enemy to divert the Ruskies from their problems at home and convince them to accept sacrifices for the sake of Mother Russia."

"I agree," said Agustoni. "We need a prosperous, market-led Soviet Union having trade links with the West. Once they get a taste of prosperity, they won't want to lose it by engaging in confrontation."

"Right!" said Dillon. "There's an untapped market out there of 290 million customers. So, Antonio, may I take it that you ain't going to rock the boat?"

Benedetti looked mortally offended. "How can you say such a thing? When a previous President of yours was calling the Soviet Union the evil empire, Cardinal Fasolo was quietly negotiating agreements with virtually all the Communist bloc countries. As a result, the Church was organized and ready to fill the ideological vacuum when Communism collapsed in eastern Europe. The Church in Lithuania is now recognized and is substantially independent of Moscow, while patient diplomacy is continuing to advance the cause of the Church in the Ukraine."

Dillon put down his brandy glass and leaned forward. "Is reaching a *modus vivendi* with the Communists Vatican policy or papal policy?"

"I'm sure the Holy Father would let us know if he felt the Secretariat were not reflecting his views."

Ryan noticed the sly smile on Agustoni's face.

"Another thing I've been meaning to ask you about, Antonio," said Dillon as he lit a cigar while the valet replenished his brandy glass, "is this guy Zingler. The strong message I get back home is that Cardinal Zingler is creating a serious problem for the Catholic Church in the States. There's even talk of the American Church declaring independence from Rome. Now theology ain't my field, but the State Department and the Vatican have worked well together in the past, and any schism could cause big problems where we have mutual interests."

Benedetti sighed and held out his hands in despair. "Those whom the gods would make mad, they first send to the Sacred Congregation for the Doctrine of the Faith."

"I thought it was fashionable in Rome these days to believe in only one God," said Agustoni, wiping his lips on a white linen napkin.

Benedetti arched his brows. "I've never been a slave of fashion."

"Has Zingler got it all wrong, then?" Dillon asked.

"On the contrary," Benedetti said, "his position is so canonically impeccable, I doubt he's even a Christian."

Agustoni smiled. "Do I detect a hint of sarcasm, Antonio?"

"As somebody once said, wit reforms, comedy cleanses, and sarcasm purifies. I strive for purity, even if I don't always succeed."

"You must not shock your new recruit," Agustoni chided.

Benedetti looked at Ryan. "James spent three years in the USA, eight years in Rome, and two years living with the Cardinal Archbishop of Westminster. Nothing can shock him."

"Is that right, James?" said Dillon, belatedly offering one of his large cigars. "Then tell me, which team do you play for? The liberals, like your old boss? The Slav fundamentalists, like your new boss? Or the Roman pragmatists, like Antonio here?"

"I hope I'm in God's team, Ambassador."

Agustoni laughed approvingly. Dillon shook his head and turned to Stapleton. "You Brits invented diplomacy, right, Derek?"

Stapleton, who had said little but had observed everything during the previous half-hour, looked over the top of his spectacles. "If we did, the Italians have perfected it."

"If only we were allowed to use it," Benedetti sighed.

"Lead Europe back to its Christian heritage and the world's problems will be solved?" Agustoni asked.

Benedetti, with a glance toward Ryan, shrugged. "We all accept we cannot compromise with evil." He paused. "Nor can we put the clock back." He smiled. "By which I mean, of course, that time has overtaken us and we must bring our little party to a close."

Ryan was the last to leave. As he thanked Benedetti, the Vatican's foreign minister asked, "Tell me, James, what did you think of the evening?"

"To be honest . . ." Ryan began.

"Splendid," Benedetti said. "Honesty is by far the best policy in the Vatican. It gives you the advantage of surprise."

Ryan walked back, a little drunk, to his attic in the Apostolic Palace and wondered what he really did think of the evening.

Chapter ✤ Ten

RYAN AND THE five Maria Bambina Sisters watched the Pope's address to the European Parliament on the television set in the private dining room.

This was the Pope whom Ryan had known from previous television broadcasts, not the Pope with whom he lived in the papal apartment. The walk was purposeful rather than sluggish, the voice authoritative rather than ponderous, the eyes clear rather than unfocused. This Pope seemed to draw strength and vitality from the presence of a live audience. The Sisters said it was the Holy Spirit.

The Pope stated that all the problems of our times stemmed from a denial of Christian values. The social divisions in western Europe were the consequence of a selfish materialism that stemmed from the denial of Christian charity. The oppressions of freedom in eastern Europe had been the consequence of a selfish greed for power that also stemmed from the denial of Christian charity.

Full economic and monetary union, he said, and the creation of a single European market, should not be limited, for selfish reasons, to the current twelve nations of the European Community. Rather, their vision should be more profound. The political liberation of an eastern Europe, burdened by economic problems created by forty years of suppression of freedom, presented the European Community with a unique challenge to "do unto others as you would have done unto yourselves." That, after all, was what the word "community" meant. The European Community should grasp the chance to create a common political and economic structure for the whole of Europe, from the Atlantic to the Urals, based on the Christian heritage shared by all European peoples. From such a position of Christian solidarity, a united Europe could once more resume its role as a beacon of civilization in the world, and use its pooled resources to tackle the urgent spiritual and material needs of the developing world.

Ryan found the speech inspiring. So too did many of the following day's newspapers including, curiously, Italy's Communist *L'Unità*. Hoffman, however, seized upon those papers which criticized the Pope for naivete, for harking back to bygone days of the Holy Roman Empire, or for interfering in political matters.

"Look at this!" he said in disgust at *La Repubblica*. "The Holy Father is *not* engaging in politics. He is simply setting out the moral guidelines that politicians must follow."

"I suppose," Ryan said, "some people might interpret that as political."

"Of course. They are the selfsame people who interpret crime as a symptom of social deprivation, and who no longer recognize the meaning of sin or accept the need for penance."

Ryan hesitated. "I'm not sure how far we can impose our own values on a predominantly secular society."

"You have put your finger on it, Father Ryan. A secular society is just what the Devil wants. Outside the walls of the Vatican, church attendance in the Pope's own diocese has slumped to less than five percent. Rome is decaying into a pagan city." He removed his spectacles in an angry gesture. "What has this 'secular society' in the West produced? Sex, violence, abortion, contraception, drug addiction, blasphemy, theft, divorce, infidelity, pornography, rape: a total breakdown of moral values and the sacred idea of the family!"

"Is it just the West?" Ryan ventured.

"Of course not. But it was to the West that the Blessed Virgin revealed the First Secret of Fatima. And how has the West responded?"

Ryan felt he was being held personally accountable for the West's response to Fatima.

"Why do you think the First Secret given to the children was a vision of hell? The Blessed Virgin prophesied that modern times would be dominated by Satan, and that only by devotion to her Immaculate Heart, through prayer and penance, can we save souls from the torment of hell."

"Is it possible that these young children gave an overliteral interpretation to Our Lady's message?"

Hoffman drummed his fingers on his desk in frustration. "Father Ryan! When the Virgin revealed this First Secret, on the thirteenth of July 1917, she promised that, three months to the day precisely, she would perform a miracle so that everyone would believe that the secrets she revealed to the children came from God. On the thirteenth day of October, one hundred thousand people gathered at the Cova da Iria outside Fatima. One hundred thousand people saw the sun spin on its axis, dance in the sky, and then swoop down toward the earth to foreshadow the end of the world. Apart from the Resurrection, this was the first time in recorded history that God had performed a public miracle at a predicted time and place in order to prove the authenticity of His message."

Hoffman collected the newspapers into two piles. One pile he took through to the Pope's study for the Holy Father to read. Ryan noticed that the newspapers he consigned to the wastepaper basket were the ones which criticized the speech.

Chapter ✤ Eleven

WHEN HIS GREEN telephone rang and a voice said simply, "It'll be devilishly cold by two o'clock," Kirillin frowned.

He had never been inside a church in his life. He had been brought up during Khrushchev's five-year onslaught against religion by parents who were loyal Party members. They had taught him to despise the Church as, at best, a superstitious cult for old women and peasants and, at worst, a relic of imperialism that sought to undermine the socialist State. Now, the officially atheist State was handing over cathedrals and churches to the Russian Orthodox hierarchy as though Christ were about to make an official visit.

He put down *L'Unità*'s account of the Pope's speech to the European Parliament, and asked his secretary whether the Assumption Cathedral was an operating church or still a museum. She giggled.

At two o'clock Kirillin crossed Ivanovskaya Square to the oldest part of the Kremlin, Cathedral Square, dominated by the white-tiered Ivan the Great Bell Tower with its golden onion-shaped dome topped by a golden triple-barred Russian cross. He paused in the center of the square, surrounded by six ornate white buildings boasting gilded domes and crosses, and wondered what led people to believe in a non-existent God.

The main door of the Assumption Cathedral, below a huge fresco of the Virgin Mary, was locked. At the left-hand side of the limestone brick building a queue of tourists waited to enter by the west door. Kirillin walked to the front, and a young American voice shouted, "Hey, fella, we're waiting in line here." Kirillin flashed his red card to the *dezhurnaya* and eased his way into the cathedral. The old woman looked stoically at the brash American student and kept the queue waiting an extra ten minutes.

Kirillin peered through the throng of camera-laden visitors being conducted around by bored Intourist guides. Like all Orthodox churches this cathedral had no pews. It was smaller but higher than Kirillin had expected. Babakin was examining a large elaborately carved wooden throne near the locked south main door.

"Ivan the Terrible's throne," Babakin said. "I trust you approve of our meeting place."

Ahead, the towering iconostasis stretched across the full width of the cathedral to shield the high altar and the side chapels ranged against the east wall. Rows of richly colored icons were set in its massive, intricately decorated gilt frame, which gleamed in the light of a giant chandelier of electric light bulbs. Four huge rounded pillars supported the vaulting high above the black marble floor of the square nave. Every inch of the pillars, like every inch of the walls, was covered by larger-than-life frescoes of saints or patriarchs. Kirillin thought it vulgarly overdone. He shrugged.

"Surely you're impressed by the most important building in pre-Revolutionary Russia?" asked Babakin, walking away from the iconostasis. "Grand Princes and Czars were crowned here. It was built in the fifteenth century by the Bologna architect Aristotle Fioravanti. The finest example of the Italian Renaissance being appropriated to serve the needs of Moscow."

"I didn't know you were an ecclesiastical historian," Kirillin said drily.

Babakin grinned. "I was trained for the priesthood. Along this south wall are the tombs of the patriarchs of the Russian Orthodox Church." He stopped at the southwest corner. "This is the most revered tomb of all."

A large tabernacle with a tent roof occupied the corner. Kirillin peered through its delicate openwork bronze walls and saw inside a bronze sarcophagus.

"Patriarch Hermogenes excommunicated the Polish invaders of Russia," Babakin said. "During the Polish occupation of Moscow he was imprisoned by the Poles and starved to death."

"Did you invite me here for a history lesson?" Kirillin asked.

"Not entirely," Babakin said. He removed a folded sheet of paper from his inside pocket and handed it to Kirillin.

Kirillin held the paper under the light of one of the chandeliers.

DRAFT MEMORANDUM OF AGREEMENT: STRICTLY CONFIDENTIAL

The European Community would welcome an application from an independent and democratic Poland for full membership of the Community. The particular conditions that the Community recognizes as fulfilling the qualifications for membership are:

(1) The applicant is governed according to European democratic norms; in the case of Poland this shall be taken to mean:

(i) the President and all members of the Sejim and the Senate shall be freely elected by the votes of all citizens, with no seats or executive positions reserved for members of any one political party or its affiliated organizations;

(ii) the rights of all citizens freely to form political

associations and parties, trades unions, and other social and cultural organizations shall be guaranteed by law;

(iii) the right to complete freedom of operation of the Catholic Church and any other religion shall be guaranteed by law.

(2) The applicant is not a member of any other multinational trading or military bloc whose interests are incompatible with those of the European Community; in the case of Poland this shall be taken to mean the Council for Mutual Economic Assistance and the Warsaw Pact.

(3) The applicant is prepared to play a full part in the security arrangements deemed necessary for the protection of the Community. In particular the applicant:

(i) shall not permit the stationing on its territory of troops or armaments or other military installations of the Warsaw Pact countries;

(ii) shall join the North Atlantic Treaty Organization, or its successor, with a view to coordinating the defense of its own territory with that of the member states of the European Community.

The European Community recognizes that such changes involve transitional costs and is prepared to offer interest-free credits to the value of [ ] European Economic Units for a period of ten years from the date of Poland's agreement to these conditions.

Kirillin looked up at the tomb of Patriarch Hermogenes. "Poland to quit the Warsaw Pact and join NATO? What is the status of this document?"

"It was prepared by the Vatican. Earlier this week the Spanish Prime Minister agreed to present it as his own proposal to the European Community heads of government meeting next Wednesday in Madrid."

"That's absurd," Kirillin said. "The Spanish Prime Minister is an atheist. He's opposed by the Church in Spain. Why should he do any favors for the Vatican?"

"On the contrary," Babakin said, "it's very clever. Spain holds the Presidency of the European Community till July. Shortly after that, there'll be a general election in Spain. My Fifth Department's assessment is that his Socialist Party will lose. It'll be close, but he'll lose." Babakin smiled. "In exchange for his putting the proposal forward, the clergy in Spain will be instructed not to preach against the evils of socialism during the election period. It should be enough to tip the balance in his favor."

"What's the source of this information?"

"An agent we have in the Vatican. Codenamed Judas."

"What sum of money is involved?"

"According to Judas, the European Community will be asked to offer credits equivalent to fifty billion US dollars, enough to wipe out Poland's debt to the West."

Kirillin thought for a while. Finally he said, "The Polish generals will never agree to join NATO. You ensured that only reliable Communists were appointed to senior staff positions in their armed forces."

"Their generals may be Communists, Dmitry Sergeyevich, but first and foremost they're Poles. If they have to choose between joining NATO or allowing Poland to disintegrate into bankruptcy and anarchy, what do you think they'll do?" Babakin smiled. "There's even a bonus in it for them. Instead of being hated by the people for enforcing martial law in 1981, they'll be applauded as patriots who freed Poland from the Russian yoke."

It seemed to Kirillin that Babakin approved the deviousness of the plan. "Is this the Pope's work?"

Babakin shook his head. "The broad objectives, yes. But there's a much more subtle mind behind this scheme."

"Who?"

"Cardinal Fasolo, the Secretary of State."

"Who else knows about it?" Kirillin asked.

"In Rome, the chief of Line PR, who personally runs Judas, and the Resident. In Moscow, only me. All signals from Judas are coded for my eyes only."

"What happens to this information now?"

"In the normal course of events, I'd copy the signal to General Blagov and to Service I, who would incorporate it in their weekly intelligence digest for the Presidential Council and the Politburo."

Kirillin looked again at the signal from Judas. "Can this information be held back?"

Babakin gave a sly smile. "I thought you'd ask that. Let's both have a think over the weekend, and see how best we can handle it. We'll meet again on Monday morning, say at ten o'clock."

Kirillin nodded. "At the Obelisk. But what about this signal?"

Babakin grinned. "Put it in your wastepaper basket."

Chapter ❖ Twelve

Kirillin worked on the President's Congress speech until two o'clock on Saturday morning. He returned to the Supreme Soviet Presidium for a meeting with the President at eight-thirty, and left at four that afternoon by the officials' entrance. He slumped into the back seat of his car, and told Georgi, his driver-cum-bodyguard, to take him to his new dacha.

The car reversed out from the row of other black Volgas facing the trees which lined the yellow facade of the Presidium's southwest wing. It circled Ivanovskaya Square, passing Cathedral Square with its crown of onion-shaped domes gleaming in the spring sun. At the end of Ivanovskaya Square the Volga turned right into the road that sloped down behind the Archangel Michael and the Annunciation Cathedrals. After passing the yellow and white Great Kremlin Palace, the road dipped sharply past the Armory and left the Kremlin beneath the tiered red-brick pyramid of the Borovitsky Gate Tower.

Kirillin was struggling to keep his eyes open as the car climbed up Frunze Street past the General Staff headquarters. By the time it had turned into Kalinin Prospekt he had given up the struggle.

Potholes in the road woke him about half an hour later. They were approaching Zhukovka, which looked like a struggling collective farm village, clusters of typical Russian peasant cabins of rough-hewn logs with outhouses in the vegetable gardens. The car turned left off the Moscow road and went down a side road into the deep forest. Where this road branched, the car took the direction marked Zhukovka-1. The car stopped at the gate in a high green fence. The driver showed his pass and the uniformed KGB guard waved the car through.

From the moment of his appointment as special assistant to the President, the Ninth Directorate of the KGB had taken over Kirillin's life. He had been driven from the Kremlin to a new apartment where, to his amazement, a team of people were unpacking all his personal possessions taken, without his knowledge, from his old apartment. When he protested, the officer in charge told him very politely that matters concerning his personal security were outside his competence. He felt less resentful at this intrusion in his life when he was introduced to the staff assigned to him. No more shopping in the special sections of GUM, no more cooking his own meals, no more bribing the cleaning lady actually to do some cleaning.

Now he was not surprised when the car pulled up at a new dacha built of imported brick, where a Ninth Directorate officer was waiting to greet him.

Inside the lavish reception room, with its marble fireplace and crystal chandelier, the officer introduced him to a cook and two housemaids. The younger one was distinctly bedable, but Kirillin had other things on his mind. He cut short the conducted tour of the dacha, took a sauna, and asked for a bottle of 100 proof Stolichnaya. Half a bottle later he was feeling more relaxed.

Dressed in corduroy trousers and a sweater, he went for a walk to explore his new kingdom. The railway line from Moscow separated his part of Zhukovka-1 from the area in which members of the Presidential Council, Politburo, senior ministers, and Central Committee Commission chairmen had their dachas with private gardens bordering the Moscow River. He turned into a pine grove in search of the river, twisted his ankle, and fell. The ground was gouged with the remnants of trenches prepared for the defense of Moscow. The Germans hadn't come this way, but they might have, they might have.

At a bluff overlooking the slow-moving Moscow River, he sat down on the grass to rest his ankle. It was a tranquil place. The sky had the soft tint of approaching sunset. The breeze carried the rich smell of pines. He looked across the river at the expanse of untidy fields littered with uncultivated shrubs and undergrowth. He could see for miles and for centuries across unchanging Russia.

Russia, Kirillin reflected, was psychologically crippled by her schizoid attitude to the West. A deep-rooted inferiority complex spawned either a pathetic eagerness to copy all things Western, or else a paranoid distrust of all things Western coupled with an aggressive identification with all things Slav.

It was ever thus.

Her leaders had called themselves Czars in imitation of the Roman Caesars. Not to be outshone by the Vatican, her Czars had commissioned Italian Renaissance architects to design palaces, cathedrals, towers, and even the walls of the Kremlin. Her priests had proclaimed Moscow to be the Third Rome. Even for her Revolution, she had been inspired by the French, and had adopted the fifty-year-old ideas of a German philosopher. In recent times, Levi jeans and Western rock music had dominated the cultural aspirations of half her children. And now, leaders like Anatoli Filipchenko believed her only salvation lay in a Western-style democracy and free market economy.

The other face of Russia revealed itself in her compulsion to impose Slav dominion as far west and as far south as she could; her southern colonies she despised, her western colonies she feared. It mattered not whether her Czar was called Ivan the Terrible or Comrade Stalin. While her people lived in wretched conditions, she built ever more and grander monuments to heroic Russian victories, all blessed by her Church. It was ironic that those twin symbols of Slav identity, the Cyrillic alphabet and the Orthodox religion, both derived from Greece, the cradle of Western civilization.

To Korolev and those of like mind, the shameful, Westernized face of Russia was threatening to take over. In the Congress it even demanded that the body of one of the few home-grown political thinkers, Vladimir Ilyich Lenin, be removed from Red Square, and that the empire, forged with so much Russian blood, be quietly surrendered along with the respect accorded Russia as a superpower.

The West, in its arrogance, viewed Russia according to Western norms. It labeled Filipchenko a radical and Korolev a conservative. The West little understood the deep-seated forces that these two men represented.

What, then, of the President? He was far more than the pragmatic reformist painted by the Western media. He was Russia's only hope. A leader who wanted to remould the very character of the nation. A leader determined to tap the deep well of Russian spirituality in order to liberate her from her psychological crutches, to nurture her development, at long last, into self-confident maturity. That meant neither Western selfish materialism nor Slavic autocracy. It meant the genuinely democratic socialist society of which Lenin had dreamt.

But time was fast running out for the President.

Kirillin stood up, threw a stone into the Moscow River, and watched the circle of ripples spread outwards. The ripples died before they reached the far bank. Kirillin returned to his dacha, finished off the Stolichnaya, and fell asleep.

Chapter ✤ Thirteen

ARCHBISHOP KORCHAN LEFT the Pope's private study through the private secretaries' office. Monsignor Hoffman was away, visiting friends. The *Sostituto* smiled at Ryan. "No rest for the wicked, even on Saturday?"

Ryan sighed. "I'm going through all these folders your Secretariat insists on sending up to the Holy Father. I'm trying to sift out the ones there's really no need to trouble him with."

Korchan winked. "You'd better not tell the Secretary of State. He believes the Holy Father should read everything that's issued in his name."

"Even a summons by the Sacred Congregation for the Doctrine of the Faith to a priest in Milwaukee for allegedly giving holy communion to a practising homosexual?"

Korchan nodded sympathetically. "Especially those. Look," he said, brightening up, "your cardinal is in Rome for next week's plenary session of the Council for Christian Unity."

"Cardinal Harding?"

"He arrived at the English College last night. Why don't you telephone and arrange to join him for a meal?"

"I'd love to, but . . ."

"I'll have a word with the Holy Father. Just fix a date with your cardinal and ask His Holiness's permission. You'll find he'll be pleased for you to see your country-man."

"Thank you, Excellency. I appreciate that."

Korchan smiled.

Chapter ✤ Fourteen

THE BIRDS WOKE Kirillin on Sunday morning. He took his time to shower, shave carefully, and dress once more in corduroy trousers and sweater. It was a fine spring morning, the sun bright but not hot. He decided to walk to the Mazunovs'.

The guards at the gate to Zhukovka-1, known locally as Sovmin, looked at him suspiciously. No, he didn't need a car, he explained, he was simply walking to a friend's dacha for lunch. After the guards had written down precise details of where and how long he expected to be, they reminded him he would need his pass to reenter the compound.

He took the second fork in the spur road from the main Moscow road. This was signposted Zhukovka-2, but usually referred to as Academic Zhukovka.

Kirillin had graduated from Moscow State University, via IMEMO, the Moscow Institute of World Economy and International Relations, to the Ministry of Foreign Trade, and thence to his sought-after foreign travel. Back in Moscow, his expertise in foreign commerce and his hard work had brought him promotion within the Government apparatus. Anatoli Filipchenko had chosen the Party apparatus, and had worked his way up from local Komsomol organizer in Sverdlovsk through to Second Secretary of the Moscow City Central Committee before he was sacked for "ambitionism" and "adventurism". Vitaly Mazunov, the athlete among the three of them, had surprisingly pursued an academic career, and was now a leading figure at the Institute of Economics of the Soviet Academy of Sciences. His published papers kept just ahead of the rising tide of *glasnost*, giving him the reputation of a radical economist without endangering his establishment position or his dacha at Zhukovka-2.

Vitaly Mazunov opened the door of the wooden dacha. Mazunov had been big and muscular, representing the university in the discus. Now the muscle had turned to fat. In the city, a smart, double-breasted suit disguised his figure. In the country, a shrunken plaid shirt and tight jeans emphasized his paunch. His chubby face broke into a grin as he wrapped a welcoming arm round Kirillin. "Mitya, it's good to see you again!"

Mazunov stood back and peered over Kirillin's shoulder. "Where are they?"

"Where are who?"

"For a man as important as you are now, I expect at least a chauffeur, a bodyguard, and a squad of motorcycle outriders."

"Vitaly Pavlovich!" a woman's voice scolded from inside. "Where are your manners? Let me see Mitya."

Mazunov bowed low and stepped aside. Kirillin grinned and pulled a bunch of tulips from behind his back. *"Les fleurs pour la fleur."*

Nina Mazunova squealed with girlish pleasure. Although in her late thirties, she retained her fresh complexion and her Mary Quantaya haircut. She was no longer the slim nymphet, but Kirillin preferred the comfortable buxom figure he now hugged.

The double doors opened directly into the large farmhouse kitchen, the main room of the dacha. In the center of the room, a table was covered with *zakuski*, plates of black and red caviar on brown bread, smoked salmon, marinated mushrooms, salted herring, salami, pickled cucumber, cold tongue, beet salad, and scallions.

While Nina put the flowers in a vase, Vitaly took a bottle of vodka from the fridge. "Is the President's special assistant permitted to drink alcohol?"

"I've just had a week sampling the delights of Narzan mineral water."

Mazunov laughed. They sat down at the table and Mazunov poured out three shot-glasses of vodka. "To the shining star of the Moscow State University Eclectic Music Appreciation Society!"

"To Mitya!" Nina said.

"To the Eclectic Music Appreciation Society!" Kirillin said.

They downed the vodka. Mazunov refilled the glasses.

Kirillin looked round the dacha. It fitted the Mazunovs like a comfortable old slipper. Vitaly, the athlete turned establishment academic. Nina, the feminist turned housewife. And what of Dmitry Kirillin? The cynical Party member turned fighter for his country's future. Why? Because, he supposed, the Soviet leader had placed his trust in him. "We've all changed," he sighed, "except Anatoli."

"We saw Anatoli's speech on television," Nina said.

"I don't know what's come over him," Mazunov said.

Kirillin shrugged. "He's sincere."

"To sincerity, provided it does not destroy *perestroika*," Mazunov said.

"To sincerity!" Kirillin and Nina said.

They helped themselves to the *zakuski*. "With talent like this, Nina," Kirillin said between mouthfuls, "I could find you employment as a maid at Sovmin."

"You're a terrible man, Dmitry Sergeyevich."

"And you're a terrible woman, Nina Maximovna."

"To Ivan!" Mazunov said.

"To whom?" Nina asked.

"Ivan the Terrible."

"Your jokes get worse," Kirillin lamented.

"To an improvement in my jokes!"

"We'll all drink to that," said Nina.

After the *zakuski* had been washed down with vodka, Nina served *solyanka*, a vegetable soup with smoked fish, followed by baked sturgeon. Mazunov poured out glasses of *Tsinandali*, a white wine from Nina's native Georgia.

While they were eating chocolate ice cream, Kirillin's favorite sweet, Nina asked about his new dacha.

Kirillin pulled a face. "It's big, it's full of the latest West German equipment, it's kept spotless by the staff, but it's . . . it's too efficient. It's not homely, not like here."

"You should get yourself a wife, Mitya," Nina stated.

Kirillin laughed. "That's what the President said yesterday morning. I told him, when you send for my friend Vitaly Mazunov and have him taken out and shot at dawn, then I shall be able to marry the only woman I've ever loved."

Nina blushed. Mazunov drained his glass and put it on the table. "Don't joke about those times, Mitya," he said somberly. "There's no guarantee they won't return."

Reacting to the change of mood, Nina said, "Why don't you two take the brandy through to the den while I clear the table and wash up?"

Mazunov picked up a bottle of Armenian brandy and two glasses, and shambled through to his den. It was the untidiest room in the dacha. Papers littered not only an old oak desk, but also most of the floor and an old sofa.

Kirillin examined the rods and stuffed fishes fixed to the wall. "You need a more active sport than fishing if you're going to lose weight, Vitaly."

Mazunov grunted. "Can't even fish now. No one here has had his license renewed this season, 'for ecological reasons' according to the authorities. But you lot at Sovmin are still fishing."

"I'll look into it," Kirillin promised.

"That's not why I asked you here. I've got bigger problems than a fishing license."

"Is there anything I can do?"

"It's the paper you asked me to prepare for the President's speech to the Congress on Wednesday."

"Yes?"

"I need your advice before I submit the final version."

"Sure. What's the problem?"

Mazunov began hesitantly. "I'm an economist, not a politician. I don't know how far I can go."

Kirillin carefully removed the papers from part of the sofa, and sat back. The vodka, the wine, and Nina had relaxed him. "I want you to be completely frank about our position and your solution for getting us out of the mess we're in. Unless the President knows the real facts and is given realistic policy proposals, how can he be convincing?"

Mazunov nodded and sat down at his desk. "The facts are bad enough. Ignore the figures put out by *Goskomstat*. Our economy is about sixtieth in world rankings and sinking fast. We're in a much worse position than the European satellites before they abandoned Communism because it didn't deliver the goods." He took a file from a briefcase by his chair. "Here. See for yourself."

Kirillin glanced at the economic analysis. "These figures don't tell us anything the Russian housewife doesn't know. On the contrary, they'll convince the people that *perestroika* is more necessary than ever." He knocked back the brandy and Mazunov refilled his glass. He didn't refill his own.

"*Perestroika* isn't merely necessary," Mazunov said quietly, "it's essential. If we don't totally restructure the economy, we won't even be a second-rate power. We'll be holding out the begging bowl alongside the poorest Third World nations."

Kirillin took another large swig from his glass. "Good," he said. "A forecast like that will scare the pants off Korolev and his friends on the Central Committee. I don't see what the problem is."

"The problem is that to finance *perestroika* we need a hundred billion dollars. We haven't got it."

"Then you must tell the President how to get it," Kirillin said. The brandy was helping him see things clearly.

Mazunov grimaced. "I can't. It's politically impossible."

"Nothing is impossible," said Kirillin expansively. "What are the options?"

"There are only three options. The first is to force a rise in domestic savings by a swingeing cutback in domestic consumption, devalue the rouble twentyfold, effectively confiscating those savings, and then switch to a market pricing system, selling off assets to whoever can pay for them."

Kirillin put down his brandy glass. "The price rises and job losses would be catastrophic. It'd be political suicide."

"Precisely. The second option is to divert resources from defense to civilian expenditure on a massive scale."

"The President's already done that," said Kirillin. "The *nachalstvo* in the Armed Forces are still seething. He had to use the chairmanship of the KGB as a bargaining counter, but the President managed to pull off another fifteen percent reduction in the defense budget."

"Peanuts," stated Mazunov flatly. "Include the hidden subsidies, and the military-industrial complex gobbles up twenty percent of our income. To bring that down to the same proportion of income as the Americans, we need a seventy percent reduction in real defense expenditure."

Kirillin was sobering up rapidly. "That's out of the question. He could never persuade the Presidential Council. Even if by some miracle he managed to force it through, we'd have a military coup."

"Which leaves only the third option. Borrow from the West."

Kirillin locked his fingers together. "Half the Presidential Council would oppose it on political grounds. The President would be against borrowing that amount on practical grounds. Look what it did to Yugoslavia's economy: 200 percent inflation, massive unemployment, strikes."

"Mitya, you now see the first part of the problem. Without the West's help, *perestroika* is doomed. But without *perestroika,* the nation is doomed."

Kirillin's brow creased.

"And it's not simply cash," Mazunov added. "We need foreign businesses to invest in our factories so that we have goods to export for hard currency, and goods to sell at home to keep the workers happy. We need hard currency loans to finance the purchase of state-of-the-art Western machinery. Above all, we need Western technology, especially computers and microelectronics, to modernize our production. But, despite all the President's goodwill visits to the West, export of the most vital technology is still blocked."

"Then we have no choice," Kirillin said thoughtfully. "We must negotiate with the West." He brightened up. "I've done it before with Fiat, and it wasn't so painful. As Lenin said of his New Economic Policy, 'We are retreating in order to take a running start and make a bigger leap forward.' "

Mazunov gritted his teeth. "That's only the first part of the problem."

Kirillin stared at him.

"The second part is that to negotiate enough of these deals on a bilateral basis, with all the restrictions currently in force, will take five years. And by that time, *krach!*" Mazunov spread his arms emphatically. "A total collapse of the currency, the consumer market, the whole economy."

"And by that time," Kirillin added, stone cold sober, *"perestroika*'s failure to put food in the shops will have toppled the President." He was silent for several minutes.

"Do you want me to 'adjust' the paper for the President's speech?" Mazunov asked finally.

Kirillin's eyes refocused. "You specified bilateral agreements."

"We have no choice."

"No choice?"

"The only other way to cut through the Gordian knot would be to negotiate membership of a powerful Western economic group that has no restrictions on trade or transfer of technology."

"The European Community with its single European market?"

Mazunov grimaced. "I said the problem was impossible."

Kirillin pursed his lips. He was thoughtful again. Then he said, "Submit your analysis of our current position and *all* possible options. Leave the rest to me."

When he returned to his dacha, Kirillin removed from his briefcase the signal he hadn't put in his wastepaper basket, the secret draft agreement between the European Community and Poland.

Chapter ✤ Fifteen

RYAN SQUEEZED INTO the number 64 bus at the Piazza della Città Leonina, near the Vatican's Saint Anne Gate, before he remembered he hadn't bought a book of tickets from an ATAC cabin or a tobacconist's. The number 64 bus had featured in his moral philosophy classes at the Gregorian University. Can it ever be morally justified to board the number 64 bus without having purchased a ticket in the certain knowledge that the bus is always so packed it is impossible to reach the red machine to validate a ticket even if you had purchased one in the first place? As in his student days, Ryan resolved to give a hundred lire to the first deserving person he met on leaving the bus.

The first deserving person he encountered was Cardinal Harding, sitting at one of a half dozen tables on the cobblestones outside the Grappolo d'Oro, where they had arranged to meet for Sunday lunch. The cardinal was dressed in a simple black clerical suit and clerical collar, indistinguishable from the dress of the priest seated opposite him. The priest looked familiar. Short-cropped white hair was brushed forward above a thin face dominated by a large nose; the ascetic appearance was marred by oddly sensuous lips.

"James, good to see you," Harding said warmly as he stood up and shook Ryan's hand. "How have they been looking after you in the Vatican?"

Ryan smiled. "No complaints, Father. At least, not yet."

"James, have you met Cardinal Bernard Demeure?"

"I've never had the privilege, Eminence," said Ryan as he shook the hand of the President of the Pontifical Council for Christian Unity.

"Everything comes to he who waits, James," said Demeure in a soft, self-mocking French voice. Here was another cardinal who never stood on his dignity.

The three men went inside to the *antipasto* table, in the middle of a room bordered by a terracotta frieze of vines and grape clusters. The two cardinals quickly selected aubergine and ordered the first dish chalked on the small blackboard above before returning outside. With a lingering look at the mouth-watering selection on the table, and the blackboard promise of delights to follow, Ryan said he'd have the same. The proprietor gave him a sympathetic smile.

When the bread rolls were brought out, Cardinal Harding ordered a bottle of Frascati. The proprietor, with a quick glance toward Ryan, suggested perhaps a bottle of Colli Albani from the Castelli, which he personally recommended and which cost little more than the Frascati. Harding was happy to agree.

The sunny spring day was marred only by the noise—pop music, shouts of teenagers, and revving of motorcycles—which echoed down the narrow alley from the Piazza Farnese. Ryan thought the noise was louder than in his student days; perhaps it was just that he was older.

Both cardinals refused the *dolci,* and ordered *cappuccino.* Ryan watched the trolley of trifles, cakes, and tarts disappear. He too ordered *cappuccino.*

After the proprietor brought the three cups of coffee and hot milk dusted with cocoa, he returned with a bottle of *amaro* and three glasses.

Cardinal Harding put up his hand to decline, but the proprietor insisted.

"A *digestivo* is necessary to finish the meal." He glanced at Ryan. "It is on the house, Father."

Ryan gratefully poured out three generous helpings. The proprietor smiled and left the bottle on the table.

"Bernard," Harding said, "the reason I asked you to join me for lunch is that I'm very worried about tomorrow's session. On the plane I read the final draft statement on the Reformation. It's unrecognizable from the draft we agreed at the working party."

Demeure took a deep breath. He looked at Ryan.

"Don't worry about James. He's the most discreet private secretary you could wish for."

"It's Zingler again," sighed Demeure. "No document can leave the Via dell'Erba without being approved by the Sacred Congregation for the Doctrine of the Faith."

"That makes your job impossible."

Demeure shrugged and glanced at Ryan. "Zingler acts with papal authority. I don't know whether it's Zingler or the Pope himself who is behind it."

"I said that James was most discreet," Harding chided. "You can't expect him to keep your confidences and betray others."

Ryan put his glass down. "There's no need, Father. I'm not betraying any confidences by saying that Cardinal Zingler does nothing without the Holy Father's knowledge and approval."

"I thought as much," said Demeure. "But that only makes matters worse. The Vatican line is isolating the Church more and more from all the other Christian communities."

"But they have confidence in you, Bernard, and the work of the Council."

Demeure looked into the bittersweet almond liquid in his glass. "We've been toiling away for over twenty-five years to implement the decisions of the Second Vatican Council. I believe we're poised for a breakthrough. The

Anglicans and the Orthodox will now accept the Bishop of Rome not only as first among equals, but also as the leading moral authority in Christendom between ecumenical councils which, heaven knows, are rare enough. But," he sighed, "the nearer the Anglicans and the Orthodox move toward us, the further Zingler moves away down the road of papal supremacy."

Harding turned to Ryan. "You see now, James, why I spend as little time in Rome as I can."

"It's creeping infallibility," said Demeure. "Every utterance of the Holy Father is enshrined by Zingler as the solemn and binding teaching of the Universal Church."

Ryan felt obliged to defend his new master. "But surely, Father, it's only on major matters of faith or morals to be held by the whole Church?"

"According to Zingler, that includes everything except the football results." Demeure emptied his glass. "And even there, I suspect he feels teams have a moral right to victory if they hang a picture of the Blessed Virgin in their dressing rooms."

"I must say," Harding observed, "this increasing emphasis on the cult of the Virgin Mary makes dialogue with the Protestant churches in my country much more difficult."

Demeure shrugged. "It's the same throughout the West. We can't have women priests but we must worship a woman. Theologically it's a nonsense."

"Does this stem from the apparitions at Fatima?" Ryan ventured.

The two cardinals looked at each other. This time Demeure reached for the bottle. "Yet another case of prepubescent fantasies based on an apocalyptic Catholic education which, I fear, is all too common in peasant communities."

"Didn't two of the visionaries die within a couple of years or so, before they'd even reached their teens?" Harding mused.

"Yes," Ryan said, "but Lucia lived. She became a nun

and continued having visions well into the Second World War."

"Ah yes," Demeure said, "dear Sister Lucia. Pity she waited until 1941 to tell us that in 1917 the Virgin had prophesied the end of the First World War and warned of a second unless people stopped offending God."

"But surely, Father," Ryan said, "on the last occasion that Our Lady appeared to all three children, in October 1917, the sun danced in the sky to prove the authenticity of the visions."

Demeure looked at him over the top of his glass of *amaro*. "Do you really believe, James, that in the twentieth century God needs to engage in cheap conjuring tricks to prove He exists?"

"But Father," Ryan protested, "that miracle was witnessed by a hundred thousand people. The apparitions have been accepted by the Church. Pope Pius XII personally saw a repeat of the solar miracle, here in the Vatican Gardens, when he made his infallible declaration of the Assumption of the Blessed Virgin Mary into heaven."

Demeure raised his eyebrows. "Sadly, our bishops, cardinals, and even popes have a pretty poor track record when it comes to the sun. I do recall they once believed it danced round the earth, and were rather horrid to Galileo for pointing out that it was the other way round."

Ryan couldn't help smiling. Nonetheless, it troubled him that the Blessed Virgin had actually predicted the precise time and location of the miracle, and that many of the hundred thousand witnesses were skeptics who had originally come to mock before testifying that the sun had indeed danced in the sky.

Harding scratched his head. "Wasn't there something about a Third Secret that was supposed to be revealed by the Pope in 1960?"

"That's right," said Ryan. "Apparently, Pope John XXIII found it so horrifying that he refused to divulge its contents."

"That rings a bell," Harding said. "It was something to do with the end of the world."

Demeure fingered his glass. "These things usually are."

"Well," Harding said, "all very interesting, but I fear it isn't helping us with the Statement on the Reformation."

Demeure raised his glass and said gloomily, "I think all we can do is pray that Zingler doesn't restore that building to one of its former uses."

Ryan looked over his shoulder to the fifteenth-century Chancery Palace which overlooked the piazza. Behind its elegant travertine façade, now darkened with Rome's grime, papal bulls of excommunication had once been prepared.

Ryan nodded toward the square that adjoined the Piazza della Cancelleria, to the left of the Chancery Palace. "Better still, that he doesn't restore the Piazza Campo dei Fiori to one of *its* former uses."

Now the site of a bustling, open-air food market, the Campo had been the place of execution during the Counter-Reformation. A statue of its most renowned victim, the cowled Giordano Bruno, brooded over the square. The monk had been burned alive in 1600 by order of the Holy Inquisition.

"Yes," Harding said philosophically, "at least we can be thankful that the Church doesn't have people killed nowadays."

Chapter ✦ Sixteen

AT TEN O'CLOCK on a Monday morning in spring, the Alexander Garden is one of the most peaceful places in Moscow. It is only after midday that office workers with their packed lunches begin occupying the benches, or queueing at the kiosk serving sickly-sweet milky coffee, or grouping around the lemonade automatic vending machines. It is usually Thursday before wedding parties begin paying their respects and having their photographs taken at the Tomb of the Unknown Soldier. And it is later in the year before the slow-moving queue of tourists for Kremlin museum tickets stretches back from the booth below Trinity Tower to the Middle Arsenal Tower.

Kirillin struck a solitary figure as he waited, hands in pockets, by the grotto at the foot of the Middle Arsenal Tower, opposite the Obelisk. Lines creased his brow.

Babakin seemed to savor the tranquility as he strolled past the dark red porphyry blocks commemorating the Soviet Union's Hero Cities that stretched in a line parallel to the Kremlin Wall from the Tomb of the Unknown Soldier to the Obelisk.

"Have you decided how to solve the problem?" Babakin asked.

"Which problem?"

"The invitation to our Polish friends to join the European Community."

Kirillin looked down at his shoes and spoke carefully. "The President welcomes any initiative to open up the European Community to the east."

"But?"

Kirillin, hands deep in his pockets, looked up. "But we can't allow Poland unilaterally to destroy the Warsaw Pact and join NATO."

"That is the key condition," Babakin said.

Kirillin sighed. "If news of this leaks out, the General Staff will demand the tanks be sent in. They'd never tolerate the prospect of a reunified Germany and Poland in NATO with no Warsaw Pact forces blocking the path to the Soviet Union."

"They'd be backed by at least half the Presidential Council," Babakin added.

"The President has publicly revoked the Brezhnev doctrine. He's pledged no interference in the affairs of east European states."

Babakin shrugged. "If Poland unilaterally abrogates its obligations under the Warsaw Treaty and applied to join NATO, it would be interfering in the affairs of the Soviet Union. The President would be able to justify intervention."

"That's just playing with words," Kirillin said. "If we sent tanks into Poland now, there'd be a bloodbath. The President's managed to win over most of western Europe from the Americans. Everything would blow up in his face."

"And if he did nothing to stop Poland, everything would blow up in his own backyard."

Kirillin looked at him.

"*Pamyat* and the Russian Workers United Front have watched the empire in eastern Europe collapse like a pack of cards. So far the collapse hasn't actually threatened Russia itself. But I warn you, Dmitry Sergeyevich, they won't stand for Poles humiliating Russia. They'd bring the

great silent Russian majority on to the streets of Moscow
and Leningrad."

"*Pamyat* doesn't represent anybody," Kirillin snapped.

Babakin raised his eyebrows. "It knows how to organize
and incite."

"It's fascist."

"Sure," Babakin agreed. "But our intelligence says that
two out of five Russians believe *Pamyat* is the only organization standing up for Russia. You'd be foolish to underestimate the resentment caused by the Balts, the Georgians,
the Armenians and just about every other nationality kicking sand in our faces."

"Is that how you feel?" Kirillin challenged.

"Of course not," Babakin said smoothly. "But most of
the Leningrad Regional Party Committee does, not to
mention the Party apparatus east of the Urals. More to the
point, most of the current leadership of the KGB does.
Add the General Staff, and the President has a formidable
force ranged against him."

Kirillin looked up at the Obelisk of the Great Revolutionary and Socialist Thinkers. "This was originally erected
to commemorate the three hundredth anniversary of the
Romanov dynasty. One of the first acts of the Moscow Soviet after the Great October Revolution was to remove the
double-headed eagle from the Obelisk and carve on the
names of socialist thinkers." He turned to Babakin. "The
President doesn't want to see the imperial double-headed
eagle restored."

"Neither does Filipchenko and the Popular Front.
They'd organize counter-demonstrations against any demands for a Soviet intervention in Poland. It'd all end in
bloodshed."

"Are you telling me the only options are a bloodbath in
Warsaw or a bloodbath in Moscow?"

"Not necessarily. An idea occurred to me over the
weekend."

"Yes?"

"We can't inform the Presidential Council. That would

put the President under too much pressure for intervention."

"So what do we do?"

Babakin smiled. "It's simple. We stop the European Community making the offer to Poland in the first place."

"We ask them politely. Very simple."

Babakin paused. "Before the Community heads of government meet, we need an incident in Poland that will shock them. Shock them enough to reject the Spanish Prime Minister's proposal. As an additional safeguard, that incident should also deepen the split between the two main Solidarity factions."

"What do you have in mind?" Kirillin asked suspiciously.

"Most of the élite of the Polish security service were trained by us at Balashika Center. We find it judicious to maintain direct contact with certain officers. There are enough who don't want Poland to descend into a Solidarity-style anarchy or else turn into a theocracy."

"What, specifically, are you proposing?"

"Before Wednesday members of the Polish security service posing as supporters of one Solidarity faction seize a leader of the other faction and give him a good beating," Babakin said. "A terminal one."

"That's barbaric! We're trying to build a society based on the rule of law."

Babakin shrugged. "You have only three options. This is the option of least violence."

"What if the attack is traced back to the security service?"

Babakin smiled. "It won't matter. The damage will already have been done."

Kirillin looked up again at the Obelisk. "Were you trained for the priesthood by the Jesuits?"

Babakin laughed.

"Not Lech Walesa," Kirillin said.

"OK. But someone close enough to him to matter. Do I go ahead?" Kirillin said nothing. Then he nodded, and walked away.

Chapter ✤ Seventeen

HOFFMAN TOOK THE call from the Primate of Poland and transferred it to the Holy Father. He told Ryan to cancel the official lunch invitation to twenty American bishops who were in Rome for their *ad limina* visit.

No flowers adorned the white linen tablecloth in the private dining room. The chairs were turned to face the television set. When the Pope stood up to say grace, it seemed his eyes would never open. Eventually he uttered the words and crossed himself. Hoffman looked at his watch and switched on the television set for the lunchtime news.

The female newscaster introduced a long item about the Italian Parliament's refusal to grant the City of Rome any further subsidy to preserve its ancient monuments, alleging that Rome's pollution was destroying them faster than the experts were restoring them.

Neither the Pope nor Hoffman touched the borscht that the nuns served. Ryan left his too.

At the newscaster's mention of Poland, all five nuns came into the dining room.

"The car into which Tadeusz Wujec, the Solidarity senator, was bundled this morning as he was leaving mass at

Saint Brigid's Church in Gdansk has now been identified. It belongs not to a member of the anti-Walesa faction of Solidarity as first reported, but to a member of the Polish security service."

The newscaster was handed a sheet of paper. "We've just received news that Tadeusz Wujec has been found. He was discovered over 280 kilometers south of Gdansk, by the side of the road that leads to Czestochowa, Poland's most celebrated shrine to Our Lady. He was taken to hospital, but died shortly afterwards of severe internal hemorrhaging."

The still photograph flashed on the screen was that of a gaunt man with lank blond hair and drooping moustache. The man who had sat on Ryan's left at the lunch table exactly one week ago.

"The weather in the Lazio region for the rest of today will be fine and . . ."

Hoffman turned off the television set. The Pope rose slowly from the table, took out his rosary beads, and walked to the door. Ryan got up to follow, but Hoffman put a restraining hand on his arm.

"The Holy Father wants to be alone in the chapel." Hoffman kneeled down on the red carpet in front of an icon of Our Lady, and began to pray silently. Ryan joined him.

Hoffman rose, and Ryan followed him to their office. Hoffman sat down at his desk. His jaw jutted out. "This will put an end to Fasolo's trading with the Devil."

"Can we be sure that . . ." Ryan began, before Hoffman's eyes silenced him.

"What do you think defeated Communism in Poland, in Czechoslovakia, in Hungary? I tell you this, Father Ryan, it was not Cardinal Fasolo's negotiations with the Communist authorities. While Vatican diplomats tried to reach secret agreements, the priests and the faithful refused to compromise. The people looked to their Church for leadership, not to their Government or to the Vatican. It was the Church that kept the national spirit alive. It was the

Church that helped set up and organize the people's movements for social justice. It was the Church that preserved their faith in God."

Hoffman removed his spectacles and peered at Ryan. "When the Church was forced underground by persecution, her priests and people never ceased praying to the Mother of God. And she rewarded the faithful, as she'd promised at Fatima. She inspired the people to rise up and defeat one of the mightiest forces the world has ever seen."

Hoffman banged his fist on the desk in frustration. "The whole apparatus of Communism—the secret police and the occupying army—would have been brought crashing to the ground in Poland if the Vatican hadn't insisted on Solidarity going into partnership with the Communists in order to keep Russia happy. This is the result! From now on, no compromise with the Devil."

"Is it right to equate Communism with the Devil?" Ryan asked tentatively.

"Of course it's right! The Second Secret of Fatima makes it perfectly clear: Communist Russia is the instrument of Satan. Men, even men as clever as Fasolo, can't outwit the Devil. The Immaculate Heart of Mary alone has God's promise of victory over Satan. Only through her can we finally defeat Communism and bring peace on earth."

"But Monsignor," Ryan said, "that means defeating Communism in the Soviet Union. Poland, Czechoslovakia, and Hungary are mainly Catholic countries. The Soviet Union isn't."

Hoffman went through to the Pope's private study next door and returned with a book. Hoffman stared at Ryan before hooking the arms of his spectacles back over his ears. "If you don't believe me, perhaps you will believe the Mother of God. Sister Lucia wrote down the precise words of the Second Secret." He began to read:

> *"If my requests are not heeded, Russia will spread her errors throughout the world, causing wars and the persecution of the Church. The good will be mar-*

tyred; the Holy Father will have much to suffer; various nations will be annihilated. In the end my Immaculate Heart will triumph. The Holy Father will consecrate Russia to me and she will be converted, and a period of peace will be granted to the world."

Hoffman looked up. "These words were spoken by Our Lady at the very time Lenin and his Bolsheviks were seizing power in Russia. Everything the Virgin prophesied has come to pass. The Church was persecuted throughout Russia and eastern Europe. Whole Christian nations, like Lithuania and the Ukraine, were annihilated and merged into the Soviet Union. Pope John Paul II was shot, here in Saint Peter's Square, on the very Feast of Our Lady of Fatima. If this wasn't a warning that Our Lady's request has not yet been fulfilled, then I don't know what is."

"But I thought that Pope Pius XII consecrated Russia to the Immaculate Heart of Mary?"

Hoffman opened the book again and tapped his forefinger hard down on one page. "Sister Lucia states that, in a vision she received in 1929, Our Lady made clear that God promises to save Russia only if the Holy Father consecrates Russia to her Immaculate Heart *in union with all the bishops of the world."*

His eyes, magnified by his spectacles, shone hard, like diamonds. "The Holy Father has asked the Blessed Virgin Mary to let him live long enough to see the collegial consecration of Russia to her Immaculate Heart, and to witness the dawn of her promised era of peace in the world. The collapse of Communist rule in eastern Europe was our signal. It is the duty of those of us, Father Ryan, who believe in the power of heaven, not Vatican diplomacy, to complete the task and bring about the Holy Father's dearest wish."

Part ✤ Two

SUMMER

Chapter ✤ One

ANDREW GRIMES WAS right. Rome was hell on earth, at least in summer. As a student Ryan had either returned to England for pastoral experience or had escaped to the English College's summer residence at Palazzola in the Alban Hills. Now he was wilting under the oppressive blanket of heat and humidity that stifles Rome from July to September.

It was made worse by the atmosphere inside the Apostolic Palace. The papal apartments were in the Palace of Sixtus V, built around a small, square courtyard and connected to the rest of the Apostolic Palace by the tiered loggias that flanked the northern side of the Saint Damasus Courtyard. The door from the private apartment on the top floor, which opened onto the Third Loggia, had turned into a border crossing between the Secretariat and the papal household.

Ryan had breached that border on two occasions when he'd accepted invitations to Archbishop Benedetti's intimate little dinner parties. He had now declined a third invitation, partly because he felt uncomfortable with the exclusively male ambience of the Palazzina della Zecca, and partly because Monsignor Hoffman interpreted such fraternizing as disloyalty to the papal household.

Ryan was depressed that his eagerness to be loyal was not reciprocated. Monsignor Hoffman continued to treat him with reserve, as though suspecting he were a liberal or else in league with the Romans. The Polish Sisters were similarly distant. The Pope was kinder, but he couldn't be the elder brother that Cardinal Harding had been; he was the Pope, a man whose awesome responsibilities separated him from other mortals.

Ryan tidied the top of the small desk which nestled between the corner windows in the Pope's private study. He put together in what he hoped was the correct order the pages of handwritten notes for a speech, which were scattered over the desk's red leather top. He placed these between the anglepoise lamp and the modern steel crucifix, and stacked the Bible, the psalter, the breviary, and Sister Lucia's memoirs in a neat pile next to the locked wooden chest. He removed the files the Pope had dealt with and took them through to his own office. Hoffman was with the Pope for the morning audiences in the State library a floor below.

The files had been given to the Pope by the Secretary of State the previous evening. Each was known as a *camicia,* literally a "shirt," a double sheet of paper with the original document from one of the curial dicasteries in the middle and a summary in front. The Secretary of State added his own suggestions, views, or additional information below the summary.

The Pope had rejected Cardinal Fasolo's recommendation that the Church's absolute prohibition of artificial means of birth control be modified in those countries where starvation or infant mortality or AIDS was a dire problem. He had also rejected all three shortlisted candidates for the vacant bishopric of Newark in the USA.

But the most dismissive papal note was scribbled on the *camicia* containing a paper written by Archbishop Benedetti. It summarized the Soviet leader's speeches calling for a Common European Home and proposing a merger between the European Community, representing the West, and the Council for Mutual Economic Assistance, representing the former Soviet bloc. Fasolo suggested that this echoed the Holy Father's own address to the European Parliament and that the Holy Father should respond positively. The Pope had written in large, untidy scrawl, *The Holy See opposes economic aid to any country that keeps other nations in thrall.*

The daily meetings between the short, bespectacled Secretary of State and the Pope had become briefer. Once, Ryan had even heard the courteous Fasolo raise his voice in frustration. Since Wujec's murder and the collapse of the plan for Poland to join the European Community, Ryan had not seen Fasolo smile once when coming up the steps from the private library.

Ryan looked at the white net curtains. He understood why Pope John XXIII had called the top floor of the Palace of Sixtus V his prison. The loneliness was, at times, almost unbearable.

The black telephone on Ryan's desk rang. *"Pronto. Qui parla Don Ryan,"* he answered.

"Father," the nun on the Vatican central switchboard said, "a Ms. Diana Lawrence wishes to speak to you."

Ryan frowned. He didn't recall anyone by that name.

"She said she was one of Katie Maguire's best friends."

"Father?" the voice in the telephone asked. "Are you still there?"

"Yes," Ryan said hoarsely. "Put her through, please."

"Father James Ryan," a husky American voice said, "forgive me calling you like this, but I'm in Rome and I just had to see you."

"Katie never mentioned . . ."

"That's not surprising. Look, this is difficult over the phone. Let's meet."

Ryan thought quickly. The next day the head of the Ukrainian Catholic Church in Exile was coming to lunch with the Pope. Monsignor Hoffman would be there. "To-morrow? Say at one forty-five?"

"Terrific. Where?"

"The Obelisk, Saint Peter's Square," he answered without thinking.

"You got it."

"Miss Lawrence. How will I recognize you?"

There was a gentle laugh. "No problem. Katie sent me enough photographs of you to make an album. *Ciao.*"

Ryan couldn't sleep that night. He blamed it on the heat. He found it difficult to concentrate at the Pope's private mass the following morning, and he paid scant attention to Hoffman's explanation of Vatican duplicity toward the Pope's lunch guest.

Cardinal Andrii Chuprynka, Major Archbishop of the Metropolitan See of Lvov in western Ukraine, together with his small staff, had been given a suite of rooms on the Piazza Madonna dei Monti, across the Tiber. The strongly nationalist half of the Ukrainian Church demanded that their religious leader in exile be accorded the title Patriarch. The Ukrainian Church, they argued, was far larger than all the other Patriarchal Byzantine Rite Churches in communion with the Pope. The Vatican, however, had refused. To do so, the Secretary of State said, would be to recognize Ukrainian claims to territorial sovereignty; this would provoke the Soviet Union, which had reconquered eastern Ukraine in 1920 and annexed western Ukraine in 1939. Like his predecessor, Chuprynka was made a cardinal. The Ukrainians scorned this title as a Western administrative office, a relic of the Imperial Roman Court and not a fitting designation for the head of their national Church. With typical Roman pragmatism, the Secretariat of State then devised the unique ecclesiastical title of Major Archbishop. Half of the Ukrainians continued to regard Chuprynka as their Patriarch.

At one-thirty Monsignor Hoffman brought Cardinal

Chuprynka into the *salone* in the private apartment. The head of the Ukrainian Catholic Church struck a dignified figure, dressed in his white cylindrical Byzantine Metropolitan's headdress with flowing white veil. Instead of a cardinal's crimson sash around his waist, a white scarf bearing the insignia of his office hung down from his shoulders, and a locket adorned with an icon replaced the Western pectoral cross.

Ryan shook hands with the tall, gray-bearded Chuprynka, and excused himself.

He changed out of his cassock and put on a black clerical suit. His heart was beating wildly as he walked across Saint Peter's Square toward the Obelisk.

There was no danger of missing Diana Lawrence in the crowded square. She hadn't Katie's red hair, but the blond, suntanned woman in a white linen suit with its hemline well above her knees radiated that same self-confidence as she walked toward him.

She held out her hand and smiled. "Hi. It's good to meet you at last."

"I'm pleased to meet you, Miss Lawrence," Ryan said shyly.

She nodded toward the students gathered round the Obelisk. "These guys make me feel old enough without you calling me Miss Lawrence. I'm Diana. And I'm hot. Let's go grab a beer somewhere."

They walked out of Saint Peter's Square and down the Via di Porta Angelica until they came to the bar with yellow plastic chairs and tables covered with clipped-on red tablecloths. They sat down at a pavement table and, in passable Italian, she ordered two beers.

"I guess I owe you an explanation. Do you mind?" she asked as she lit a menthol-tipped cigarette. "It's a filthy habit." She inhaled and blew out a long stream of gray smoke in the direction of Saint Peter's. "Katie and I went to the same convent school in Boston and we both went on to Radcliffe. After Katie graduated she took her master's in business administration at Harvard. I sort of drifted into

the diplomatic service, and got posted abroad as an assistant cultural attaché. Moscow, would you believe? That
place is the pits."

"She never said . . ."

Lawrence laughed. "By this time, Katie had flipped. All
she wrote about in her letters was this real dishy English
guy with an Irish name she'd met at Harvard. Half of me
was bored stiff, half of me was jealous." She gave him an
appraising look. "You haven't aged since those photographs. Katie always had good taste."

Ryan blushed and sipped his beer.

Lawrence lit another cigarette. "I was coming back for
your engagement party when things got difficult. Big
clampdown on dissidents. Shcharansky got thirteen years.
Ginzberg also got hit big. All leave in our part of the embassy was canceled." She stubbed out her cigarette in the
ashtray. "Afterwards, I guess I was glad I didn't come
back."

Ryan looked away, into the gutter.

"I'm sorry," she said softly. "That was a dumb thing to
say. What I mean is . . ."

"I know," he said.

"Katie's mother wrote me. She said the climbing accident wasn't your fault."

He nodded. But he didn't believe it. How could it not
have been his fault?

After a while she asked, "Have you eaten, James?"

He shook his head.

"Neither have I." She walked to the counter and came
back. "Ham rolls. I've seen better at Fenway Park at the
end of a Red Sox double-header."

He grinned.

"That's better. Two more beers?"

He nodded. "Then I must get back."

"OK. Look," she said, as she handed him his second
beer, "I'm going to be here for some time. Let me take you
out for a proper lunch."

"I'd love that, but I rarely know in advance when I can get away."

"No problem. Here's my card." She wrote her home address and telephone on the back. "My apartment's in Trastevere. Not the most fashionable part of the city, but it's a large apartment and there's no danger of bumping into other Embassy staff this side of the Tiber."

He looked at the printed side of the card. "The Cultural Attaché of the Embassy of the United States of America to the Republic of Italy," he read out loud. "I'm impressed."

"So you should be. Do we have a deal, James Ryan?"

"We do."

"Good. I look forward to it."

Ryan watched Diana Lawrence walk away, hips swaying just like Katie's, up the Via Porta di Angelica toward Saint Peter's. He wondered what he'd let himself in for.

Chapter ✤ Two

KIRILLIN LOOSENED HIS tie and undid the top button of his shirt. It was one of those hot, sticky summers. He pushed back his chair, stood up, pulled back the white net curtains, and looked out from his office window.

The sky over Red Square was heavy and threatening. To his right, at the southern end of Red Square beyond the Savior Tower, the extravagant multicoloured domes and towers of Saint Basil's Cathedral, shaped like onions, pineapples, and cones, proclaimed Russian triumphalism at its most magnificent and its most vulgar. Built by Ivan the Terrible to commemorate the capture of Kazan, it had been named the Cathedral of the Intercession of the Blessed Virgin, but was popularly known by the name of the holy fool buried within its walls. Visitors to what was now a branch of the Historical Museum increased each year; visitors to the shrine of New Soviet Man, Lenin's Mausoleum, decreased each year.

Over the Kremlin Wall immediately to his left rose the receding rectangular tiers of the austere red-granite tomb. A human chain projected out into Red Square, turned left, and disappeared from view behind Saint Nicholas's Tower.

By restricting the Mausoleum's opening hours and by keeping visitors no more than two abreast, the KGB guards were able to extend the queue beyond the main Historical Museum building at the northern end of Red Square; it must remain the longest queue in Moscow.

The thunderclouds burst and a downpour swept Red Square. The line of visitors to the Mausoleum stood impotently in the rain. Kirillin's attention was distracted by the activity along Kuybyshev Street, which led away from Red Square by the side of the huge GUM department store directly opposite. Cars pulled into the curb, and their drivers scrambled out and fixed on windscreen wipers as quickly as they could. Spare parts were virtually unobtainable, and so few drivers left their windscreen wipers in place; if they did, the wipers would vanish. Soviet citizens didn't regard this as theft, merely a way of coping with yet another shortage in supply.

Kirillin sighed and returned to his desk. His plan to obtain Mazunov's hundred billion dollars of capital investment and technology from the European Community had failed. The Western media had applauded the President's vision of a Common European Home, but the European politicians had stopped short of opening up the European Community to the Soviet Union. With a renewed stridency Vatican Radio was insisting that a Common European Home only made sense if its inhabitants were free to choose which rooms they occupied: specifically, if all Soviet republics were free to exercise their right under the Soviet Constitution to secede from the USSR.

The President was at his Black Sea villa preparing for his trip to the United States. The Camp David summit meeting with the US President was their last hope of rescuing the Soviet economy. It was a mark of the President's desperation that he'd been forced to turn to the country which, for more than forty-five years, had filled the traditional role of the *glavny vrag,* the main enemy.

The President had departed in a somber mood. He'd

asked Kirillin to hold the fort; that fort was now under siege. Kirillin reopened the red file on his desk.

The report had been sent to the office the President maintained at the Central Committee building on Staraya

Komitet Gosudarstvennoy Bezopasnosti
Moscow
ul. Dzerzhinskovo 2
Tel. (095) 221-07-62

--TOP--
SECRET

THE WESTERN INNER RIM

Report of a Sub-Committee of the Presidium of the KGB

To: Politburo of the CPSU

From: Chairman of the State Security Committee

Classification: TOP SECRET

Square. It had taken two days to travel the quarter of a mile along the secret underground passage that linked the Central Committee headquarters with the Kremlin. Even if Kirillin managed to fax the report to Pitsunda, the President would see it two days after the other members of the Politburo.

The report made grim reading. Blagov's efficient summary and recommendations began with the three Baltic republics. The position was dangerously unstable. Estonia, the northernmost and the smallest of the republics, had consistently flaunted All-Union laws. Blagov recommended that the experiment of granting it economic freedom be deemed a failure, that its trade with the West be blocked by bureaucratic means, and that the official Communist Party be sustained by every means at the expense of the independent Communist Party.

In Latvia, excesses of nationalism had resulted in oppression of the 40 percent non-Latvian minority, mainly Russians. Blagov recommended the sacking of the Latvian Communist Party First Secretary for failing to prevent the abuse of human rights, and his replacement by Comrade Ignatov, who would crush the nationalist movement by a program of rigorously upholding the human rights of all Soviet citizens. The Latvian Republic Headquarters of the Second Chief Directorate would provide necessary support.

In Lithuania, policies of appeasement had proved disastrous. The Catholic Church had been granted concessions; far from showing gratitude, it had helped form the popular movement *Sajudis,* and had then encouraged *Sajudis* to adopt a separatist platform. Permitting reformists in the Communist Party to establish a Lithuanian Communist Party independent of Moscow in order to outflank the nationalists had been counterproductive: the Lithuanian CP had been unable or unwilling to resist extremist demands; even so it had failed to gain the popular support accorded *Sajudis,* and this had led to the unilateral declaration of independence by the Lithuanian parliament. Blagov recommended that leaders of *Sajudis* be discredited by press revelations about their private lives, and that economic sanctions be imposed on Lithuania—restricting the supplies of vital goods and materials from the Soviet Union, cutting electricity and other fuels during vital periods, etc.—to force compliance with geopolitical realities.

The next section worried Kirillin most of all.

UKRAINIAN SSR

The next most populous republic in the USSR after Russia is critical for three reasons. First, it is the key element of the Western Inner Rim, forming a strategic 450-kilometer-wide corridor from Russia to Po-

land and thence to Germany. Two nuclear missile
fields, vital for the protection of Russia, are sited in
the Ukraine, at Pervomaysk and Derezhnaya. In addition, more than a thousand nuclear warheads are
hidden in secret storage bunkers in the Carpathian
mountains. Second, the Ukraine provides more than
20 percent of industrial output and 25 percent of agricultural produce of the USSR, and possesses re-
serves of coal, iron and minerals essential to the
Soviet Union. Third, the Soviet Union has invested
heavily in plant and electricity generating stations in
the Ukraine.

Nationalist sentiments, inflamed by the Ukrainian
Byzantine Rite Catholic Church into anti-Soviet and
anti-socialist hatred, the Chernobyl nuclear disaster,
troublemakers among sections of the workforce, especially in the vital Donbass mining area, plus excesses of *glasnost* in neighboring republics, have
spawned a series of anti-Soviet groups, ranging from
right-wing nationalists, through militant Christians,
the intelligentsia, students, hooligans, labor agitators,
and self-styled ecological groups.

Ukrainian Party First Secretary Budko has shown
exemplary skill and cooperation with the KGB in
controlling the attempts of such groups to violate socialist legality.

However, continuing industrial unrest in eastern
Ukraine provides cause for concern. In western
Ukraine groups masquerading under a banner of
perestroika are proving dangerously disruptive; some
are openly campaigning for secession from the Soviet
Union. A particular problem is the Ukrainian Byzantine Rite Catholic Church (also known as the Uniate
Church for its union with Rome). It was abolished in
1946 because of its anti-Soviet nationalist tendencies,
but has now benefited from the law on freedom of
conscience. We estimate it has at least 5 million
members regularly engaging in violations of Article
227, 600 unregistered priests and fourteen unregistered bishops, plus three unregistered seminaries. Its
leaders are agitating for the return of the churches

and properties appropriated in 1946 for State use or else handed over to the Russian Orthodox Church as part of the policy of social integration with the Soviet Union. It is in regular contact with its leaders in exile in Rome, who undertake a propaganda campaign in the Western media for concessions on its behalf under the pretext of religious freedom. Any such concessions would rob the Russian Orthodox Church of more than half its total property and income, and provide organizational bases for the separatist movement.

Recommendations

(1) Comrade Budko and the Politburo of the Ukrainian Communist Party be given every support in their endeavors to maintain observance of legality within the republic.

(2) Security Troops of the KGB's Ninth Directorate, drawn exclusively from Russian personnel, be deployed at regiment strength to reinforce security at the Pervomaysk missile field, the Derezhnaya missile field, and the Carpathian nuclear warhead storage facilities, and at battalion strength at the nuclear bomber bases at Starokonstantinov, Poltava, Gorodok, Zhitomir, and Lvov. Ninth Directorate troops of Ukrainian or Byelorussian ethnic origin who are currently guarding these locations be redeployed outside the Ukraine.

(3) No concessions be granted to the Ukrainian Byzantine Rite Catholic Church. On the contrary, vigorous action be pursued against all its leaders who flout All-Union laws and Ukrainian SSR laws. The Ukrainian plenipotentiary for religious affairs should demonstrate the Soviet commitment to religious freedom by arranging a greater development within the Ukraine of the Russian Orthodox Church, which obeys Soviet legality and is not an agent of a foreign power.

Kirillin closed the file. Babakin had warned him that Blagov's report was due in the autumn. Blagov had completed it early while Babakin was on holiday at his hunting lodge.

Zavidovo was two hours' drive north of Moscow. Kirillin looked up the hunting lodge's phone number, picked up the green telephone, and dialed. He said, "It'll be dry by four o'clock," and replaced the handset.

At half-past three he looked out of the window. The summer thunderstorm had ceased, and the sun was already drying Red Square. If he could control the weather, perhaps he could sort out this problem without troubling the President.

Chapter ✥ Three

RYAN MANAGED TO see Diana Lawrence twice during the following three weeks. It wasn't always easy. Hoffman was away for three days visiting his sick mother in Gdansk, and then made a five-day pilgrimage to Fatima. The one advantage of his absences was that Ryan spent more time with the Holy Father.

Hoffman returned from Fatima with a bad cough, and developed a temperature. The Deputy Director of the Vatican Health Service wanted Hoffman to go into hospital for observation or, at the very least, escape the oppressive heat by moving to the papal summer residence at Castel Gandolfo. Hoffman stubbornly refused. He would only go to Castel Gandolfo when the Holy Father was free to go, in the middle of August. His compromise was to stay in bed until nine in the morning, take a long siesta after lunch, and go to bed after supper.

Ryan was working through the *camicie* late one morning while the Pope was giving his fifteen-minute individual audiences in the State library on the second floor of the papal apartments, a floor below the private apartment. Ryan heard coughing from the attic above. He put down the *camicia* containing reports from apostolic nuncios on Western governments' policies toward religious freedom in the Soviet Union. He went to the kitchen to ask the nuns for a glass of water and took it up to Hoffman.

Hoffman was sitting up in bed. Sweat dripped from his face. Large damp patches darkened his sky blue pajamas. His face was thinner. It made him even more intense.

"Good man," Hoffman said as Ryan handed him the glass of water.

"Shall I phone Dr. Masala?"

"Certainly not."

"Is there anything I can do for you, Monsignor?"

"No. But there's something you can do for the Holy Father."

"Certainly," Ryan said.

Hoffman put on his steel-framed spectacles and examined Ryan. "You've been with us now for three months, Father."

"That's right, Monsignor."

Hoffman nodded. "The Holy Father trusts you."

Ryan's heart leapt. The loneliness of the past months vanished with that simple statement. "I'm very grateful for that trust, Monsignor."

Hoffman nodded again. "Masala has forbidden me to travel until this thing, whatever it is, clears up. The Holy Father would like you to take my place on a trip abroad."

"The Holy Father's only to tell me . . ."

Hoffman waved his hand impatiently. "The Holy Father doesn't want to ask you himself. Because of the oath you've taken, you wouldn't be able to refuse him. It's not a trip you might normally expect to make as part of your duties here. He wants you to feel free to decline, and he would not think badly of you if you did."

"Of course I'll do it for the Holy Father," Ryan said.

"Good man. I knew you'd say yes. But, James, the trip is not without an element of danger."

It was the first time Hoffman had ever addressed him by

his Christian name. "Just tell me what to do," he responded eagerly.

"The Holy Father wants you to take a picture to Kiev in the Ukraine."

"Is that illegal?"

Hoffman chose his words carefully. "No. There is a private house in the Sviat Oshino district which is registered for Roman Catholic worship by the Ukrainian plenipotentiary for religious affairs. A licensed Catholic priest comes up from Odessa every Sunday to say mass. The Roman Catholic community in Kiev is small, mainly Polish and Hungarian immigrants, and the Holy Father thinks that a picture from Rome would show we haven't forgotten them."

"That sounds marvelous. I'm honored to do it."

"The painting of Saint Peter is of no great financial value." Hoffman broke into another bout of coughing. "But the Holy Father would like you to make a stop on your way through the Ukraine to deliver a couple of other things."

"Fine," Ryan said. "Will Archbishop Benedetti's department make the arrangements?"

"No." Hoffman coughed again. "They're very busy with all their diplomatic work. The Holy Father doesn't want to burden them with more responsibilities. Archbishop Korchan knows what to do."

Ryan smiled. "You don't have much time for Church diplomats, do you?"

Beady, peasant eyes looked up at Ryan. "Holy Mother Church doesn't need diplomats, she needs saints."

Ryan grinned. "Let's hope she doesn't want martyrs for this trip."

Archbishop Korchan asked Ryan to meet him inside the Vatican Bank, rather than come to the Secretariat of State.

Ryan walked out of the private lift into the Courtyard of Sixtus V. He nodded to the *vigilanza* in his glass booth to the right of the arched entrance in the ochre-colored stone wall. A brass plaque proclaimed: *Istituto per le Opere di Religione.* Ryan went through the frosted glass swing doors into a brown-carpeted entrance hall.

A secretary led him to a spacious modern office. No one sat behind the large executive desk; Archbishop Korchan relaxed in a black leather armchair in front of a low coffee table, and to his left a young nun sat demurely on a black leather sofa.

Korchan rose. "James, it is good to see you," he said in English. "May I introduce you to Sister Iryna of the Basilian Sisters."

Sister Iryna's pretty elfin face, dominated by large, liquid brown eyes, smiled shyly. Her dress was halfway between the traditional habit worn by the nuns in the papal apartments and the ordinary clothing preferred by progressive American religious orders. A gray headscarf covered most, but not all, of her black hair. Her gray blouse was buttoned to the neck and had a narrow white collar. A silver cross dangling from a chain around her neck, coupled with the gold wedding ring denoting a bride of Christ, completed her religious insignia. She smoothed her gray knee-length skirt as Ryan sat down next to her.

"Sister Iryna will be accompanying you," Korchan continued in Italian. "She has no English, but her Italian is fluent."

Ryan looked again at the young nun; she appeared the kind who would be nervous crossing the road. He glanced at Korchan.

"Only if you agree," said Korchan, "and if your Polish, Ukrainian, and Russian is better than I've been given to believe."

"Polish?"

Korchan nodded. "Here are the tickets for the return flight to Warsaw made out in the names of Sister Iryna and yourself."

"Kasamir Hoffman said the Ukraine."

"Indeed. You will be met at the airport, stay overnight in

Warsaw, and then be given tickets for a series of train journeys. It will be better if you leave your passport and your clerical dress with your hosts in Warsaw." He opened a large envelope. "Here is a passport and other papers in the name of Jacek Komar. You'll be provided with working men's clothes in Warsaw, and travel from there as Sister Iryna's dumb brother."

Korchan looked at the expression on Ryan's face. "Just a precaution, you understand. We want to avoid possible embarrassment to the Holy Father." His eyes twinkled. "It'll make a change from shuffling through the Secretariat's *camicie.*"

Ryan phoned Diana Lawrence to cancel their lunch date, explaining that he'd just been asked to go abroad the following day, and at lunchtime he needed to collect some clerical robes.

"Gammarelli's?"

"Yes," said Ryan, surprised.

"That's near the Pantheon, right?"

"Right."

"Two blocks on the other side of the Pantheon there's a small square, the Piazza Rondanini. In one corner you'll find a restaurant called L'Angoletto. It's one of the few places in Rome that does a decent fish lunch. See you there at two. *Ciao.*"

Ryan was left speaking to a dialing tone.

Ryan walked through the dark, narrow Via del Cestari, past the shops that specialize in religious vestments, and turned left into the Via di Santa Chiara where he found Gammarelli's.

Fifteen minutes later, holding two cardboard boxes, he left the Pope's tailor and walked through the Piazza della Minerva, passing the grimed facade of an undistinguished Renaissance *palazzo* that housed the most exclusive educa-

tional institute in the Catholic Church. The Pontifical Ecclesiastical Academy, which counted five popes and more
than eighty cardinals among its former students, trained
the Vatican's diplomatic corps. Like the present Pope,
Ryan was excluded from the *fiducia*, that peculiarly Italian
bond of trust, which the Academy fostered among Fasolo,
Benedetti and its graduates who worked in the Vatican.

Ryan found Diana Lawrence sitting at one of L'Angoletto's pavement tables. In a city of immaculately
dressed, beautiful women, she excited attention.

She kissed him on the cheek, and poked into one of his
cardboard boxes. Her eyes widened when she saw the
gold-threaded cope. "So they're making you a bishop already, James?"

"No, no," he said, "I've to take these to somebody."

She sat down and looked thoughtful. "Let me see. If it
were anyone in Rome, he or his valet would collect them.
So you must be taking them with you on your trip tomorrow. The only reason that our bishop would need his kit
made in Rome is that he can't have it made in his own
country. Which more or less reduces us to Vietnam, China,
or the Soviet Union. Let's assume you're not going too far
east. In Lithuania the nuns can stitch a few bits of gold
thread together without the KGB demanding a sample.
Ditto for Latvia. So, James Ryan, we deduce you are going
to the Ukraine. Am I right or am I right?"

"You should have become a detective."

She gave that carefree laugh which Ryan found so attractive. "Elementary, my dear Watson."

He smiled. She hadn't even looked into the second box
which contained a Byzantine bishop's crown-shaped miter.

Chapter ✤ Four

IT WAS DUSK as the Alitalia plane banked on its approach to Warsaw. The glassy gray River Vistula meandered through a city which was switching on its tiny fairy lights.

"Is that the cathedral spire?" Ryan asked.

Sister Iryna leaned across Ryan who was next to the window. She turned, those large eyes inches from his. "We call it the Butcher's Cathedral."

She sat back in her own seat. "The Palace of Culture and Science was a gift from Stalin. Take the lift to the thirtieth floor and you have the view of the city that Poles love most. It's the only one from which you can't see the Palace of Culture." She smiled uncertainly, as a schoolgirl might after telling her first adult joke.

Ryan smiled politely back. Sister Iryna's doe-like eyes reminded him of the way his kid sister had looked at him when she was 12 years old and he was her big hero. He hoped Sister Iryna wasn't going to be an encumbrance on this mission he was performing for the Pope.

Ryan's first experience of an east European country was anticlimactic. Okecie Airport could have served any small provincial Western city. He'd had more hassle with immigration officials at Kennedy Airport.

A burly middle-aged man detached himself from the small crowd beyond the customs barrier. He embraced Sister Iryna and kissed her on both cheeks. She introduced him to Ryan as Henryk Dabrowski. Dabrowski shook Ryan's hand firmly, and said something which Sister Iryna interpreted as an inquiry after the health of his cousin, Kasamir Hoffman.

"Please say that Monsignor Hoffman has some virus, but we don't think it's serious. And please tell Mr. Dabrowski that I hope his aunt in Gdansk is recovering."

Sister Iryna looked puzzled. "Henryk says he has no aunt in Gdansk."

"Monsignor Hoffman's mother," Ryan prompted.

"He says Aunt Danuta died twenty years ago."

Dabrowski took Sister Iryna's two old, large suitcases, while Ryan carried his own, which contained little else apart from the set of bishop's vestments and the painting.

Dabrowski lifted up the hatchback of the battered blue Polonez parked outside, and carefully loaded the three suitcases into the back. Ryan sat in front. He peered out of the window during their half-hour journey into Warsaw, but it was now dark and the street lighting was so poor that he saw very little. The lack of activity made it seem like the early hours of the morning rather than the early evening in a capital city.

The car slowed as they drove along yet another poorly lit street. This one was lined with mansions set back from the pavement. Sister Iryna pointed to a neoclassical façade mostly hidden by trees behind a wrought-iron fence. "That's the Archbishop's Palace, where the Primate lives," she said.

"Will we be visiting the Primate?" Ryan asked.

"No. The building next door is owned by the Government. The security service has listening devices there which pick up all conversations inside the Archbishop's Palace."

Ryan thought the young nun was still living in a bygone age, no doubt due to the sheltered environment of her

Ukrainian convent in Rome. "Poland has a Solidarity prime minister now, Sister," he said kindly.

She nodded. "And the Party apparatus still controls the security service, the police, and the army."

Dabrowski turned the car into a driveway on the other side of Modowa Street. "We're staying the night at a convent," Sister Iryna said. "Henryk will collect us in the morning."

The nuns greeted them warmly, and insisted they prepare a meal for Ryan and Sister Iryna before showing them to the guest rooms. The convent was simply furnished: every room contained a crucifix, a painting of the Madonna, and a photograph of the Pope.

The last thing Ryan saw before closing his eyes to go to sleep on the narrow bed was the Holy Father smiling down at him.

Chapter ✤ Five

A KNOCK AT the door disturbed Ryan's dreams.

"Come in," he said sleepily.

Sister Iryna pushed open the door with her knee. She was holding a tray in one hand and a carrier bag in the other.

Ryan pulled the sheet as high as it would go when he sat up in bed. Hoffman had told him to travel lightly and he had no pajamas.

Sister Iryna put the tray down on his lap.

Ryan looked at the pot of tea, the plate of two fried eggs and a sausage, and the plate of bread, butter, and cherry jam. "I'm afraid I don't eat before holy communion, Sister," he said, feeling rather pompous.

"There's no time for mass this morning, Father," she apologized. "We're to catch the six forty-two train. You'll need a good breakfast for the journey." She stepped back and examined him. "I don't think you should shave this morning, Father. This bag contains your clothes. Henryk thinks they'll fit you." She smiled shyly. "I hope so. I'll call back in half an hour."

The old serge suit was a size too large, and so were the shoes.

"I think I'll wear my own shoes," Ryan said when Sister Iryna returned.

She frowned and shook her head. "You'll do fine as you are, Father. My older dumb brother in his best hand-me-down clothes. Leave your own clothes and shoes on the bed. The sisters will look after them until we return."

Ryan followed Sister Iryna down the stairs. At least this charade didn't involve Sister Iryna changing out of her nun's clothes.

Dabrowski drove them to the station, where Sister Iryna bought their tickets. Ryan insisted on carrying her suitcases which, to his surprise, were very much heavier than his own. They boarded a compartment with spring-cushioned seats and a table. At exactly 6:42 whistles blew, voices were raised, the engine hooted, the compartment lurched, and the train began its trundle southeast.

In the harsh early morning light, the countryside appeared flat and dismal. The train stopped at towns and villages which looked grim and depressed. At one station a Polish peasant family crowded into their compartment. They began chattering to Sister Iryna. Ryan didn't understand Polish, and the dumb Jacek Komar couldn't speak. Sister Iryna made a fuss of the four children. Ryan started to feel glum and depressed.

At noon Sister Iryna took out from a brown paper carrier bag slices of salami, hunks of bread, and a flask of soup. The fat peasant mother matched this with a whole roast chicken, while the thin peasant father produced a bottle of vodka. All the food was shared. When the man spoke to Ryan, Sister Iryna looked at the bottle of vodka and smiled encouragingly. Ryan wiped the top of the bottle on his sleeve and took a large swig.

Shortly after two o'clock in the afternoon, Sister Iryna stood up and pointed to the suitcases. The train shuddered to a halt, and Ryan hauled the cases on to the platform. "Have we reached the Ukraine?" he asked.

"No," Sister Iryna whispered. "Shush."

Ryan, carrying the heavy suitcases, followed Sister Iryna out of the station and into a nearby café.

"What do we do now?" Ryan whispered after Sister Iryna had returned from the counter with tea and cakes.

She spoke in a low voice. "We wait for the 19:54 train from Cracow."

Ryan looked at his watch. "That's over five hours. Nothing sooner?"

"By the time we buy our tickets, the clerk and the porters will be the evening shift ones and they won't recognize us. When the immigration officials inspect our tickets, they'll see they were bought here in Przemsyl and assume we're locals. Do you want to look round the town?"

Ryan looked at the suitcases and then out of the window at the drizzle now falling which made the streets even duller. He shook his head.

To Ryan's surprise the time didn't drag. From their corner seat by the window they couldn't be overheard if they spoke softly. An unintelligible hubbub of voices cut off the rest of the café; condensation misted the window cutting off the rest of the world. Their conspiratorial whispers began to feel like intimacies in a clandestine affair.

Ryan was intrigued by the deceptively capable young woman he had first thought naive. She told him about her family fleeing the persecution of the Ukrainian Catholic Church in western Ukraine and settling in 1949 in Cracow, where she'd been born. She had been educated by the Ukrainian Catholic Basilian nuns, and had joined the order. Her mother superior had sent her for further study to Rome, and she lived at the convent in which their superior general and her council resided in exile. Sometimes Cardinal Chuprynka or his secretary asked the superior general to send one of the sisters as a courier to the Ukraine. "It's all very simple." She smiled.

The more she felt at ease in his company, the more she smiled. She had now relaxed into a huge smile. Sister Iryna wasn't beautiful. Her eyes and mouth were too large for such a small face. But when she smiled like this she did so with her whole face: her lips parted to show a perfect row of white teeth, her nose wrinkled with delight, and those eyes lit up with such joy that Ryan found it impossible not to smile back. It was the most captivating smile he had ever seen.

"Now tell me about yourself, Father."

Ryan took a deep breath. "Let's save that till another time. We ought to be heading back to the station."

When the train from Cracow arrived, Sister Iryna led him to their compartment. It looked like pre-War rolling stock. Ryan managed to squeeze the luggage under the slatted wooden seats.

The train left Przemsyl and headed east across a dark flatland of forests. The headlights of the few cars on the parallel highway easily overtook the train. The highway led to a floodlit customs post. The floodlights also showed the two lines of barbed wire fencing, separated by a broad clearing, which protected the Soviet Union from its neighbor.

The train followed the border, which vanished back into the night, and then it clanked to a halt. Lanterns flashed and approached the train. Ryan heard voices speaking in an unfamiliar language. With his heels he tried to push his suitcase further underneath the seat. "What's the problem?" he asked nervously.

Sister Iryna shrugged. "No problem. Soviet trains have a different gauge from Polish ones. No one is allowed to leave the train, and so we can't change coaches. The Soviets change the wheels instead."

Ryan peered through the window. By lamplight about eight workmen were adjusting the bogeys of each coach. Twenty minutes later the train moved on. Ten minutes after that it pulled into a brightly lit station. A large digital clock showed local time as 23:04; other signs were in Cyrillic. Soldiers in khaki uniform, with green bands on their peaked military caps, green epaulettes and shoulder flashes, and green stripes down their trousers, waited on the platform. Some of the KGB border guards had automatic rifles, others had dogs.

"This is the Mostiska checkpoint," Sister Iryna whispered. "It'll be all right, believe me."

A blue-uniformed immigration official checked their tickets, passports, and visas. As he left, Ryan heard a commotion from further up the train. A man wearing a dark green uniform jumped down from the train and walked swiftly to one of the station buildings. Guards with barking dogs surrounded the compartment door. The man returned, accompanied by a woman wearing a similar uniform who looked as though she would be more comfortable in a weightlifter's leotard. A few minutes later they left the train with a man in a black suit who was protesting loudly. A guard followed, carrying a suitcase. The party disappeared into the building.

Their compartment door was opened by a man wearing a similar dark green uniform and a military cap with a red star badge. Sweat started to run down Ryan's back.

The young customs official looked bored and tired. Sister Iryna smiled at him, unnecessarily offered him their tickets, passports, and visas, and then launched into a long and unsolicited explanation with much gesticulation and smiling. The official tried to interrupt, and finally backed out of the compartment. He hadn't even glanced at Ryan.

After the train pulled out of Mostiska—minus the man in the black suit—Ryan leaned across to Sister Iryna. He whispered, even though there was nobody else in the compartment. "I think the man they detained was a priest."

Sister Iryna nodded. "Father Korniychuk has an American passport. He was the diversion. After they've one arrest to write up in their duty report, all they want to do at this time of night is get back home to bed."

She looked at Ryan's expression. "Don't worry, they'll only confiscate the books and periodicals he was carrying—a biography of Metropolitan Sheptytsky in Ukrainian, copies of Solidarity publications, things like that—and put him on the four o'clock train." She smiled.

She tucked her legs up underneath her, snuggled up in the corner seat, and closed her eyes. Her face carried the memory of that smile as she went to sleep.

Two hours later the train pulled into Lvov station and Ryan took his first step on Soviet soil.

Chapter ❖ Six

SISTER IRYNA LEFT Ryan with the suitcases and ran toward a large-framed man in an anorak who was waiting beyond the ticket barrier. She returned, arm linked in his, and introduced Pavlo Stus, a member of the Committee for the Defense of the Ukrainian Catholic Church. Pinned to his anorak was a metal lapel badge of a blue and yellow flag.

Bright, inquisitive eyes examined Ryan from a face surrounded by straggly hair and beard. Ryan judged Stus to be about sixty years old. He took Ryan's outstretched right hand in both of his and shook it vigorously while he spoke.

"Pavlo says welcome to occupied Ukraine. He apologizes for the weather, but says what can you expect with Soviet meteorologists?"

Stus laughed. He bent down, picked up the two heavy cases, and strode off.

"He's going ahead to get a taxi," Sister Iryna said.

Outside, rain lashed the large puddles on the station forecourt. Stus was talking animatedly with the driver of the third of three yellow taxis displaying a small green light in the corner of the windscreen. Two gray-uniformed militia watched from the shelter of the station entrance. Stus, now soaking wet, came back with the suitcases and shook his head in exasperation.

"Pavlo apologizes. He says they'll only accept US dollars or West German marks."

"Archbishop Korchan gave me five hundred US dollars for an emergency," Ryan whispered. "They're hidden in the handle of my suitcase. Tell me how many dollars Mr. Stus needs and I'll go to the washroom and get them."

"Pavlo says he wouldn't dream of breaking the law. He's off to find a proper Ukrainian."

Stus put up the hood of his anorak and disappeared into the rain and gloom beyond the station lights.

A few minutes later a small battered red car pulled up where Ryan and Sister Iryna were waiting. Stus climbed out, beamed, and began fitting the suitcases, Ryan, and Sister Iryna behind the front seats.

The Zaporozhets gave a reluctant cough, spluttered into life, and chugged forward as though propelled by a lawn-mower engine. Ryan, feet bunched up on top of one of Sister Iryna's suitcases and arms clasped round his own, peered past the greasy dandruffed hair of the driver through that part of the windscreen intermittently cleared by the one windscreen wiper that worked.

"I feel better now we're clear of all those police inside the station," Ryan confessed to Sister Iryna.

She put a finger to her lips and then spoke in Ukrainian. The driver's pockmarked face looked over the shoulder of his imitation tweed jacket and nodded with an ingratiating smile. Next to him, Stus shrugged.

Stus lived in a residential estate of gray concrete ten-story blocks just off Semsotletiya Lvova Street, a wide road that linked a modern shopping zone just north of the old town with residential zones further north, part of the Lvov Construction Master Plan for the Year 2000. The Zaporozhets stopped underneath the weak bluish glow of one of the

widely spaced street lamps that gave the area at night an
eerie, unnatural appearance. While Stus paid the driver,
Ryan and Sister Iryna stepped through the large muddy
puddles covering most of the road where the tarmac, laid
thinly without proper foundation, had worn away.

Ryan, struggling with the three suitcases, nodded
ahead. "Is this the place?"

"No," Sister Iryna said. "It's three blocks further down.
I didn't want the driver to know where we're going."

"I hardly think that man was KGB," said Ryan as he
bent down to pick up the suitcases.

"Of course he's not," Sister Iryna said. "But he's using
his car as a taxi without a license. In return for not having
drivers like that fined and imprisoned, the KGB expect to
be kept informed of anything unusual, like a passenger
speaking a foreign language. They'd want to know where
he was dropped off, and they'd check the block with ad-
dresses of known dissidents."

The outside door of the apartment block, built in 1980,
was hanging loose from one hinge. Stus shone a pocket
torch into the small entrance lobby and pressed a button
for the lift. The light inside the lift was working, but the lift
was only large enough for three people without luggage.
Stus put the cases in the lift, waved Sister Iryna in after
them, and led Ryan up seven floors of narrow, badly
chipped concrete steps. Lights worked on less than half the
landings. Ryan learnt later that one of Lvov's newest industrial plants manufactured electric light bulbs.

Waiting in the doorway of the apartment was Alia Stus,
a handsome woman no taller than Sister Iryna but much
stockier, her best blue blouse, skirt and stockings offset by
a pair of cheap red carpet slippers. She smoothed back a
wisp of hair that had fallen loose from her bun before saying in English, "Welcome, Father." She turned to Stus,
who was wheezing, and spoke rapidly in Ukrainian. The big
man nodded penitentially, and then winked at Ryan.

"I'm afraid we've got Pavlo into trouble," Sister Iryna

whispered. "He's not supposed to climb those steps because of his heart."

Alia led them to a small living room, brightly cluttered with bookcases, icons, crosses, photographs of family, friends and Ukrainian Catholic prelates in exotic Byzantine Rite robes, Ukrainian embroidery, and wall carpets. Large damp patches discolored the green distemper on the visible area of the walls.

Alia swept a mass of papers to one end of the table. She took her best plates from a glass cabinet, put them on the table, and from the kitchen she brought a large sausage, some Spam, cheese, and bread. When Stus beamed and pointed at the suitcases, Alia scolded him and looked toward the clock. "Please have chair, Father," she instructed.

Ryan excused himself first, and went to the cramped bathroom. A single chrome pipe from the geyser swiveled between the bath and the handbasin, but nothing happened when he turned the tap. Worse, he couldn't flush the toilet. Sheepishly, he apologized to Alia. "There is water from six to nine in the morning, and from six to nine in the evening," she said, showing him the pan hanging off a hook. She filled it with water from the bath and poured the water down the toilet.

"How long has there been a water shortage?" he asked.

She shrugged. "About ten years."

After their supper, only Ryan and Sister Iryna were served coffee. When Ryan took the empty cups through to the small kitchen he noticed a jar of instant coffee on the draining board. It was almost empty.

Stus beckoned to Ryan and showed him the bedroom. "Pavlo!"

Alia's voice summoned them both. She spoke to her husband with the tone of a mother correcting her small child, looked up to heaven, and turned to Ryan. "Fifteen years have addled his brain. He is thinking that all guests sleep in our bed. I ask him, what do the Committee for the Defense of the Ukrainian Catholic Church think if he is having priest and nun in double bed?"

Before he went to sleep on the floor of the living room, Ryan whispered across the dark to Sister Iryna on the sofa, and asked what Alia had meant by fifteen years.

It was the length of time Stus had spent in prison, she said, the last twelve years in a special regime labor camp in the Ural mountains. Stus, Ryan learnt to his surprise, was only ten years older than himself. He was imprisoned shortly after graduating in history from the Ivan Franko University in Lvov, and had been released in 1987. Alia, who taught literature at the University, would normally have lost her job once her husband had been convicted of anti-Soviet agitation and propaganda under Article 70 of the Criminal Code; this was the charge brought against him for demanding his right under Article 52 of the Soviet Constitution to worship as a Byzantine Rite Catholic. Fortunately, Professor Stepan Konovalets, the head of her department, was one of the republic's leading literary figures, a Party member, and a Ukrainian Writer's Union representative on the Central Committee of the Ukrainian Communist Party. He respected Alia's work and had not only protected her job but had also arranged for her to be allocated her own apartment in this new residential block; prior to that she had been sharing sub-standard accommodation with her mother, brother, sister-in-law and their two children.

Sister Iryna also told him that for three years following Alia's move to the apartment, Stus had been denied the visits and the two letters per month to which he was entitled. The camp authorities had told him his wife was sleeping with Konovalets.

"Now we must go to sleep," Sister Iryna whispered. "Good night, James."

Ryan found it difficult to sleep. He lay there, wondering how Pavlo Stus found the courage to resist such physical and mental torture for so long.

Chapter ✦ Seven

RYAN WOKE WITH a stiff neck and an aching back. The rugs hadn't softened the hard wooden floor, and his head had rolled off the cushion. Sister Iryna, tucked up beneath a blue blanket on the old sofa, was watching him. Her black hair was cut short; it suited her elfin face.

"Good morning, Father. I hope you slept well?"

Ryan put on a brave face. "I've slept in much worse places." His rough trousers and shirt itched. He felt the stubble on his chin. "Do I have your permission to shave this morning, Sister?"

Her small face screwed up in thought. "I think I prefer you as a Ukrainian peasant."

He threw the cushion at her just as Alia Stus came into the room. She looked at each of them, feigned an expression of shock, and said in English, "I think it is good you are not having our bed, yes?"

During breakfast Alia wagged her finger at Stus. She apologized in English to Ryan, saying that Pavlo's period of corrective labor had not corrected his manners; he was again asking Sister Iryna what her suitcases contained. Ryan, too, was curious.

At last, with breakfast over, Stus was allowed to open the cases. He was like a child on Christmas morning. Few children, however, could match the expression of delight on his face as he removed from the first case an IBM-compatible portable computer, printer, and three boxes of disks. The second case produced a fax machine, boxes of paper, and a video cassette recorder. Ryan needed no interpreter as Stus gabbled excitedly in Ukrainian, hugging Sister Iryna and Ryan.

Alia assumed an air of exaggerated patience. "He is not content with fifteen years?"

Ryan remembered the scene at Mostiska. "Is it illegal to bring these things into the USSR?" he asked hesitantly.

Alia shrugged. "Not if you pay import duty." She surveyed the Italian-made equipment. "At a rough guess, a hundred thousand roubles."

Ryan swallowed. "Does Pavlo risk a fine for using it?"

"A fine?" Alia gave a dry laugh. "Under the new, enlightened amendments to Article 7 of the Law on State Crimes decreed in 1989, he can get ten years for using technical equipment from abroad in order to demand changes in the Soviet state." She looked at Stus excitedly opening up all the plastic bags of cables and plugs. She sighed. "I am thinking he now has better equipment than the KGB."

Ryan searched for an excuse. "I thought things had changed in the Soviet Union."

Alia shrugged again. "For forty-four years the Ukrainian Catholic Church is illegal. Now it is legal to be a Ukrainian Catholic. That means the authorities use administrative laws against us instead of anti-religious laws."

"But surely under *perestroika* . . ."

"I tell you something, Father," Alia said. "When the Brezhnevites in Moscow get sick of *perestroika,* they are coming here to the Ukraine for a holiday."

Stus now talked animatedly to Ryan, who looked helplessly to Sister Iryna.

"Pavlo!" One word from Alia and the large Stus smiled meekly.

"Forgive him," Alia said, "he is forgetting you do not understand our language." She looked at her husband. The unfeigned flash of pride and love in her eyes touched Ryan to the core. She turned back to Ryan. "Pavlo wants you to give a message to the Holy Father. He is saying that, thanks to the Holy Father's prayers, the grace of God is healing the division between *Ukrainska Helsinka Spilka* and *Ukrainska Demokratychna Spilka,* and that the workers are also now working with the intelligentsia. In one week's time, in Kiev, all patriotic groups are agreeing to form a single organization, the Ukrainian Solidarity Movement. He is asking for the Holy Father's blessing."

Ryan looked at Sister Iryna.

Her eyes were shining. "Isn't it wonderful news! You *will* ask the Holy Father for his blessing, please?"

Ryan's unhappiness at not being warned about Sister Iryna's luggage melted with that smile. She had done it to protect him. "Of course I will ask the Holy Father," Ryan said to Alia. "You must be very proud of your husband."

She was proud but she shrugged. "He keeps trying," she said as casually as she was able, "he is as stubborn as mule."

Stus spoke again to Ryan.

The mask of long-suffering returned. "He is also as curious like cat. He wants to know what is in the third suitcase."

"Ah," said Ryan. "That's not for him. It's for Bishop Mychaylo Antoniuk. Will you tell me where I can find the bishop?"

"Pavlo says you find him in the Zhiguli Palace."

"Where's that?"

Alia translated and the three Ukrainians laughed.

"The Zhiguli is the bishop's car," Sister Iryna explained at last. "It's his only home. The authorities refuse to register him, and so he moves around from village to village without ever telling anyone. That way the *stukachi* can't inform on him, and the militia don't catch him."

"But how will I find him?"

"Pavlo says that Bishop Antoniuk has a way of finding us when we need him."

Ryan looked exasperated.

"Is there anything else you are needing?" Alia asked.

"Yes," Ryan said. "The Holy Father wants me to go to Grushevo to check on the reported appearance of the Blessed Virgin Mary."

"There is no such place," Alia said.

"But Monsignor Hoffman said . . ."

"Monsignor Hoffman should be knowing better. Grushevo is a Russian name. The Blessed Virgin appeared to Ukrainians. The place is called Hrushiv in our language." The mask slipped again. "Pavlo himself saw the miracle."

Chapter ✦ Eight

KIRILLIN LEANED ON the railing of the veranda and looked past the cypresses and pink oleanders down to the pebbled shore of the Black Sea. A soft breeze cooled the bright sun and carried the scent of pines. He might almost have been back in that villa in the hills outside Pesaro on the Adriatic Coast, the villa in which he'd spent a blissful week with that blonde assistant cultural attaché.

The President's villa was modest compared with many on this coast. Budko, the Ukrainian Party chief, had taken over a sumptuous four-story palace near Gurzuf built by one of his predecessors; not content with one marble-lined swimming pool, he had one for salt water and one for fresh water.

The President had been dissatisfied by Kirillin's assurances over the telephone about the KGB Western Inner Rim Report. He had asked Kirillin to bring the report personally and brief him on what action was needed.

A Tupolev-154 was laid on at Vnukovo-2 airport, near Kirillin's new dacha, to fly him to the Crimean capital of Simferopol on the banks of the Salgir River. Instead of the usual Aeroflot seats and fittings, this aircraft had luxurious upholstery supplied by a Finnish company. Two hours after leaving Moscow, Kirillin transferred from the plane to a Hip helicopter, which flew down the dried-up Salgir River valley, past fields of corn and lavender, and climbed over the Crimean mountains, densely greened by rowans and tall poplars, with the crags of the soaring Chatyr-Dagh to his right. Through the pass, the helicopter swooped down over darker cypresses and pines, past vineyards and white cottages dotted by the side of the winding road, and headed toward the sea. The helicopter wheeled right, away from the seaside town of Alushta and the pale waters of the Black Sea which rapidly shelved to cobalt-blue. It skirted the bear-shaped mountain of Ayu-Dagh and flew past the port and resort of Yalta. It began to slow as it passed over the Renaissance-style Grand Palace in Livadia Park, where Roosevelt and Churchill had carved up Europe at the Yalta Conference. (These days no one ever mentioned that Stalin was present.) Twenty minutes out of Simferopol the helicopter descended to a landing pad in the fenced-off grounds of the four-story sanatorium used exclusively by Central Committee staff. A large black Zil limousine, its path cleared by motorcycle outriders with flashing lights, took a further ten minutes to climb the twisting road to the President's isolated villa. Kirillin was impressed—and surprised—by the efficiency of it all.

He sipped the glass of cool, dry white wine which the President's wife had poured, after assuring him that mineral water was not the only drink available in the house. It had been due to her personal intervention that the Massandra vineyards outside Yalta, which had started to produce dry whites and not just the cloying sweet stuff that Russians traditionally drank, was spared the total vandalization begun by local bureaucrats in response to Moscow's anti-alcohol campaign. In gratitude, the director of the Magarach Central Research Institute of Viticulture and Viniculture ensured that the First Lady was supplied with her favorite wines.

After reading Blagov's report, the President had burst

into one of his private rages. Kirillin wasn't sure whether the President's anger was directed at Blagov's proposed measures or at the reported nationalist unrest; probably both. The President had wanted to go back to Moscow. Kirillin had persuaded him there was no need.

In turn, the First Lady had tried to persuade him to stay here a few days, away from the energy-sapping humidity of Moscow's summer. He'd been tempted. This was his favorite view of the Ukraine, not the picture of right-wing, foreign-inspired, religious nationalism painted by Blagov. But duty beckoned.

He finished his wine and went inside to assure the President once more that everything was under control.

Chapter ✦ Nine

CARDINAL FASOLO WALKED up the short flight of steps from the Pope's private library and stopped. He took off his rimless spectacles with his right hand, picked up the trailing end of his crimson sash with his left hand, and began carefully wiping the lenses. This was the only outward sign of his emotions. He had just spent thirty-five minutes attempting to explain the realities of life to the Pope.

The apostolic nuncio in Washington had made it very clear that Zingler's draft for the Pope's letter to the American bishops' conference was disastrous. The United States was a nation founded on democratic ideals: the right to freedom of speech, the right to question traditional teaching, the right to express a view on social issues, all these were held to be the birthright of every American citizen. It had taken the Church nearly two hundred years to establish itself as genuinely American, and not some foreign import. Now the Catholic Church, with fifty-three million members, was by far the largest Church in the United States. The Church in Rome simply could not sack theologians from Catholic-funded posts at American universities for merely asking questions; it could not remove an American archbishop for offering the opinion that nuclear weapons were immoral in all circumstances; and it certainly could not send a letter in the Pope's name declaring that the National Conference of Catholic Bishops may not issue any document touching on faith or morals without that document having first been approved by the Sacred Congregation for the Doctrine of the Faith in Rome.

The Pope had sat there, head inclined to one side, eyes almost closed, whether in concentration or in boredom Fasolo was unsure. He had said nothing.

Fasolo had tried another tack. The Vatican was technically bankrupt. The income of the Holy See from investments—mainly its property in Rome—and from publishing, fell short of its expenses on salaries and administration, on Vatican Radio, on publishing, and on the papal visits. Each year, on the Feast of Saint Peter and Saint Paul, a collection called Peter's Pence was taken in every Catholic church in the world. Until recently Peter's Pence had covered the Vatican's deficit. No longer. And one-third of all Peter's Pence came from the United States. If that were reduced, or even cut off, the consequences were unthinkable.

The Pope's eyes had opened. *Istituto per le Opere di Religione* were the only words he had uttered.

Fasolo had given an inward sigh of exasperation. The Vatican Bank was not part of the Holy See, or of the Roman Curia, or of the Vatican City State. The Bank, which was housed in the Bastion of Nicholas V, three floors below that very room, had been constituted as a non-accountable institution, the profits of which were placed at the personal disposal of the pope. It had been used by Pius XII to found, finance, and organize the Christian Democratic Party in Italy after Mussolini's downfall to ensure that the Communists would not gain power after the War. It had been used to finance and organize Solidarity in Poland. True, it had also been used in recent years to help bridge the Vatican's deficit. But how many times had

Fasolo explained to the Pope that the Bank had sustained massive losses with the collapse of Michele Sindona's financial empire and with the Banco Ambrosiano fiasco? It had no more funds to pay out—either for any religious works the Pope wished to undertake or for the Vatican's deficit. It was imperative the Church not simply maintain but increase its income from the United States. Zingler's draft letter would stop the American subsidy altogether.

The Pope had stood up to end the audience and said that no pope could change what Christ had established.

It was clear to Fasolo that, after the failure of his Polish initiative, his own influence with the Pope had dwindled to nothing. But for the sake of the Church, which had withstood popes of all idiosyncracies and inclinations, he must find a way of getting through to this pope. Antonio had suggested Father Ryan, who had spent three years in the United States and had a business degree from Harvard. He would understand. And he had the Pope's confidence.

Fasolo became aware that Giuseppe was watching him from the doorway of his own room, next to the Pope's bathroom. He still had his spectacles wrapped in the end of his sash. He smiled and replaced his spectacles. "Giuseppe?"

"Eminence?"

"Is Father Ryan about?"

"No, Eminence. He is on holiday."

"Monsignor Hoffman?"

"Dr. Masala has sent him to bed. I don't think he's asleep yet, Eminence."

"Thank you, Giuseppe."

Hoffman ill. Well, it was worth a try. Fasolo walked up the narrow stairs to the attic area and knocked on Hoffman's door.

Hoffman was sitting up in bed. He put down the book he had been reading. From its lurid cover depicting Red Indians attacking a defensive circle of covered wagons, the book appeared to be a Polish translation of a pulp Western.

Having inquired after Hoffman's health, Fasolo steered

the conversation in general terms to the problems of the Church in the United States.

Hoffman took off his steel-rimmed spectacles and peered at Fasolo. "The tragedy of the West, Eminence, is that democracy has been such a political success it has taken over every sphere of life, including morality. Even the truth is something that is decided by voting." Fasolo found distasteful the intolerance in Hoffman's smile as the Pope's principal private secretary continued. "We are fortunate that we have a pope who knows that truth is a gift of the Holy Spirit, and not merely the majority opinion of mortals."

Outwardly, Fasolo's mild manner did not change. "Is there any danger, Monsignor, that the Holy Father will catch your infection?"

"The Holy Father needs me here."

"Of course. Especially with Father Ryan on holiday. A rather unfortunate time for him to be away from the office if you are confined to bed, Monsignor."

Hoffman did not respond.

"Would it help, Monsignor, if I sent one of my staff to assist you until Father Ryan returns?"

The smile verged on the supercilious. "There is no need, Eminence. I assure you, everything is under control."

Chapter ✣ Ten

THE APPARITION OF the Blessed Virgin Mary in the Ukraine was first reported on the anniversary of the nuclear catastrophe at Chernobyl. An eleven-year-old girl told her mother, a devout Ukrainian Catholic, that she had seen the Virgin Mary, shining with light, in the belfry window of the abandoned chapel near their house on the outskirts of the village of Hrushiv. Several other children then reported seeing the vision, and many of the villagers also claimed to have seen the Mother of God in the belfry shortly before sunset each day.

The chapel originally belonged to the Ukrainian Byzantine Rite Catholic Church. After Stalin liquidated the Church in 1946, the chapel was given to the Russian Orthodox Church, but later abandoned. Members of the underground Catholic Church declared that Our Lady had appeared in an abandoned church to reproach those who had abandoned their national faith.

As word spread hundreds, and then thousands, came by foot, by motorcycle, by bus, by car, and by train from as far afield as Donetsk to witness the apparition in this rural village.

The local Communist authorities condemned the miracle as a Vatican device to extend its influence in the socialist east. They also blamed the apparition for diverting workers from their jobs, for lowering local agricultural productivity below the targets set by Moscow, and for harming public health. The KGB and the militia attempted to stop people coming to the village. They failed. So they fenced off the chapel, boarded up the offending window, and blocked off a nearby spring that pilgrims claimed had miraculous healing powers.

These efforts failed too. A shadowy image of the Virgin and Child was reported on the small balcony of the belfry. Each day the fence was covered with embroidered cloths, flowers, and petitions to the Mother of God. Some of the envelopes containing petitions also contained money. Each day the local militia stripped the fence bare. Each day it filled again. In one year the pilgrims' offerings amounted to 62,000 roubles. The local soviet announced it was donating the money to the Soviet Peace Fund; that year the Communist Party Central Committee's International Department reduced its grant to the Peace Fund by 62,000 roubles.

Alia had heard of another young girl saying that a Lady, surrounded by shining light, had appeared to her on the way to school near Hrushiv and had asked why she did not pray. The Lady taught her prayers and asked her to tell everybody to pray each day to the Immaculate Heart of Mary so that the world would be delivered from evil.

"I go there after being released from Perm-36," Alia interpreted for Pavlo Stus. "Truly it is a miracle. Before me I see thousands upon thousands of people no longer afraid of persecution, but declaring their faith in front of the militia. They are praying and singing hymns with such joy in their hearts. And in the distance I see an outline of the Mother of God with the Infant Jesus. I say to myself, it was not for nothing that I was in prison all those years. It was worth the pain."

"What's happened to the shrine now?" Ryan asked.

"The KGB try another policy," Alia said. "The plenipotentiary for religious affairs re-registers the chapel for Russian Orthodox worship and instructs the Metropolitan of Kiev to send an Orthodox priest. The Orthodox liturgy is conducted there, but once the people hear the Russian they no longer come, and the Virgin no longer appears."

Pavlo Stus returned after lunch with a beam that threatened to split his face in two. Even Alia smiled when she heard his news.

"The Mother of God has granted both of your wishes," she said to Ryan. "Tomorrow is the Feast of the Assumption. At midnight tonight Bishop Antoniuk celebrates the liturgy in the chapel at Hrushiv. So, you see both the bishop and the place where Our Lady appeared. You also talk to the villagers."

"Is a midnight eve liturgy traditional for major feast days in the Ukraine?" Ryan asked.

Alia shrugged. "It is when the Catholic liturgy is celebrated in secret because it is not permitted in the chapel."

While Ryan waited in the Stus's apartment for the rest of that day, he tried to recall the particular significance of the Assumption of Our Lady into heaven. Then he remembered. It was during the week that Pope Pius XII had declared the Assumption to be an infallible doctrine of faith that the Pope had seen a repetition of the Fatima solar miracle in the Vatican Gardens.

At quarter to eleven that night Pavlo and Alia Stus led Ryan and Sister Iryna from the apartment. Outside the block stood a gleaming black Volga. Pavlo gestured proudly. "He says no Zaporozhets tonight," Alia interpreted. "A friend, a secret Catholic, works as a chauffeur for the city soviet." Two men and one woman were already in the car. Ryan put his suitcase in the boot and squeezed in the back seat with

Sister Iryna on his knee. She seemed to think it was all great fun.

On their journey along muddy potholed roads south of the city the car was stopped twice, but when the GAI patrol cars saw the registration number they waved the Volga on.

It was just past midnight when the car turned into a field and parked behind some bushes. The Carpathian mountains blocked out stars low in the sky behind them as they walked carefully along a dirt path. A man emerged from the shadows. Ryan thought everyone could hear his heart pounding. The man and Stus exchanged a few quiet words, and they continued on their way.

Another man came out from behind a tree and showed them the gap in the fence. The wooden chapel was small, and yet there must have been two hundred people inside. Blankets covered the windows. The only light came from a score of flickering candles held by men who acted as stewards. Ryan saw many young men and women standing there, not just the old ladies he'd expected.

The congregation shuffled back to allow a man with gray hair and a short gray beard to pass through. He wore ordinary clothes, but when he stood in front of the iconostasis he pulled over his head a white vestment on which Greek crosses were embroidered. His *omophor,* a Byzantine Rite bishop's scarf of authority, formed a broad circular band around his shoulders, with a straight length hanging down both his back and his front. He looked around, nodded, and opened the central royal door which bore an icon of the Annunciation.

An old man wearing an *epitrachil,* similar to the bishop's scarf but hanging only down the front, handed the bishop a thurible. The bishop incensed the altar, the book of the gospels, the icons, and gave the thurible back to the old priest.

In the dim light Ryan peered at the English translation of the divine liturgy of Saint John Chrysostom which Korchan had given him.

In a low but sure voice, Bishop Antoniuk intoned the

opening words: *"Blessed be the kingdom of the Father and of the Son and of the Holy Spirit, now and for ever and ever,"* and the congregation joined in the sung liturgy. The Ukrainian language, harsh to Ryan's ears when spoken, was ideally suited to the slow, mournful chant. Muted, lest its sound carry to informers in the village, it conveyed the psyche of the nation; even the Alleluias embodied the pain of a suffering people.

A low cry pierced the chant.

The candles were extinguished. The singing stopped.

It was pitch black. The sound of a car was the only noise to be heard. Its headlights illuminated the chapel. Ryan heard the intake of breath. Sister Iryna gripped his hand.

The headlights faded and the car continued down the road.

One by one the candles flickered into life. Bishop Antoniuk's firm voice once more led the muted chant. They were safe.

Babakin yawned. "How much longer will they be?"

Captain Chuprov, the Dragobych District Commander of the KGB, leaned forward from the rear seat of the unmarked Volga. "The whole thing usually takes about an hour and a half, but it could be longer tonight with the bishop present. He will hear confessions after the liturgy."

Babakin looked round. "In my day they heard confessions before, not after."

"They'd like to, but they're afraid they may be interrupted, and the liturgy has priority."

Babakin yawned again and settled down in the front passenger seat. "Wake me when the action starts."

Chapter ✠ Eleven

THE BYZANTINE LITURGY differed from the Western mass Ryan was used to. Much incensing. Much chanting by the people. Much making of the sign of the cross, with thumb and little finger bent into the palm and the middle three fingers touching forehead, chest and then right shoulder followed by left shoulder, rather than left followed by right. As the liturgy neared its end, however, these differences seemed superficial. It was the congregation returning after receiving holy communion that crystallized for Ryan the real difference. The faces of these people, who were risking heavy fines if not imprisonment, said it all. Until then Ryan had not known what real faith was, the faith that sustained Pavlo Stus through all those years of prison camp.

Ryan followed Sister Iryna to Bishop Antoniuk, standing at the opened door of the iconostasis. Ryan stood there like the others, arms crossed on his breast. Bishop Antoniuk gave him a momentary glance of non-recognition before dipping the spoon into the chalice and giving him the mixture of what appeared to be bread and wine, but which in reality was the Body and Blood of Christ.

* * *

Captain Chuprov nervously tapped the hunched shoulder in front of him. "They're starting to come out now, General. Do you want us to move in?"

"No."

Babakin carefully opened the car door so as not to make a sound. He moved silently to where the driver had kept a lonely vigil shielded by a hedge, and raised a camera to his face. Captain Chuprov hovered nervously behind him.

After twenty minutes Chuprov whispered, "The Lvov Regional Commander will want a report."

"He's not to have one."

"But . . ."

Still looking through the camera, Babakin said in a low voice, "As far as you're concerned, this never happened and I was never here."

Chuprov stuck his hands in the pockets of his regulation-issue civilian leather mackintosh. He was unhappy.

Babakin handed him the camera. "Take a look at those two—the younger man with the suitcase and the younger woman—behind the bishop."

Chuprov peered at Ryan and Sister Iryna.

"What strikes you about them?" Babakin asked.

The only thing that struck Chuprov was how powerful and how clear the infrared telescopic lens was.

"They're both foreigners," Babakin said. "That's why the First Directorate is involved. If you or your driver breathe a word of this, you'll spend the rest of your days as a trooper patroling the border at Kyakhta." Babakin smiled. "Understand?"

"Anything you say, Comrade General." Chuprov's wife thought this place was the end of the earth. He daren't even imagine her reaction to a Siberian outpost on the border with Mongolia.

* * *

Ryan and Sister Iryna followed the bishop, Alia, and the priest, Father Melnyk, with a crowd of others, while Pavlo Stus took up the rear.

Melnyk led them to a stone cottage with a corrugated iron roof. The crowd filled the whitewashed main room. A man put some more logs in the stove, which had a platform with bedding behind it.

Ryan stood to one side while both the men and the women queued to drop to both knees and kiss Antoniuk's episcopal ring. Antoniuk, however, was as far from a self-important Vatican prelate as Ryan could imagine. It wasn't merely his ordinary dress—gray shirt, blue tie, tweed jacket and gray trousers—but his relationship with his flock. After accepting the reverence of the faithful to their bishop, Antoniuk pulled them from their knees and hugged them warmly. Ryan shuffled uncomfortably while Sister Iryna followed this distinctly non-Roman display of obedience and love.

Antoniuk turned from Sister Iryna. "So you are the Holy Father's man?" he said in English with an American accent. Like Pavlo Stus, his gaunt features beneath thinning gray hair testified to years of labor camp starvation diets, and like Pavlo Stus, his eye shone with an unbroken spirit. To Ryan's surprise, his broad grin revealed a mouthful of gold teeth. He grasped Ryan's hand firmly. The man was a natural leader.

Two middle-aged women went out into the yard, to the kitchen shared between four similar cottages. They returned with plates of goose soup, goose pâté, goose stew, and slices of cold goose. An older man, who might have been a farmer, produced bottles of home-made vodka distilled from sugar.

When the old priest was told by Stus who the strangers were, he escorted Ryan to the seat at the corner of the room, below an icon of the Virgin draped with a *rushnik*, a ceremonial white towel decorated with Ukrainian embroidery. Immediately below the icon, above Ryan's head, a red votive lamp flickered.

Ryan watched self-consciously as the rest took their seats, looked toward him, and waited. Antoniuk, next to him, leaned across and whispered. "You're in the red corner, Father. You say grace."

Ryan blushed. "Bless us O Lord, and these thy gifts which we are about to receive, through Christ Our Lord, Amen," he said in English.

The watching faces relaxed into broad smiles, and then turned to the food. Ryan gratefully followed Antoniuk's example and tossed back the glass of vodka in one gulp.

"Would you like a glass of water, Father?" Sister Iryna giggled.

Ryan, trying to suppress the fire burning his throat and stomach, nodded.

After the meal, Ryan took the bishop to one side. "The Holy Father has sent some gifts."

Antoniuk raised his eyebrows.

Ryan opened his suitcase. He pulled out the gold-threaded bishop's cope and the golden Byzantine miter, together with a full set of liturgical vestments worn by a Byzantine Rite bishop.

Inquisitive faces gasped in admiration. Antoniuk held out his hands. "What can I say? You must thank the Holy Father, and ask him to pray that the day will soon come when I can wear these splendid vestments in public." He scratched his head. "I have only a letter to offer the Holy Father in return." He pulled an envelope from inside his tweed jacket and handed it to Ryan. "It's from the Urals, written in Russian. Archbishop Korchan can help with the translation if necessary."

"I'll personally hand it to the Holy Father," Ryan said. "And I have one more thing."

Stus, Alia, and Sister Iryna joined those gathered round to discover what else Ryan had brought from the Pope.

Ryan took out the painting of Saint Peter.

The others looked at it politely. The old priest hid his disappointment less well.

Ryan began dismantling the frame. From behind the canvas he removed an icon, approximately eight inches high by seven inches wide. "The Holy Father has blessed it. He entrusts it to your care, Bishop. He says you will know how best it will serve the needs of your people."

The humor left Antoniuk's face. He put out his hand and gingerly felt the icon.

Stus was shocked. "He says that's how the Mother of God appeared outside the belfry," Alia said.

"It's the original," Bishop Antoniuk whispered in awe. "The one found under the ruins of Kazan in the fifteenth century after an apparition of the Blessed Virgin told a young girl to search there." He sank to his knees, crossed himself, and kissed the icon, which showed the head and shoulders of a sad-faced Mother of God in a veiled dress cradling the Infant Jesus on her left shoulder. The faces of the Virgin and the Infant, painted on wood, stared out from the bejeweled rizza. This beaten-gold icon mounting was intricately crafted to form the garments of the Virgin and the Infant, standing out in relief from the dark, flat painting. The Virgin's halo was studded with large, rectangular emeralds, while her veil was crowned with a diadem of amethysts and diamonds. The Infant's robe was clasped by a huge emerald.

"But how . . . ?" Alia asked.

"Monsignor Hoffman brought it from Fatima last week," Ryan said.

Antoniuk, still on his knees, looked up. "It was taken there for safekeeping, ready to play its part in fulfilling the Second Secret of Fatima." He rose to his feet. "It was smuggled out of Moscow after the Revolution, before the Communists destroyed the Basilica of Our Lady of Kazan in Red Square to prove there was no God." He gripped Ryan by the shoulders. "You have just brought us the most venerated icon in Christian Russia, the miraculous Kazan Icon of the Mother of God."

"But why has the Holy Father . . . ?" Alia began.

Antoniuk's eyes gleamed. "For five hundred years this icon has performed miracles, uniting Christian factions and saving the Motherland from infidels. For this it was awarded the title 'Liberatrix of Holy Russia'."

Chapter ✣ Twelve

JUST BEFORE NINE o'clock in the morning Bishop Antoniuk, dressed in the clothes he had worn the previous night, called at the Stus's apartment to take Pavlo Stus, Sister Iryna, and Ryan to Kiev. Shortly afterwards the Zhiguli Palace, which resembled an old-fashioned box-shaped Fiat, left Lvov and headed along Highway 12 toward the sun.

The bumpy road ran almost straight, lined with a windbreak of trees. It crossed a river and passed through two small towns. After nearly four hours, with the sun high in the sky, the scenery changed to a flatland of marshes and dank woods. Ryan had slept little after returning at four in the morning from Hrushiv. His eyes kept closing.

"What do you think of our countryside, Father Ryan?" Bishop Antoniuk asked cheerily.

Ryan opened his eyes. "Interesting."

"You must always tell the truth, Father," Antoniuk chided. "Even in the sunshine, this countryside looks sad. And so it might. Volynia has never seen peace. At one time it was part of the Kievan Federation with its own prince, but it has been fought over by Lithuanians, by Poles, by

Russians, and by Germans. Despite the russification policy since the War, its people, thank God, still retain their national faith, although many do so in secret."

Ryan frowned. "They're Catholic?"

Antoniuk nodded. "Of course."

"But surely, Bishop, one mark of the Catholic Church is that it is universal. It can't be national at the same time."

Antoniuk looked so long at Ryan next to him in the front seat that Stus had to lean over and grab him by the shoulder as the car drifted toward an oncoming truck on the other side of the road. Antoniuk pulled at the steering wheel just in time and gave a gold-toothed grin to the truck driver.

"This is your Western thinking, Father. Christ tells us to love our neighbors as ourselves. When we love our neighbors, then we are good patriots and also good Christians. The Church is the spirit of the nation." He grinned at Ryan. "The Council for Religious Affairs refuses to register me as a bishop because they say I'm a nationalist when I'm simply practising Christianity."

Ryan noticed that Antoniuk, like Stus, wore a lapel badge of the banned flag of independent Ukraine.

Shortly afterwards they reached the town of Rovno. The petrol station was closed. Antoniuk passed the railway station and its nearby cafés, and drove out to a residential area. He parked outside a medium-rise apartment block. Ryan was hungry as well as tired.

"We have a stop here," Antoniuk said.

The ground floor apartment was full, with a bride and groom and half a dozen babies among the twenty other adults and children. Only after he had officiated at the wedding, baptized five babies, confirmed three teenagers, and heard eight confessions in the bedroom, did the bishop sit down to eat some food, waving Ryan, Sister Iryna, and Stus to join him.

When they set off again, Ryan noticed that the petrol gauge registered full.

The road continued through marshland. The light faded rapidly.

Ryan felt a tap on his shoulder. He woke up. "This is where we stay the night," Sister Iryna said.

The bishop knocked at one of the larger houses in the village. Soon the house was full and the bishop celebrated the liturgy. Ryan found great difficulty in keeping his eyes open during the liturgy and the meal that followed. He whispered to Sister Iryna that he didn't know where Bishop Antoniuk found the strength.

She smiled. "It is God's strength."

They set out before six o'clock the following morning, and within half an hour they were driving down Kiev's main thoroughfare.

Kreshchatik used to be a wooded valley running through the plateau on which most of the city was built. The fashionable boulevard, randomly developed since the early part of the nineteenth century, was bombed during the Second World War. After the War Stalin's town planners widened Kreshchatik and created a six-lane road bordered by broad, tree-lined pavements and flanked by uniformly designed seven-story, pale yellow concrete-tiled and red-roofed buildings. The boulevard was punctuated by three monumental squares whose names have changed with fluctuating political fortunes.

"The Russians here call this the Champs Elysées of the East," Antoniuk said disparagingly.

"What's that?" asked Ryan, pointing ahead. A great steel arch, like a silver rainbow, bestrode a wooded slope beyond the end of the boulevard.

Antoniuk gave a dry laugh. "That is the monument dedicated to the reunion of Russia and the Ukraine."

Kreshchatik curved gently to the right and ended in what used to be known as Stalin Square and was now called Leninsky Komsomol Square. Antoniuk drove round the flower bed at the center of the square, used as a turning circle for trolley buses, passing the gloomy bulk of the Hotel Dnipro, a large cinema hoarding, the yellow nineteenth-century Philharmonia building and the modernist concrete Lenin Museum. Here Antoniuk turned right off the square and up a steep hill.

The narrow road led to another square with a flower bed at its center. It was overlooked on one side by the monumental columned white façade of the Kiev City Communist Party Central Committee building and on the other side by the five-story pink neoclassical Ukrainian Republic Militia Headquarters. "The only example of efficient Communist planning in Kiev," Antoniuk grinned. "It takes only ten seconds for the people's militia to come and protect the people's Party from the people."

They left Kalinin Square by the Militia HQ, and zigzagged round a one-way system to come to a halt by a small, flat park. "Come," Antoniuk ordered. "This is what I really want to show you."

Ryan stood at the highest point in Kiev. At his feet lay the reconstructed foundations of a church, behind him four of the five gold-edged green domes of Saint Andrew's Church rose above a line of chestnut trees, and beyond and below flowed the wide Dnieper River.

"This was Church of the Holy Virgin, the first stone church in the land of the Slavs," Antoniuk said. "Here was the great capital of Kievan Rus, when Moscow was just a wheel track in the forest. Here the Slav tribes of the east were first united. Here Saint Vladimir brought Christianity to the Slav peoples a thousand years ago, when the Byzantine Church still accepted the Pope of Rome as head of Christendom. This is why, Father Ryan, we are Catholic. Unlike the Russian Orthodox, we maintain the tradition of loyalty to the Successor of Saint Peter."

"I've been thinking about your nationalism, Bishop," Ryan said. "What I don't understand is your attitude to the Russians. They're Slavs like yourselves, and they liberated you from Nazi Germany. You talk of loving your neighbor, but . . ." He let the words hang in the air.

Antoniuk interpreted Ryan's English for Sister Iryna

and Stus. The latter spoke animatedly. The bishop nodded, and then said, "It's time to move on."

"Are we going to the Roman Catholic community now, Bishop?"

Antoniuk looked at him. "Soon, soon."

They returned to the car. Antoniuk took them down the Andreyevsky Descent, past the white and blue baroque Saint Andrew's Church, to the old Lower Town, the Podol, by the banks of the Dnieper.

They drove under the high concrete pylon of the Moscow suspension bridge, part of the North Bridge crossing the islands of the Dnieper River, and on through the concrete tower blocks of the modern residential district of Troeschina on the flat east bank. After Troeschina they turned off the road and joined the Chernigov Highway, carved through a flat pine forest. After five minutes on the highway Antoniuk turned right down a gravelly dirt path into the forest.

The car pulled up in front of a barrier. Antoniuk, Ryan, Stus, and Sister Iryna climbed out of the car. No one spoke. Antoniuk pointed ahead. The other three waited by the car while Ryan walked slowly along the newly cobbled path on the other side of the barrier.

At the end of the path, amid the slender pines, lay a mound about ten meters by fifteen meters bordered by pink granite slabs. Two Cyrillic words were carved on the large central slab. Fresh flowers lay beneath it.

The morning was dank and misty. No sun pierced the upper branches of the pines. The eerie silence was broken only by the cawing of a single crow. Ryan went deeper into the forest. The carpet of pine needles and moss over the sandy soil was soft and yielding beneath his feet. In places it had subsided into large hollows. Ryan walked through cobwebs between trees that appeared dead. A few bushes were attempting to grow, but their leaves were covered with a white deposit. That solitary, invisible crow was the only sign of life in the forest.

"This is Bykovnya Forest."

Ryan jumped. He hadn't heard anyone following him.

"We're one hundred and forty kilometers south of Chernobyl," Antoniuk said.

"Is that why the forest is dying?" Ryan asked.

Antoniuk stared at the undulating forest floor. "It is the forest of the dying and of the dead. One hundred and fifty thousand, possibly two hundred and fifty thousand, decomposing Ukrainian bodies caused these hollows. They were shot in 1937 by Stalin's NKVD for the crime of being Ukrainian. Four years earlier seven million Ukrainians were starved to death when the Russians forcibly took the food from our land and sold it abroad for foreign currency to finance their great Communist Revolution." He gave a deep sigh. "The Russians liberated us from the Poles, the Germans liberated us from the Russians, and the Russians liberated us from the Germans. We've had enough of liberators, Father Ryan. You ask the Holy Father. He understands why we want to be free, not only of Communism but also of Russia."

Ryan and Sister Iryna climbed out of Antoniuk's car at Kiev Railway Station after they had delivered the picture of Saint Peter to the house in Shepetovskaya Street licensed for Roman Catholic services.

Before Antoniuk and Stus left for a meeting of the provisional council of the Ukrainian Solidarity Movement, Ryan asked if there was anything he could do for them back in Rome.

Antoniuk nodded slowly. "Please ask the Holy Father to recognize the Metropolitan Chuprynka as Patriarch of the Ukraine. And ask him to look favorably on the beatification of Metropolitan Slipyj, who suffered seventeen years in Soviet labor camps for the faith. A Ukrainian saint would be a great inspiration for the faithful."

◊ ◊ ◊

The taxi stopped in the Saint Damasus Courtyard. Before Ryan alighted, Sister Iryna shyly kissed him on the cheek. "Thank you, Jacek, from the Ukraine."

Ryan stood there, in the suffocating heat of Rome, as the taxi took Sister Iryna back to the seclusion of her convent. It was almost exactly five days to the hour that he had been away. Five days that had steeled his faith.

Chapter ✣ Thirteen

THE FOLLOWING MORNING, the Pope, Archbishop Korchan, Kasamir Hoffman, and Ryan descended by the private lift to the Courtyard of Sixtus V. Giuseppe was standing next to the gleaming black Mercedes-Benz which had yellow and white papal pennants hanging limply in the heat from small masts on both front wings. Suitcases were already packed in the boot. Six Swiss guards stood to attention either side of the lift exit.

Giuseppe drove the car sedately through the narrow arch into the Saint Damasus Courtyard, out through another equally narrow arch on the opposite side, and threaded the car down a narrow cobbled road through three small courtyards—the Pappagalli, the Borgia, and the Sentinel—overlooked by fortified ochre-colored walls.

When it reached the Square of the Oven the car took the same steep road up the Vatican Gardens that Ryan had walked with Monsignor Grimes on his first working day at the Vatican. At the highest point of the Vatican City an Alitalia helicopter, flying the papal pennant, waited for them. It was surrounded by a gaggle of prelates, altar boys, and Vatican staff in their best clothes.

Korchan, Hoffman, and Ryan climbed into the helicopter with two *vigilanze*. The Pope said his goodbyes, and then joined them in the aircraft.

Ryan had never been in a helicopter before. The blades began to spin, disappearing in a whirring circle as the helicopter ascended heavenwards from the waving faithful below.

Ten minutes after leaving the Vatican Hill, Ryan peered forward to see the huge, oval-shaped deep blue water of Lake Albano partially filling a massive volcanic crater whose inner slopes were dark green with oak and chestnut trees. Above the left-hand rim loomed Mount Cavo. Perching on the right-hand rim, the town of Castel Gandolfo stretched back in a ragged line of red-tiled roofs from the white dome of Bernini's Church of Saint Thomas of Villanova, across a small square from the Pontifical Palace that dominated the town.

Ryan was still on a high after his Ukrainian venture. For the first time since his arrival at the Apostolic Palace he was being treated as part of the papal family, and not some visiting stranger. Kasamir Hoffman's suspicious reserve melted into the affection and pride an uncle might show his favorite nephew who had performed some heroic feat. That evening, after a supper of cheese and an apple in the private dining room on the top floor of the Pontifical Palace at Castel Gandolfo, Ryan even felt able to broach the question of Hoffman's mother in Gdansk. Hoffman nodded. "Mother never recovered after my father was shot by Stalin's NKVD. She died twenty years ago. But my spiritual mother in Gdansk is not well. What you did last week will help her as well as the Ukraine." Ryan thought he understood.

The Pope spent most of his time in prayer in the chapel. Hoffman was still recovering from his virus and stayed indoors, but he and Korchan urged Ryan to take a holiday.

Korchan was staying in the Secretary of State's apart-

ment in the Villa Barberini. Cardinal Fasolo rarely used
the apartment; he was spending his summer break with his
sister and brother-in-law in Faenza. Because the grounds
were strictly private and surrounded by high walls, the
Pope was quite happy for his staff to dress informally. Korchan, in gray open-necked shirt and trousers, chatted with
Ryan about the Ukraine as he showed Ryan round the next
day.

The façade of the Pontifical Palace formed one end of
the small Piazza della Liberta in the town of Castel Gandolfo. The palace was built round a small courtyard, with a
triangular shaped garden on the opposite side from the
piazza. The top two floors of the palace extended over the
Via Massimo d'Azeglio, linking it with a building in the
grounds of the Villa Cybo. The walled gardens of the Villa
Cybo ran parallel to the town, and a tree-lined viaduct over
the Salita San Antonio, which descended the outer slope of
the volcano, connected the Villa Cybo with the Villa Barberini, the grounds of which extended as far as the next
town of Albano. The whole area was larger than the Vatican City State.

Ryan had been impressed by the Vatican Gardens, but
they paled by comparison with the grounds of the Villa
Barberini, which included the remains of the theater and
the villa built by the Emperor Domitian for his summer
residence. Underneath the first of three large terraces of
gardens that stepped down the volcano slope, a huge underground hall had been hollowed out of the peperino
rock. Standing on a rock platform twenty-five feet above
the floor of the concealed chamber, Korchan said, "From
here Domitian surveyed the Roman senators sitting
meekly below." He smiled. "Like most autocratic rulers,
he was assassinated."

Korchan took Ryan beyond the *Cryptoportico* to the
swimming pool, hidden by hedge, fence, and roof so that
no one might see the Holy Father in his swimming trunks.
Ryan was welcome to use the pool other than between four

and five in the afternoon when the Holy Father had his daily swim. Korchan suggested Ryan join him on a shoot.

Ryan frowned. "Shoot what?"

Korchan's broad Slav face creased into a smile. "Anything that moves. Sparrows are best. The Italian nuns make a delicious pasta sauce out of them. Since shooting sparrows became illegal in Italy, their sparrow sauce is a rare delicacy."

"But if it's illegal . . ."

"Ah, but we're not in Italy. Castel Gandolfo is extraterritorial, so we can shoot away to our hearts' content. It's one thing we and the Italians have in common."

Ryan declined the offer.

Ryan began to appreciate why popes spent as much time as possible at Castel Gandolfo. It wasn't just to be free of the never-ending assault of audiences, meetings, reports, and telephone calls. For a body wilting under the heavy, sticky, dirty heat of a Roman summer, the clear cool air of the Alban hills was purifying and invigorating.

For Ryan it was best of all at night. Gone was the jarring cacophony of Rome's traffic, which avoided collision by the blaring of horns, the squealing of brakes, and the roaring of engines. Here, only the splashing of a fountain, the chirping of crickets, and the occasional fluttering of doves in the chestnut trees disturbed the peace of the papal summer residence.

Below, where the road hugged Lake Albano, the street lights edged the lake with a row of white and amber pearls that sent a curtain of light shimmering into the lake. The curtain gave way to a flat, starlit gray expanse that merged into the blackness of the far rim and Mount Cavo above it.

The view overhead was even more exhilarating. No shroud of pollution turned the night starless and closed off escape from the prison of the papal apartment. Here the stars shone large and bright in an open, vast blackness that stretched to the very edge of the universe. Here the infinite was real.

The call from Diana Lawrence came as if from another world. Ryan had no idea from where she had obtained the private telephone number.

She was eager to hear about his Ukrainian trip, and about Castel Gandolfo. She had been lent a villa with a swimming pool above Lake Nemi, near Genzano. It was less than four miles from Castel Gandolfo. She'd love him to join her for a day or, better still, two days. When he hesitated, she said that she had to go back to the States in a couple of days, and she didn't want to leave without seeing him.

Ryan explained to Hoffman that an old friend had invited him to a nearby villa. Hoffman said that was fine, telling him to stay the night if he wanted. He did suggest Ryan should be back by the Feast of the Immaculate Heart of Mary.

Chapter ✣ Fourteen

IT WAS EXACTLY 18:30 when the big white Ilyushin-62 taxied away from the apron in front of the terminal building at Vnukovo-2 airport. Five minutes later the plane containing the President, his wife, and Foreign Minister Zavornitsky roared down the runway. It cleared the forest at the airport's perimeter, rose steeply in an arc, and headed toward the sun. Kirillin continued to watch until it shrunk to a dot and was lost among fluffy white clouds that would either vanish by morning or else swell with thunder.

Kirillin walked back to his car, climbed into the back seat, and crumpled like a puppet whose strings had been cut. Adrenaline had kept him going without sleep during the previous forty-eight hours. He'd compiled the draft agreements needed on the most vital areas of trade and transfer of technology for the two days of negotiations at Camp David; he'd helped steer the draft arms reduction treaty through the Soviet General Staff and the Ministries of Defense and Defense Industries; and he'd drafted the President's speech to the United Nations on human rights. There was nothing more Kirillin could do. His hopes—and, though they did not appreciate it, the hopes of the Soviet people—were now in that plane.

Georgi turned round from the driver's seat. "The dacha, sir? You could do with some sleep."

Kirillin nodded.

The drive through the silver birch forest from Vnukovo-2 to Zhukovka took less than ten minutes.

After a shower and a meal of grilled steak washed down with a bottle of Georgian *Saperavi*, Kirillin felt refreshed. He went to his favorite think place, the bluff overlooking the now sultry Moscow River, to watch the red sun sink into the west. The worst was through, with no major disasters. This long hot summer was the period he'd feared most. The wave of demonstrations and strikes had led the Supreme Soviet to extend its session into the second week of August. The President, as usual, had been attacked from all sides but, as usual, he'd weathered the storm. His opponents had dispersed to their dachas or their villas by the sea, no doubt to bemoan further shortcomings of *perestroika* rather than put their energies into transforming society. Babakin had assured him that it was safe to postpone any action on Blagov's Western Inner Rim Report until after the President's return from the USA. The agreements on trade and transfer of technology promised in return for the Soviet defense cuts would revitalize the Soviet economy and enable food and consumer goods to be pumped into the republics to take the steam out of the nationalist unrest. Then he could deal with Blagov.

Back in bed he read Lermontov's *A Hero of Our Time* while sipping his way through half a bottle of Armenian brandy. His mind drifted to anticipating the next two weeks by the Black Sea. His digital clock was showing nearly midnight when he leaned across to switch off the bedside lamp. He had no reason to know that the next day was the Feast of the Immaculate Heart of Mary, the feast day instituted by Pope Pius XII to fulfill a request made by the Mother of God on her third appearance at Fatima.

Chapter ✤ Fifteen

FIVE HOURS AFTER Kirillin had relaxed into a contented sleep, shadows began to move.

From the residential zones in the north and the villages beyond, they moved down side roads, avoiding the street lamps on Semsotletiya Lovova Street. From other zones of identical ten-story concrete blocks in the southwest they skirted the LAZ bus factory and the lighted windows of the newspaper office opposite, and sought the darkness of the woods in Stryisky Park and then of the deserted arcades and pavilions of the Bogdan Khmelnitsky Leisure Park, as they too moved inward. From the southeast they moved eerily through heroic Soviet monuments in the Hill of Glory Military Cemetery and through tombstones in the old Lychakovskoye Cemetery. From the northeast they disturbed the silhouette of Castle Hill taking shape below the graying wash of a predawn sky.

The city called Lviv by its inhabitants but Lvov by its Soviet authorities—and Lemberg, Lwow and countless other names by previous rulers—had begun to stir.

An hour later the shadows packed into Rynok Square, surrounding the City Soviet that used to be the Town Hall.

On the stroke of six o'clock, ten thousand candles flickered
into life and banished the gloom. Sirens wailed from afar,
but otherwise the square was silent as a large blue and yellow nationalist banner unfurled between the heraldic lions
guarding the entrance to the old Town Hall. Blue and yellow flags rose from the sea of candle flames alongside papal
yellow and white flags, embroidered white banners bearing
images of the Virgin and other saints, and icons draped
with *rushniki*. The crowd moved back to let the large banner pass through, and then it funnelled into a procession
behind the banner which headed out of the square toward
Lenin Prospekt. A mustard-colored militia jeep—siren
wailing, headlights blazing, red and blue roof lamps flashing—raced down Sovetskaya Street, but found its way
blocked by a solid mass of people, candles, and banners
stretching back from Rynok Square along Ruskaya Street
to the junction with Sovetskaya.

Lenin Prospekt too was blocked. Both its northward and
its southward carriageways were filled with candle-lit people spilling over from the broad, tree-lined pedestrian avenue that separated the carriageways. The candles parted to
allow the procession from the City Soviet to reach the
square at the center of the pedestrian avenue, known unof-
ficially as Nationalist Square. Other torch-bearing leaders
stood here, beside the flower-bedecked people's monument to the Ukrainian poet Taras Shevchenko. Silently the
mass of candles and flags to the north and south waited to
follow the procession which crossed Lenin Prospekt and
headed up Gorky Street. At the northern end of the Prospekt, a black frowning Lenin, trapped from the waist down
in a solid block of red granite, looked on.

By now the sky had lightened enough to show the faded
yellows of the three- and five-story neoclassical façades on
Gorky Street, and the mainly empty shop windows of their
ground floors. Even the military tailor's could boast only a
solitary Army greatcoat in its double window.

Militia jeeps and cars, followed by dark green canvas-
topped lorries, flashed and wailed their way through un-

blocked streets to head off the procession. They poured into Ivan Franko Park from the south and disgorged MVD regular militia plus Special Orders troops, some of them wearing their black berets but others protected by white helmets and plastic riot shields. Gray phalanxes formed in front of the main university building and round the huge red granite Ivan Franko staring uphill into his park, away from the helping militia dogs.

When the lead banner reached Pobedy Square, it continued past the park entrance and up Mickiewicz Street, climbing the hill parallel to the park. For one quiet moment the militia watched as the banners and candles began passing them by on the other side of the border of trees. Then a cacophony of shouts and whistles and barking was followed by the sounds of engines revving, doors slamming, and sirens howling.

Before the first car had moved, the banner had passed by the three tall radio masts topped by red lights which had been erected to jam the BBC World Service, Radio Liberty, and Vatican Radio. The procession continued beneath trolley bus wires gleaming with the first light of dawn. By the time the banner had followed the curve of Mickiewicz Street up into Bogdan Khmelnitsky Square, one black unmarked Volga and two covered six-wheeler trucks had circled round and were speeding in from the north. Special Orders troops, rifles at the ready, jumped out from the trucks to line the faded pink walls that protected Saint George's Cathedral. Four plainclothes KGB officers hurried from the Volga to the gate pillars at the foot of the slope that led up to the cathedral courtyard.

The banner stopped in the center of the square, facing the KGB officers. The procession silently fanned out behind, filling up the cobbled square and then flowing back underneath the trees of the parkland to the rear.

A squat, leather-coated KGB captain held out his hand. A colleague gave him a megaphone. He put it to his mouth and ordered the demonstrators to disperse immediately.

Opposite him, no one moved. There was none of the

usual shouting or slogan chanting, just a sea of silent, watchful faces holding lighted candles, flags, and icons.

Beneath the large nationalist banner, Pavlo Stus turned to the gaunt gray-bearded man wearing a black topcoat and a black astrakhan hat. "Are you ready?"

Bishop Antoniuk nodded. "May God give me strength."

"The Blessed Virgin will protect you."

A young priest removed Antoniuk's topcoat to reveal a magnificent gold-threaded cope. Another priest replaced Antoniuk's hat with a golden Byzantine miter.

The KGB captain took a Makarov semi-automatic from his shoulder holster. "Get back or I shoot," he shouted in Russian.

Stus unwrapped the icon and handed it to Antoniuk, who held it to his breast. "Then you must first shoot Our Lady of Kazan," Antoniuk declared loudly in Russian. In the eerie silence that followed, Antoniuk intoned the third section of the Russian *akathist* in honor of Our Lady of Kazan:

> *"Rejoice O thou who dispels the darkness of evil*
> *with the revelation of your Icon*
> *Rejoice O thou who enlightens all*
> *with the rays of miracles*
> *Rejoice O zealous Protectress*
> *of the Christian Brethren!"*

The echo of his ringing voice faded. The KGB captain repeated his shouted threat, more hoarsely this time, and stretched out his right arm to aim the gun at Antoniuk. Those next to the bishop began to sing softly the *O Spomahay Nas Divo Mariye*. More joined in this Ukrainian hymn to the Mother of God, and still more, so that the hymn became a tidal wave spreading out from the icon at the center. As it spread it grew in volume.

The bishop, icon held to his breast, walked slowly toward the KGB captain. By now those at the back of the two hundred thousand strong crowd had added their voices to invest the anthem with a frightening intensity. The gun wavered. Behind the captain, the sun was rising above the statue of Saint George the Dragonslayer on the roof of the cathedral. The bishop thrust the icon aloft. The sun's rays hit the bejeweled, beaten-gold dress of the Mother of God. The KGB captain instinctively put up his left arm to shield his eyes from the blinding reflection. The long-suppressed emotions of the faithful flooded full-voiced into the anthem which echoed through the square so that the walls behind the troops seemed to tremble before the dazzling Virgin.

Pavlo Stus's large hand grasped the captain's right wrist. "You don't need that, my friend. Bullets cannot kill the Mother of God." The gun clattered to the stone flags. The militia watched as if mesmerized. Suddenly one young trooper threw aside his rifle, ran forward, and fell on his knees before the icon. Several others followed. The rest stood motionless as the procession passed through them and up the cobbled slope to the cathedral courtyard.

A black-robed Russian Orthodox priest ran out from the former residence of the Ukrainian Catholic Metropolitan. His protests froze at the sight of the icon.

Antoniuk, still holding the icon, turned to face the cathedral. Stone staircases rose from the left and from the right to meet in front of the cathedral's main door. A twice-life-size Saint Leo stood atop one side of the portico, and Saint Anastasius the other. Above them, the simple arched main window was the only plain feature of a pink baroque façade that soared up to an embellished gable; at its peak the triumphant Saint George was spearing the dragon.

On either side of Antoniuk priests were sprinkling incense on the lighted charcoals of a thurible and were blessing the water in a brass aspersorium. Inside the cathedral Stus was levering back the lock of the main door.

Preceded by one priest swinging incense and another sprinkling holy water, Antoniuk mounted the left-hand staircase. He held the icon aloft while the main door was blessed. It swung back. The two priests and Antoniuk walked through, followed by two lines of priests holding lighted candles and, after them, the faithful.

Slowly the candle-lit procession moved down the gloomy center nave, between the four huge square pillars that supported the high, wide central dome, passed through the opened altar rail, and came to the iconostasis. As the priest with the thurible intoned a blessing before this symbolic gate between heaven and earth, Stus switched on the lights. The cathedral glowed with the sudden illumination of the intricate gilt frames and gold leaf detailing of the paintings and icons that cluttered the pale green walls and pillars. But nothing surpassed the blaze of the breathtakingly elaborate gilt iconostasis frame lit by a massive chandelier.

Bishop Antoniuk opened the royal door and entered the holy place. He stood the Kazan icon in front of the altar, removed his miter, took three steps back, and prostrated himself before it.

By the time Antoniuk had blessed and incensed the altar, the cathedral had filled and Stus's colleagues had connected the cathedral's amplification system to cables that led to loudspeakers in the cathedral courtyard and Bogdan Khmelnitsky Square.

Antoniuk climbed the steps to the ornate white and gold pulpit a third of the way up the pillar to the left of the altar rail. His deep voice resonated through the cathedral, the courtyard, and the square beyond. "In 1770 this cathedral was consecrated to Saint George, who slew the dragon who was Satan. Stalin, the creature of Satan, took our cathedral from us. This morning we return to celebrate the divine liturgy on the feast of the Immaculate Heart of Mary, the woman clothed in the sun who, Saint John tells us in the Book of Revelation, will confront the red dragon with seven heads and will triumph over him."

In the bell tower Stus was at work. The oldest bell in the Ukraine pealed out its summons to an oppressed nation.

Chapter ✦ Sixteen

THE INSISTENT RINGING of the telephone roused Kirillin from a deep sleep.

The Prime Minister's voice was tense. "Voloshin here. There's a meeting of the Politburo at three o'clock this afternoon."

Kirillin rubbed his eyes. "There can't be. The President's in the United States."

"The nationalists have taken over Lvov. Budko demanded an emergency meeting."

Kirillin sat up in bed. "He'll have to wait until the President returns."

"Dobrik has the agreement of more than half the members."

Kirillin was out of bed and trying to wrap a dressing gown round him while holding the telephone. There had been no love lost between Leonid Dobrik and the President since the latter had transferred Dobrik to head the Central Committee Commission on Agriculture, a political graveyard which had destroyed the reputation of most of Dobrik's predecessors. Within the Politburo Dobrik took every opportunity to point out problems arising from the implementation of *perestroika,* but he'd never seemed to Kirillin to possess the brains to organize a coup. "Dobrik?"

"Yes. But Nikolei Korolev has phoned to ask if I want to take the leading role in stabilizing the country."

Kirillin bit his lip. Only a mind like Korolev's would ask the Prime Minister to take the leading role when, in the absence of the President, the Prime Minister already had that role. "What are you going to do?"

"I'm at Usovo. I'm coming over to collect you in fifteen minutes' time on my way into the Kremlin."

Kirillin turned on the television to see exactly what was happening in the Ukraine. But all the television screen showed was the regular children's program, in which a cheerful young woman was demonstrating to two abnormally attentive specimens of Soviet childhood how to make a paper chain of soldiers.

He picked up the phone and dialed. "What the devil's happening? Why didn't you warn me?"

"The storm took everyone by surprise," Babakin's voice said. "My immediate priority was to assess the storm damage. Where are you now?"

"I'm at Zhukovka . . ."

"As far as the future weather pattern is concerned," Babakin interjected, "it seems that the general outlook was established earlier this morning at Frunze Street, and our chief forecaster returned with a sunny disposition. The ninth meteorological officer has been summoned, presumably to work out detailed pressure charts."

That meant the KGB chief had already reached an agreement with the Army General Staff. The head of the KGB's Ninth Directorate, whose responsibilities included the personal security of Party leaders, was being asked to draw up detailed plans. It looked bad. "I need to know the precise forecast before three o'clock this afternoon."

"That'll be difficult, but I'm sure the weather will be fine by two o'clock."

Kirillin put the phone down, had a cold shower, and had

only just finished dressing when he heard a heavy knock at the door.

A man with a bulge under the left armpit of his cheap gray suit filled most of the doorframe. Over the man's shoulder Kirillin saw the single flashing blue light on the roof of a black Volga. The KGB.

"Comrade Kirillin?" an uneducated voice asked.

Kirillin's heart pounded. It had come to this so soon?

"The Prime Minister is waiting."

Kirillin nodded and turned back, ostensibly to collect his briefcase but principally to hide the flush burning his cheeks. I must be getting paranoid, he thought to himself. He followed the Prime Minister's bodyguard to the Zil parked behind the first escort car. A second KGB car waited down the road. He climbed into the deep leather seat next to Voloshin in the rear of the limousine with curtained windows.

The Prime Minister looked younger than his fifty-seven years. With his European face, slim figure, and well-tailored suit, he would not look out of place at a meeting of top businessmen in London or Paris. Usually he radiated an impression of total imperturbability, which contrasted with the President's bursts of emotion. Now, his face showed strain. It was clear he had only been informed of the emergency Politburo meeting once Korolev had secured a majority by using Dobrik to contact the others.

"What happened?" Kirillin asked.

Voloshin looked straight ahead. "A Ukrainian Catholic bishop produced a miraculous icon of the Mother of God. The icon summoned two hundred thousand people to Saint George's Cathedral in Lvov. It sent out shafts of light which blinded the KGB officer in charge and sent his gun spinning from his hand. The icon turned the MVD troops into statues, while it sent another shaft of light to open the cathedral doors."

"You can't believe that?"

Voloshin turned to face him. "It doesn't matter what I believe. It only matters that half of the Ukraine believes it.

The uprising has spread to Kiev. Rumors say three Russians have been killed."

Kirillin sank back in the seat. He needed time to think. He had barely begun to work out the options when, through a parting in the window curtains, he saw the gray gothic skyscraper of the Hotel Ukraina looming up on the left. Because the Zil's suspension had smoothed out the rough road, he hadn't appreciated how fast they had been traveling. The motorcade sped past the Ukraina onto Kalinin Bridge over the Moscow River, and continued down the reserved center lane of Kalinin Prospekt. Habits died hard. Despite several bouts of de-Stalinization, the Prospekt retained the name of the man who had been Soviet President during the Stalin years.

With GAI militia holding up the traffic at every junction, the first escort car, blue light flashing, turned right and led the Zil down into Borovitsky Square. The twin traffic lights either side of the Borovitsky Tower Gate switched to green as the motorcade passed into the Kremlin with barely a drop in speed; the lights immediately returned to red.

Up the hill past the Armory and the Great Kremlin Palace, they turned left into Ivanovskaya Square and slowed only as they passed the Supreme Soviet Presidium on the right. At the end of the Presidium they swung right through already-opened gates in a black wrought-iron fence.

As soon as the Zil stopped, two KGB men from the first escort car opened the passenger doors. The half hour's journey had taken fourteen minutes.

Above the green dome of the Council of Ministers Building the Soviet flag hung limply. In the Prime Minister's second-floor office his secretary was waiting with a signal from the President sent by the Ambassador in Washington.

1. Ban journalists from Ukraine on grounds of personal safety.

2. Country cannot afford cancellation of negotiations on trade and technology transfer. Am proceeding with planned two days at Camp David.

3. White House and Camp David not secure for transmission or receipt of sensitive material.

4. Defuse situation until my return.

After dismissing his secretary, the Prime Minister sat down at his desk. He must have read the signal half a dozen times.

Kirillin stood discreetly near the large window that overlooked the Lenin Mausoleum. He didn't envy the Prime Minister. Voloshin had been brought to Moscow from Stavropol by the President, who had steered his progress through the government and Party apparatus. He was being groomed by the President as his successor. But the succession wasn't planned for today.

If Voloshin took on Korolev and lost, the President would conclude Voloshin hadn't the steel to succeed him, and Voloshin would be shunted off to obscurity. If Voloshin accepted Korolev's invitation to "take the leading role in stabilizing the country," it would almost certainly be to implement a policy the President would fight on his return from the USA. If the President lost, he would be forced to resign and Voloshin would end up fronting a regime he knew in his heart was doomed to disaster. If the President won, Voloshin wouldn't even enjoy the privilege of obscurity.

Kirillin looked away from Red Square when he heard a sharp knock on the door. Voloshin's secretary came in. "This fax has just come through, Prime Minister."

Voloshin read it twice, and then handed it to Kirillin.

DEMANDS OF THE UKRAINIAN SOLIDARITY MOVEMENT

The Ukrainian Solidarity Movement, embracing all free social, cultural, economic, religious, historical, trades union, rural, and political associations in the Ukraine, defines as its principal aim the defense of the rights of the people of the Ukraine to self-determination as provided in Article 1 of the Helsinki Accord ratified by the Soviet Union and as provided in Article 72 of the Fundamental Law of the Union of Soviet Socialist Republics.

In particular, the Ukrainian Solidarity Movement makes the following twelve demands:

1. Immediately, the right of the Ukrainian people to form free trades unions and cultural, historical, social, economic, and political associations without interference or intimidation.

2. Immediately, the right of the Ukrainian Catholic Church, and also of the Ukrainian Autocephalous Orthodox Church, to operate freely in liturgical, spiritual, educational, social, and pastoral work without administrative restrictions, interference, or intimidation.

3. Immediately, the uncanonical so-called Synod of Lviv of 1946 be recognized as null and void, and all churches, monasteries, property and land seized by the government or transferred to the Russian Orthodox Church be restored to their rightful owner in law, the Ukrainian Catholic Church.

4. Once the above rights have been established, free elections shall be held for a reconstituted Ukrainian Congress of People's Deputies which shall appoint a President and Government of the Ukrainian Republic, whose initial task shall be to prepare a draft new constitution for the Republic for submission to a referendum of all Ukrainian citizens.

5. Only those All-Union laws which have been registered by the Ukrainian Congress of People's Deputies shall have validity in the Ukraine.

6. All non-Ukrainian speaking units of the Soviet Armed Forces, the Interior Ministry, and the KGB shall be replaced by Ukrainian-speaking units re-

sponsible to the elected Government of the Ukrainian Republic.

7. The right of the Ukrainian people to all land, air, water, minerals, forests, other natural resources, and the principal means of production within the Ukrainian Republic shall be recognized in law, coupled with local self-determination for all industrial, agricultural, commercial and financial enterprises in accordance with the resolutions of the 19th Party Conference of the Communist Party of the Soviet Union.

8. A separate currency shall be established for the Ukraine.

9. Ukrainian economic enterprises shall have the right to enter into free trade agreements with any other trading enterprise, inside or outside the Soviet Union.

10. Ukrainian shall be the principal language in all educational, governmental, and administrative organs of the republic.

11. Ukrainian citizenship shall be established and the Government of the Ukrainian Republic shall control residence permits for non-citizens in order to protect the cultural integrity of the republic.

12. European Time shall operate in the Ukrainian Republic.

Kirillin also read it a second time. "What do you think the Politburo would be prepared to concede?" he asked the Prime Minister.

Voloshin took back the statement. "Possibly the last demand. Most of them believe the Ukrainians and the Poles have always lagged behind the Russians."

A telephone on the Prime Minister's desk rang. He picked it up and listened. He put his hand over the mouthpiece. "It's the Ambassador in Rome. The Vatican's Foreign Minister is waiting in his reception room. The Pope has offered to go to the Ukraine and mediate."

* * *

At ten to two Kirillin left the Council of Ministers Building
and crossed Ivanovskaya Square. The gray uniformed militiaman who patroled the square with a whistle had been
joined by five colleagues. All six carried long batons and
had revolvers in holsters strapped to the outside of their
jackets. The wide, concrete-flagged pavement in front of
the Palace of Congresses was deserted. Kirillin continued
past the Palace toward the red-brick Trinity Tower. A cobbled bridge led down from Trinity Tower Gate, over the
Alexander Garden, to the small white ornamental Kutafya
Tower. At this hour in August streams of visitors would
normally be passing up and down the bridge. Now it was
empty.

Restless crowds milled outside the barriers at the
Kutafya Tower. The militiaman who opened a section to
let Kirillin through asked him what was happening "up
there."

"Business as usual," Kirillin replied. "Are these"—indicating the closed barriers—"really necessary?"

"We have our orders," the militiaman said.

Kirillin turned right, down the steps into the Alexander
Garden. Babakin was waiting for him by the Obelisk.

Kirillin raised his eyebrows. Babakin removed from his
inside jacket pocket two sheets of photocopied paper. He
held them in his hand.

"The plan Molchanov will present to the Politburo less
than an hour from now."

Kirillin held out his hand.

Babakin kept his grip on the sheets. "They weren't easy
to obtain." It had taken all his skills over the past three
months to untighten Valentina Kruglova, but once she had
let go, the cow had become insatiable.

"The President won't forget this."

Babakin's lips curled into a grin. "Perhaps he'll want to
forget it."

Kirillin read the two sheets. He shook his head in disbelief. "If this is implemented . . ."

"Then the President might as well stay in the United States and seek political asylum," Babakin concluded.

Chapter ✤ Seventeen

RYAN, DRESSED IN collarless black shirt with rolled up sleeves, and black slacks, sat on the stone terrace outside the north wing of the Pontifical Palace. Above, the late morning sun shone brightly on the two white domes housing telescopes no longer used by the Jesuits who occupied the lakeside top two floors of the palace. These days the Vatican astronomers studied the heavens by peering at computer printouts, not by peering through optical telescopes.

Ryan, too, needed no telescope. The light was so clear he felt he could almost reach out and touch the antennae on top of Mount Cavo above the blue water of Lake Albano to his right. To his left, the aquamarine ribbon of the Tyrrhenian Sea seemed tantalizingly close. Ahead, beyond the dark green hedges and combed cypresses bordering the top of the two castellated walls that came to a point at the northern perimeter of the palace grounds, the countryside fell away; in the distance nestled the tiny haze-shrouded city of Rome.

Ryan put down his glass of chilled Frascati on the table. His elation had nothing to do with the wine, or even the view. Earlier that morning, after Ryan had helped the Holy Father celebrate mass in honor of the Immaculate Heart of Mary, Hoffman had asked him to tune the radio set to the BBC World Service. The Pope had understood the broadcast, but Ryan had interpreted for Hoffman the marvelous news being relayed from the television and radio center at Lvov. The Pope and Hoffman had congratulated Ryan as if he were personally responsible for liberating the Ukrainian people from the Soviet yoke. Naturally he'd said that he'd merely been an insignificant messenger. But now, on his own, he couldn't suppress a glow of pride at recalling the Pope's words, and feeling that he had indeed helped bring about an historic turning point in the battle for the soul of Russia.

The Holy Father had telephoned Archbishop Benedetti, and afterwards had gone to the chapel to spend the rest of the day in prayer, watched over by Monsignor Hoffman.

As he sipped the wine he saw a dark blue Fiat 131 approaching Castel Gandolfo up the Via del Palazzo Pontificio from the direction of Rome. The car passed out of sight below the fortified wall of the Garden of the Moro. A few minutes later, Ryan heard the creaking of the main gates from the palace to the Piazza della Liberta, and the revving of a car's engine as it entered the courtyard.

Ryan put down his glass and went to meet the visitor. He was surprised to see the slight figure of Cardinal Fasolo, hot in his heavy caped cassock and crimson *zucchetto* and sash. Ryan led him through to the terrace.

"Wine, Eminence?" Ryan offered, gesturing to the ice bucket on the terrace.

"No thank you, Father. But I would appreciate a glass of water."

"Certainly, Eminence."

When Ryan returned with the water, Fasolo was seated in the shade of the white and yellow quartered parasol. He had removed his *zucchetto* and was wiping his brow with a large white handkerchief which he tucked back up the sleeve of his cassock. He was grateful for the water.

"We weren't expecting you, Eminence. We thought you were on holiday in Faenza."

Fasolo looked carefully at him. The cardinal seemed unsure. "I was. Naturally I returned as soon as I heard the news from the Ukraine. I think it would be helpful if I saw the Holy Father as soon as possible."

"I'm sorry, Eminence. The Holy Father is spending the day in prayer. He left strict instructions not to be disturbed."

Fasolo forced a smile. "I don't imagine he meant to include the Secretary of State in that instruction."

Ryan was embarrassed. "I'm afraid the Holy Father's instructions were very clear, Eminence."

Fasolo's voice gained a slight edge. "The Holy Father telephoned Archbishop Benedetti earlier this morning."

"I don't believe His Excellency has telephoned back, Eminence."

"He hasn't. Will you explain to the Holy Father that I have come with the reply."

"Eminence, I'm very sorry. The Holy Father said he wishes to see no one from the Secretariat. I'm instructed to take the reply to him."

Fasolo took a deep breath. He looked over Lake Albano and then toward Rome.

Ryan was uncertain how the most senior cardinal in the Catholic Church would respond to being told to go away by a priest graded as one of the *officiali minori* in the Vatican hierarchy.

"Very well. I do not wish to increase your embarrassment, Father Ryan. Please tell the Holy Father that the Soviet Ambassador to the Republic has informed Archbishop Benedetti that the Soviet Government unequivocally rejects the Pope's offer to mediate."

"I'm sure the Holy Father is deeply grateful for the trouble you've taken, Eminence," Ryan soothed. "He will be distressed to learn that you interrupted your holiday to deliver the news personally. Perhaps if His Excellency had telephoned . . ."

"Thank you for your concern," Fasolo interrupted. "But why do you think that neither Archbishop Benedetti nor I considered it prudent to use the telephone?"

Ryan hesitated. "I'm not sure, Eminence."

Fasolo sighed and shook his head. "It's bad enough that half the Apostolic Palace knows the Soviets have snubbed us again. If we contact Castel Gandolfo by telephone, within minutes the Italian Government knows." He looked at Ryan. "It is one of the functions of the Secretariat of State, Father, to know what is possible and what is not possible, to know when to make public a gesture and when to operate behind the scenes. I'm sure you understand that, but . . ." He shrugged. "In this case the inevitable result is humiliation for the Holy See."

Ryan smiled. "I think not, Eminence. The Soviets are playing into the Holy Father's hands."

Fasolo studied Ryan through rimless spectacles that made his blue eyes seem twice as large. "Father, the Secretariat does possess some expertise in diplomacy and some considerable experience in negotiating with Communist authorities. It is, to say the least, unfortunate that this experience was not employed and the Secretariat not even consulted before the Holy See responded to this reckless action in the Ukraine. It can only end in disaster for the Church in the Ukraine, in Lithuania, in Latvia . . ."

"That is not the Holy Father's view, Eminence. If the Soviet authorities do not accept his offer of mediation, the Holy Father will confer the title of Patriarch on Cardinal Chuprynka in Saint Peter's in front of the world's media."

Fasolo shook his head in disbelief. "This is what the Ukrainian extremists have been demanding for years. They'll interpret it as the Church's blessing for their actions. If only the Ukrainians had consulted us first, the Holy Father could have stopped them embarking on this suicidal venture."

"Eminence," Ryan said, "I think you should know that

the Holy Father actively encouraged this public demonstration of the national will of the Ukraine."

Fasolo removed his spectacles and carefully cleaned them with the end of his sash. Eventually he looked up. "Doesn't the Holy Father realize the Soviets will send the tanks in? There'll be a bloodbath in the Ukraine."

"Eminence," Ryan said as gently as he could, "the Ukrainian people have been betrayed once too often. The Holy Father is determined that this time they'll win their freedom."

Fasolo was on the edge of despair. "Papa Montini would never have dreamt of a thing like this," he said, half to himself.

"They tell me Pope Paul liked to be a diplomat, Eminence. This pope prefers to be the Vicar of Christ."

"Tell me, Father Ryan, does the Holy Father really know what he is doing?"

"He does indeed, Eminence. He's fulfilling the request made by the Mother of God at Fatima."

"But the Russians . . ."

"The Holy Father is certain the tanks won't be sent in. With the Soviet President in the United States about to address the United Nations General Assembly on human rights, the Russians have too much to lose."

"I hope he's right, for God's sake."

Ryan raised his glass. "I'm sure he's right."

Chapter ✦ Eighteen

KIRILLIN RETURNED TO the Kremlin through the Trinity Tower Gate. As he crossed the silent Ivanovskaya Square he noticed for the first time the two nests of television cameras on the roof of the Supreme Soviet Presidium. One of the four cameras at the near end was tracking him.

In his absence a flock of gleaming black Zils had arrived and were now lined up like waiting birds of prey outside the Council of Ministers Building. Usually the chauffeurs chatted idly in groups of twos and threes. Now they stood in a closed circle, deep in hushed consultation. Kirillin smiled and greeted them. Usually the chauffeurs responded warmly to this recognition by a high Kremlin official that they were fellow human beings. Now they responded silently with looks that suggested Kirillin had a contagious disease.

The bars of the Internationale chimed from the Savior Tower clock to signal half-past two. As Kirillin was about to walk past the guards at the entrance to the Council of Ministers Building, a Zil pulled up just behind him. Kirillin looked round. Alexander Budko climbed out of the limousine.

Budko ruled the Ukraine as First Secretary of the Ukrainian Communist Party, surrounded by a gang of henchmen from Dnepropetrovsk, all appointees of Yegor Velbitsky, his predecessor. Budko had continued his mentor's policy of brutally suppressing dissent in the Soviet Union's second largest republic. In private the President had called him the Ukrainian dissidents' best recruiting officer. But over the years Velbitsky had appointed his own people to all key positions in the Ukraine; removing his influence would necessitate removing not only Budko but also the whole of the Ukrainian Politburo, the Presidium of the Ukrainian Supreme Soviet, and the Ukrainian Council of Ministers. The President hadn't felt able to risk the anarchy which would have followed. That had proved to be a miscalculation. The suppressed resentment had exploded into an anarchical takeover of the capital of western Ukraine and threatened Kiev itself. Yet Budko greeted Kirillin with the air of a man who had it all under control. "Good afternoon, Comrade Kirillin. Do I assume you're here to learn how to deal with an insurrection?"

When Kirillin entered the Prime Minister's office, Voloshin was standing alone, looking out of the window into Red Square where crowds were massing noisily. No member of the Politburo had called in to chat before the meeting started. Voloshin knew that cabals were huddled in other parts of the building.

Kirillin had no time to break it gently. "In twenty minutes' time, the Politburo will be presented with a paper by Molchanov."

"He's never had an original thought in his life," said Voloshin, still staring out of the window. "Who prepared it?"

"General Lukin, Deputy Chief of the General Staff. The General Staff have agreed it. General Blagov pledged KGB support this morning."

Voloshin's voice was lifeless. "Read it."

Kirillin took a deep breath. "Let's start with Lvov. At 06:00 hours tomorrow, two thousand Ministry of Interior

Special Orders troops from Gorky will land at Lvov airport. At 06:30 hours the colonel commanding the troops will ask for assistance from the Army. At the same time, the 17th Guards Motor Rifle Division, with the support of two regiments of the 13th Tank Division, will leave the Carpathian Military District HQ and head for the city center. Fifteen minutes later, five Mil Mi-26 Halo helicopters will take off and land companies of the District's Air Assault Brigade at Castle Hill to reclaim the television and radio center, at the open square on the corner of Sovetskaya and Ruskaya Streets to reclaim the City Soviet, and at Ivan Franko Park to reclaim the University and Saint George's Cathedral. A Spetsnaz unit will seize Bishop Antoniuk, Pavlo Stus, and other leaders of the Ukrainian Solidarity Movement, and will take custody of this icon. The operation will be directed by the Commander of the Carpathian Military District, Lieutenant-General Karavansky. In Kiev . . ."

Voloshin turned from the window. "Vladislav Karavansky?" He swallowed. "The Butcher of Kabul?"

Kirillin looked at Voloshin's deathly white face. "You pinned the Order of Hero of the Soviet Union on his chest," he said.

Voloshin gestured helplessly. "After Afghanistan we had to keep the General Staff happy."

"And they were happy to promote Karavansky?"

"They'd no choice. The commanders who'd won their spurs in Afghanistan were impatient with the old guard in Frunze Street who'd failed them. Lukin was Karavansky's divisional commander in Kabul." The air of a defeated man hung about Voloshin. "It's the Afghanistan vets who're now running the General Staff. They can't be bought off with more medals, a retirement dacha, and a guaranteed plot in the Novodevich Cemetery."

Voloshin had been chosen by the President because he was a good manager. He had now to become a good politician. Kirillin thrust the two photocopied pages into Voloshin's hands. "Comrade Voloshin. You are Prime Minister of the Union of Soviet Socialist Republics. Under our constitution only the President or the Council of Ministers can authorize this action."

Voloshin returned to his desk.

"Whose support can you count on?" Kirillin asked.

"Korolev must have gained the support of the key ministers." Voloshin counted them off on the fingers of his left hand. "Yagodin hasn't forgiven the President for forcing through the huge cut in the defense industry budget he wanted to take to Washington. As Defense Minister, Ulanov will fall in line with the General Staff. Molchanov is proposing the plan because, as Interior Minister, he can't be seen to do nothing when Russians are reported killed in Kiev. That will give enough muscle to outvote me in the Presidium of the Council of Ministers."

"What about the rest of the Politburo?"

"Dobrik is the front man; he's already committed. Korolev can count on Budko for strong-arm tactics to restore his position in the Ukraine. Mishin built his Party career in the Ukraine and will use the excuse that, as chairman of the Central Committee's Commission on Legal Policy, he can't sanction the illegal action taking place there. Gubarev opposed the President's line with Poland, Hungary, Czechoslovakia and East Germany, and will back Korolev on an issue like this. With the President and Foreign Minister in the USA, that leaves only Sirotin, with the socioeconomic portfolio, to argue against the plan."

"And what about you?" Kirillin challenged.

Voloshin snapped back angrily at the President's special assistant. "Why do you think I'm here on my own, and not discussing tactics with Korolev?"

At last, some spark of life. "I'm sorry, Prime Minister," Kirillin lied. "I didn't intend to insult you."

Voloshin nodded.

"That means a vote of eight to two," Kirillin said.

Voloshin shook his head. "Korolev has chosen the issue and the timing to perfection. There'll be no vote. The Politburo will instruct the Council of Ministers to implement the plan." The Prime Minister put his head in his hands. "The tanks will move in the day the President is due to address the United Nations on human rights."

Kirillin looked at the clock on the wall. Voloshin couldn't be allowed to sink back into accepting the inevitable. Kirillin's tone was urgent. "My information is that the Ukrainian nationalists can count on at least five million active supporters, with the majority of the rest giving tacit support. The uprising has the blessing of the Ukrainian Catholic Church. It'll become a holy war. Can't Korolev see that?"

Voloshin nodded. "He sees it clearly enough. But for him, and for most of the Party apparatus, it's the last stand. Either they fight now, or the Communist Party is finished. And on this issue they'll exploit Russian nationalism against the Ukrainians to carry the Supreme Soviet with them."

"But if Korolev does win, it'll be Czechoslovakia in '68 and Peking in '89 all over again, except this time the Ukrainians will fight back." Kirillin put his hands on the desk and leaned forward to look Voloshin in the eyes. "Prime Minister, do you wish to preside over the end of *glasnost*, the end of *perestroika*, and the end of the Common European Home? If so, it means the end of the Soviet Union. If Korolev does win, all that Lenin created will collapse in the bitterest civil war this country has ever seen. Russia will be left bankrupt, morally and economically: a de-developed nation that no civilized country will want to help."

Voloshin stared blankly at the clock on the wall. It was seven minutes to three. He spread his hands helplessly. "What can I do?"

"There is one way out," Kirillin said. "I only recommend it because I can see no other way of saving the Soviet Union. It carries a high risk, and it demands a great deal of courage on your part."

Voloshin said nothing while Kirillin outlined the plan Babakin had proposed.

Chapter ❖ Nineteen

A SHEET OF flame leapt toward him. The Cardinal Secretary of State dropped to his knees. With his left arm protecting his face, he crawled forward and groped for the switch. The flames finally died down. His knees felt hot and sticky. He looked down. He was kneeling in what remained of his omelette.

He put his hand on the edge of the cooker to pull himself up and cried out. His fingers burned with the heat of the cooker.

Nothing ever happened in August. His private secretary was on holiday. The nuns who cooked and cleaned for him were on holiday. Eduardo, his valet-chauffeur, was on holiday. He was supposed to be on holiday with his sister and brother-in-law in Faenza.

The driver from the Vatican car pool, who had taken him to Castel Gandolfo, had kindly offered to buy some eggs and bread for his lunch from the Vatican grocery store opposite Saint Pilgrim's Church. Cardinal Fasolo had assured the driver that he was perfectly capable of cooking an omelette.

He walked through to the dressing room next to his

bedroom where Eduardo kept his clothes. His second black cassock wasn't in the wardrobe; Eduardo must have sent it to the cleaners. The only cassock hanging there was the crimson one for formal ceremonies—the one he had worn in the Sistine Chapel when he had cast his vote to elect this Pope.

He went to the bathroom to try and remove the stain.

He returned to his office, next to his private apartment on the first floor of the Apostolic Palace. From a cupboard he took the bottle of malt whiskey he used for the occasional small celebratory drink with colleagues after a job well done. He poured himself half a glass. The only colleague in whom he could confide, Antonio Benedetti, had left a note on his desk saying he'd gone to try and calm the American Ambassador to the Holy See; the White House and the State Department were livid that the Vatican hadn't prevented, or at the very least warned them, of the uprising led by a Catholic bishop while the Soviet President was a guest of the American President.

Fasolo took a large gulp of the malt whiskey. He was glad Antonio had left before he had returned from Castel Gandolfo. How could Antonio possibly have explained that not only was the Cardinal Secretary of State unaware of the planned uprising, he had also been unaware that the Pope had personally encouraged it?

He slumped into his chair behind the desk. From the wall opposite a photograph of the Pope looked down with those eyes that saw no shades of gray in the world, only black and white. Fasolo took from his top left-hand drawer a dog-eared copy of *Pastor Bonus*, the Constitution of the Roman Curia. Article 39 proclaimed:

> *The Secretary of State collaborates closely with the Holy Father in the exercise of his supreme mission.*

For countless generations his family from the village outside Faenza, in the former Papal States, had served the Holy See. He was the third cardinal this century to bear the

name Fasolo. Now this Pope from a strange land had made
him a stranger in the Apostolic Palace his forebears regarded as their second home. He couldn't possibly continue as Cardinal Secretary of State.

He took a sheet of letter paper embossed with the
crossed keys of Saint Peter in the top left hand corner and
placed it on his blotter. He removed the top of the fountain
pen given to him by Pope Paul VI and, in his neat handwriting, composed his letter of resignation.

He read it through.

Where would he go? There was no pending vacancy in
an Italian archdiocese, not even an archbishop who might
be persuaded to retire to make way for him. He couldn't
bear the idea of retiring himself. What would he do? After
devoting his whole life to the Holy See he couldn't even
cook an omelette.

He tore up the letter of resignation.

Chapter ✦ Twenty

AT ONE MINUTE before three, Grigori Voloshin walked down the marble-lined corridor from his office on the second floor of the Council of Ministers Building and into the Oval Hall.

Korolev was already seated at his usual place, at the center of one long side of the large oval table. The others had coalesced into three groups. Seven full members of the Politburo were standing on the window side, with Dobrik and Molchanov at their center. Four candidate members were grouped round a fifth, Mikhail Demidenko, Chairman of the Supreme Soviet, who was in earnest conversation with Valentin Sirotin, the full member who unequivocally supported *perestroika*. The remaining three candidate members stood uneasily between the other two groups. Murmurings broke off abruptly when Voloshin entered.

Voloshin's footsteps sounded on the carpeted floor. He walked straight to the chairman's chair, facing Korolev, and sat down. Peals of the Internationale preceded the Savior's Tower clock striking three.

"Comrades, please be seated," Voloshin announced.

They took up their places.

Dobrik began to speak, but Voloshin cut straight through him. "The President congratulates you on your prompt action, and is grateful for your taking the time to meet today. He has authorized me, on your agreement to two conditions, to inform you of his plan for solving the Ukrainian problem. The two conditions are, first, the plan must remain absolutely confidential to voting members of the Politburo and, second, no action is taken by the Council of Ministers until he returns."

The chairman of the Central Committee Commission on Agriculture, who wasn't blessed with quickness of mind, peered through hooded eyes. "We need to know the plan first before we agree to take no action."

Voloshin looked straight at Dobrik. "I said the President will take prompt action on his return. But he has asked me to warn you that sending in General Karavansky with tanks and an air assault brigade will provoke civil war. Any member of the Politburo who sanctions such a course of action without the approval of the President or a full meeting of the Presidential Council will be tried for treason."

Korolev's eyes darted round the table. Eighteen copies of the paper Molchanov was due to present to the Politburo were stacked in front of the Interior Minister. Dobrik was visibly shaken. Others glanced nervously around, wondering who had leaked the plan to Voloshin.

In the consternation, Demidenko stood up. "I accept. I withdraw to comply with the President's first condition."

Four of the other non-voting members immediately followed. The three remaining candidate members decided that nothing was served by putting their heads on the line. They too rose and left the room.

That disturbed Korolev much more than the threat of arraignment for treason. Voloshin had had the nerve to send committed supporters of the President out of the room. No sane man would do that unless he was certain of a majority among the voting members of the Politburo.

Ulanov had come to the same conclusion. The President's first condition confirmed his own suspicions that more than one member had leaked the plan for military intervention to the Prime Minister while pretending to go along with Korolev. The Defense Minister said uneasily, "I propose we agree provisionally. We can rescind the agreement if the plan proves unacceptable."

Voloshin watched Korolev's coalition crumble. Mishin led the climb-down by saying that they either had to agree unconditionally or else flout the constitution which established a society based on the rule of law. Molchanov slid the stack of papers into his briefcase.

At that point, Voloshin informed them of the plan Kirillin had provided for him. Dobrik was isolated. Even Korolev, who had said not one public word challenging the President's authority, could hardly fault the plan on ideological grounds.

Chapter ✢ Twenty-one

THREE DAYS AFTER the emergency meeting of the Communist Party Politburo, Kirillin briefed the President in the lounge overlooking the runway of Vnukovo-2 Airport. The President accepted the plan. Despite the First Lady's protests, the President's plane was ordered to refuel and fly on to Kiev. Kirillin made two phone calls, the first to Alexander Budko and the second to General Blagov.

Later that day, Budko was ushered into Kirillin's office in the Supreme Soviet. The Ukrainian Party boss appeared less confident than when he had met Kirillin on the steps of the Council of Ministers Building.

Kirillin handed him a letter and a pen. His manner was brusque. "You will find it in your interests to sign this."

Budko read the letter which announced his retirement. "As a member of the Politburo of the Communist Party of the Soviet Union," he protested, "I have the right to see the President in his capacity as General Secretary of the Party."

"Your planes crossed. The President is now meeting

with the Politburo of the Communist Party of the Ukraine."

Budko was a cornered animal. "He can't! The Ukrainian Politburo can't meet without its First Secretary!"

"You seemed to think it perfectly acceptable for the Soviet Party Presidium to meet three days ago without its General Secretary."

"I won't be the scapegoat for the anarchy in Lvov! If I have my way . . ."

"You have two ways. The first is to sign this letter and retire on full pension. The second is to be investigated for corruption by the Central Committee Special Investigator, lose all the property you have acquired as a servant of the Party, including the salt water swimming pool and the fresh water swimming pool at the Gurzuf mansion built with Party funds, and be sacked without a pension. I have another meeting in five minutes, so please don't take your time."

Budko crumpled.

After signing, he asked, "Who is to take over as Ukrainian First Secretary?"

Kirillin allowed himself a smile. "Read *Pravda*."

Kirillin heard animated conversation outside before his secretary ushered in General Blagov.

The uniformed KGB chairman placed both hands flat on Kirillin's desk and leaned forward. "You asked me here to meet the President," he bristled. "Budko tells me he's in Kiev."

Kirillin looked up at the heavily jowled face and the eyes drilling into him from under bushy black eyebrows. "The President sends his apologies. There was a little local difficulty in the Ukraine he had to attend to."

Blagov slammed his fist down on Kirillin's desk. "There's an insurrection . . ."

"Please sit down, General."

Blagov did not sit down. He continued to stare at Kirillin. Kirillin understood why the word most frequently used

to describe Blagov was "intimidating." He returned the
stare and saw in Blagov's eyes a bully's fear.

The KGB chief drew himself up to his full height,
pursed his lips, and took his time to sit in the hard chair on
the other side of the desk and try to make himself comfortable. "Has the President read the KGB's Western Inner
Rim Report?"

Kirillin was dismissive. "Do you seriously think you can
crush a movement like the Ukrainian nationalists' by sending in tanks and imprisoning their leaders? No, General.
You only create martyrs and fuel the movement." Kirillin
stood up and walked slowly round his desk. "The Baltic
republics are small and peripheral; they don't matter. The
Muslim republics are a drain on our resources; we'd be
better off without them. But the Ukraine. That's different.
If this uprising succeeds in gaining independence for the
Ukraine, it'll mean the collapse of the Soviet Union."

"That's precisely why I warned of the dangers of *glasnost* and *perestroika*," Blagov said.

Kirillin had circled Blagov and now spoke to his back.
"What policy would you adopt, General?"

Blagov turned in his chair to face the President's special
assistant. "Insurrections must be put down by the Army."

Kirillin raised his eyebrows. "What Army?" He continued his walk round Blagov, and returned to his desk.

The furrows on Blagov's forehead deepened. "This
President hasn't yet persuaded the Presidential Council to
disband the Army."

Kirillin resumed his seat. He placed his elbows on the
desk, intertwined his fingers, and stared at Blagov.
"There'd be no need. Times have changed, General. It was
bad enough in Afghanistan. Tell those boys to shoot their
own people and there'll be no Soviet Army as you know it.
The non-Russians will desert to their homelands, and we'll
be left with a demoralized half a Soviet Army plus fourteen
well-equipped and trained national liberation armies to the
west and south of Russia."

Blagov said nothing. He chewed furiously on strands of tobacco left in his mouth from a cheroot.

"The Politburo did not approve Lukin's plan for armed intervention in the Ukraine," continued Kirillin, "because no member of the Politburo wishes to preside over the destruction of the Soviet Union." Kirillin relaxed back in his executive chair, his hands resting on the armrests. "These, General, are the stakes we're playing for."

"The President was deeply disappointed," Kirillin continued after a pause, "that you endorsed that suicidal scheme without following constitutional procedures."

Blagov hunched in his chair. When he spoke, the bluster had gone from his voice. "How does the President intend to deal with the insurrection if he doesn't want to use the Army?"

"The Politburo approved a policy of eliminating the source of religious nationalism in the Ukraine."

"This Bishop Antoniuk?"

"I said the source."

Blagov frowned. "Kill the Pope?"

"You bungled the job in 1981," Kirillin stated.

"That was the Bulgarians," Blagov said quickly.

Kirillin raised his eyebrows. "Are you suggesting the *Darzhavna Sigurnost* weren't acting under orders from the KGB?"

Blagov shuffled in his chair. "I was in the GRU at the time. It was nothing to do with me."

"My dear Comrade General," said Kirillin, "no one is suggesting that you had any personal responsibility for that fiasco. But," he added pointedly, "you were responsible for endorsing Lukin's plan."

Blagov was unsure where this conversation was leading.

"It would be a pity to lose a chairman of the State Security Committee after so brief a time in office," Kirillin mused.

Blagov said nothing.

"I wonder," Kirillin continued, "if you can see a way of restoring your good name."

Blagov mouthed the words slowly. "Kill the Pope?"

"The President does not, of course, wish to involve himself in operational matters of the KGB," said Kirillin. "That is your prerogative under the constitution."

Blagov's eyes narrowed in suspicion. If that were the case, this President was unique. Every Soviet leader from Stalin to Andropov had personally intervened in State Security operations, from plotting murders to petty forgeries.

"But in terms of overall policy," Kirillin said, "he would want three conditions fulfilled if you decided to pursue this course of action."

Still Blagov said nothing.

"First," continued Kirillin, "you must succeed."

Blagov's lips drew back in a sly smile. He was being offered the chance to redeem himself. He pulled a packet of black cheroots from his inside pocket.

"Second, the Pope's death must never be traced back to the Kremlin."

Blagov struck a match, lit his foul-smelling cheroot, and nodded as he tossed the match in the general direction of Kirillin's wastepaper basket.

"And third?"

"Third, it must be completed before the end of the year."

Part ✦ Three
AUTUMN

Chapter ✤ One

THE PAPAL PARTY returned from Castel Gandolfo buoyed by the Ukrainian success. The Holy Father was right: the tanks had not been sent in; the Soviet authorities were powerless to impose their will on the Ukrainian people, and the Catholic liturgy was being celebrated openly throughout the land. Faith in the Blessed Virgin Mary had proved more effective than the claimed diplomatic skills of the Secretariat of State.

Cardinal Fasolo greeted the Pope with warnings about what was happening in the United States, but he was told the problems of the West would be solved by prayer as they were in the East.

To Ryan it seemed a lifetime since he had arrived a stranger at the Vatican. His complete acceptance into the papal family was confirmed when Kasamir Hoffman asked Ryan to take his place at the next Wednesday public audience. Ryan sat proudly in the back of the open top white jeep as it circled the rear of Saint Peter's Basilica. Immediately in front of him stood the Pope, feet astride, holding the roll bar of the jeep. The wall of sound that greeted them as they entered Saint Peter's Square through the

Arch of the Bells was something he would remember the rest of his life. The crowd had swelled to more than twice the usual size; the cheers and applause were redoubled yet again. The faithful had come to celebrate the triumphal return to Rome of the Vicar of Christ.

Among the crowd he saw familiar blue and yellow flags and Ukrainian tridents. Only once, when the jeep approached the spot near the Bronze Door where Mehmet Ali Agca had waited, a Browning 9mm calibre pistol in his pocket, did Ryan glance nervously up at the broad white back of the man giving his blessing. Pilgrims stretched out their hands to try and touch the Successor of Saint Peter. How do you distinguish between fervent admirers and fanatical assassins? But no, that betrayed a lack of faith. Ryan was sure this Pope would not die before he saw the consecration of Russia to the Immaculate Heart of Mary.

The jeep pulled up at the canopied audience stand, a temporary structure erected every Tuesday evening when the weather was fine at the foot of the steps leading up to the basilica. Ryan was directed by Bishop Spiazzi to a seat at the Pope's right hand. Ryan had never seen the Pope look so well. Before the Ukrainian triumph, his homilies had been somber. Now he stood up and radiated the joy of his faith in the Mother of God, urging the faithful to pray to her Immaculate Heart and assuring them that she would answer their prayers. After the Pope's Italian homily had been read in English, French, German, Spanish, and Polish, the Pope addressed the hundred and forty-eight official groups of pilgrims on Bishop Spiazzi's list in their own language. At each greeting the pilgrims cheered and clapped. The biggest applause came when the Pope gave a special welcome to pilgrims from the Ukrainian Cathedral of Saint Nicholas in Chicago. Ryan was glad of the canopy as the September sun beat down, but the Pope seemed oblivious of the heat.

After the pontifical blessing, Ryan followed the Pope to the jeep. The Pope, however, walked straight on and, to the consternation of the plainclothes *vigilanze*, went to the barriers to touch hands, pick up children, and give his blessing to ecstatic pilgrims.

Two and a half hours after the audience had begun, with Bishop Spiazzi repeatedly looking at his watch and mumbling that the Vatican workmen would demand overtime, the Pope was finally persuaded to return to the jeep. Ryan was drained. The Pope was invigorated.

That evening Ryan climbed up the Vatican Hill toward the setting sun and reached a white post bearing the message *Et in terra pax hominibus*. In front of him lights burned in the Vatican Radio building, where Jesuits worked twenty-four hours a day broadcasting the message of peace to mankind throughout the four corners of the earth.

Ryan delivered the sealed envelope from Monsignor Hoffman to Father Sosiura, whose office was next to one of Vatican Radio's soundproofed studios on the ground floor. After leaving the Palazzina of Leo XIII, Ryan sat on a bench in the gardens. A galaxy of tiny stars flickered into life between amber ribbons beyond the black snake of the Tiber to signal the dawn of Rome's nightlife. The world that existed before he'd offered his life to God seemed light years away. Even the horror of seeing Katie slip from his grasp and slither screaming down the cliff face was almost anesthetized from his memory. How good God had been to him! Standing above her body crushed into the obscenity of a violent death, he had screamed curses at God. God had meekly accepted those curses, as He had accepted the curses of those who nailed Him to the cross. He can bear your curses, Katie's wise old Boston priest had told him, but not your despair. Despair means the sacrifice of His own life has been in vain. Ryan had, in the end, a simple choice: spend the rest of his life in bitter recrimination or else offer up his suffering to God in atonement for his own recklessness that had taken Katie's life.

He had always found it impossible to do things by halves. It was inevitable that his submission to the will of

God should have led to the priesthood. But he could scarcely have imagined that the will of God would have taken him so close to His Vicar on earth at a time when a fundamental change in the balance of spiritual power in the world was imminent.

Chapter ✣ Two

THE SURPRISE ANNOUNCEMENT that the new First Secretary of the Ukrainian Communist Party was to be Professor Stepan Konovalets bought the President time.

On his return to Moscow the President sacked Dobrik, ostensibly because the grain harvest was certain to fall below 200 million tonnes. Korolev, with his strong support in the General Staff and Party apparatus, was, for the time being, untouchable.

It wasn't long before Konovalets flew to the capital. The Ukrainian Solidarity Movement insisted on negotiating direct with Moscow, maintaining that any agreement they made with Konovalets could be torn up by the Kremlin. On the advice of Babakin, Kirillin offered to go to Kiev for an unofficial meeting with Ukrainian Solidarity leaders to establish a basis for negotiations.

The Zil that had collected Kirillin and Konovalets from the airport left Kreshchatik at Leninsky Komsomol Square and turned sharply right into Kirov Street. As the limousine climbed uphill, past wooded parkland on the left, Kirillin saw the most striking change since his last visit to Kiev. The forbidding dark granite arc of the Ukrainian Council of Ministers Building which loomed on the right now flew the blue and yellow flag of independent Ukraine instead of the red and blue of Soviet Ukraine. Further uphill, on the parkland side, blue and yellow paint had been daubed over the giant hammer and sickle symbols carved above and either side of the six-columned portico of the light gray Ukrainian Supreme Soviet. At the top of the hill, the baroque turquoise and cream Mariinsky Palace built for Czaritsa Elizaveta Pyotrovna, where Kirillin had attended Ukrainian Supreme Soviet receptions, was guarded by nationalist militia wearing blue and yellow armbands.

The Zil turned right into Rosa Luxemburg Street, part of the *Lipki* district which had housed Kiev's aristocracy in Czarist times. Kirillin was relieved to see no nationalist militia outside the Kiev Hotel, which was reserved for guests of the Ukrainian Communist Party; Kirillin had stayed here when he was deputy manager of the VAZ factory. Adjoining the Kiev was a building with a stylish three- and ten-story concrete extension stretching along the rest of Rosa Luxemburg Street as far as October Revolution Street. Permanently closed white net curtains shielded all the ground floor windows. The only sign on this building was a small notice on the door of the entrance at Number Five Rosa Luxemburg Street, "Admission by special permit only." The discreet Zhovtneva was the hotel for guests of the Ukrainian Communist Party Central Committee; Kirillin had stayed here when he was Deputy Minister of Machine Building for Light Industries.

Instead of pulling up outside the Zhovtneva, however, the Zil stopped on the other side of the street, outside a renovated two-story villa with a yellow neoclassical façade. Konovalets joined Kirillin on the pavement. The villa and its garden wall, which was topped by steel shuttering, occupied the whole of that side of Rosa Luxemburg Street opposite the Kiev Hotel and the Zhovtneva.

"I found out," Konovalets said with a wry smile, "that

this is where the Ukrainian Party aristocracy accommodate *their* guests. All very *maskirovannoye* on the outside. I don't think the nationalists will disturb you here."

Kirillin followed the white-haired Konovalets through the glass door set in a red granite surround. The thick-pile red carpets, the Swedish furniture and decor, and the West German kitchen fittings impressed him. "The maids tell me," said Konovalets, "that they're trained to perform any service required."

Kirillin telephoned Semyon Malanchuk to suggest that the informal talks with Ukrainian Solidarity leaders begin the following morning at the Ukrainian Communist Party Central Committee building, just down Ordzhonokidze Street from the Writers' Union, which Solidarity was using as its headquarters.

"The Council of the Ukrainian Solidarity Movement has voted that its representatives meet you only on neutral ground," Malanchuk replied.

"Fair enough," Kirillin said. "Where do you suggest?"

"Perhaps an hotel," Malanchuk said cautiously, "where people going in and out won't attract attention."

"The Dnipro?"

A dry chuckle came from the telephone. "Not an hotel foreigners use."

"Why not?"

"They're all bugged."

Kirillin was becoming exasperated. "I've just traveled over eight hundred kilometers to meet you. I hope I haven't wasted my journey."

"The Hotel Moskva, off Kreshchatik."

"I'll book a room and see your delegation at nine tomorrow morning."

From Kreshchatik, the Hotel Moskva had looked impressive. Deep, wide, black granite steps led up to a terrace above Kreshchatik, from which two parallel staircases of red granite climbed a grass slope to a second terrace on which stood a massive monument to the October Revolution: four bronze fighters for the Revolution at the foot of a giant red granite Lenin from whose broad back flew a red granite flag. Behind that, a row of chestnut trees. And behind the chestnut trees, the solid yellow Hotel Moskva rose to dominate the skyline.

Kirillin, who was driven to the rear of the Hotel Moskva from the *Lipki,* saw why Intourist no longer used it for foreign tourists. On the outside it was shedding its brickface-shaped yellow concrete tiles, thereby shedding its pretense of solid brick construction. On the inside it was stinking of urine. It was, he reflected sadly, characteristic of the Soviet centralist system: capable of building majestic public monuments to Soviet achievements that would stand a thousand years, and yet incapable of building decent public lavatories that would withstand a few years pissing.

He looked out from the window of the top floor suite. In Moscow the leaves had already died and were falling to the ground. Fifteen stories below him, the chestnut trees were still green. Next to them, a large blue and yellow Ukrainian nationalist flag fluttered defiantly from the Palace of Culture. Kiev was holding on to its summer as long as it could.

A porter ushered in three men. Their first response was to look suspiciously round the lounge and at the closed doors which led off.

"Welcome, gentlemen," Kirillin said. "I'm all alone, but please feel free to look in all the rooms if you doubt me. Coffee?"

The three men who sat round the coffee table constituted a formidable team if their KGB files and their *kharakteristiki* were accurate.

With his flaxen hair, blue eyes, and muscular body, Stefan Nikitin from eastern Ukraine could have posed, shovel in extended arm, as a model Soviet miner in one of those Stalinist portraits intended to encourage the workers. Instead he was the leader of the Donbass Miners Welfare Association, an unofficial trade union in all but name that had developed from the Donbass strike committee of 1989. He was the only one without a criminal record.

In the 1970s his uncle had attempted to set up an independent miners union to campaign for better housing and less dangerous working conditions. Anyone who didn't believe that the Party and the workers were one, and that the official miners union represented the miners' interests, was clearly insane; accordingly, Alexei Nikitin had been committed to a psychiatric hospital. In 1981 he had again called for officials of the miners union to be elected by the miners themselves. He had again been declared insane and had died in an asylum in Kazakhstan. The death certificate showed the cause of death as cancer. Kirillin had little doubt the cancer was a side effect of the drugs used on him. Alexei Nikitin's nephew was dressed in his best suit and seemed the least relaxed of the three Ukrainian Solidarity representatives.

Semyon Malanchuk lounged back on the sofa. Kirillin found it difficult to read this Kiev-based council member of the Ukrainian Helsinki Union. While serving seven years in a labor camp in Siberia for his membership of the Helsinki Monitoring Group in the 1970s, Malanchuk had been snow blinded, and now wore dark-tinted spectacles to protect his retinas. The permanently amused smile underneath the drooping moustache on his sallow face seemed another part of his disguise. He held the most difficult position of the three, attempting to reconcile the young radicals on the council of the Ukrainian Helsinki Union who wanted to campaign openly for immediate independence, with the older ex-prisoners who wanted to adopt a tactical approach of first transforming the USSR into a genuine confederation of sovereign states.

Kirillin thought Pavlo Stus the most interesting. This large-framed, untidy, cheerful man had proved his determination by serving fifteen years in the camps. The KGB had tried everything—beatings, isolation in freezing punishment cells, denial of visits and correspondence while telling him his wife was sleeping with Konovalets, injec-

tions of Aminazin, Magnesium Sulphate, and Haloperi-
dol—but they hadn't broken him. There was something
about a faith that could carry a man through all that, without apparent bitterness, which intrigued Kirillin. Stus was
now risking further imprisonment. Not only was he a leading member in western Ukraine of the Committee for the
Defense of the Ukrainian Catholic Church and of the
Ukrainian Helsinki Union, he was also a leading member
of the banned Ukrainian Christian Democratic Party.

"Gentlemen," Kirillin began, "I take it we are agreed
that this meeting is unofficial and confidential."

"No." Nikitin shook his head vigorously. "I'm not here
to make any secret deals with the authorities."

"Forgive me," Kirillin said, "I've failed to make the position clear. We are not here to negotiate any deals, only to
establish whether the basis for negotiations exists."

"You've no alternative but to negotiate," Stus said. "The
Ukraine is at a standstill."

Kirillin shrugged. "Sadly, previous Soviet governments
employed alternatives to negotiating. The President hopes
those days are gone, and we can settle disputes by more
civilized means."

"Are you threatening us?" Malanchuk asked.

"Gentlemen, I understand your suspicions, believe me.
But try and understand the President's position. He is prepared to offer you negotiations in good faith. It is essential
to that good faith that neither of us goes running to the
press, trying to score cheap publicity points. Instead, we
work together to resolve our differences and we jointly announce our solutions."

"I don't make any secret agreements," Nikitin repeated.

"All I'm asking you to do is to listen to what the President has to offer. If you don't like it, you're free to walk
straight out and do whatever you want. But," Kirillin's affa-
ble manner became serious, "you must bear the consequences of not responding to the President's offer of
negotiations."

"Let's hear what the man has to say," Stus said.

Nikitin looked at Malanchuk. The latter shrugged.

"The President," Kirillin said, "is offering you round table negotiations, with yourselves and the Ukrainian Council of Ministers as equal partners, to resolve your grievances. Let me add that the President is personally sympathetic to many of the demands you've outlined. That's why he wants you to take this opportunity of working with the government here to bring about *perestroika* for the benefit of the Ukrainian people."

"But?" asked Malanchuk.

"Two items cannot be on the agenda."

"They are?" Malanchuk pressed.

"First, there can be no negotiation of secession or redrawing of boundaries. Second, there can be no agreements which prevent the Soviet government from honoring its commitments to the Warsaw Treaty Organization."

Kirillin sat back and sipped his coffee. Despite his unwillingness to make any deals, Nikitin should have no objection to those terms. The miners had little interest in political matters: they wanted better working conditions, increased wages, and food and consumer goods to buy with those increased wages. Kirillin calculated, rightly, that Malanchuk would be the problem.

"What's the point in negotiating with the government here in Kiev if the Soviet government keeps its military and security machine in place?" Malanchuk asked dismissively. "Moscow could plow through any agreements a day, a month, or a year later."

Conscious that Stus was studying his reactions, Kirillin said carefully, "I didn't say that nothing could change on the security issue. Your sixth demand centers on non-Ukrainian-speaking units of the security services . . ."

"And, crucially, to whom they are responsible," Malanchuk interjected.

"I'm trying to be reasonable," Kirillin said, "to suggest fruitful areas for negotiation within the context of your twelve demands. You expect, quite rightly, the Ukrainian government to honor any agreements it makes with you. You must also expect the All-Union government to honor agreements it has made with others, in this case, the members of the Warsaw Treaty Organization. That's why certain matters cannot be negotiated by the government of just one republic of the Soviet Union."

"That's a blind," Malanchuk challenged. "The Warsaw Pact is just a branch of the Soviet General Staff. The people of eastern Europe don't want it. They want the Soviet troops out."

"Personally," Kirillin said, "I've little doubt that the Warsaw Treaty Organization will be dismantled constitutionally once acceptable security arrangements can be guaranteed. But, while All-Union treaty obligations remain in force, the Soviet government must honor them."

Kirillin saw that Stus was impressed with the reasonable manner he'd adopted.

"Everything else can be negotiated?" Stus asked.

"Sure," Kirillin said. "You appreciate that I can't guarantee the outcome on each item. Negotiation means give and take on both sides."

"But we can negotiate legal and administrative freedom for the Ukrainian Catholic Church and the Ukrainian Autocephalous Orthodox Church?"

"That's what I said."

"What about the churches and the property seized by Stalin in 1946?"

"Negotiate."

"Do we have your agreement to adjourn and come back to you?" Malanchuk asked.

Kirillin spread out his arms. "I'm at your service, gentlemen. I'll wait here until you return. You can use any one of the rooms in this suite if it's more convenient for you."

It didn't take them long to return and announce they were prepared to proceed on the basis Kirillin had set out. Kirillin now had to carry the momentum forward over the next, and bigger, hurdle.

"There are just two matters to resolve," Kirillin said,

"before the round table talks can proceed. First, normal conditions must be resumed in the Ukraine. Second, the date for starting the talks must be fixed."

"We'll start tomorrow," Malanchuk said.

"I had in mind starting in three to four months," Kirillin said. "Say in the New Year."

Malanchuk laughed incredulously. "Tell the people to go back to work, resume life as before, and we'll start to talk in a few months' time? You think we Ukrainians are really so stupid?"

Kirillin waited until the other two had also rejected his proposal in equally disparaging terms. "Permit me to explain the President's thinking, gentlemen. The President wants to see these round table talks produce constructive results, which could be used as a model in other republics. Although Budko's gone, if you begin tomorrow you'll still be faced across the table by Budko's cronies. Ask yourself, how much will they be prepared to concede? Give Professor Konovalets a reasonable period to restructure the Ukrainian Party Politburo and the Ukrainian government. What I'm suggesting is that a few months waiting now will pay enormous dividends in the long term."

"The miners stay out until the talks have produced the results they want," Nikitin stated. "We're not concerned about the starting date, only the finishing date."

"We must be practical, Stefan Ivanovich," Kirillin said. "The round table talks will take time if we're to reach agreements that stick. The miners must return while the talks proceed."

Nikitin was aggressive. "We're always spun that line. The miners go back, talks drag on, and nothing changes. That won't happen now. If you want to understand why, you leave your fancy office in Moscow and come with me a thousand meters underground at the Kalinin Mine, walk and crawl another kilometer to the coalface, hack out the coal with a drill and a pick for eight hours in dust and methane at nearly a hundred degrees, and then return to the surface to find no soap and one shower for twenty men."

Kirillin nodded sympathetically. "Believe me, I understand. The President understands. That's why we need restructuring of the economy and restructuring of the management of enterprises, the kind of measures you're proposing in your seventh demand. But, let me say this, if the miners stay out for the duration of the talks, the economy of the Ukraine will collapse and there'll be nothing left to restructure."

"I fear you underestimate, Dmitry Sergeyevich," Malanchuk said in a tone that hovered between the friendly and the mocking. "All one hundred and twenty mines in the Donbass region are on strike. The railway workers have offered to come out on strike if our demands aren't met. Once that happens, it won't merely be the Ukraine that'll be at a standstill. The whole of the Soviet Union will be brought to its knees."

The reasonable, almost supplicatory, attitude Kirillin had adopted with Nikitin hardened as he turned to Malanchuk. He stabbed a forefinger at the lounging finger. "It is you who underestimates the seriousness of the problem, my friend. I tell you in the strictest confidence that the tanks were very nearly sent into Lvov and Kiev while the President was in the United States. If you think the Soviet Party Politburo, the State Security Committee, or the General Staff will permit the Soviet Union to be brought to its knees then, my friend, you are living in a dream world. You have an ally in the President. Try and speed up the process of *perestroika* too quickly and you destroy everything."

Stus, who had watched the interplay carefully, now spoke. "This is a good time to adjourn the session. We need to consult our colleagues."

That afternoon in the Ukrainian Politburo villa Kirillin watched the televised broadcast of the first day of the Supreme Soviet's autumn session. Anatoli Filipchenko walked straight to the rostrum and demanded an emergency session of the full Congress of People's Deputies to debate the crisis in the Ukraine. He was strongly supported by deputies from the Baltic republics, Georgia, Armenia, Moldavia, and Byelorussia. The President looked drawn. A cutaway shot showed Korolev staring contemptuously at Filipchenko. The Party's ideology chief went to the rostrum. He didn't mention the Ukraine. Instead he thanked the President for his efforts in the United States, but warned that the Americans would only agree to major changes in European security arrangements if they faced a strong and resolute Soviet Army. Peace was achieved through strength. It would be the height of folly, Korolev warned, to depart from that policy.

Korolev knew what the Supreme Soviet deputies didn't know. In response to the Soviet Union's unilateral defense cuts, the American President had simply issued a communiqué praising the Soviet leader and his policies. He had not made the promised compensatory reductions in the barriers to trade and transfer of technology. He couldn't do so, he'd apologized privately, for domestic political reasons while the situation in the Ukraine was so unstable. This shattering of the President's scheme to rescue the Soviet economy, coming after his failure to obtain similar trade and technology agreements with the European Community, had been disguised with fine sounding speeches. But Korolev knew the score. He was consolidating his position with the Army and biding his time.

That night, Kirillin slept badly.

Chapter ✤ Three

AT QUARTER PAST seven in the evening, Giuseppe ushered Cardinal William Lacey into the private secretaries' office. Hoffman was in the kitchen, talking with the nuns. The portly Lacey perched on the edge of Hoffman's desk.

Ryan had vague memories from his three years in the States of the radical Bishop William Lacey of Youngstown, Ohio, friend of the Berrigan brothers and supporter of Catholic peace movements. Summoned to the Vatican for elevation to archbishop and appointment as Secretary of the Sacred Congregation for Seminaries and Institutes of Study, Lacey quickly became Romanized and was duly rewarded with a cardinal's hat and the post of Prefect of the Sacred Congregation for the Causes of Saints. Vatican gossip labeled him a yes man, but considered him unlikely to gain further promotion in the Curia. In former days such a cardinal might have returned to an important archdiocese, like Washington. However, the demonstrations against the Pope's nomination of theological conservatives to fill vacant American bishoprics had served notice on the Secretariat that sending a Curial cardinal to take over a key American archdiocese might prove the last straw. It seemed, to Grimes at least, that Lacey was doomed to spend the rest of his days in Rome.

Lacey was early for his seven-thirty appointment with the Pope. "And whose cause for canonization does the Holy Father want me to speed up this time?" he asked jovially.

"I've no idea, Eminence," Ryan replied.

At eight o'clock Lacey came back into the private secretaries' office as Ryan was tidying his desk for the evening. Lacey's face was white. "You should have warned me," he accused.

"I'm sorry, Eminence, I don't know what you mean."

Lacey looked at him, and finally decided that Ryan really didn't know why the Pope had summoned him. He shook his head and walked out without a further word.

Chapter ✤ Four

THE THREE REPRESENTATIVES of the Ukrainian Solidarity Movement returned to the Hotel Moskva the following afternoon.

Stus opened proceedings. "We propose the following four conditions for the round table talks. One, striking workers will return on a temporary basis and will remain at work provided progress continues to be made. Two, government and Communist Party buildings now occupied by Ukrainian Solidarity supporters will be returned for normal use with the same proviso as before. Three, Saint George's Cathedral and the Ivan Franko University in Lviv will not be handed back. Four, the President will appear on tonight's edition of *Vremya* to announce that round table talks on our demands will begin on the eighth of November, and this commitment will also be published in tomorrow's *Izvestia*."

Inwardly, Kirillin leapt with relief. Outwardly, he grimaced. The others watched carefully. He raised his eyebrows and nodded to himself. Slowly the grimace turned into a resigned smile. "Gentlemen, you drive a hard bargain." He shook hands first with Stus, secondly with Nikitin, and lastly with Malanchuk.

After they'd gone Kirillin telephoned the President with the good news. The two months' delay should give enough time to finalize Babakin's plan. He ordered a bottle of vodka when he finally got through to the hotel management.

He was pouring himself a second glass when he heard a knock at the door.

"Dmitry Sergeyevich," said Babakin, "my congratulations on your performance. Permit me to introduce Major Ubartas from Vladimirskaya Street."

Kirillin examined the seedy man in a black leather coat. "From where?"

"The Ukrainian Republic HQ of the KGB," said Babakin. "The major and I were colleagues in the Fifth Chief Directorate."

The major's thin lips formed into a smile. His narrow eyes were expressionless. He offered a damp hand to shake.

Kirillin ordered two more glasses. "It was a close call."

"Closer than you think," Babakin said.

Major Ubartas placed his case on the table, unlocked it, and opened it to reveal a tape recorder. He wound back the spool and pressed the PLAY button.

Kirillin sat on the edge of his chair and listened to the heated discussion as the Council of the Ukrainian Solidarity Movement debated his proposed terms for the round table talks. Nikitin was deeply suspicious of the delay in the start of the talks. Stus said that the President had shown his good faith by sacking Budko and appointing Stepan Konovalets as First Secretary. He argued that they should respond in good faith to this move.

"Listen to how the little Jew responds," Major Ubartas said.

MALANCHUK: *The President had no choice. He had to appoint a front man acceptable to the public in a way that none of the Dnepropetrovsk mafia could ever be. Konovalets is still a Communist. He never resigned from*

the Central Committee when Budko ordered the Special
Orders goons to break up our twenty-second of January
rally.

STUS: My wife knows Konovalets. He's an honorable
man. Maybe he was mistaken, but he thought he could
do more good from within the Central Committee, to try
and curb Budko's excesses.

[CYNICAL LAUGHTER]

UNIDENTIFIED VOICE: Konovalets is Moscow's puppet. If he doesn't jump when Moscow pulls the strings,
Moscow will get rid of him.

UNIDENTIFIED VOICE: They always use the trick of
demanding the return of normal conditions while talks
proceed. As soon as we go back to work our position is
weakened. They know it's harder to bring the men out a
second time.

MALANCHUK: Dead right. We have them by the balls.
We shouldn't let go.

UNIDENTIFIED VOICE: We should give their balls another twist.

[LAUGHTER]

"And that's how the first session ended," Ubartas said as he
fast-forwarded the tape. "But at the next session, Bishop
Antoniuk is present. This is him now."

ANTONIUK: I appreciate all you say about not losing
impetus. But I've every reason to believe that if the
round table talks begin after the seventh of November,
we'll be in a much stronger position. And I'm not simply
talking about our position within the Ukraine.

MALANCHUK: What, precisely, do you mean?

ANTONIUK: I can't be precise. But I did advise that
the Feast of the Immaculate Heart of Mary was the day
to launch our Lviv initiative, and that proved to be correct. Now I'm advising that if we wait until after the sev-

enth of November to launch our next major offensive,
it'll produce more than liberty just for the Ukraine.

NIKITIN: *The bishop was right about Lviv. I vote we*
follow his advice.

UNIDENTIFIED VOICE: *I agree. This isn't just a fight*
about wages or getting one over the authorities. It's a
fight for freedom for all the Russian colonies.

"That's why they accepted your proposals, Comrade Kirillin," Ubartas said as he stopped the tape. "The Jew was
outvoted by the Catholics on the Council."

Kirillin looked out from the window, beyond the October Revolution Monument to the October Revolution
Square on the other side of Kreshchatik. "Why should Antoniuk say that they will be in a much stronger position, and
not just within the Ukraine, on the day we celebrate the
Anniversary of the October Socialist Revolution?"

Babakin shrugged.

Kirillin turned back from the window. "Can you find
out?"

Chapter ❖ Five

AFTER THE THUNDERSTORM on Wednesday morning, the sky was unusually clear in the afternoon. From above the basilica's dome the sinking sun slanted into Ryan's office through the net curtains and on to his empty desk. The mass of paperwork had been cleared, and Hoffman had left with the Pope for the five o'clock meeting with the heads of dicasteries that took place monthly when the Pope was in Rome. What puzzled Ryan was that there was nothing unusual in Cardinal Lacey's report from the Sacred Congregation for the Causes of Saints, just brief progress reports on the long investigations of those who had been proposed for beatification or canonization.

Three items on the interminable agenda appeared likely to provoke discussion and extend the meeting past its scheduled seven-thirty finish. Tucked away in a long report from the Sacred Congregation for the Eastern Churches was a passing reference to the proposed redesignation of the Major Archbishop of Lvov as Patriarch of the Ukrainian Byzantine Rite Catholic Church. Next, the Cardinal Secretary of State was presenting the half-yearly report from the Council of Cardinals for the Study of the Organizational and Economic Problems of the Holy See. The report showed a record deficit in the only accounts published of 146,000 million lire; just less than half this had been met by the Peter's Pence worldwide collection but, ominously, a note stated that this year no reserve funds were available to cover the remainder of the deficit. Ryan had heard rumors on the grapevine that the secret accounts of the Vatican Bank and of the Evangelization of Peoples dicastery were both heavily in deficit. The third controversial item was another report presented by Cardinal Fasolo: a review by the Secretariat of State of the worsening relationship with the Church in the United States.

Despite these items, Ryan heard the Pope, Hoffman, and Archbishop Korchan return at six-thirty. When Hoffman came through from the Pope's private study he seemed in a particularly good mood: his eyes were glinting behind his spectacles and the thin slit of his lips curled down at the edges in what Ryan recognized as a smile. Ryan asked how the meeting had gone.

Hoffman stopped, cocked his head to listen behind him, and then nodded. "The Holy Father and Archbishop Korchan are going for a walk on the roof terrace. The fresh air will do the Holy Father good. You were saying, James?"

"I asked how the meeting went."

"Which meeting?"

Ryan frowned. "The heads of dicasteries, Kasamir."

"Fine, fine."

"No problems?"

"Why should there be?"

"The record deficit?" Ryan ventured.

Hoffman shrugged. "God will take care of that. I've more important things to talk to you about, James." He rubbed his hands together in pleasure. "We're ready to launch the second stage of the plan to convert Russia."

"That's great news, Kasamir." Ryan thought of Sister Iryna. "I only wish we could let Bishop Antoniuk and his people know."

For an instant Hoffman's smile became a peasant's cunning smirk. "But they do, James, they do. You delivered the message."

His beady eyes gazed at Ryan's expression. "Come," he said, grasping the back of Ryan's arm just above the elbow and leading Ryan to his desk. He released Ryan's arm, sat at his desk, unlocked the drawers, and removed a buff folder. His head nodded in satisfaction as he placed a yellow sheet on the blotter. "This is the Italian translation of the homily that Father Sosiura gave during the Vatican Radio broadcast to the Ukraine of the liturgy from Saint Sophia Cathedral."

Ryan read the paper.

> Continuing our study of the Book of Revelation, written by Saint John at a time when Christians were being persecuted because of their faith in Jesus Christ as Savior, we come to Chapter 14, Verse 15. Here, the second angel exhorts the first to *use your sickle to reap the harvest, because the time has come; the earth is ripe for the harvest.*
>
> The definitive study of this part of Revelation was made by Saint Ernest, and it is to Saint Ernest that we should look to understand how this passage of Scripture will be fulfilled.

"This is some kind of message, Kasamir?" Ryan asked.

Hoffman beamed. "A very specific one."

"Do the Ukrainians have a code book or something?"

"Indeed they do. The Bible, plus a knowledge of their Catholic faith."

"But how . . . ?"

"The Ukrainian clergy know the broadcast contains a message for them when the homily is introduced by the words 'Christians being persecuted for their faith in Jesus Christ as Savior.' The message is clear from the particular passages of Scripture."

Ryan scratched his head.

Hoffman peered over the top of his spectacles at his not

very bright pupil. "The last message we sent referred to Revelation, Chapter 12, Verse 1, *And a great sign appeared in heaven: a woman clothed in the sun,* together with Verse 3, *And there was another sign in the heaven: and behold a great red dragon having seven heads,* which is clearly the Soviet Union and the seven members of the Warsaw Pact. The homily mentioned that Verse 1 matched the image at Fatima—and so Bishop Antoniuk knew we were talking about the icon which had come from Fatima—and that the triumph of the woman over the beast would be brought about by devotion to her Immaculate Heart. That's how he knew on what date to use the Icon of Kazan."

Ryan looked again at this new message. "I've never even heard of Saint Ernest, still less read anything by him."

Hoffman gave a dry chuckle. "It's your Western mind looking for complications. It's all very simple. The homily tells the Ukrainian clergy that the next stage in fulfilling the request of the Virgin of Fatima will strike at the heart of Russia itself, symbolized by the sickle, and the date will be the feast of Saint Ernest, the seventh of November."

Chapter ✦ Six

THE SKY OVER Moscow was already heavy with the promise of winter. By the late afternoon premature flurries of snow swirled down and clung to the bare trees on Tsvetnoi Boulevard. Babakin was early. He stopped his Volga outside the indoor Central Market to see what was on offer.

The scent of fresh flowers greeted him as he pushed open the doors from the street. The blaze of color inside contrasted with the gloom outdoors. He walked past the flowers to the fruit and vegetable stalls manned mainly by swarthy southerners from Georgia and Armenia trading in the free market that existed long before *perestroika*. There was nothing here that he couldn't obtain from the special shops he was entitled to use. The prices were exorbitant compared with those which would be charged by State shops in the unlikely event they actually had the fruit and vegetables to sell, and over twenty times the subsidized price he'd pay in the special shops. But the produce here was fresher, driven up overnight by relatives of the stall-holders. He bought tomatoes, lettuce, cucumber, and two pomegranates.

Behind the vegetable market were two smaller buildings. He ignored the meat market, where the maximum price per kilo was fixed by the State but where the weight was negotiated, and went to the dairy department. He tasted several samples of honey offered to him on scraps of wax paper by old peasant women. He bought three bottles.

Continuing down Tsvetnoi Boulevard, he drove across the wide Trubnaya Square and into Neglinnaya Street in the old brothel quarter. He parked, crossed the road, and walked a short way up Second Neglinnaya Lane to an ochre two-story neoclassical building that had seen better days. Two *tsyganki* vied with each other to sell him a rouble's worth of leafy birch twigs from the piles on top of old packing cases outside the door. He brushed aside the old gypsy women and opened the door to the entrance hall.

The smell of steam and the sight of those columns, arches, and molded ceilings painted in turquoise, white, ochre, and gold triggered off memories. His father had brought him here on his fourteenth birthday. The Sandunosky Bathhouse was an exotic Moorish palace where only men went. It was huge. That's why he'd suggested it to Kirillin as a meeting place. He walked up the four marble steps to buy his ticket at the wooden kiosk. The single, naked electric light bulb hanging from the arch overhead showed how much the place had shrunk since his last visit, aged fifteen. It also showed the peeling paint and the broken moldings.

A marble staircase rose from each side of the kiosk, curved round, and met one floor above, outside the door to the changing room. The *banshchik,* wearing only white cotton trousers and open white cotton jacket, handed Babakin a rough white linen sheet in exchange for his ticket. Babakin gave him a ten-rouble note. The man hesitated, looked at Babakin's suit, and finally offered the note back. "The private cubicles are already taken, sir. If you can come back tomorrow . . ."

Babakin shrugged and, leaving the note in the attendant's hand, walked through into the changing room.

It was difficult to believe that this room had once

seemed so large and luxurious. Beneath the dark oak carved ceiling, half a dozen partitions projected from the oak paneled side walls. Curtained off from the rest of the changing room, these formed the dozen private cubicles. Ahead of him, half a dozen dark oak high-backed benches—like rows of church pews—filled the center of the room. White linen sheets draped the benches. Clothes—mainly cheap serge suits—hung from pegs at the top of the benches. Men, some naked and some swathed in their white sheets, stood in the aisles or sat on the benches talking, chewing, and drinking. This was the room in which he'd first tasted beer. His father had handed him a mug of watery *Zhigulovsky*, confirmation that he'd passed the initiation test of the steam room and had joined the world of men. It was nectar. Now, he wouldn't give *Zhigulovsky* to his German shepherd dog.

Babakin's good-natured smile camouflaged the disgust he felt at seeing these naked bodies flabby with fat. At least in the KGB officers' *banya* beneath Dzerzhinskovo Street, the naked bodies were neither tattooed nor pressed so closely together.

He eased his way through the crowded changing room to the large alcove beyond, which his father had called the Turkish Room because of its plaster ceiling molded and painted in Moorish patterns. He arranged his suit as neatly as he could on a wire hanger and hung it next to an army uniform from a peg above the bench lining the semicircular wall.

Naked, he walked through the Moorish arch to the marble-tiled soap room, where overweight men were sponging themselves and other naked men on marble slabs with hot soapy water from rubber basins. Not the Asgard of his youth, more like a boiler room, with rusty piping running across cracked green and beige patterned wall tiles. To his right, a cheap unpainted pine door was fixed crookedly in the original molded doorframe. He pushed the door open and walked up the wooden steps.

The air in the steam room burnt his nostrils. His eyes

adjusted to the gloom. A heavily moustached naked Tartar threw water from a bucket into the glowing oven. It vanished in an explosion of hissing steam amid shouts of "More water!", "Enough!" and "No more!"

Babakin breathed the scalding air slowly, and threaded his way through masses of perspiring pink flesh up more steps to the hottest region of this particular Russian hell.

Kirillin was already there, flagellating his body with a bunch of birch twigs.

Babakin sat on the wooden bench next to him. "Blagov has given me the task of assassinating the Pope," he smiled. "He thinks that if I succeed he'll get the credit, and if I fail he'll be able to get rid of me."

"You told me that would happen," Kirillin said.

"Of course. That's not why I asked to meet you here."

Kirillin offered him the birch twigs. When Babakin declined his offer, Kirillin laughed. "You allow nobody to beat you, comrade. That's good."

"Our friend in Rome is determined to beat the President," Babakin said softly.

Kirillin's jovial mood evaporated as he listened to Judas's report on what the Pope was planning for the seventh of November.

After Babakin left, Kirillin made his way slowly back through the soap room to the changing room. He sent the *banshchik* out for a mug of beer and sat down on the wooden bench in his cubicle. Beyond the curtain, a group of workers were complaining among themselves about the shortages of fresh food in the shops; the loudest voices demanded a strong leader to stop speculators from the southern republics charging extortionate prices in the so-called free market that *perestroika* had created. When the *banshchik* returned, he asked Kirillin what he thought about the Ukrainian crisis; without waiting for a reply, he condemned the President for doing nothing about the disgraceful treatment meted out to Russians. Kirillin heard educated voices from the adjacent cubicle reflecting on the inevitable Russian cycle of stagnation, reform, and dictatorship. "This period of reform has run its course," one voice said. "I'm afraid so," his companion agreed. "After *perestroika, perestrelka* and *pereklichka.*" The first voice laughed.

After the restructuring, the fighting and the imprisoning. Kirillin seethed. If the intelligentsia got off their arses and tried to make *perestroika* work . . . He wondered if Babakin's plan would come too late to rescue the Soviet Union from collapse.

Kirillin walked angrily from the changing room, crossed the slippery tiles of the soap room, opened the green door opposite the pine door, and plunged into the dark icy water of the marble-lined swimming pool. The post-Revolutionary concrete that patched its broken Imperial tiles and moldings was already disintegrating.

Chapter ✤ Seven

TRASTEVERE, THE DISTRICT situated twenty minutes'
walk downriver from the Vatican on the west bank of the
Tiber, was once the city's port and housed Jews, Syrians
and other Mediterranean traders alongside its dockwork-
ers. Now it was the most Roman of all Rome's districts, re-
sisting assimilation into the modern international city on
the east bank.

The market in the center of the wide Piazza di San
Cosimato had closed for the day. Weatherbeaten traders
were drinking beer and exchanging stories around the
white-topped plastic tables which spread out from the res-
taurants across the pavement and over the cobbles of the
square. At other tables large matrons in floral frocks were
dallying over wine and olives before hauling their full shopping bags home to prepare the evening meal. Groups of
young Trasterverinos in their best stonewashed denims
and basketball shoes wandered between the tables, arguing
among themselves where they would find the best piece of
action that night. Little danger here of bumping into embassy or Vatican people on Saturday evening. But, just to
be sure, Ryan skirted round the barracks-like Palazzo San

Calisto, which housed five of the Pontifical Councils
spawned by the Second Vatican Council.

Feeling furtive, he passed through a couple of narrow
alleys festooned with washing, and found the crumbling
honey-brown building not far from where the Via Gari-
baldi sloped down from the Janiculum. He pressed the an-
saphone button, but there was no reply.

A rapid patter of feet was followed by panting. "Hi!
You're early or else I'm slow."

Diana Lawrence stood there, hands on the hips of her
brief running shorts, taking deep breaths. The edges of her
hair were matted with sweat. Sweat ran down her brow and
dripped off the end of her nose. Dark damp patches were
spreading down from the neck of her vest. "Don't just
stand there grinning," she said. "Do I get a kiss after coming four thousand miles to see you, or don't you like sweaty
women?"

He gave her a chaste peck on the cheek. It tasted salty.

She removed a key from a wristband and opened the
door. He followed her tight white shorts and long brown
glistening legs up two flights of stone stairs. At the top she
rapidly punched out six digits on a panel by the door and
pushed the door open.

The interior contrasted vividly with the outside of the
building. Ryan had only seen its like in glossy color magazines. Designed entirely in black and white, the austerity
was offset by the quality of the furnishings: in the reception
room a soft white leather sofa stood on a richly black carpet; black and white wood cabinets alternated along white
walls.

Her running kit didn't match the decor. No designer
T-shirt or fancy jogging shoes, but a faded Radcliffe College Track Club vest, now a size too small, and well-used
trainers. Her breasts were still heaving. She looked at her
wrist stopwatch. "You're right, I'm slow. My God, I feel
like I've run a marathon. I've forgotten how humid this
place is.

"Andrew Grimes says it's the greenhouse effect caused

by pollution. He's convinced the city is, quote, on a spiral of irreversible physical decay, unquote. Kasamir Hoffman believes the decay's moral."

She laughed.

"Where've you been?"

"The Doria."

Ryan had walked in the Villa Doria Pamphili when he'd been a student in Rome. The large public park covered the highest part of the Janiculum. Across the road from the main entrance to the park, the *carabinieri* maintained a permanent guard at the entrance to a well-shielded villa.

"Help yourself to a drink in the cabinet, James. I'm taking a shower."

He poured rather more scotch into the tumbler than he'd intended.

"Put on a CD," a voice called from down the passage.

"A what?"

"A compact disc."

He looked through the collection, hesitated over the Leonard Cohens, and picked out Rachmaninoff's Piano Concerto No. 2, which he'd last heard live at an open air concert given by the Boston Symphony. "How does this thing work?" he asked, looking down the passage.

A Radcliffe running vest was tossed out of an open door into the passage. It was followed by a pair of shorts. "Just turn it on and push the thing in the slot."

He turned away from the passage and faced the CD player.

Relaxed in the soft leather sofa, with a large whiskey in his hand, listening to Rachmaninoff, he tried to clear his thoughts.

Diana Lawrence came through the passageway. She was wearing the white towelling robe she'd worn at the villa near Lake Nemi. It came less than halfway down those brown thighs. Her hair was wet.

She poured herself a long Campari and soda and perched on the arm of the sofa. "I always knew you were a romantic," she smiled, nodding toward the CD player.

He shifted his gaze from her legs and looked past her to the Bridget Reilly on the wall. "I'm not sure it's a good idea, Diana. My coming here for supper, I mean."

"Why?" The innocence of the smile made him feel guilty.

"People might talk. Me, a priest, and you . . ."

"Yes?"

"You a single lady," he said completely lamely.

"That's why I suggested here," she laughed. "Don't look so shocked. I suggested here so people *wouldn't* talk. Look, we have a meal together twice at Roberto's or Marcello's, and the old women in the Vatican start gossiping about your mistress. You can come here and relax. Nobody ever comes to this part of town." She crossed her legs.

"Even so . . ." He stared steadfastly into his glass.

"Do you think I lured you here so I could fall upon you and have my wicked way with your body?" a husky voice said.

He didn't reply.

"I do believe you're blushing."

He looked away.

She stood up. "James, I'm sorry. I'll go and put something decent on."

He wondered about leaving. There was one of those infernal digital locks on the door.

She returned quickly, wearing a black full length kaftan embroidered with gold thread. The gold cotton buttons were fastened up to her throat. "Better?"

He nodded.

When she smiled this time, he smiled back.

"Come on. I popped a little something in the oven before I went out."

The little something was a *coda alla vaccinara,* a rich oxtail stew with red wine, vegetables, nuts, pepper and spices. As she poured him a glass of Barolo she said, "One reason I invited you, James, was to ask how much the Pope knows about what's happening with the Church in the States."

"The Secretariat supplies reports from the nuncios, and Monsignor Hoffman shows the Holy Father the newspapers."

"All of them?"

"Of course not."

"He selects."

"Well, he has to choose the most . . . to select some, otherwise the Holy Father will be drowned in newsprint."

"James, do you realize how bad it is? Just before I came back, they organized a sit-in in Newark Cathedral that stopped that conservative guy's installation ceremony. There's no way they're going to have him bishop there."

"Wasn't that just some gay Christian group?"

"Is that what the nuncio says? James, figure it out. Do five thousand people, including most of the priests and half of the nuns of the diocese, constitute just some gay Christian group? The chancery have gone ahead and nominated their own candidate for bishop, and other bishops are prepared to ordain him if Rome refuses to ratify the appointment."

He hadn't realized it was that bad.

"So I come from a Church in turmoil in the States back to a Church in turmoil in Rome. What's happening here?"

"Nothing's happening. No turmoil here."

"Come on, James Ryan. Don't play the innocent with me." It might have been Katie talking. "The big buzz around town is this mysterious canonization."

"How do you know about the canonization?"

She shrugged. "You know Rome. Everything is a mystery but nothing is a secret."

He chose his words carefully. "There's been no announcement made."

"Exactly! The Vatican press office is normally falling over itself trying to interest hardbitten journos in the virtues of some eighteenth-century Italian noblewoman who gave up her riches to found an order of nuns, or else some obscure Polish priest who had visions of the Virgin Mary. Now, nix. Good leaks that there's an upcoming canonization, but nothing from the press office except a bland statement that details will be given nearer the time. So naturally the journos want to know why and who."

"I can't tell you, Diana. But I will say this. Don't be out of town on the seventh of November."

Chapter ✤ Eight

"HOW MAY I be of service, Comrade Kirillin?" Gennady Afanasyev's voice on the telephone sounded particularly unctuous.

It made Kirillin brusquer than usual. "I need to see the Patriarch."

"Certainly," Afanasyev said. "When?"

"As soon as it's convenient for him."

"Tell me when you want him at the Kremlin. He will find it convenient."

"I want to go to his headquarters, to see at first hand how the Church operates."

"Certainly, Comrade. May I collect you in, say, an hour's time?"

"Yes."

The Chairman of the Council for Religious Affairs, whom Kirillin hadn't met before, was fat, with slicked-back hair too black to be natural. His black Chaika was the latest model.

Instead of turning right at the end of Ivanovskaya

Square and leaving the Kremlin by the more discreet Borovitsky Tower Gate, Afanasyev's chauffeur turned left, drove past the yellow neoclassical façade of the Supreme Soviet Presidium's main entrance and out through the Savior's Tower Gate into Red Square. Traffic militia blew whistles and waved back the tourists to clear a path for the Chaika as it swung downhill, past Saint Basil's Cathedral, and sped on to Moskvoretsky Bridge.

After crossing the artificial island between the Moscow River and the Drainage Canal, they entered Zamoskvoreschye, the old merchants' and artisans' enclave in the bend of the Moscow River and one of the few districts in the city spared Stalin's monumentalist reconstruction. The onion-shaped domes of Zamoskvoreschye's many churches rose above the two- and three-story nineteenth-century buildings that lined Bolshaya Ordynka Street. The street led to Dobryninskaya Square, the junction with Stalin's eight-lane Garden Ring Road that marked the southern boundary of Zamoskvoreschye. Beyond, their road widened into Lyusinovskaya Street.

Ignoring traffic regulations, the chauffeur turned left across Lyusinovskaya and down a side road. Ten minutes after leaving the Kremlin, the Chaika pulled on to the wide pavement next to a white wall pierced by two rows of loopholes, and came to a halt next to a pink and white fortified gate church. Afanasyev looked to Kirillin for approval. The *vlasti*'s ability to travel from A to B in the shortest possible time was as important to their self-esteem as the size of their limousine. Kirillin ignored him and climbed out of the car before the chauffeur had time to open the passenger door.

The unexpectant eyes of a one-legged beggar sitting with his back to the wall looked upwards. Without interrupting his mumbled prayers or the continuous crossing of himself with his right hand, the beggar held out a cap in his left hand. A black-robed priest hurried from the gate church to tell the beggar to leave. He apologized to Kirillin.

Kirillin ignored him too. He took a ten-rouble note and stuffed it in the beggar's coat pocket.

"Who are those?" Kirillin muttered, indicating the small crowd of Russian Orthodox priests who emerged from the arched entrance. All were bearded and wore black cassocks. The cylindrical headdresses of two of them were white, instead of black, and these clerics also wore lockets on their breasts and carried staffs.

"Your reception committee," Afanasyev replied.

Kirillin frowned.

"Archimandrite Aleksandr," said Afanasyev, introducing an elderly priest. "Father Superior of the Danilov Monastery."

"On behalf of the brethren, may I bid you welcome."

"Thank you," Kirillin said.

Archimandrite Aleksandr introduced him to the first white-hatted cleric, whose long bushy black beard almost covered the two lockets hanging on his breast. "His Eminence Metropolitan Nikolei of Minsk and Byelorussia, Head of the Department of External Church Relations."

"Their foreign minister," Afanasyev said, as if showing a friend round a zoo.

"His Eminence Metropolitan Pavel of Odessa, Chancellor of the Moscow Patriarchate," continued Archimandrite Aleksandr.

Kirillin was obliged to shake hands with all the clerics, lined up in strict hierarchical order, ending with Father Paulos, secretary to the Patriarch.

Archimandrite Aleksandr hesitated. A squat, powerfully built man, with bald head and pig-like eyes, came out of the door from the gate church into the arched passageway.

Kirillin stared at General Grechko. "I don't recall asking for the KGB," he said, "or did you just happen to be in church praying?"

Grechko's smile was a leer. "The Moscow Patriarchate comes under the jurisdiction of the Second Directorate. I would be doing the President's emissary less than his due if I didn't attend personally."

Kirillin looked long and hard at Afanasyev before following Archimandrite Aleksandr into a spacious courtyard.

"It was all crumbling away," Afanasyev said, "when we gave the place back to them. They did a splendid job in restoring it in time for the celebrations of a thousand years of Christianity in Russia."

"That's the monument commemorating the millennium," said Archimandrite Aleksandr proudly. An inscribed arch topped by a golden onion-shaped dome stood in the center of the cobbled courtyard.

"Perhaps you would like to inspect the Church of the Seven Ecumenical Councils," said Metropolitan Pavel, beckoning to his left at the church with an octagonal tower supporting its central dome, "it's seventeenth century and of a rather unusual design."

"I came here to see the Patriarch," Kirillin said ungraciously.

"Of course."

Archimandrite Aleksandr led the party to the right. The sound of unaccompanied male voices chanting psalms floated out from a yellow, green-domed cathedral with a white pillared façade. Opposite was a four-storyed neoclassical building painted in lime green.

"The Department of External Church Relations," said Metropolitan Nikolei.

"We used to use it as a prison for junior delinquents," Grechko grinned.

They turned the corner into another large square in front of an elegant new building. A solitary crow on the lawn flapped its wings at their approach and flew to Saint Vladimir's statue, from where it watched them enter the building by the main door beneath a circular mosaic of Christ's face.

The man who greeted Kirillin at the door to the library was old. His white headdress was not cylindrical, like those of the metropolitans, but shaped like a First World War German helmet with a small gold cross projecting from the top. A sacred image was embroidered on the front, and also on each end of the white veil that hung from the hat down either side of his wispy white beard and reached to his breast, next to the single engraved locket. His bearing was dignified, but the blue eyes were watchful.

"I have the honor to present His Holiness Patriarch Ioann of Moscow and all Russia," Archimandrite Aleksandr said reverentially.

"You are welcome," the Patriarch said simply.

Kirillin was disconcerted to see the whole party follow the Patriarch into the paneled library. "I wanted to see the Patriarch on his own," he whispered to Afanasyev.

"Would you like to dismiss your entourage, your Holiness?" Grechko said.

The Patriarch looked from Grechko to Kirillin. "Please leave us," he announced with a wave to the other clerics.

The Patriarch sat down at the head of a long mahogany table on which stood a solitary, elaborate gold cross. Kirillin sat at the top of one long side of the table, near the Patriarch, and Afanasyev took the seat next to him. Grechko stood behind Kirillin.

"How may I be of assistance?" the Patriarch asked.

"Comrade Kirillin," Grechko said, "wishes to form a better understanding of how the Russian Orthodox Church operates. I'm pleased to say that the days of persecution of the Church are over. The State now holds the Church in great esteem. Indeed we hold its Patriarch in so great an esteem that we have awarded him the Order of Friendship of the Peoples, and the Soviet Peace Committee holds him in so great an esteem that it nominated him as one of its representatives to the Congress of People's Deputies. But let the Patriarch himself tell you how his Church operates in the Soviet Union of *glasnost*."

Kirillin turned round angrily to the KGB general.

"It is true that the State has been most generous to us since *glasnost*," the Patriarch said. "The celebration of our millennium was supported by the State. It marked a change in our relationships. Before, the State saw the Church as its enemy. Now we are allies."

Kirillin looked from the gold cross on the table to the sacred images on the Patriarch's headdress. "We don't believe in the same things."

The old man replied mechanically, "We are Orthodox believers. At the same time we acknowledge the Soviet Union as our civil Motherland, whose joys are our joys and whose misfortunes are our misfortunes."

Kirillin's anger was growing at being served up with stilted formulae which insulted his intelligence.

"And your relationship with the government of the people?" Grechko prompted.

"It is the moral duty of all believers to support the legitimate government of the Motherland, especially one which seeks to meet the earthly needs of its people by applying social principles which accord with the Gospel message."

"Good, good," Grechko patronized.

"The government is atheist," Kirillin challenged.

The Patriarch sighed. "The responsibility of the Church is to preserve the liturgy so that the sacrament of Christ's body and blood is available to the people. What happens after that is Christ's will."

"And so it must be Christ's will that we have an atheist government," Grechko concluded.

Kirillin studied the Patriarch's expression. He wondered why any man could be so compliant.

"Only an atheist State like ours could be so forgiving, could it not?" Grechko asked.

The Patriarch hesitated. "The State has shown me great consideration," he said finally.

"Indeed it has," Grechko agreed. "I don't imagine Comrade Kirillin knows that you deserted your post in the Great Patriotic War."

The eyes of the Patriarch stared straight ahead from an expressionless face.

"And that you were sentenced to ten years' imprisonment?" continued Grechko as he paced the length of the table. "But such a sensitive creature, a monk indeed, found prison very hard. And the State Security Committee was so understanding that it arranged for an amnesty." Grechko smiled. "And since then your career in the Church has never looked back."

Grechko picked up one of three framed photographs on a cabinet at the end of the library. It showed the Patriarch in solemn robes presiding over some religious ceremony. "His Holiness is very fond of dressing up in golden costumes and having his path sweetened by incense," Grechko said as he walked back up the other side of the table. "Is that not so, your Holiness?"

Before Kirillin could stop this humiliation, Grechko put down the photograph and walked round the back of the Patriarch's chair. "But for you to exercise moral and spiritual authority, your Holiness, you must be unblemished in the eyes of the people. The State Security Committee keeps your secrets secure, does it not?" Grechko leaned forward so that his face was level with the back of the Patriarch's head. "At the same time, we are men of the world. We know you wish to be kept informed of the two children and the mistress you left behind in Rostov all those years ago. But the common masses have no need to know of such things. Their ignorant minds would see this as a lack of monastic piety." Grechko stood up straight. "I have a photograph of my own."

The KGB general put his hand into the inside breast pocket of his suit, removed a photograph, and held it in front of Ioann's face. "This was taken last month, your Holiness. What a fine man he is. He does you credit."

The old Patriarch turned involuntarily to the photograph and then resumed his impassive stare. Although the face was expressionless, Kirillin had never before seen such depths of pain reflected in any man's eyes.

"That's enough," Kirillin snapped. He turned to the old man. "I'm sorry."

The Patriarch looked at him. "Is that all you came for, my son?"

"No," Kirillin said. He turned to Grechko and Afanasyev. "I want to speak to the Patriarch alone."

For a moment Grechko stared straight back. Then he shrugged and left. Afanasyev followed.

"I came to ask you about Metropolitan Nikodim of Leningrad," Kirillin said.

"Ah," the Patriarch sighed, "Metropolitan Nikodim. For twelve years he was head of the Foreign Department of the Patriarchate. He supported the government at peace conferences throughout the world. But perhaps you should ask your friends outside about him."

"I'm aware that Metropolitan Nikodim was an officer of the KGB," Kirillin said. "I want to know from you what kind of man he was. Was he a good man?"

"Through God's grace he became a good man."

"A holy man?"

The Patriarch's gaze shifted to the solitary gold cross on the table. "Nikodim died in the arms of Pope John Paul I in Rome."

"Was he a saint?"

The Patriarch looked up, perplexed.

"This is for your ears only, Holiness."

Patriarch Ioann nodded.

"I'm given to understand that the current Pope intends to canonize Nikodim as a saint of the universal Church."

Chapter ✤ Nine

THE WHITE AIRPLANE landed at the airport outside Perm, in that one-fifth of the country which remained closed in the era of *glasnost*.

Babakin, protected against the near-zero temperature by a dark blue cashmere overcoat and a black Barguzin sable hat, stood at the top of the steps leading down from the passenger door. He was the only passenger. He waited, gloved hands in pockets, while a black Volga raced out from the motley collection of single-story buildings. It was several years since Babakin had been here. Nothing had changed, except that the main airport building had lost more of its brickface-shaped yellow tiles and so the gray patches were now larger than the yellow ones. A fierce wind whipped across the vast open area of tarmac and flat fields. Rows of camouflage-colored fighter-bombers and dark gray interceptors lined most of the runway; large dove-gray military transporters, with five-pointed red stars on their tail fins, littered the aprons; similarly marked khaki helicopters huddled together in the fields beyond. Babakin doubted that half these aircraft were serviceable. Still more would be useless when the massing clouds released their threat of snow.

A big man wearing a rabbitskin hat and a long black leather coat climbed out of the Volga's back seat. The slit eyes set in the broad, pitted face betrayed Major Salykov's mixed race: he was one half Buryat, one quarter Cossack, and one quarter his grandmother couldn't remember. He had been recruited as an energetic lieutenant from the Second Chief Directorate's Irkutsk Regional Command into the Fifth Chief Directorate's Moscow office. His natural brutality had served the Fifth well in its early days, but it proved inconvenient when Babakin shifted to a more sophisticated treatment of dissidents. Babakin had had him transferred back to the Second, with promotion to captain. It was part of Babakin's skill that such cast-offs held him in high regard and were pathetically eager to perform the unofficial service he asked of them from time to time.

"I hope you enjoyed the flight, General," Salykov said, taking Babakin's attaché case.

"I can think of better ways to spend three hours."

Creases formed at the sides of Salykov's eyes. "We had some good times, General, cracking skulls in the Lubyanka."

"Times have changed now, Major," said Babakin, settling into the back seat of the Volga. "This is the age of *perestroika.*"

Salykov gave a throaty laugh. "In Moscow, maybe. How is Moscow?"

Babakin shrugged. "You wouldn't like it. The Lubyanka's all offices now. Vodka has been banned from the building. Prisoners are held at Lefortovo. Blagov has circulated a memo stating that any item of expenses above five roubles will only be reimbursed against a claim form supported by documentary evidence."

Salykov shook his head. "How does he expect us to do our jobs? Never mind. Memos like that get lost before they reach here. And a shortage of vodka is one thing you won't find in my command, General."

The Volga left the runway and headed toward the air terminal, passing an apron on which a giant Condor trans-

porter was being unloaded with little enthusiasm by a
squad of surly young conscripts in winter boots but without
their winter fur hats. Before reaching the terminal, the
Volga turned right by one of the few hangars on the air-
field. Mechanics were playing cards beneath the wing of a
big SU-27 Flanker aircraft that was missing one engine.
The Volga stopped only long enough for KGB troopers to
lift the manually operated barrier and swing open the double chain-mesh gates.

The car headed toward the city of Perm and then left
the highway at Kuchino, where it followed a winding road
up the rocky, wooded slopes of the Ural Mountains that
mark the end of Europe and the beginning of Asia. The car
turned off this road at a signpost marked "VS-389/35/1."

"We have a new Camp Director," Salykov said. "Name
of Major Krylov, from Moscow. Do you want to meet
him?"

Babakin shook his head. "I've no time to waste."

The road ended in a clearing in coniferous woods. The
car halted at a battered solid steel gate in a four-meter-high
fence. The gate was next to a guardhouse and overlooked
by a watchtower. A large sign said: *Forbidden Zone. Do Not
Enter.* The driver sounded the Volga's horn. Dogs barked.
After a rattling of metal, the gate swung back. The car
drove slowly over the fenced-off stone road that crossed a
six-meter-wide strip of freshly turned earth containing an
electrified fence and electronic alarms. The armed guards
patroling the strip pulled hard on the leashes, but their
dogs continued to bark. The car stopped at a similar gate in
the inner barbed wire fence. Armed guards clanged the
gate shut behind the Volga. It drove along a narrow concrete road through roughly cut grassland past a long
wooden barracks to a collection of stone buildings. Babakin
followed Salykov out of the car to the KGB office. The dogs
were still barking.

"Snow won't be far off." Salykov said as he opened a
bottle of vodka and poured two glasses. He took a strip of

vobla from a cupboard, tore it in two with his grimy fingers, and offered half to Babakin.

Babakin disguised his revulsion at the piece of dried salted fish by unlocking his attaché case and removing a bottle of scotch whiskey which he placed on the table. "To keep you warm in winter, Major."

Salykov picked up the bottle and stroked it tenderly. It might have been a newborn baby. "I always said you were the best commander a man could have, General. Tell me, which *zek* are you interested in?"

Babakin took a buff-colored file from his attaché case and opened it. He removed the summary at the front of the file and gave it to Salykov.

STOGUL, KONSTANTIN PETROVICH

27 September 1937:	Born: Yelizavetovka village, Volnovakha district, Donetsk oblast, Ukrainian SSR. Father: engineer. Mother: Christian.
5 July 1957:	Graduated from Leningrad Theological Academy as a correspondence course student.
11 October 1957:	Professed monastic vows and ordained priest of Russian Orthodox Church.
23 July 1959:	Joined staff of Moscow Patriarchate.
15 September 1966:	Elevated to hieromonk and appointed lecturer in ecclesiastical history at Leningrad Theological Academy.
14 February 1981:	Arrested under Article 70 of the Russian Soviet Federative Socialist Republic Criminal Code for anti-Soviet agitation and propaganda.

23 April 1981:	Tried and sentenced to three years in prison followed by two years in a strict regime labor camp. Served prison sentence at Chistopol.
23 April 1984:	Transferred to Perm-37 Labor Camp.
18 March 1986:	Rearrested in camp for violating Article 227 of the RSFSR Criminal Code by engaging in forbidden religious services, and sentenced to a further three years in a special regime camp.
28 March 1986:	Transferred to Perm-36 Labor Camp.
8 January 1987:	Rearrested for violating Article 190-1 of the RSFSR Criminal Code by slandering the State, aggravated by possession of an object designed to cause bodily harm. Sentenced to a further seven years in a special regime camp followed by five years' internal exile.
1 January 1988:	Transferred to Special Unit of Perm-35 Labor Camp on closure of Perm-36.

"What was the weapon found on him?" Babakin asked.

Salykov grinned. "My friend Stogul. I remember it well. The weapon was a wooden dagger."

"A wooden dagger?"

"Sure. He kept calling it a cross."

Babakin removed three photocopied sheets from the file. He pushed them across the table to Salykov. "Stogul smuggled this out. It is proving an embarrassment to us."

Salykov's grin disappeared. He squinted at the three

pages. "Did this shit reach any of those human rights organizations?"

"No. The Vatican."

"The Vatican?"

Babakin's voice was icy. "Perhaps you've heard of it? It's where the Pope lives."

"Fuck Krylov's mother," Salykov growled. "He came here with *glasnost* pouring out of his arse. This is the result."

Babakin placed both hands flat on the table. "This has nothing to do with Krylov or his mother. Interior Ministry people are here simply to administer the camp. It is the State Security Committee that is responsible for security. You are supposed to be its representative here."

Salykov shrank from those eyes. "What do you want me to do, General?"

"I need to find out whether this document represents the truth, or whether your electrodes on his balls sparked off a piece of creative fiction."

Salykov reached across to the telephone on his desk. "Povarnitsyn. Bring Stogul to the interview room."

Babakin followed Salykov down the corridor to a whitewashed room containing a cheap wooden table, four chairs, and a battered leather couch. The bulb in the center of the ceiling was protected by a mesh net; the only light switch was outside the room.

A few minutes later Lieutenant Povarnitsyn, the duty officer, came in, followed by Stogul and a guard.

Hieromonk Stogul was emaciated. He was shaven bald and wore a striped uniform that resembled a pair of pajamas with a number stitched on the breast pocket. The bridge of his nose was broken, giving a lopsided appearance to a face patched with dry, peeling crust; the lobes of his large ears were cracked and covered with ulcers. He sat down at the table, clasped his fingers together, and slowly examined the other people seated across the table. He possessed an inner calm that Babakin had seen before. Babakin understood how easily such a man could irritate Salykov.

"Prisoner 18723," said Salykov, "you have an important visitor from Moscow."

Stogul spoke softly. "May I know your name, sir, or are you too known by a number?"

Salykov jumped to his feet. "You will address the General with respect. He wants to know about this document." He threw the three photocopied sheets on to the table.

Stogul ignored them. "When will *perestroika* reach our camp, General?"

Salykov rose to his feet again. "You insolent . . ."

Babakin waved him quiet. "Doesn't my presence here," he said silkily, "indicate that the process of restructuring has begun?"

"In which case, General, will you kindly arrange for my release."

"I will do my best. But on what grounds? You have the record of a hardened criminal."

Stogul smiled. "I have been guilty only of two so-called crimes. First, telling the truth about the collaboration between the Russian Orthodox hierarchy and the atheistic Communist authorities. Second, celebrating the liturgy with a crust of bread and the juice from wild berries. Do these merit fifteen years plus five years' internal exile?"

Babakin made a gesture of helplessness. "I cannot go against what the law has decreed."

"Precisely. That is why you must release me. My last sentence was for an alleged violation of Article 190-1. That article has now been removed from the statute book and all prisoners sentenced under it have been granted an amnesty."

Salykov leaned forward across the table. "For someone who has been denied visits or mail for the last four years, you seem remarkably well informed."

"This is a serious point, Major," said Babakin. "We now have a society based on the rule of law. Why was Father Stogul not amnestied?"

Stogul grinned. "The amnesty didn't apply to prisoners in punishment cells. Prisoner 18723 was serving fifteen days in the *shizo* on the day of the amnesty."

Babakin looked back at Stogul.

"That was a put-up job," Stogul said without rancour.

"This is a serious allegation, Major," Babakin said. "I insist on seeing the papers."

"Get the file," Salykov growled at the lieutenant. He stabbed his finger at Stogul. "This man is a troublemaker, a bad influence on the other prisoners."

"What have you to say to that, Father Stogul?" Babakin asked.

"In this camp," said Stogul serenely, "Catholic, Lutheran, Baptist, and Orthodox have put aside centuries of bitterness. We have joined together in the love of Our Savior, Jesus Christ. Insofar as I have contributed to that Christian unity, I consider it an influence for the good."

Salykov seemed on the verge of an apoplectic fit. Lieutenant Povarnitsyn returned with the file. Babakin made a great show of studying it. He sighed. "You were sentenced for not fulfilling your work norm. You appealed to the local procurator on the grounds that your work norm had been doubled and was unobtainable. The procurator for the Chusovsky district considered your appeal, found it without foundation, and confirmed the sentence. I'm afraid there's nothing I can do."

"What you are saying, General," Stogul said, "is that you're no different from the rest, and we in the Urals can forget *perestroika.*"

"I said that there are no grounds for overturning a lawful sentence of the court. However, I may be able to assist with an amnesty if you cooperate."

Stogul's laughter turned into a bout of coughing, for which he apologized. "I'll sign nothing. No false confessions, no lies. Major Salykov should have told you not to waste your journey."

"No, no," Babakin assured him. "Those days are past. I

simply want you to tell me about this document you smuggled out."

Stogul took a pair of spectacles from his breast pocket and put them on. They were held together at the center with sticky tape; one lens was broken. Stogul peered at the typewritten sheets. "They're not mine."

"Do you deny you wrote this?" Salykov demanded.

Stogul smiled. "These sheets are typewritten. I don't recall you ever granted me the loan of a typewriter."

"Are the words yours?" Babakin asked.

"If you haven't got the original," said Stogul, "or even a photocopy of the original to check my handwriting, tell me where the original is."

Salykov could contain himself no longer. He reached across and grabbed Stogul by the front of his prison uniform. "We ask the questions. You give the answers."

"If you refuse to tell me where the original is," Stogul wheezed, "then I refuse to speak about the document."

"Shall I make him talk?" Salykov asked, bunching the fist of his free hand.

Babakin looked into Stogul's eyes. He knew the type. Pull out his fingernails and he'd faint with pain before he'd tell you anything. He shook his head. "Pentothal."

Salykov reluctantly let go of the prisoner's uniform. "Get the doctor," he ordered.

When Lieutenant Povarnitsyn returned, Babakin was pleased to see the doctor was a woman, in her mid-thirties, white coat tight over her breasts, and long black hair pinned up on top of her head. Interesting.

Salykov walked round the back of Stogul's chair, leaned over, and put his arm round Stogul's neck. This brought on another bout of coughing. The lieutenant rolled up the prisoner's left sleeve and held his arm straight.

Stogul's eyes darted toward the syringe being filled by the doctor. He crossed himself with his free hand. "May the blood of Jesus Christ cleanse my lips and my soul from any betrayal I may make under the influence of this drug."

"Shut up and keep still," Salykov ordered.

Stogul closed his eyes in concentration and kept repeating, "Jesus is my Savior. Jesus is my Savior. Jesus is my Savior . . ."

The needle went in and Stogul's eyes glazed.

"He's all yours, General," the doctor said.

Babakin stood up, walked round the table, and perched on the table edge, directly in front of Stogul. "Tell me all you know about Metropolitan Nikodim of Leningrad," he asked conversationally.

"Jesus is my Savior. Jesus is my Savior."

Babakin repeated his question, but Stogul repeated his mumbled reply.

"Does he need another shot, Doctor?" Babakin asked.

She pulled back Stogul's eyelids, peered at his pupils, and shook her head. "He's an old hand. He's conditioned himself to repeat that truth which overrides all others in his mind."

"Is there nothing we can do?" Babakin demanded.

"Let me at him," Salykov pleaded.

The doctor squatted by the side of Stogul's chair, took Stogul's hand, and stroked his palm sensuously. "Jesus is your Savior. Jesus wants to save you. Jesus wants you to tell this gentleman all you know of God's servant, Nikodim of Leningrad."

"Jesus is my Savior. Jesus is Nikodim's Savior."

Babakin grimaced. He nodded to Salykov.

The doctor shook her head and continued gently. "Jesus wants to know when you met Nikodim. Tell Jesus."

Stogul's words came out slowly. "I first met Nikodim when he was still an archimandrite."

The doctor smiled and nodded at Babakin. He smiled back. She looked the kind who wanted a Moscow posting. Maybe he would delay his return.

"Was Nikodim a Catholic?" Babakin asked.

"Yes."

"Are you?"

"I was received into the Catholic Church by Nikodim himself."

"Why?"

"We joined the Catholic Church because it is the one founded by Christ."

"Isn't the Orthodox Church?"

The words began to flow more quickly. "The Orthodox Church was the Church of our Motherland. But the more I learnt the more I discovered that it was not the Church Christ had founded."

"Why not?"

Stogul's face creased in pain.

"Jesus wants you to say why," the doctor encouraged.

"In Moscow I saw how the Patriarch and the metropolitans collaborated with the Communist authorities. They took orders from atheists. They appointed only those who would do whatever the plenipotentiary for religious affairs told them. I saw what happened to the good priests, like Archbishop Vermogen of Kaluga, Father Gleb Yakunin, and many more."

"Why didn't you join them?" Babakin asked.

Stogul's head shook sadly. "I hadn't their strength of faith. I retreated to Leningrad and tried to bury myself in theological studies. But the more I studied the more I saw a leaderless Church was not the answer. The Church of my Motherland had become at best a rustic Church for illiterate peasants who watched a magic liturgy and worshiped magic icons. We no longer had a theology that could compete with Marxism for the minds of thinking men. Such men joined the Communist Party to build paradise on earth."

"Why didn't you do what many people did?" Babakin asked. His voice softened. "What I did. I too abandoned superstition and joined the Party."

A smile spread on Stogul's face. "You abandoned one corrupt superstition for another."

Babakin's fist smashed into Stogul's face.

"General, please!" the doctor cried. "Not if you want more out of him."

"Why did you turn to the Catholic faith?" the doctor asked, stroking his palm.

"Nikodim opened my eyes. He showed me how the theology of the Catholic Church was based firmly on the Bible, on the scholarship of learned fathers like Augustine and Thomas Aquinas, and on the teaching authority of Peter's successor. Here was an ideology to which an intellect like Nikodim's could submit both in faith and in reason."

"Tell me the truth about Nikodim," Babakin snapped "You've fantasized in this document. In the first place, Nikodim was never an Orthodox believer. He was a good Communist who infiltrated the Orthodox Church."

"He told me all this, of course. For many years he believed fervently in Communism."

"What made him change?"

"When the KGB made him head of the Foreign Department of the Patriarchate, one of his tasks was to spy on the Catholic Church, to find out what it was up to in eastern Europe and the Soviet Union. His cover was to collect material for a doctoral thesis on Pope John XXIII. But the more he learnt, the more he was attracted by the Church. He saw in John XXIII the embodiment of doctrinal authority combined with God's love. Here, truly, God was speaking to his people, both to their minds and to their hearts, through his Vicar on Earth."

"So, he converted, just like that?" Babakin scoffed.

"No," Stogul said slowly. "He wrestled with his Russianness, to which he had been born, and with his loyalty to the Communist Party, which had nurtured him. But eventually he became a Catholic in his heart."

"But only in his heart," Babakin insisted.

Stogul shook his head. "During a spiritual retreat after he was appointed Metropolitan of Leningrad, he decided what he must do. He visited Rome and made his submission of obedience to Pope Paul VI. It was Paul VI who urged him not to declare himself openly, but to go back to Russia, give succour to the Catholic Church there, and

work and pray for the reunion of the Russian Orthodox
Church with the Catholic Church."

Babakin's voice was edged with anger. Nikodim had
been one of the KGB's prized agents. "What exactly did
Nikodim do when he returned?"

A smile began to cross Stogul's cracked face. Blood from
his mouth, where Babakin had punched him, dribbled
down his chin on to his uniform. "He did three things. As
head of the Patriarchate's Foreign Relations Department,
he initiated the Russian Orthodox–Roman Catholic Dialogue." Stogul's smile widened. "His KGB colleagues
thought it was a ploy to persuade the Catholic Church to
stop its opposition to Communist governments in eastern
Europe and the Soviet Union. They never for one moment
realized that its true intention was precisely what it proclaimed publicly, to bring about union between the two
Churches."

Babakin gritted his teeth. "The second?"

"Nikodim proposed that the Synod of the Russian Orthodox Church approve the giving of holy communion and
the other sacraments to Catholics denied the services of a
Catholic priest. Because the Synod knew he was KGB, it
agreed, despite opposition from the other Orthodox
Churches."

"The third?"

Stogul's eyes focused on infinity. He spoke as though
addressing God. "The third was his greatest triumph. You
see part of it before your eyes."

Babakin folded his arms and sneered. "You?"

"Nikodim confided in those of us he could trust at the
Leningrad Theological Academy. He inspired us with the
true faith. We learnt to spot the *stukachi*. But for the genuine students, we passed on the faith." He nodded happily.
"A majority of Orthodox priests trained at Leningrad are
clandestine Catholic priests. Several of them are now bishops. Soon the time will be ripe."

Babakin leaned forward. Below the bald domed head,

his ice-blue eyes focused on Stogul's glazed eyes. "Ripe for what?"

"Ask Nikodim."

"Nikodim is dead."

"Nikodim is with God."

Babakin raised his hand, but the doctor shook her head. "There's more, I'm sure," she whispered. She turned to Stogul. "When will the time be ripe?"

Stogul looked toward the doctor's open, encouraging face. "Nikodim became seriously ill. He thought the KGB suspected he was a traitor, and its agents were slowly poisoning him. He told me he must go to Rome. But Paul VI died. Immediately Nikodim went to brief his successor, John Paul I, and ask when the plan should be implemented." A blissful expression filled Stogul's face. "God granted him a glorious reward. Nikodim died in the arms of the Vicar of Christ."

Babakin's voice was low and menacing. "What was the plan? When did he think it should be implemented?"

"Ask Nikodim."

The doctor grabbed Babakin's arm as he raised his fist. "He doesn't know, General. If he did, the Pentothal would tell you."

Babakin sat down. "You're right. Nikodim was trained by us to tell subordinates only what they need to know."

"What now, General?" Salykov asked.

"Send him back." Babakin stared at every one in the interview room. "None of you has heard any of this." Only when he saw the look in their eyes did he relax.

As the doctor followed Povarnitsyn, Stogul, and the guard, Babakin put a restraining hand on her arm. "You did well, Doctor. I don't even know your name."

She smiled. "Ledovskaya. Tanya Yeygenyevna."

"Join us for a drink."

Back in Salykov's office, Babakin slumped in Salykov's chair and pointed to the bottle of scotch.

"Did the prisoner confirm that document, General?" Salykov asked as he poured out three drinks.

"He did more than that." Salykov was out of his depth, but the woman understood.

"Did we suspect Nikodim?" Ledovskaya asked.

"The records show the Second suspected him, but they'd no proof."

"Did they poison him?"

"No. He had heart trouble. He died of a stroke."

"Human rights groups are pressing for Stogul's release," she said.

Babakin studied her over his glass of whiskey. "Do you think he should be released, Tanya Yeygenyevna?"

She shrugged. "It depends in what state he's released."

He bared his teeth in approval. "Arrange for Stogul's speedy release," he said to Salykov.

The next day Father Stogul was summoned to Salykov's office.

"I'm pleased to inform you, Prisoner Stogul," Salykov announced, "that in return for the cooperation you provided, General Babakin has authorized your release."

Stogul was at first incredulous and then overwhelmed. He sat down. "Praise be to Jesus Christ! When am I going?"

"As soon as a few formalities are completed. I'm arranging a residence permit for the village of Barysh in the Ternopol region. I understand from all the letters sent to you that your sister lives there."

"Yes, yes."

"There's an outbreak of typhoid in that area." He looked at Stogul. "You're hardly in the best of health. The doctor thinks you should have an inoculation before you're released." Salykov's face split into a grin. "We can't have you dying on us as soon as you're released."

Joyfully, Stogul went to the camp hospital for his inoculation. Twenty minutes later his body, wrapped in a canvas bag, was wheeled out and emptied into a grave which had been dug that morning and partially filled with lime.

Salykov sauntered into the Camp Director's office. "This is the letter you're to sign and send to Stogul's next of kin."

Major Krylov read it. "This says he died of heart failure."

"So, his heart stopped, didn't it?"

"This wasn't how it happened."

Salykov leaned over Krylov's desk. "Major, letters like these describe what could have happened."

"It's not true, you mean."

"It contains a part of the truth. It doesn't confuse the people."

Chapter ✣ Ten

THE PACKAGE BORE the seal, *Sala Stampa Santa Sede Vaticano,* of the Vatican's press office. Ryan opened it and read the letter inside:

> Your Holiness,
> The enclosed will be released on 1 November, All Saints Day, as instructed.
> I beg to remain Your Holiness's most obedient servant,
>
> > *Robert Frawley*
> > Director
> > Sala Stampa della Santa Sede

Underneath the letter an idealized portrait of a bearded Russian wearing black robes and a white metropolitan's headdress looked benignly at him from the golden glow of a halo against a celestial background. On the other side, an invitation:

> *The Rector and Faculty of the Pontificium Collegium Russicum have the joy of announcing the happy news*

*of the Canonization of their Patron, Nikodim of
Leningrad, and cordially invite you to the solemn
ceremony to be held in Saint Peter's Square, Rome,
on 7 November at 9.30 A.M.*

A pamphlet bore the same saintly image.

SAINT NIKODIM OF LENINGRAD (1929–78)

HIS EARLY YEARS

Like Saint Paul, Nikodim began his life persecuting
the Church. Born into an avowedly Communist
household, he was taught to hate and despise Christians as enemies of the Socialist State. So exemplary
was he in informing on those of his schoolfriends and
their parents who secretly practiced their faith that
he was recruited at an early age into the MGB, the
Ministry of State Security, which was to become the
KGB.

His task was to infiltrate the Russian Orthodox
Church and ensure that it followed the policies of its
atheist masters. Ordained a monk when only eighteen years old on the orders of the MGB, he was
quickly promoted within the Church. Ten years later,
as an archimandrite, he headed the Russian Orthodox mission in Jerusalem, where his role was to praise
the achievements of the Soviet Union, to persuade
the Middle Eastern states that they had nothing to
fear by embracing Communism, and to deceive the
world about the evil plan of the Soviet Empire for
world domination.

Pleased with his work, his Soviet masters brought
him back two years later, in 1959, to head the office
of the Moscow Patriarchate at the time Khrushchev
launched his campaign to eliminate Christianity from
the Soviet Empire. Nikodim made certain that the
hierarchy of the Orthodox Church meekly accepted
the burning of icons and the closure of churches and
seminaries. He arranged the dismissal, imprisonment, and even the deaths of bishops and priests who
objected.

Like Saul, he "tried to destroy the Church" (Acts 8:3), washing his hands in the blood of martyrs who recognized in Communism the First Beast of the Apocalypse, the beast with seven heads which "began to curse God, his name, and the place where he lives" (Revelation 13:6); which "put to death all who would not worship it" (Revelation 13:15); and which "forced all the people, small and great, rich and poor, slave and free, to have a mark placed on their right hands or on their forehead. No one could buy or sell unless he had this mark" (Revelation 13:16–17).

These were dark days in which citizens of the Soviet Empire were compelled to sign a declaration denying God on pain of being deprived of their bread, clothing, and residence permits.

Fearful that their evil deeds would cast doubt on the peaceful intentions they proclaimed to the rest of the world, the agents of Satan appointed Nikodim Bishop of Podolsk to head the Foreign Department of the Moscow Patriarchate. Here he was to deceive the world outside as to what Godless atrocities were taking place within Satan's kingdom. While continuing to head the Patriarchate's Foreign Department, he was promoted Archbishop of Yaroslavl, then Metropolitan of Minsk, and then, while still only thirty-six years of age, Metropolitan of Leningrad and Novgorod, becoming the second most powerful man in the Russian Orthodox Church after the Patriarch.

HIS CONVERSION

For Saul it was on the road to Damascus where God asked, Why are you persecuting me? and converted him into the Apostle Paul, the early Church's greatest missionary. For Nikodim it was on the road to Rome, the Holy See, where God miraculously opened his eyes to the truth. Having begun his journey from Moscow an agent of Satan, Nikodim arrived in Rome and flung himself at the feet of the Sovereign Pontiff who had taken the name of Paul. He begged forgiveness for his sins, and God, in his inestimable mercy, granted him pardon. When he asked of the Vicar of Christ what he should do for reparation, Pope Paul told him to go back to Russia and follow, in secret, the example of the Apostle Paul so that Russia might be converted back to Christianity as Our Lady of Fatima had requested.

HIS MISSION

Nikodim, confirmed Bishop of the Universal Church with the Pope's own hands, returned to Russia where he carried out the mission entrusted to him.

For the next nine years he worked ceaselessly to try and bring the Russian Orthodox Church, which had strayed from its origins, back into communion with the Holy See. He gave succor to Catholics denied the ministry of their priests and bishops. And, through the Leningrad Theological Academy, he inspired students with the true faith, the faith of Peter, the Rock upon which Christ built his Church, against which the gates of hell shall never prevail (Matthew 16:18).

As a result of his missionary work, hundreds of priests and many bishops of the Russian Orthodox Church have secretly vowed their allegiance to the Holy See and its Bishop, the Supreme Pastor of the Universal Church. They await the day when the Successor of Peter will call upon them to declare openly their faith in the One, True Church and shall, with him, consecrate their beloved Motherland to the Immaculate Heart of the Mother of All, the Blessed Virgin Mary, Liberatrix of Holy Russia.

HIS MARTYRDOM

The agents of Satan discovered Nikodim's true vocation, and began to poison him. Warned by God of his impending death, Nikodim left his sickbed to travel to Rome. With his dying breath he told the new Pope of the clandestine Catholic Church in Russia dedicated to the Immaculate Heart of Mary. Nikodim's mission on earth having been fulfilled, God took him from the arms of Pope John Paul I and carried his soul to its just reward among the blessed in heaven.

PRAYER

Almighty and eternal God, You have placed in your Saints a great light and a strong support for our human weaknesses. Through the example of the blessed Saint and Martyr Nikodim, You have shown us that, however far we descend into the clutches of Satan, You will never abandon us. Grant us, Lord, the grace to follow Nikodim's renunciation of Satan and his devotion to the Immaculate Heart of Your Mother. We ask, through his intercession, that we may show the same fidelity to Christ and the Church He founded, so that one day we may share in Your glory together with all the Saints.

Through Jesus Christ Our Lord. Amen

Imprimatur
William Cardinal Lacey

Ryan sat back. "Kasamir, since when has Nikodim of Leningrad been Patron of the Russian College?"

From the desk facing him, Hoffman peered over the top of his spectacles. "Since last week."

Ryan frowned. "I take it you've seen this pamphlet."

"The final draft."

"How much can be proved?"

"It's all in a letter from one of Nikodim's clandestine priests, smuggled out of a labor camp in the Urals. The letter Bishop Antoniuk gave you in Lvov."

"It said all this? Has the letter been corroborated?"

Hoffman removed his spectacles. "James, what you have in front of you is not a legal document."

"It's not necessarily true, is that what you're saying?"

"It contains a greater truth. It inspires the people."

Chapter ✛ Eleven

THE GREATEST FEAST day in the liturgical calendar of the
Soviet Union is the Anniversary of the Great October Socialist Revolution, commemorating 25 October 1917 when
Lenin's Bolshevik forces captured the seat of government,
the Winter Palace in Petrograd, and announced the establishment of the Soviet state. Four months later the Council
of People's Commissars rejected the Julian calendar used
in Czarist Russia and adopted the calendar of Pope Gregory XIII to fall into step with the West. The abolition of
thirteen days meant that the 25 October Socialist Revolution is celebrated on 7 November.

On this particular 7 November the gods did not look
kindly on the gigantic red banner bearing the sanctified
image of Lenin which hung from the roof of the GUM department store, opposite the Kremlin. Sleet fell from the
heavens, and the giant Lenin shivered in the cold wind that
blew through Red Square past the flapping "1917" which
covered most of the Historical Museum façade.

At precisely nine o'clock the military brass bands began.
Kirillin parted the net curtains of his office window. On the
other side of Red Square, past the red, yellow, blue, and

white guidelines painted on the cobbles, and beyond the dark blue ranks of naval cadets, crowds huddled in front of GUM.

Open-topped Chaikas drove between the yellow guidelines from the direction of the Historical Museum, a general standing in the back of each—right hand raised in salute, left hand anchored to the roll bar, face set impervious to the weather. Next came a detachment of soldiers in gray military greatcoats, yellow-belted and yellow-tasseled, their black boots synchronized at 110 paces per minute for the 266 paces to cross Red Square.

The bands struggled valiantly against the deafening clanking of tanks over the cobbles. Standing in the turret of the lead tank was a heavily tasseled and bemedalled figure.

"It seems a Chaika is too comfortable for our friend Karavansky."

Kirillin turned round in surprise. "I thought you'd be on one of the viewing stands," he said to Babakin.

Babakin grinned. "Far too exposed down there." He peered over the Kremlin wall to look at the back of the fedoras, fur hats, and military caps of the Presidential Council and the Politburo members on top of the Lenin Mausoleum. "Another one gone."

Molchanov had been "retired" as Interior Minister and had been replaced by a man loyal to the President. The problem, Kirillin reflected, was that Molchanov had been appointed in the first place because of his supposed loyalty to the President.

"How many at the counter-demonstration at Tverskoy Boulevard?" Kirillin asked.

Babakin shrugged. "They haven't got any tanks."

"Do they need them?"

Defense Minister Ulanov finished his speech at noon. The time in Rome was nine o'clock.

It was one of those autumn mornings that banished memories of the oppressive heat and humidity of the Roman

summer. A gentle overnight breeze from the north had
swept the sky clean. Basking in the bright sun, the stone-
work of the great eastern façade of Saint Peter's Basilica
seemed almost white against the clear blue sky. The large
central door was covered by red drapes. Above, from the
balcony used by popes on Easter Sunday to give their
blessing *urbi et orbi,* a great tapestry hung down. It bore
the same celestial image of Nikodim of Leningrad that
adorned the invitation cards.

Two tall enclosed passageways ran straight from each
side of the façade toward the Via della Conciliazione
before opening out into the curved arms of Bernini's
colonnade that embraced the large oval portion of Saint
Peter's Square. From between the statues on the roof of
the passageway that connected with the Apostolic Palace,
on the northern side, Ryan looked down into the rectangular area directly in front of the façade. Below him, in front
of the right-hand doors to the basilica, the Sistine choir
were already seated, facing the square. In the center, in
front of the main door, stood a large temporary altar, and in
front of that, above the twenty-two steps that led down into
the oval part of Saint Peter's Square, a white satin chair and
kneeler awaited the Bishop of Rome, Archbishop and Metropolitan of the Province of Rome, Primate of Italy, Patriarch of the West, Supreme Pontiff of the Universal
Church, Sovereign of the Vatican City State, Successor of
the Prince of the Apostles, Vicar of Jesus Christ, and Servant of the Servants of God.

Rows of empty chairs faced each side of the altar. Ornate gilded chairs with red cushioning formed the first two
rows of each block, wooden chairs the next four rows, and
black plastic stacking chairs the rear ten rows. Beyond a
barricade, the front half of the oval part of the square was
corraled off into numbered enclosures of black plastic
stacking chairs. Behind a gangway running across the middle of the oval, larger pens were fenced off for standing
pilgrims.

Crowds streamed down the Via della Conciliazione. No

random throng of spectators this, but regimented columns walking behind the bearer of their standard—a sign with the name of their parish or convent and their corral number—and displaying their livery: large scarves, mainly the pre-Revolutionary Russian colors of white, blue and red, but some groups with the Ukrainian blue and yellow. The women wore these large scarves on their heads, while the men and the nuns wore them around their shoulders. Most of the columns also carried banners bearing that same image of Saint Nikodim. To Ryan they seemed less like pilgrims and more like cohorts of Roman legionaries returning victoriously to witness the emperor bestow the laurel leaves on their general.

Tinny loudspeakers filled Saint Peter's Square with prerecorded triumphalist hymns while *vigilanze* and stewards directed the cohorts to their numbered enclosures. By a quarter past nine the square was a solid mass of faces and scarves interspersed with parish ensigns and Nikodim banners.

The guests of honor emerged from the Arch of the Bells, on the far side from Ryan, and were guided to their places on either side of the altar by Swiss guards and stewards in morning coats. The director and faculty of the Russicum, bishops, priests, nuns and leading laypeople from the International Center of the Blue Army of Our Lady of Fatima and Russian Catholic Byzantine Rite churches, plus leaders of Russian emigré organizations, took up their unaccustomed places in all but the front two rows of the block to the left of the altar. The Italian Foreign Minister, other government officials, ambassadors from the one hundred and thirteen countries represented at the Holy See, and those Roman noble families who have served the Holy See for countless generations, needed little shepherding to take their places in the block to the right of the altar. Most of the men were dressed in black morning suits, with sashes of office and full decorations, and the women in discreet black dresses, but one man strode to his place in a heavily bemedalled military dress uniform complete with sword, while one beautiful black woman wiggled across in a tight leopardskin dress.

"A major calamity averted," said a voice behind Ryan. "That pompous ass from Guatemala insisted on having one of the cushioned seats. Your dear Derek, bless him, offered his place. I'd give him a knighthood of Saint Gregory if he weren't Church of England."

"I'm surprised to see you," Ryan said to Archbishop Benedetti. "I thought you'd be with the VIPs."

"I prefer the company up here. These saints," Benedetti said, stroking one of the statues, "don't bite back."

By now Saint Peter's Square was full, and the faces and the scarves extended back into the Pius XII Square and beyond, up the Via della Conciliazione.

Ryan shook his head in wonder. "It's impressive."

"So it should be. We've had over sixteen hundred years to perfect it." Benedetti looked down his nose at one of the loudspeakers perched on the roof. "Or fail to perfect it. The Sistine choir want overtime for singing before the mass, and this is Spiazzi's response. If he hadn't joined the Church, he'd be a Calabrian bank clerk like his father."

Ryan peered over the stone balustrade to where the clean-cut director of the Vatican Press Office was leading journalists to their enclosure. "Is Father Frawley English?"

"No, alas. He's the acceptable face of the American clergy. Pity he wasn't born in Salt Lake City, he'd have made a splendid Mormon. Be careful of him, James, be careful."

The loudspeakers stopped their tinny anthems. The crowd stopped its chattering. The choir began to sing, beautifully, the entry hymn, *Veni, sponsa Christi*. The red drapes parted, and the crowd clapped as a procession of altar boys emerged from the basilica into the bright sunlight. The applause increased when the altar boys were followed by two lines of cardinals, each wearing a formal crimson cassock and white lace surplice underneath a crimson *mozetta,* a large shoulder cape. While they took their seats at the front of the left-hand block, the volume of the applause increased at the sight of the cardinals and bishops in their mass vestments of cope and miter—some wearing Byzantine Rite robes. The clapping paused, in expectation of the last concelebrant to emerge from the basilica. But instead of a solitary figure in white cope and miter carrying the crosier of Saint Peter, the red curtains opened to rapturous cheering and clapping, and revealed the Pope accompanied by a tall figure in golden Byzantine miter and cope, broad white *omophor,* and gold-topped staff.

The Pope led his partner to the microphone in front of the altar at the top of the steps, facing the television camera on a gantry that rose from the bottom of the steps. When the last notes of the *Veni, sponsa Christi* died away, the Pope's deep singsong voice echoed throughout the square and into millions of homes across the globe: *"In nomine Patris, et Filii, et Spiritus Sancti. Pax vobis."*

The sound of a quarter of a million voices chanting, *"Et cum spiritu tuo,"* showed the power of the papacy at its most dramatic. Ryan watched, spellbound, as the Pope waved the tumultuous applause to silence before departing from the Rite of Canonization. In Italian now his voice spoke to a hushed stillness.

"Brothers and Sisters, on this most glorious day for the Universal Church and, especially for the Church in the East, we wish you to share our joy in recognizing our Brother in Christ, Andrii Cardinal Chuprynka, as Patriarch of the Ukrainian Catholic Church."

Ryan thought the cheers would be heard in Lvov as the Pope gave the kiss of peace to Chuprynka, who then fell to his knees and kissed the Petrine ring.

"This pope's missed his vocation, of course," Benedetti said. "If he'd gone to Hollywood, he'd have acted Reagan off the screen."

The Pope sat in front of the altar while the Rite of Canonization proceeded. Cardinal Lacey walked up the steps to the Pope's seat, knelt, and offered a red-bound book containing the case for canonization. The Pope touched it. Cardinal Fasolo intoned, "Flectamus genua," and all knelt, while the litany of the saints was chanted. After each saint's name, the throng responded, *"Ora pro nobis."*

Fasolo signaled them to rise: *"Levate."*

The Pope stood, took two steps to the microphone, and pronounced the solemn formula: *". . . auctoritate Domini nostri Iesu Christi, beatorum apostolorum Petri et Pauli ac Nostra, matura deliberatione praehabita et divina ope saepius implorata, ac de plurimorum Fratrum Nostrorum consilio, Nikodimum de Leningrad Sanctum esse decernimus et definimus . . ."*

The rest was drowned by the waves of ecstatic cheering and clapping that rose heavenward from a billowing sea of a quarter of a million white, blue and red scarves. Images of the sainted Nikodim danced above the colors of Holy Russia while the choir fought bravely with the triple *Amen.* The tumult subsided only when the Pope rose again and chanted *"Gloria in excelsis Deo,"* to begin the high mass in honor of the new saint.

"And Stalin was foolish enough to ask how many divisions the Pope had," Benedetti observed.

While the epistles were being read, Benedetti said casually, "James, the Secretariat didn't receive an advance copy of the homily, though I gather the Press Office has one. Have you seen it?"

Ryan hesitated. "The Holy Father wrote it himself, with Monsignor Hoffman's help. I wasn't involved," he said, clumsily avoiding a direct answer.

"I see," said Benedetti. "I think I need a stiff drink." He looked away at the end of the gospel as the Pope went to the microphone.

Silence descended before the deep voice began: "Dear Brothers and Sisters, We celebrate the canonization of a great Russian saint at a time when we are witnessing the greatest upheaval in the East since the Bolsheviks seized power in 1917 and declared Russia to be a Marxist State. That State denied the existence of God and his commandments. It claimed a scientific interpretation of world history to justify all acts, however immoral, which advance the cause of class struggle. In denying God, it denied the dignity of man who is made in God's image. In denying God's commandments, it denied the command to love one another for God's sake. It claimed, instead, an objective historical right to violence. Thus the religion of God made man was challenged by the religion of man who makes himself God.

"While those tragic events were unfolding in Russia, the Blessed Virgin Mary appeared to three innocent children in Fatima and prophesied that, without devotion to her Immaculate Heart through prayer and penance, Russia would spread her errors throughout the world.

"Communism did indeed embark on the path of world domination by force and by deceit. By force it spread across the old Russian empire and beyond, west into central Europe and south into China and Southeast Asia. By deceit it convinced other nations that Godless Marxism was the means of liberating their peoples from the bondage of imperialism and poverty, thus spreading its insidious message to Africa and to Central and South America.

"Those who paid no heed to the Virgin of Fatima feared that nothing could be done to stop its global advance save to meet violence with violence, thus leading to the wars that the Virgin of Fatima predicted. But those who followed her precept to pray to her Immaculate Heart knew that, in the end, their prayers would be answered and her Immaculate Heart would triumph.

"And so it is coming to pass.

"The eyes of those who freely embraced the deceitful doctrines have been opened, and they are abandoning a creed that has brought only hunger, misery, and subjugation to totalitarianism.

"Even more dramatically, those who were forced into the bondage of Communism have thrown off their shackles. Led by Poland, a nation that has remained faithful to Our Blessed Mother throughout centuries of persecution, the prayers of the faithful are causing the walls of Godless

Marxism to fall as surely as the trumpets of Joshua caused the walls of Godless Jericho to fall.

"But we are not gathered here today to celebrate the defeat of a social system. It is not the social aims of Marxism that are in error. It is the Marxist denial of God that reveals the hand of Satan. And let no one think that Godless Marxism can be replaced by Godless materialism, as some in the West would have us believe.

"No, we are gathered here today to celebrate the deep spirituality of the Russian people, a spirituality which has manifested itself in the deeds of its glorious son, Nikodim of Leningrad. Thanks to him, the way has been prepared for the final victory over Satan's Godless domination of the East. The day will come soon when the faithful sons and daughters of Russia will rise up and join with the Universal Church in consecrating their beloved country to the Immaculate Heart of Mary to herald the era of peace which the Virgin of Fatima has promised.

"May God bless all of you here in person and all of you in Russia who are here with us in spirit."

Benedetti sighed. "To misquote Maréchal Bosquet, *C'est magnifique, mais c'est la guerre.* From now on, James, it's war."

Part ✠ Four
WINTER

Chapter ✦ One

IT WAS THE bleakest weekend Kirillin could remember.

During the week he usually processed at least a dozen invitations for the President to come for an informal meal with a family spending the weekend in one of the dacha communities west and southwest of Moscow. The invitations came from members of the Presidential Council, ministers and members of the Central Committee, or from leading intellectuals, writers, and scientists. Occasionally the President—often at his wife's insistence—would accept one, and the lucky host would have an opportunity to impress the President, or to try and gain support for a particular project, while the President felt he was keeping his finger on the pulse of the nation. Usually the invitations were politely declined, but the offers of hospitality noted: they provided some indication of the President's stock among the *vlasti*, the élite of Soviet society. This week, for the first time, there had not been a single invitation.

On Monday the Russian Popular Front had staged a large demonstration in Pushkin Square. The same people who, not long since, had carried portraits of the President and demanded the implementation of *perestroika*, now carried pictures of the Pope, demanded freedom, and claimed that the Pope supported their calls for an end to Communism.

In the Supreme Soviet Filipchenko had confidently predicted that the previous week's Great October Revolution Parade would be the last to be seen in Red Square. The one planned for Kiev had been abandoned when the tanks had been daubed with blue and yellow paint, and demonstrators waving banners proclaiming *Russian Occupiers Go Home* had blocked Kreshchatik.

At Thursday's Presidential Council meeting Ulanov had delivered what was termed a formal request from the General Staff that political action be taken to prevent the country from sliding into anarchy; he had warned that the Army faced a potentially fatal collapse of morale if its troops were expected to stand by and do nothing while hooligans insulted them and threw paint at them.

By Friday evening the President was on the point of nervous exhaustion. Kirillin had persuaded him to take no papers to his Usovo villa and to try and catch up on his sleep. Kirillin himself hadn't slept.

Now, on a gray Saturday morning, he walked over frost-hardened ruts in the pine groves of Zhukovka. Gray clouds hung low over gray fields and a gray Moscow River. Large flakes of snow, like goose down, were falling. Soon the Moscow River would freeze over.

Were Russians congenitally incapable of forging the democratic socialist society the President was offering them? How many times had he told them that the future lay in their hands? That neither he nor the Government could solve their problems for them? That he was releasing their energies, initiatives, and creativities, which had been suppressed by every leader since Stalin, so that they could solve their own problems within a socially just and responsible society? Now, it seemed, half of them wanted to retreat to the certainties of an all-powerful leader, while the other half wanted to throw out everything—all the good things that socialism had brought—and embrace the free market jungle of capitalism where only the fittest survived. Or was it that the Russians, who had never experienced democracy, simply needed more time to mature?

But there was precious little time before the two conflicting forces tore Russia apart. He was at a loss to know what more the President could do.

Back at the dacha, watching the snow fall more heavily, he dialed a Zavidovo number and said, "It'll be fine by two o'clock on Monday."

At the Trinity Tower Gate Kirillin pulled up his collar. Three crones, swaddled in layers of black clothing, were using witches' broomsticks to sweep the snow from the bridge leading down to the Kufta Tower Gate. Below, hooded crows were protesting noisily at the white carpet that covered their feeding grounds in the Alexander Garden.

He waited in the shelter of the Kufta Tower Gate while a snow-clearing truck churned its way down Manezhnaya Street. Parallel with Manezhnaya, the busy Marx Prospekt showed little sign of the overnight snowfall: only the terrace in front of the light gray, columned Lenin State Library, at the junction of Marx and Kalinin Prospekts, was covered with slush.

Kirillin turned down the first street on the right off Kalinin Prospekt. A drab beige building on Granovsky Street bore a plaque: *In this building on 19 April 1919 Vladimir Ilyich Lenin spoke before the commanders of the Red Army left for the front.* The painted-over windows revealed nothing. A sign by the door warned that entry was by special permit only.

Inside, Kirillin was reaching for a bottle when a voice behind said, "1977 was a poor year. That's why the French send it here, they think Russians have no taste." Babakin grinned. "They're right, of course. I'd recommend the '82, and if you think it's too expensive, try the Chateau Palmer.

It's next to Chateau Margaux, shares the same soil and aspect, but not the same public relations firm."

Kirillin took a Palmer '82, though it would devour a large slice of his monthly Kremlin ration and he had little to celebrate.

The checkout girl of the privilege shop, which resembled a small Western supermarket rather than the uninviting counters, empty shelves, and triple queuing of the State shops, took Kirillin's identification, noted his monthly allowance, calculated the total on an abacus, and gave him a receipt plus a brown paper bag for the wine and the four bottles of Stolichnaya 100. He glanced back at Babakin's purchases, but they had already disappeared into a brown paper bag.

"Ukrainian Solidarity has refused to budge," Kirillin said. "According to Konovalets, its idea of negotiation is to put its demands on the table and expect the other side to agree them in full."

Babakin's eyes darted round the shop. "Let's talk somewhere less noticeable. Your apartment's not far. I'll give you fifteen minutes."

Babakin put his brown paper bag in the boot of the Volga, which was parked over the curb near a "No Parking" sign, nodded to the militiaman, and walked on, down snow-cleared Kalinin Prospekt until he reached the Praga Restaurant at Arbat Square. He strolled down the pedestrianized Arbat Street, the home of royal servants in the sixteenth century, then of aristocracy, then of merchants, then of intelligentsia, and now of the beneficiaries of Moscow's 1980s conservationist lobby: bookshops, cafés, art shops, and tourist attractions. Babakin stopped. Five people were sitting around a brazier in the center of the street. Signs round their necks proclaimed they were on hunger strike to protest against the repression of the Ukrainian Catholic Church. Babakin looked angrily round for a militiaman, but none was to be seen.

He strode on, turned down Starokonyushenny Lane,

and reached the new apartment block at the junction with Sivtsev Vrashek Lane.

He spent five minutes questioning the *dezhurnaya*, who kept watch from her desk in the lobby, before he took the lift up to Kirillin's apartment.

Babakin surveyed the decor in the warm, centrally heated apartment while he removed his gloves and coat. "Well, Dmitry Sergeyevich, this is rather splendid."

"So I thought until I saw how guests of the Ukrainian First Secretary are accommodated," Kirillin said drily. "Vodka, or do you only drink claret?"

Babakin grinned. "On a day as cold as this, vodka."

Kirillin poured the drinks and sat back in a brown leather armchair. "What precisely did the Pope mean when he said the day will soon come when the faithful sons and daughters of Russia will rise up?"

Babakin made himself comfortable in the matching armchair. He stretched out his legs. "I don't know," he said reflectively. "This Pope doesn't make idle speculations. He's planning something. My guess is either a mass demonstration in Moscow with that damned Icon of Kazan, or else part of the Russian Orthodox clergy will announce their allegiance to Rome, or possibly both."

"The icon is a fraud. My secretary says the original is in the Church of Our Lady of Kazan in Kolomenskoye."

Babakin's smile was half sneer. "On the contrary, the icons in Kolomenskoye and in the Kazan Cathedral in Leningrad are copies."

Kirillin refilled the glasses. "Superstitious claptrap. What does it matter, anyway, which is the original icon?"

Babakin ignored his drink. "It matters a great deal. According to believers, only the original icon performs miracles."

Kirillin poured himself a third glass. "I'll start believing in miracles when the Russian Orthodox Church pledges allegiance to Rome. You told me that many of the Orthodox clergy are secret Catholics. But let me tell *you* something, Lev Stepanovich. The Orthodox hierarchy refuse to hand over a single church in the Ukraine to the Catholics, and so the Catholics are taking them over by force. Konovalets fears that it could turn into another Nagorno Karabakh, or even a Lebanon. I telephoned the Patriarch and all he'd say is that whatever happens is God's will." He swallowed his third glass in one gulp. "I want the KGB to *order* them to hand over a few churches peaceably, just to get the Ukrainian negotiations moving. If not, Ukrainian Solidarity will bring out the miners again and the country will have no heating this winter. And that really could bring down the Government."

"Ah," said Babakin before finishing his vodka and holding out his glass for a refill. "That's not so simple."

"Why not? I've seen how that thug Grechko orders them about."

"First, you must understand that the clandestine Catholics among the Orthodox clergy are those trained at only one of three Russian Orthodox seminaries, and they come from the generation after Nikodim. The people running the show in the Patriarchate—the people you have to deal with over Church property—are from Nikodim's generation, nearly all anti-Western and Furov Category One."

"Furov what?"

Babakin grinned. "It's a classification devised by a former Deputy Chairman of the Council for Religious Affairs that defines their degree of loyalty to the State. Naturally, only Category One, together with some token Category Two people, are appointed to positions of influence."

"If they're so bloody loyal, tell them loyally to hand over some churches."

Babakin leaned back back in his chair, elbows on the armrests and the tips of his long fingers pressed together. His bald head gleamed. "Put yourself in their shoes, Dmitry Sergeyevich. The Russian Orthodox Church has always been a tool of the Russian State. The pagan Grand Prince Vladimir adopted Byzantine Christianity and forcibly converted his people as part of a deal by which he mar-

ried the Byzantine Emperor's sister and formed an alliance
to consolidate the State of Kievan Rus.

"The State, aided by the Church, transplanted the Byzantine concept of a divinely protected autocracy to Russian
soil and fostered Russian patriotism. All went well until Patriarch Nikon got too big for his boots. So Peter the Great
abolished the Patriarchate and replaced it with a Holy
Synod presided over by his agent, effectively making the
Church a department of State. That lasted for two hundred
years until the Revolution. Before the Bolsheviks seized
power, Church leaders met and elected a Patriarch. At first
Patriarch Tikhon attacked the new Soviet State but," Babakin grinned, "after a few months in the Lubyanka he became a committed supporter of the new Russian
Government."

"Splendid," said Kirillin drily, and refilled the glasses. "I
still don't see why . . ."

Babakin waved the index finger of his right hand.
"Those who don't understand the lessons of history are
doomed to repeat the mistakes of history. When Tikhon
died, Stalin forbade a successor. He launched a bloody
campaign to eliminate religion, and closed down 95 percent of Orthodox churches. But Stalin wasn't stupid. By
1943 the War was going badly. Stalin summoned the three
remaining metropolitans to the Kremlin in the early hours
of the morning. The poor bastards thought they were going
to be shot. Instead, Stalin told them to elect one of themselves patriarch and mobilize the Russian people against
the Western hordes who were threatening the Russian
Motherland. The Church raised enough money to equip an
armored division of the Red Army, and sent hundreds of
thousands of volunteers to the front. Frankly, without the
Church's support, I doubt whether we'd have withstood
the German advance."

"So," Kirillin shrugged, finishing his glass, "the Church
leaders are patriots."

"They are *Russian* patriots. Remember that. After the
War Stalin was faced with resistance from Ukrainian na-

tionalists, led by the Ukrainian Catholic Church. So he abolished the Ukrainian Catholic Church, killed most of its leaders, sent its priests to the camps, and handed its parishes over to the Russian Orthodox Church. Stalin told the Moscow Patriarchate this was their reward for supporting the Great Patriotic War, and they were duly grateful. In fact he was using them to implement a policy of russification: only approved Russian nationalists were appointed to the Orthodox hierarchy in the Ukraine. A neat solution, don't you think?"

"It may have been fifty years ago," Kirillin said, "but not in the nineties."

"Patience," Babakin chided. "Remember the lessons of history. Khrushchev built his party career in the Ukraine," he continued. "He was confident the KGB and the Russian Orthodox Church between them had succeeded in crushing the national spirit in the Ukraine. So, when he took over the Kremlin, he decided the Church had outlived its usefulness and he launched yet another campaign to eliminate it. After Khrushchev's fall, the KGB kept the Church's Foreign Department going as a useful propaganda machine, and eased off the persecution internally while still keeping strict control.

"When *perestroika* began to run into sand, we decided to learn from Grand Prince Vladimir, Peter the Great, and Stalin, and use the Russian Orthodox Church to mobilize support for *perestroika.*"

"*We* decided?" Kirillin queried.

"I wrote the policy paper that first suggested it. It was very tenable theologically," Babakin continued. "Praise the virtues of hard work and the family, condemn the evils of alcohol and theft, and join the moral restructuring of society. The price was rehabilitating the Church once more." Babakin held out his glass for a refill. "The hierarchy have never had it so good since Stalin gave them the Ukraine. We supply the Patriarch with a new bullet-proof Zil every year, just like the President's own. The Supreme Soviet passes a new law on freedom of conscience. The Government removes administrative restrictions. The result? Churches are reopened and the money rolls in from the faithful. The Church is now the richest institution outside the State. The Metropolitan of Kiev has a palace in Kiev, a villa in Odessa, and an apartment in Moscow."

"Let them show their gratitude by giving up a few parishes."

"Not these guys," Babakin said. "Now they're out of shit and into clover, they don't want to let go. Over half their income comes from the Ukraine. They may be spineless but they're not fools. They know they've got the backing of Russian nationalists like Blagov and Grechko in the KGB, and Korolev and friends in the Presidential Council."

"The President runs this country," said Kirillin angrily, "not Blagov or Korolev."

Babakin raised his eyebrows. "The Patriarchate have done their sums and they think they can count on the President's support: sixty million Orthodox against five million Ukrainian Catholic nationalist extremists. He's got to go with them, especially when his position is not exactly at its strongest."

"You've forgotten one thing," Kirillin said. "They haven't delivered on *perestroika.*"

"Good," said Babakin approvingly. "And the reason?"

"You tell me."

"The Patriarchate have lost their credibility among the masses. They're perceived as a tool of the Communist State. That's why a defection of lower level Orthodox clergy to Rome could take a hell of a lot of believers with them."

Kirillin poured himself another glass. "Now tell me the good news."

Babakin smiled. "The good news is that the Patriarchate are still doing their sums on an abacus. They've come up with the wrong result."

Kirillin looked at the smiling face. He thought Babakin must have drunk too much. "What, according to you, is the correct result?"

"My computer tells me that sixty million Russian Orthodox don't outweigh 900 million Catholics."

The vodka was slowing Kirillin's mind. "You're going to
kill the Pope."

Babakin shrugged. "Knock one pope down and up pops
another."

"What *are* you suggesting?"

Babakin gave that grin which was half smile and half
baring of teeth. "Instead of playing with the tiddlers in the
small pond, we play with the big fish in the ocean. We control the Catholic Church."

"You must be mad."

"It's an idea I've been toying with for some time. Think
about it. The ecclesiastical policy of Grand Prince Vladimir, Peter the Great, and Stalin applied on a global scale.
Apart from solving the Ukrainian Catholic problem and
swinging the moral authority of the Catholic Church behind *perestroika,* do you know how many European heads
of government are Catholic? How many South American
presidents have to carry the Catholic Church with them?
How many American congressmen are dependent on the
Catholic vote?"

"Sure," said Kirillin, pouring out the last of the Stolichnaya, "it's a nice dream over a bottle of vodka. But I have to
live in the real world."

Babakin picked up his glass and swirled the contents
round. His voice was confident. "My role, Dmitry Sergeyevich, is to make your dreams come true."

Kirillin realized that Babakin was serious. That sobered
him up.

"You've lived in Rome," Babakin continued. "You know
the score. The Catholic Church doesn't owe allegiance to
any one country, only to God. Control God and you control
the most important single piece on the world chess board."

"God hasn't put in many appearances over the last two
thousand years," Kirillin muttered.

"Unlike our dear leader, he never exposes himself. It all
adds to the mystique. But he's got a well-oiled party ma-

chine, and his Vicar on Earth speaks with his authority. That's what makes it so easy. We don't have to bother with parliaments or other messy democratic bodies. Control God's pope and we control God's church."

Babakin was making it sound feasible. "You really believe you can do it?"

"Sure. In the past we've controlled a head of Britain's M16, a deputy director of the CIA, an Italian prime minister . . ."

"How?"

Babakin grinned. "Everybody has a hidden crack in his head. It's simply a matter of finding the crack and widening it. There isn't a person born who's not susceptible to money, ideology, coercion, or ego. We select our man, identify the particular crack, widen it, and then ensure he gets the job we need him in."

"I knew there'd be a flaw. OK, you nobble a cardinal, it's been done before. But how do you get him made pope?"

Babakin stood up, and put on his coat and gloves. "Don't expect me to tell you every trick of the trade. But do you really believe it's the Holy Spirit inspiring those guys in red frocks how to vote? I'd enjoy the challenge. Let me know whether to go ahead. *Ciao.*"

Kirillin watched him go. He went and brewed a pot of strong black coffee, and started making notes. The phone rang.

"Sorry to disturb you," his secretary said, "but you did tell the Minister for Power that you wanted the information as soon as possible."

"Yes, yes."

"Well, he says he thinks that, on average, the stocks of coal at the generating stations might last till Christmas."

"Christmas?"

"The end of the year."

Kirillin took a deep breath. "I asked him for precise figures. What does he mean, 'thinks,' 'on average,' 'might'?"

"He did apologize. He says there's a problem with the

Ministry computer which makes accurate forecasts rather difficult."

"I see. Well, thanks for letting me know. And Petya . . ."

"Yes?"

"Don't look to the icon at Kolomenskoye for a miracle."

"Pardon?"

"Forget it."

He put the phone down, completed his notes, and went to his desk. Out of the window he saw the snow falling. The meteorologists were predicting another bitterly cold winter. He unlocked a drawer, pulled out a file, and put it on the desk. He put his notes in the file, after Vitaly Mazunov's proposed solution to the impending economic collapse, and the draft secret agreement between the European Community and Poland.

He knew what his answer to Babakin would be.

Chapter ✦ Two

ARCHBISHOP BENEDETTI'S VOICE on the telephone sounded unusually grave. Ryan apologized and said that he wasn't free for dinner on Saturday evening.

"James, this is not, alas, a purely social invitation. Somebody has asked to meet you to help prevent a crisis in the Church."

When Ryan arrived at the Palazzina della Zecca at seven-thirty, Benedetti's valet led him to a dark blue Fiat from the Vatican car pool and said that His Excellency would be joining him immediately.

"James, it was good of you to come," said Benedetti as he settled into the back seat next to Ryan. The archbishop was dressed with an unaccustomed lack of color; only a silver pectoral cross decorated a black clerical suit.

"Did I have any choice, Excellency?"

Benedetti patted his knee. "Out of the office, please call me Antonio. I knew you would respond."

The car circled round the back of the basilica, left the Vatican through the Arch of the Bells, and turned right to sweep past the forbidding façade of the Palace of the Holy Office, which housed Cardinal Zingler and the Sacred Congregation for the Doctrine of the Faith.

"Am I permitted to ask where we're going?" Ryan asked, dropping the "Excellency" but not feeling comfortable with "Antonio."

"Indeed," replied Benedetti. "The Villa Stritch." But Benedetti wouldn't be drawn further on whom they were to meet there, saying that all would be revealed soon enough.

Fifteen minutes after leaving the Vatican, Benedetti's valet parked the car outside a building that resembled a Holiday Inn. Benedetti and he were led by a young American priest to an apartment on the top floor.

The priest who opened the door was big and rough-hewn and, Ryan guessed, late middle-aged. The top of his head was completely bald, and the gray hair at the sides short-cropped, yet the shoulders of his black jacket were speckled with dandruff. Gray, oddly blank eyes gazed out from a pockmarked face. "Hi, there," he said to Benedetti. He nodded toward Ryan. "This your man?" A large hand engulfed Ryan's. "Pleased to meet with you, James."

"James," Benedetti said with deliberate ostentation, "permit me to introduce Michael Cardinal Fallon, Archbishop of Chicago."

"Michael will do fine," the big man said. "Whaddya drink?"

"A scotch," Benedetti replied.

"The same for me," Ryan said.

Fallon went to a cocktail cabinet in the corner of the room. He poured two scotches plus a large Jack Daniels for himself.

"No ice, please," Ryan said quickly before a large handful of ice cubes was emptied into all three glasses.

"They're bringing dinner up in half an hour," Fallon said as he lowered himself into an easy chair. "Siddown."

Ryan looked round the lounge. The building was Holiday Inn on the inside as well as the outside.

"James doesn't know why he's here," Benedetti said.

Fallon nodded. He tamped tobacco into a meerschaum pipe and took a gold cigarette lighter from his pocket. As he held the flame above the pipe bowl and sucked, his unblinking eyes studied Ryan. "We gotta problem, James," he said between puffs. "A big problem. The National Conference of Catholic Bishops is gonna vote to reject the Pope's instruction to submit all its documents on faith or morals to the Sacred Congregation for the Doctrine of the Faith."

He drew deeply on the lighted pipe and watched Ryan's reactions. "I told 'em just to acknowledge the Pope's letter, lie low for twelve months, and then carry on as before. The thing'd die a natural death. But they saw it as a matter of principle and insisted on taking a stand. I warned Francesco that would happen if Zingler's draft became official."

"Archbishop Francesco Casale," Benedetti explained, "our pro-nuncio in Washington. Cardinal Fasolo strongly urged the Holy Father not to send Zingler's letter but," he shrugged, "the Holy Father didn't seem to appreciate the implications. Cardinal Fasolo tried to find you, but you were on holiday in Poland."

Ryan blushed. So neither the Secretary of State nor Archbishop Benedetti knew of his mission to the Ukraine. "I don't know what I can do," he said.

"You're close to the Holy Father," Fallon said. "You gotta make him understand that Zingler's driving the American Church toward breaking with Rome."

"Monsignor Hoffman is much closer to the Holy Father," Ryan said.

"Cardinal Fasolo tried to reason with him," Benedetti said, "but Hoffman was too arrogant to listen."

"He's actually a very humble man," Ryan said loyally.

Benedetti raised his eyebrows. "There's arrogance in too much humility."

"Perhaps Archbishop Korchan?" Ryan suggested.

Benedetti and Fallon looked at each other. "Look, James," Fallon said, "the Holy Father's eyes seem fixed on the east. I understand you spent three years in the States. You know the scene. People like Brown . . ."

"Archbishop Joseph Brown of Seattle, President of the United States Bishops' Conference," Benedetti interjected.

"Brown and company are saying they can see no theological reasons why women can't be ordained priests, and so forth. Me? I don't go for all that crap. I've always been loyal to the Holy Father. But," he leaned forward and pointed the stem of his pipe toward Ryan, "if I were to get up in my pulpit and announce that the priests of my archdiocese have been instructed to refuse communion to all those who continue to take the pill, then let me tell you, James, my churches would be empty." He sat back. "Of priests as well as parishioners."

"It's not just a theological matter," Benedetti said.

"Too damn right," Fallon agreed. Those gray eyes stared straight at Ryan. "The Archdiocese of Chicago has a bigger turnover than the whole of the Vatican."

"What Cardinal Fallon is saying," Benedetti added swiftly, "is that if the North American Church were forced to cut off its donations to the Vatican, the Holy See would be bankrupt within the year."

"I still don't know what I can do," Ryan said.

"OK," Fallon nodded understandingly. "In the old days we'd simply get hold of our most senior man in the Vatican and ask him to bend the Holy Father's ear. But that guy happens to be William Lacey."

"I'm sure Cardinal Lacey would try his hardest," Ryan said. "He's an honorable man."

"So was Brutus," Benedetti observed.

Fallon shook his large head. "I even hear talk that the Holy Father wants to send Lacey to take over New York. How out of touch can a pope get? Doesn't he understand that New York is positively the last place on earth to send a creep like Lacey? The chancery simply wouldn't have him. Period."

"What do you want me to do?" Ryan asked.

Fallon re-lit his pipe. "I'm here for three days. It's unofficial. Brown doesn't know." He blew out a stream of blue-gray smoke and fixed Ryan with those strangely expressionless eyes. "I don't think it's in the Pope's interest or our interest to allow this thing to go any further. We gotta come to some sort of deal. If the Holy Father will take Zingler off our backs, I'll do my damnedest to keep the Church in the US loyal to Rome. But," he pointed the stem of his pipe once more at Ryan, "I don't go in cold. You gotta soften him up for me." He sat back. "Do we have a deal?"

"I'll try my best," Ryan said.

In bed that night Ryan tossed and turned. He was just beginning to grasp the significance of what Fallon had told him. Schism between Rome and the Church in north America would be the most disastrous event since the Reformation. Worse, the most disastrous since the split between the Western Church and the Byzantine Church in the eleventh century. If the bishops of north America did reject the authority of the Pope, most of the bishops in south America would surely follow. Their theology might be a world away from that of their affluent northern neighbors, but they shared a resentment at being told what to do by people in Rome. They felt the Curia simply had no understanding of how the gospel message had to be applied to the dispossessed masses of their continent. And how soon after that would the Churches in Africa and Asia rebel against the imposition of Roman tradition on their native cultures? The responsibility that Fallon and Benedetti had placed on his shoulders terrified him. He climbed out of bed, dressed, and crept down to the Pope's private chapel.

He didn't switch on the lights, but kneeled there, bathed by the flickering glow of the candle in the red votive lamp above the altar. In the shining black-streaked white marble floor the lamp's reflection glimmered like tongues of infernal fire. Demon-like shadows danced behind the bronze saints on the walls. Without the broad white-cassocked back to fill it, the gray prie-dieu in the center of the chapel seemed insubstantial, abandoned to the night. Only the face of the Madonna, to the right of the altar, remained serene in her suffering. Ryan prayed that she might give him the strength to help heal the rift in her Son's Church, to reconcile the bishops of the world with the first of the bishops who was her devoted servant.

Watching the image of the Mother of God that both the Pope and Hoffman revered, it occurred to Ryan that, whatever he might say to the Holy Father, the Pope would talk it over with Hoffman. It was essential to win Kasamir Hoffman's support. Cardinal Fasolo had failed, but the two men held each other in mutual contempt. Ryan threatened neither. Ryan thanked the Blessed Virgin for showing him the way and, eyes fixed on the icon, he continued praying. He never noticed the darkness fading nor even the white figure kneeling at the prie-dieu.

Chapter ✣ Three

RYAN'S OPPORTUNITY TO enlist Kasamir Hoffman's support in trying to prevent a schism with the Church in America came later that day. As on most Sundays, the Pope went out at four o'clock in the afternoon to visit one of the city's parishes in his capacity as Bishop of Rome. That left Ryan alone with Hoffman, mellowed by a large Polish Sunday lunch.

Ryan suggested they go for a walk in the Vatican Gardens. The weather was what Ryan's mother would have called healthy. The sun, hanging low over the Vatican Hill, was bright but lacking warmth. The leaves were browning and falling in the breeze that blew from the Vatican Museums. Hoffman, wrapped in long black overcoat and black scarf, led Ryan at a brisk pace to his favorite part of the gardens, going north from the Governor's Palace through a thickly wooded hill above the Vatican Museums, past a waterfall that coursed down a bouldered slope, and up to a clearing containing a Roman wayside shrine. The statue of a goddess had been replaced by one of the Mother of God.

Hoffman, breathing heavily, motioned Ryan to sit down next to him on a bench sheltered from the breeze by a row of fir trees. "Well, James, what's troubling you?" he asked kindly.

"I've been thinking about the Church in the United States," Ryan began.

"Ah yes," said Hoffman. "The Holy Father finds it painful to read of such lack of guidance on moral questions by so many people who occupy positions of great responsibility. The devil does everything in his power to seduce the leaders of the Church from the One Truth."

"You know I lived in America for three years."

Hoffman nodded understandingly. "You must have seen all these things at first hand."

"There are very many good people in America, Kasamir."

"Indeed. It is to protect the good people that the Holy Father sent his letter to the American bishops. We must do our utmost to ensure that the people of America receive the authentic teaching of Christ's Church."

Ryan picked up a twig and traced a path in the dirt. "I'm not sure how the American bishops will respond to that. It would be a tragedy if there were to be a breakdown in relations between Rome and the United States."

Hoffman gave a deep sigh. "A tragedy, yes, but one that we have been expecting."

Ryan looked up to the square face, the thrust-out jaw, the beady eyes behind the steel-framed spectacles. "Why on earth do you say that, Kasamir?"

Hoffman's voice was soft, and yet it was filled with an unnerving certainty. "Sister Lucia has made it clear that the Secrets revealed to her by Our Lady of Fatima mean that we have entered the last times of the world, the times of the final rebellion against God."

Ryan hesitated. "I'm not sure I understand. The First Secret was a vision of hell together with a promise that sinners could be saved by devotion to the Immaculate Heart of Mary. The Second Secret was a prophecy of the sufferings that would be caused by Communism together with a promise that peace would be granted when Russia was converted back to Christianity. But I don't recall anything about the last times."

Hoffman studied the young priest, and then made a decision. "James," he said, "do you remember the wooden chest on the Holy Father's desk in his private study?"

"The locked one, next to the crucifix by the window?"

"It contains the Third Secret of Fatima."

"The Secret that Sister Lucia asked the Pope to reveal in 1960?"

Hoffman nodded. "Pope John XXIII decided that it was too horrifying to make public."

"Wasn't that because it prophesied mass destruction by nuclear war, or something like that?"

Hoffman shook his head slowly. "It was something far more terrible than that."

"Kasamir, I . . . I don't understand."

"Why do you think, James, that Pope John instituted the Feast of Our Lady of the Rosary of Fatima, and called the apparition 'the center of all Christian hopes'? Why do you think he summoned the Second Vatican Council?"

"The Council was convened to renew the Church, to adapt it to the modern world."

"Not to adapt it to the modern world!" Hoffman was vehement. "That is the error perpetrated by dupes of Satan! After he read the Third Secret, the good Pope John summoned an ecumenical council to renew the Church in order to strengthen the faith, so that the Church might withstand the final assault he knew was coming. That is why Satan tried to subvert the Second Vatican Council, to seduce so-called liberal theologians into questioning the fundamental truths of Christianity. After the Council Pope Paul VI was moved to say that 'the smoke of Satan has entered the Church.' "

Ryan felt bemused, as though Hoffman's words were coming from a distance. He wondered if it was because he hadn't slept the previous night. "Have you read the Third Secret, Kasamir?" he asked hesitantly.

"Of those still alive," Hoffman said, "only His Holiness

and Cardinal Zingler have read Sister Lucia's transcription
of the Blessed Virgin's own words. But the Holy Father has
told me that the Third Secret reinforces the accounts in
Scripture of the last times of the world, and warns of the
signs that indicate the world is nearing its end."

Ryan looked around. The statue of Our Lady. The Vatican Hill preparing for winter. The dome of the basilica, the
Eternal City, preparing for . . . for eternity? Now? "Can
you be sure, Kasamir? Really sure?"

Hoffman nodded slowly. "We can be sure from the apparition at Fatima that the woman clothed in the sun who
confronts the red dragon in the Book of Revelation is the
Mother of God fighting on our behalf against Satan. At
Fatima the Blessed Virgin identified the First Beast of
the Apocalypse as Communist Russia, the creature of
Satan that attempts to impose its Godless tyranny on the
world. As she prophesied, devotion to her Immaculate
Heart is now wounding this First Beast: the Communist
empire outside Russia is being destroyed. But after the
First Beast comes the Second Beast of the Apocalypse,
the false prophet that deceives the people and heals the
wound of the First Beast. These are the last days of the
world."

He took a pocket Bible from his overcoat pocket. It
fell open at a well-thumbed page, and Hoffman began
reading:

> As Jesus sat on the Mount of Olives, the disciples
> came to him in private. "Tell us when all this will be,"
> they asked, "and what will happen to show that it is
> the time for your coming and the end of the world."
> Jesus answered, "Be on your guard and do not let
> anyone deceive you. Many men, claiming to speak for
> me, will come . . . Many will give up their faith at that
> time; they will betray one another and hate one an-
> other. Many false prophets will appear and deceive
> many people . . . You will see the Awful Horror of
> which the prophet Daniel spoke. It will be standing in
> the holy place."

"Matthew, Chapter 24, which is repeated in Mark, Chapter 13 and Luke, Chapter 21," Hoffman said. He turned the pages of the Bible. "In his second epistle to Timothy the Apostle Paul describes how people will behave in the last days of the world:

> *The time will come when people will not listen to sound doctrine, but will follow their own desires and will collect for themselves more and more teachers who will tell them what they are itching to hear. They will turn away from listening to the truth.*

"Now do you understand, James, that we should not be surprised to read of American bishops teaching that homosexuality, artificial contraception, and even abortion, are matters of personal conscience? That the Church in America rebels against the teaching authority of Christ's Vicar on earth?

"As for the precise time," Hoffman said, "the Apostle is very specific in his second epistle to the Thessalonians:

> *That day cannot come before the final rebellion takes place, when wickedness will be revealed in human form, the man doomed to destruction. He is the adversary who raises himself up against every so-called god or object of worship, and even enthrones himself in God's temple, claiming to be God.*"

He closed the Bible. "In the Third Secret of Fatima the Blessed Virgin says that we have entered the last days of the world, and urges us to read what Scripture tells us about the signs. We must help prepare the Church, James, to withstand the final rebellion before Christ's Second Coming. We must guard against the adversary who enthrones himself in God's temple."

Chapter ✣ Four

RYAN HAD PERSUADED Bishop Spiazzi to fit Cardinal Fallon in at the end of the individual audiences on the Monday morning.

At half-past twelve, after the audience, Fallon came up the stairs from the State library on the second floor and, without knocking, pushed open the door to the office shared by Hoffman and Ryan. His large frame, draped in plain black clerical suit, almost filled the doorway. Long arms hung at his sides, hands opened loosely as though ready to draw six-shooters from invisible holsters fixed to the black belt with a silver and pearl buckle revealed by the open jacket. Gray unblinking eyes, narrowed to slits, peered at Ryan. "Don't anyone ever say I didn't try." He turned and walked out.

Hoffman looked at Ryan over the top of his spectacles. "I doubt that he'll be joining us for lunch today."

The one person who did join them at lunch was Archbishop Korchan. He'd just received bad news from Kiev. The round table talks had reached deadlock over the restoration of Ukrainian Catholic Church property seized by Stalin in 1946. Hoffman said that if the Soviet Government were sincere about wanting a just solution in the Ukraine it would simply order the Russian Orthodox to hand over the churches.

The following morning Hoffman and Korchan went to visit the Ukrainian Patriarch at his offices in the Piazza Madonna dei Monti, leaving Ryan alone in the private secretaries' office.

Ryan picked up the green phone on its second ring. Before he could speak, a commanding Italian voice asked in English, "Father James Ryan?"

"Yes."

"Luigi Bergantino here. I wish to take you to dinner."

Ryan hesitated. Bergantino was not only the doyen of the Vatican press corps, he was also a Communist.

"Do you have to ask Fasolo's permission to eat dinner?"

Ryan smiled. "No. But I'm afraid that I'm occupied most evenings for supper."

"You are free tomorrow evening. Rasella's at nine o'clock?"

Ryan looked at his diary. Instead of taking supper with his two private secretaries as usual, on Wednesday evening the Pope, accompanied by Kasamir Hoffman and Archbishop Korchan, was having a private dinner at the Russicum. Ryan was intrigued. "OK."

"Good."

Ryan leaned back in his chair. His first instinct was to phone Father Frawley and find out more about Luigi Bergantino. Then he remembered Benedetti's warning, which had been reinforced by Andrew Grimes. According to Grimes, Frawley was zealous in his mission to put across the views of the Holy Father, or what he saw as the views of the Holy Father, and he had ways of dealing with officials who, in his opinion, differed from those views or who communicated with journalists without going through him. Off the record briefings to his trusties in the press had damaged the careers of several senior Vatican officials.

Ryan doubted that Frawley could add much to Grimes's gossip. Bergantino was the Vatican correspondent of *L'Unità,* the Communist daily. He was regarded by the unprejudiced few in Rome as the most informed and objective of the Vatican press corps. More importantly, as far as Ryan was concerned, Grimes had said that Bergantino was a frequent traveler to Russia and was on first name terms with the Soviet President. It *might* be coincidence that this invitation had come the day after the Holy Father had learnt that the Ukrainian round table talks had reached deadlock. On the other hand . . .

Ryan pursed his lips. There was no need to inform Frawley or Fasolo. All he had to do was give nothing away and see what he could discover that might be of use to the Holy Father.

Ryan arrived at Rasella's promptly at nine o'clock. A shirt-sleeved man of indeterminate age, who had the lined face and powerful shoulders and arms of a peasant, ushered him to a discreet table for two at the back of the restaurant. An uncorked bottle of a 1982 Chianti Classico, a bottle of white wine in an ice bucket, and four glasses stood on the white tablecloth. This was not typical of the trattorias Ryan knew.

"Would Father like a drink while he waits for Signor Bergantino?" the proprietor asked.

Ryan nodded and put his hand over the wine glasses. "A mineral water, please."

"Certainly, Father."

The proprietor returned with a tray holding a bottle of Clavdia and a tall narrow glass almost full with ice cubes. When he left, Ryan fished out the slice of lemon and several ice cubes with his fingers and put them in the ashtray before pouring the sparkling clear liquid into the glass. He settled down to wait.

It was nearly half past nine when an untidily but expensively dressed man entered the restaurant and made straight for Ryan's table. The man was late middle-aged, short and thickset. His opened jacket revealed a large paunch, and yet he moved swiftly and almost gracefully.

"Do forgive me," he bowed by way of introduction. "Some young night editor neither understood nor appreciated fine literary style. I don't know what's become of our education system."

"I admired your article yesterday about the Soviet leader's attitude to religious freedom in the Ukraine," said Ryan as the older man sat down.

Luigi Bergantino nodded acknowledgment as he filled up two wine glasses with white wine. "It's good that the Pope's office sees a decent newspaper from time to time."

"I particularly admired the way such a frank and open article managed to say absolutely nothing," Ryan continued.

Bergantino put down the bottle and stared at Ryan. A big smile spread across his face. He opened his hands wide. "I have been an assiduous student of the Vatican for over twenty-five years. What better teacher could a man ask for?"

"How did you know that my diary was free this evening?"

Bergantino looked suspiciously around the restaurant before leaning toward Ryan and saying in a low, confidential voice. "I will reveal to you one of my great secrets." When he had Ryan's full attention, he whispered, "I guessed!" He leaned back in his chair and burst out laughing. "I know where the Pope is eating tonight. When he eats out, he takes only one of his private secretaries with him, and I don't imagine your Russian is too fluent."

Ryan joined in laughing at the man's disarming delight with his own subterfuge. Bergantino gestured toward his glass. Ryan tasted the wine. "It's good. Better than the Frascati we're always served."

"Of course it's good. The vineyard is owned by a good Communist."

"Tell me, Signor Bergantino . . ."

"Luigi!" demanded the journalist.

Ryan couldn't help liking the man, who was much more Italian than Roman. "And I'm James."

"Good!" Bergantino refilled Ryan's glass.

"Tell me, Luigi. Why does a good Communist like you spend twenty-five years in and around the Vatican?"

Bergantino shrugged his shoulders. "Tell me, James. Why does a good Catholic like you intend to spend twenty-five years in and around the Vatican?"

Ryan smiled. "Touché. Now give me an honest answer, not a politician's answer."

Bergantino picked up his glass and peered into the wine, as though seeking the answer in its depths. "OK. I tell you. When I was young and idealistic, I wanted the editor to send me to Moscow. I wanted to become *L'Unità*'s expert on the Kremlin. I wanted to tell Italy, the whole world, just how Lenin's heirs were building the socialist society, creating the scientific conditions from which the New Man would emerge."

"And he sent you to the Vatican?"

Bergantino emptied his glass. "At first I am fascinated by the bureaucracy. Now the Vatican is a habit. I'm almost fond of the place."

"One bureaucracy is the same as another?"

Bergantino snorted. "How long have you been in the Vatican?"

"Six months."

Bergantino waved a dismissive hand. "You know nothing, my young friend. Drink up."

"Then tell me what differences a Communist like you sees between the Vatican and the Kremlin," Ryan challenged.

Bergantino waved his forefinger at the priest. "There are two important differences, and you should never forget them if you wish to rise any higher up the tree. First, the Curia has a 330-year start on the Kremlin. Second, it is much more efficient. That's why the Vatican is still going strong while the Communist bureaucracy has crumbled all over Europe."

"Doesn't faith in God have something to do with the difference?"

"Possibly. There are some members of the Politburo who still believe in Lenin. Now study the menu, James, before you become too serious."

Ryan looked at the unaccustomed range of dishes in the menu. He hesitated. "The *baccala alla vicentina,* I think."

Bergantino shook his head. "Beware of fish in Rome, and eat it only on Tuesdays and Fridays. May I suggest the *rigatoni,* the *spaghetti alle vongole,* and the *penne all'arrabbiata* to start. If you don't like spicy sauces, I guarantee I'll finish the *penne.* I also recommend the *funghi porcini.* They're freshly picked on Wednesdays and absolutely exquisite. And for the main course, you will do no better than the *abbacchio brodettato.* Paolo's cousin is a shepherd in the Abruzzi mountains and sends him the very best of his lambs."

"It sounds more like a feast than a dinner," Ryan said.

Bergantino smiled. "You must allow me to bribe you with good food. Then you might arrange for me an interview with the Pope."

"On matters of cuisine, I'm content to be guided by you. But as for bribery, surely it's Father Frawley you should be spending your money on?"

Bergantino sighed. "Frawley is an American. Americans do not understand the meaning of the word 'cuisine.' They think of it as a method of cooking. My friend, you will learn in Italy that cuisine is about culture and creation. Frawley will never learn. He's worse than his predecessor as Press Secretary. And he's a member of Opus Dei. I do hope you are not?"

Ryan shook his head.

"Thank goodness. You are an Englishman I could begin to like."

After finishing the large mushrooms and the white wine, and before Bergantino poured out the red, Ryan said, "Are you serious about wanting an interview with the Pope?"

Bergantino adopted a serious tone for the first time that evening. "The Soviet President wants to solve the Ukrainian problem."

"Then why can't he . . ."

Bergantino put up his hand. "The days are gone when the Party leader simply picked up the phone, gave an order, and it was carried out. Thank goodness, of course. But the other side of the coin is that it takes time to get things done." He poured out the Chianti. "He wants a more direct channel of communication with the Pope. An unofficial one."

Ryan said nothing.

"You know what it's like, James. If the Pope wants to make a proposal to the Soviet President about the Ukraine, Fasolo sends it first for comments to the Sacred Congregation for the Eastern Churches, the Pontifical Council for Christian Unity, and the Pontifical Council for Justice and Peace. Then Zingler gets in on the act. He sits on virtually every Vatican committee except the Pontifical Commission for Sacred Archaeology. He hasn't yet managed to convince the Pope that the conduct of excavations underneath Saint Peter's is a matter of faith or morals, but I understand he's working on it. Now, if no one succeeds in losing it in the sand, an emasculated proposal is finally given to Benedetti. He takes it to the Soviet Ambassador to Italy, who sends it to the Soviet Foreign Ministry. Then the fun begins. They send it for comments to the Central Committee Commission on Ideology, the State Security Committee, and the Council for Religious Affairs. That's just for starters. The Council for Religious Affairs sends it on to the Moscow Patriarchate, and so on. Are you surprised, James, when we don't make progress?"

Ryan was cautious. "What exactly are you suggesting, Luigi?"

Bergantino looked approvingly at the lamb in egg and lemon sauce which Paolo placed on the table before re-

moving the ashtray swimming in melted ice cubes. When
Paolo had gone, he said, "There are difficulties with the
Russian Orthodox Church and with Russian nationalists in
the Government and the KGB." He poured out two more
glasses, picked up his own glass, and studied Ryan over the
top of the ruby-colored liquid. "What I am about to say is
for the Pope's ears only. The Soviet President is planning
an initiative that will cut through all these difficulties and
solve the Ukrainian problem. But he needs time to put this
initiative in place. He is asking the Pope to give him this
time."

Ryan sipped his wine to give himself time to think.
"How can the Pope give him time, even if he wanted to?"

"Are you telling me, James, that the Pope doesn't have
direct lines of communication with the bishops in the
Ukraine?"

"If you say so," Ryan replied cautiously.

"Then ask the Holy Father to use those channels to persuade Ukrainian Solidarity not to press their claims for the
return of Ukrainian Catholic churches until after the New
Year."

"Precisely what is this initiative?"

Bergantino held out his hands. "James, I'm talking
about an initiative that even the Presidential Council
knows nothing of. I don't know the precise details."

"What guarantees does the Holy Father have that this
initiative will provide a solution acceptable to the
Church?"

"Guarantees? None. If Ukrainian Solidarity brings the
Soviet Union to a standstill, I can't even guarantee that the
President will be in office by the New Year. If he's not, I
can guarantee that his successor will crush Ukrainian nationalism and the Ukrainian Church."

Ryan took a deep breath. "I'm still not sure that the
Holy Father can act on something without knowing more
details."

"James, by telling you this, the Soviet President is putting himself in your hands and in the Holy Father's hands.

The only details I've been told by a source close to the President—very close—are that the President's solution could have profound implications for Catholic-Russian Orthodox unity."

Ryan didn't touch his lamb. He wasn't hungry any more.

Bergantino took a book of matches from the small pile on the table. He gave it to Ryan. "This has Rasella's telephone number on it. If the Holy Father wants to communicate more directly with the Soviet President, you are to ring Paolo, give your name, and ask if the special table for two is free that evening. He will contact me. If I can make it, he'll phone you back and confirm the reservation. If I can't, he'll suggest some alternative dates."

Chapter ✤ Five

THE LUDOVISI DISTRICT, between the Borghese Gardens and the Piazza Barberini, so differs from Trastevere as to be barely recognizable as Italian, still less Roman.

Diana Lawrence gazed down from the sixth floor window on to the Via Veneto, on to the newsstands which displayed more English language publications than Italian ones, on to the boutiques and the pavement cafés whose elegant clientele paid by Diners Card or American Express, and on to the luxury hotels which would be at home in any Western capital.

"Sit down, Diana. Relax." Ricky Richardson, the CIA Rome station chief, fitted well into the Via Veneto. It wasn't simply his sleek good looks, his expensive preppy clothes, and his credit cards—by those criteria she merged equally well into the international jet set—it was his soul. He had no feel for Rome.

She sat down on the other side of the desk from Richardson.

"That's better," he said, opening a file. "You've done a terrific job so far, honey, really terrific. Fact is, if you'd told us the meaning of this icon, and how and when it was going

to be used in Lvov, you'd have a one hundred percent
strike rate." Richardson grinned. "Boy, the White House
sure hit the roof on that one. The big Ukrainian uprising
takes place while the President is toasting the Soviet President in the State Dining Room! The director was given one
hell of a bawling out for not telling them in advance."

"James had no idea himself."

Richardson was unconcerned. "You win some, you lose
some. But," he leaned forward, now very much concerned,
"Langley were worried by your last report. Very worried.
They want you to move up from a phase one to a phase two
on Ryan."

Lawrence lit a menthol tipped cigarette and blew a
stream of smoke toward the window. Richardson frowned
and looked at the "No Smoking" sign on his desk, but she
ignored him. "What rattled them so much?"

"They don't want a schism between Rome and the
Catholic Church in America."

"Since when did the born-again Christians at Langley
convert to Catholicism?"

"Don't play smart, Diana. We don't want any cut-off of
American money to the Vatican."

"Why not?"

"I'll tell you why not. If the Catholic Church in America
stops sending money to Rome, the Vatican goes bust. If the
Vatican goes bust, it hasn't got the funds to channel to the
nationalist movements in the Ukraine and elsewhere.
Without Vatican money and equipment, the Christian opposition movements in the USSR can't organize. Without
Solidarity-style organization, they're not going to bring
down the Soviet Government."

She looked for an ashtray, couldn't find one, and so she
leaned across the desk and tapped ash into his wastepaper
basket.

"You know I don't like smoking," he said.

"From all the position papers I've read, bringing down
the Soviet Government is not Administration policy. Quite
the reverse. After the Camp David summit, the President

told Congress it was in the West's interests to assist the Soviet Government implement *perestroika*. Quote: A market-led Russia that satisfies its own consumer demands through trade agreements with the West won't risk its prosperity by engaging in destabilizing and economically crippling aggression. Unquote."

"Horseshit."

"You mean the President was deliberately misleading Congress?"

Richardson laughed. "No way. The dumbo's been taken in by the Soviets. What he doesn't understand is *why* the Soviets want Western help to modernize their industrial and technological base. Without it, they can't compete with our more sophisticated weaponry. But give them the technology and the investment capital, and you're modernizing their weapons systems. They continue to be an effective threat to the free world." He took the dagger-shaped paper knife from his desk and used it as a lecturing aid to his class of one. "There are only two ways to eliminate that threat. Either you get rid of the Communist governments, like the east Europeans did, or you ruin their economy so they can't even finance a bow and arrow factory. If the Ukrainian nationalists don't succeed with the first, they'll sure as hell succeed with the second. *Provided* we keep them resourced. The Vatican's doing a first rate job there. It's our job to make sure they keep at it."

"Even though it runs counter to the Administration's foreign policy?"

"This President wouldn't recognize a viable foreign policy if one came up and bit his ass."

"Ricky, he does happen to be the elected President."

"Don't give me all that democracy crap. He's only President because he happened to have ten million dollars more than any other candidate in the primaries. Look, Diana," he said, adopting a more reasonable tone, "presidents and congressmen come and go. Let them do their politicking and ego-tripping inside the country, but we are responsible for maintaining its security. Without us, there wouldn't be a free country for them to fool around in."

She stood up, went to the window, opened it, stubbed out her cigarette on the stone sill, and tossed it into the Via Veneto. "What exactly does Langley want from a phase two?" she asked with her back to Richardson.

"First, they want Ryan to identify and expose a high-level Soviet agent in the Vatican."

She turned around. "You've got to be joking. A Soviet spook in the Vatican?"

"We've monitored signals from their embassy here to Moscow Center. Highest security classification. We haven't cracked the cipher, but the volume of traffic has been unusually high. It's coincided with all the Vatican moves you've advised us of."

"You're jumping to conclusions, Ricky."

"You think so? Moscow station has a high-level source. He's told them the Soviets have an agent in the Apostolic Palace, codenamed Judas, who informed them about the secret proposal for Poland to quit the Warsaw Pact and join the European Community. Judas gave enough notice for the KGB to do a wrecking job before the proposal reached the European Council of Ministers."

Still standing, arms folded across her breast, she took a deep breath. "What else do I have to go on?"

"That's all the definite data. My guess is that this Judas will try and keep the Soviets informed about Vatican communications with Ukrainian Solidarity, so they can wrong-foot the nationalists at the round table talks. You've got to steer Ryan into tracking down this agent, and either getting enough proof to expose him to the Vatican chiefs or else letting us know so we can take care of him. Preferably the latter."

She pursed her lips. "You said first."

He nodded. "Second, you've got to persuade Ryan to prevent this schism. I don't pretend to understand all this doctrine stuff, but it seems the key issue is one of authority. The Pope's got to pull back and stop trying to run the

American Church from Rome. Give them some delegated power, that kind of thing. Then they'll keep the money flowing."

She shrugged. "I've already told him how bad things are with the Church in the States, and pointed up the dangers of a split. I don't know what more I can do to steer him in the direction you want."

Richardson leaned forward intently. "You've got to do more, Diana. We're playing for the big one here. And I mean the Big One. If we can push the Ukrainians far enough, we can get rid of the Communist threat once and for all."

"What do you suggest?"

Richardson relaxed. "When he's nice and malleable after a good fuck . . ."

She flushed and cut in. "I haven't slept with him."

"Jesus! That right? You're the closest thing the Agency has to the woman he nearly married. We give you a cover that tugs at his heart strings. We give you a villa near Castel Gandolfo where you have him on your own for two days, and we fit you up with a discreet love nest at Trastevere. And you tell me you still haven't pulled his pants off? You must be slipping, Diana. Or are you getting too old for this caper?"

Her eyes blazed.

"OK, OK," he said, hands held out in a peace gesture. "I take it back. But we can't afford to fuck this one. Langley are prepared to go to a phase three." He unlocked the top left hand drawer of his desk and removed a stiff-backed photograph envelope. He unsealed it and spread the black and white prints on the desk.

She picked up the top one. It showed her head and shoulders above the water in the Lake Nemi villa pool. With the light reflecting off the water's surface it was impossible to tell whether or not she was wearing a swimming costume. In the foreground Ryan was standing with his back to the camera, facing the pool. His bare buttocks were to the left of her face.

She looked at Richardson. "He was never like this."

He grinned. "The guys in the lab have done a great brush job, don't you think?"

"You need a doctor, Richardson. You're sick!"

"OK. So I forgot to tell you about the cameraman . . ."

She threw a bunch of keys on top of the prints. "The keys to your apartment. I don't ever want to set eyes on you again."

She swirled round and stormed out of the room.

Chapter ✤ Six

THE EMBASSY CAR turned off the Viale Castro Pretorio opposite the Emperor Augustus's Pretorian Guard barracks, used now by the Italian army, and pulled into the side of the Via Gaeta in a parking zone reserved for diplomatic cars.

The chauffeur opened the door and Babakin climbed out. For a moment he stood there savoring the atmosphere of this mild winter's day. Little had changed. Two *carabinieri*, each wearing a navy blue bullet-proof vest over his uniform and carrying a submachine gun, ambled up and down this section of the street. Above the battleship-gray steel shuttering that topped the pale gray stone wall, the leafy green heads of palm trees partially hid the rust-colored façade of the Soviet Embassy building. Only the aerials on the roof had grown in number and complexity, while the television cameras had become more discreet. The second-floor central window in the Ufficio Centrale per I Beni Archivistici opposite was still unlit.

Babakin had enjoyed his two tours in Rome. He turned to Yuri Shmyrev, second secretary at the embassy, who had met him at Fiumicino Airport. "I love winter here. Moscow was covered in snow when I left."

"Moscow is beautiful in the snow," Shmyrev said. Shmyrev wasn't KGB; it was standard procedure to send a regular diplomat rather than a KGB man to meet a visiting senior KGB officer in order to minimize the chance that he would be followed and the visitor identified. Babakin thought Shmyrev stupid. Once inside the embassy he discarded the second secretary and took the lift to the top floor. Waiting to greet him was Lieutenant-Colonel Maksim Lemesh, one of Babakin's protégés, who was now chief of Line PR, the political department, at the Rome Residency. Lemesh was wearing an expensive Italian suit—bought from Babakin's tailor in the Via Condotti—but he would never pass for a Roman. The knot of his tie was too large, his hairstyle was too unsophisticated, and his eyes were too eager.

While Lemesh was unlocking the gray steel door in the windowless anteroom of the Residency, Babakin said casually, "Zinaida Agniya is hoping you will have some leave this year."

Lemesh, bending down to locate and press a button hidden in the floor in order to open a second door, paused. When he stood up his face was flushed. Zinaida Agniya Baskina was a secretary working in the Fifth Department of the First Chief Directorate, where Lemesh had been posted between his first and second tours in Rome. Lemesh thought no one knew that Zinaida and he were having an affair.

Lemesh walked on down the corridor toward the Resident's office, but Babakin opened the first door on the right. The large room accommodated a couple of dozen work booths. A notice forbade smoking and conversation. The walls, the plexiglass windows—shuttered as usual—the ceilings, and the floors of the entire Residency were double, and electronic impulses were beamed through the voids to jam any listening devices. This construction also provided near-perfect soundproofing from outside noise. The two dozen case officers drafting their reports, studying operations, and translating documents in sepulchral silence gave Babakin an impression of medieval monks working away in a scriptorium. He walked round with abbot-like disdain for the no talking sign and stopped to compliment certain officers on reports he'd received. A relieved silence returned when he left.

The other room he called in while Lemesh hovered outside the Resident's office was shared by the Illegals Support officer and the chief of Line X. By the time Babakin left, the chief of Line X was smarting from acerbic observations about the quality of technological and scientific data stolen from Italian sources over the last six months.

Lemesh knocked and opened the door which led into a spacious wood-paneled office containing a conference table, a leather sofa, and a large mahogany desk. The man who stood up behind the desk was short and powerfully built. Konstantin Protchenko was the age Babakin had been in 1981, but Protchenko was a full colonel and was the Resident—the job Babakin had been denied.

Protchenko's handshake was firm. "I'm sorry they didn't appoint the right man as chairman," he said.

Babakin's eyes were penetrating but his face was expressionless. "I'm more concerned to ensure the right person is appointed to head the Fifth Department when Chestnoy retires next year."

Protchenko was equally expressionless. The Fifth Department covered France, Italy, Spain, the Low Countries, Luxembourg, and Eire. In normal circumstances the post would be filled by the deputy or else a Resident with longer experience than Protchenko. But he had learnt that Babakin didn't say anything without a purpose.

"I'm here to set up Operation Judas," Babakin said.

"Isn't that the codename of one of Lemesh's agents?" Protchenko asked as if Lemesh wasn't in the room. "How long will you be here, General?"

"Two days, perhaps three."

"Please use this office as your own."

Babakin nodded. "I'm expecting a visitor at two o'clock."

Protchenko looked at his watch. "I'll clear my things out now. Do you want me at the meeting?"

Babakin shook his head.

He continued his inspection tour, but bypassed Line KR, the internal security service. Babakin suspected its chief of being Grechko's man; in any case Babakin didn't want to be seen fraternizing with the officer who also controlled the network of informers within the Soviet colony in Rome. He spent ten convivial minutes in the office shared by the chief of the American Group, the chief of the Italian Group, and the Active Measures officer. As he left he told the latter to report to him at nine o'clock the following morning in the Resident's office. It was essential that Operation Judas was supported by a well-oiled and highly sophisticated propaganda machine. The head of the Active Measures Service back in Moscow Center had assured Babakin that his man in Rome was first class, but Babakin did not rely on the judgment of others for an operation of this importance.

The office next door to Lemesh's was the Secretariat, where two female clerks logged all incoming and outgoing communications. Sitting with her back to the door, below a chart containing photographs of all known SID surveillance personnel and CIA operatives in Rome, plus the license numbers of SID and CIA vehicles, was Lemesh's wife. "It's good to see you again, Tanya Petrovna," Babakin said softly. She turned round. The other clerk stood up, excused herself by saying it was her lunch hour, and left the room.

Afterwards, Babakin called at the Zenith Room, where a technician monitored the radio frequencies used by SID surveillance units and the *carabinieri* who were supposed to guard the embassy but who also reported to the SID. The technician said there was no unusual traffic on the frequencies. Babakin watched the television monitors as a figure walked past the Turkish Embassy at the junction of Via Palestro and Via Gaeta, and up Gaeta toward the Soviet Embassy entrance. He looked at the technician.

"Just the same."

Babakin nodded.

Five minutes later Tanya Lemeshaya came into the Zenith Room. "Embassy reception have phoned to say your visitor's arrived."

"I know," Babakin said. "Have Maksim bring the visitor to the Resident's office."

Chapter ✤ Seven

ACROSS ROME, ON the other side of the Tiber from the Soviet Embassy, Ryan was waiting at a table outside Sabatini's. Beyond the battered marble fountain in the center of the Piazza di Santa Maria in Trastevere, the mosaic of the Virgin and Child on the façade of the twelfth-century Basilica of Santa Maria in Trastevere glinted in the cool winter sunshine. Diana had said it was urgent.

He heard high heels hurrying on the cobbles.

"Hi, sorry I'm late. It's cold. Let's go inside."

He couldn't remember seeing her so harassed.

She ordered wine first, and then lit a cigarette before looking at the menu and ordering almost randomly. Ryan wasn't hungry. He said he'd have the same.

"Sorry to drag you away," she began. She sucked on her cigarette.

She wasn't harassed, Ryan thought. She was nervous. That was something he'd never seen before.

She ignored the pasta brought by the waiter. As soon as the waiter poured out the red wine she took a large drink. "James, I have a confession to make," she said as though repeating a formula she'd learnt by heart.

"You never knew Katie, did you?" Ryan asked quietly.

"Oh God," she sighed, and ground the cigarette into the ashtray. "I must give up smoking."

"You know smoking is bad for you."

She stared at him in exasperation. "It's bad enough you being a priest, James Ryan. Don't become my doctor too."

"There is no Saint Diana."

"Say again?"

"It occurred to me that no Boston Irish priest would christen a girl with the name of a pagan goddess. Diana, goddess of the night."

She looked down at the table and breathed in deeply. "When did you . . . ?"

"I suppose I started wondering shortly after we first met."

She looked up. "Then why . . . ?"

It was his turn to look down at the white tablecloth. "I . . . I don't know."

The waiter came with the dishes of *saltimbocca alla romana.* He looked pained at the uneaten dishes of *spaghetti carbonara,* now cold. She waved them away.

"I suppose I could have tried to check you out . . ." he faltered.

"Why didn't you?" she asked softly.

"I've been asking myself that."

"Oh God."

"But why did you . . . ?"

She took another deep breath and met his eyes. "CIA," she grimaced.

He was incredulous. "The Central Intelligence Agency?"

She refilled both glasses and took another large swig of wine. "They know the Secretariat's policy in eastern Europe, but they also know the Pope takes his own initiatives. They wanted to know what these were. They suspected the Pope of going behind the Secretariat's back. They wanted to know when, where, why, and how—in advance—especially with regard to the Soviet Union."

"To try and stop them?"

She shook her head. "On the contrary, to try and support any disruption in the Soviet Union. They think our President's gone soft on the Soviets. They want the Pope to do their dirty work for them."

"You keep saying 'they'. I thought you said you were . . ."

"After what I've just told you, losing the Company pension is the least of my worries."

His gaze returned to the tablecloth. "I should have realized, from the questions you asked. But you reminded me so much of Katie . . . I thought we were becoming good friends."

"Oh God, James, don't turn the screw."

"I don't understand. Why are you telling me this now?"

She put her hand on his arm. "I couldn't bear to see you get hurt."

He pulled his arm away. "OK, I've been a fool. But it's only my pride that's hurt, thinking you and I were really friends."

"James! You've no idea. These guys play rough. The other side have got someone at the very highest level in the Vatican."

He looked at her. For the first time she saw disbelief in his eyes. "Now you are trying to deceive me," he said.

She shook her head. She clasped both hands together against the edge of the table, eyes down as if in prayer. "James Ryan. If you believe nothing else I've ever told you, believe this. The KGB has an agent in the Apostolic Palace. I don't know who he is, except that his codename is Judas. And I do know he's not there to practice his Hail Marys." She looked up. The disbelief was still in his eyes. "For a highly intelligent and attractive woman, I've really blown it, haven't I? Both with the Company and with you."

"I don't understand."

"For a highly intelligent and attractive man, you can be a real dumbo." She blinked several times and stood up.

"What's wrong?"

"Just something in my eye," she sniffed. She reached for a handkerchief and knocked over her glass of wine.

"Can I help?"

"Yes. Sit down and stay there."

She started toward the door.

"Diana, when will I see you?"

She half turned. "When your stupid Church goes in for married priests, give me a ring. Meantime, may God look after you, James Ryan, because someone certainly needs to." She spun on her heel.

For several minutes Ryan sat, staring at the white tablecloth and the red stain spreading out slowly from the upturned glass.

Finally he asked for the bill.

"All is settled, Father," the waiter assured him. "The lady said she had to start paying her debts."

Chapter ✤ Eight

"WHAT IS SO important that it brings you to Rome?" Bergantino asked from his chair in front of the Resident's desk.

Babakin smiled. "I like to visit the troops at the front line from time to time."

Bergantino wasn't convinced.

"Drink?" asked Babakin.

Bergantino declined. Any meeting with Babakin demanded a clear head.

Babakin went to the drinks cabinet behind the conference table and poured himself a scotch. He didn't return to the Resident's desk, but sat down on the leather sofa. "This isn't a formal interrogation, Luigi." He was at his most charming.

Bergantino rose from the chair and joined Babakin on the sofa.

Babakin leaned back against the armrest, so that he was facing the Italian journalist who was sitting upright. "Tell me, Luigi, what did you make of Father James Ryan?"

"I liked him."

"What did you make of him?" Babakin repeated.

Bergantino studied the multicolored striped pattern on

the Ukrainian rug. "He's an intelligent and personable young man," he began thoughtfully, "honest, completely without guile. Rather impulsive. He's a romantic, an idealist, and in some ways quite naive, one of life's innocents." He looked up from the rug. "He's loyal and devoted to the Pope."

"The crack in his head?"

Bergantino pursed his lips. "He hasn't lost his sexual drive, though I'm sure he controls it. I'd also say there's some deep insecurity there, some self-doubt."

"Why?"

"He seems attracted to strong characters. He's impressionable. I'd guess quite easily influenced."

"Good," said Babakin.

"It wouldn't work," Bergantino said. "However much access we could achieve, never forget that he and Hoffman spend more time together than the average married couple."

"They're queer?"

Bergantino shook his head. "No, no. Ryan is clearly heterosexual. As for Hoffman, he's asexual, but he's a very strong personality. Any steer we attempted would be counteracted by Hoffman's anti-Soviet views."

"Ambitious?"

"More for the Church, and for the Pope in particular, I'd say, than for himself."

"So, what do you suggest?"

Bergantino looked up. "Use his sincerity, his honesty, and his loyalty to the Pope. He knows where my sympathies lie, but he trusts me. He'll make a good conduit for messages to and from the Pope, bypassing the Curia."

Babakin nodded. "You've done well, Luigi. Of course I'm not surprised. Back in Moscow I always use you as the example of the perfect agent: a man with unrivalled knowledge of the real power structures in his home territory; a man of great influence through his writing and his personal contacts; a man of impeccable character judgment; and, crucially, a man who never overplays his hand. I've written case studies of your work for the students at the Andropov Institute. Some day, Luigi, they'll know the true identity of Agent Gramsci." He went back to the drinks cabinet. This time Bergantino accepted a scotch.

"Tell me, Luigi," Babakin said as though chatting after the end of a meeting, "who are the favorites to succeed this Pope?"

Bergantino put his scotch down on the floor and stared hard at Babakin. "You're not thinking of another 1981, are you?"

Babakin looked puzzled. "I don't understand."

"An attempt to assassinate the Pope. You were my line officer at the time, or have you forgotten?"

"Oh that? Regrettably," Babakin lied, "I was kept in the dark as much as you were. Andropov handled the whole thing personally; he used the Bulgarians."

"You haven't answered my question," Bergantino said. "Is the KGB planning to kill the Pope?"

"Of course not. But he's getting old. We hear rumors about a possible retirement. With the situation in general, and the Ukraine in particular, so critical, we must prepare policy options for the future, and that involves knowing who is likely to be the next pope."

"Policy options?" Bergantino snorted. "That's the first time I've heard the KGB talk of more than one policy."

Babakin smiled. "Times have changed, Luigi, times have changed. Look, the President needs to know what the long term policy of the Vatican is likely to be—and that means knowing who is likely to be the next pope—before he can decide what kind of deal to strike with this pope in the short term."

Babakin was at his most persuasive, but Bergantino knew him of old. "It's purely information you want? No action planned?"

Babakin shrugged. "If one candidate were more likely to take a realistic line in relations with us then, naturally, we'd take care not to spoil his chances."

"And if the leading candidate were likely to follow this pope's policies?"

"That would simply dictate the kind of agreement we make in the short term, the kind of guarantees we'd have to insist on, whereas we'd be more relaxed if we thought the next pope would be reasonable."

"You promise no physical harm to anyone? I know the Pope's causing you problems, but I don't want any part in violence."

Babakin spread his hands. "My dear Luigi. I told you. Times have changed. The President doesn't approve of wet jobs. He sees the KGB as an agency for gathering intelligence and for giving assistance to those who take a sympathetic view of what we're trying to achieve in the Soviet Union."

"OK." Bergantino picked up his scotch. "Then I think you may be in luck. A lot of people are unhappy about the direction the Vatican has taken, particularly in recent times. The Church is on the edge of bankruptcy, but the Pope doesn't seem to care. The Italians do care: they'd hate to see a foreigner throw away all they've built up over centuries. Relations with the Church in Latin America and in Africa are poor. Portugal, Eire and most of Spain are still fervently loyal, of course, along with the east Europeans, but the north Europeans are restless, led by the Dutch. Worst of all, relations with the Church in the United States are at breaking point."

"The implications?"

"There'll be a big move at the next conclave to elect a pope who will bring back some stability to the Church, heal the rifts, sort out the financial mess. If those were the only criteria, the strong favorite among the *papabili* would undoubtedly be Fasolo, the current Secretary of State."

"What other criteria will they look at?"

"Ever since the Second Vatican Council there's been a distrust of the Curia. Fasolo's spent his whole life in the Curia. He's the pragmatist *par excellence*. He never allows religion to interfere with the management of the Church."

"A diplomatic coup would increase his chances?"

"Sure, if there were a big pay-off for the Church. Not financial, you understand. Some big religious gain."

Babakin nodded. "Who else?"

"If the Italians couldn't get Fasolo elected, they'd switch their votes to an Italian they think will be more acceptable to the anti-Curialists. Cardinal Innocenzo Davino fits the bill. Archbishop of Florence, essentially a pastor, a caring, holy man. Incorruptible. No interest in politics. He's not one of them, but the Curia wouldn't find it too difficult to manipulate him."

"Weaknesses?"

"Precisely his lack of interest in management and Church politics. Can the Church afford a pope who might let the Church drift into financial collapse? Is Davino really up to the most demanding chief executive job in the world?"

Babakin laughed. "I'm not sure you'd say that if you lived in Moscow. Who else would be up to the job?"

"Zingler, without a doubt. Never forget that this Pope's theological conservatism commands a lot of support. He speaks with the moral authority of God. No fudging. What's right is right, and what's wrong is wrong. Simple as that. Zingler would continue that fundamentalist approach. Many moderates, and even some liberals, concede privately that it was an uncompromising line with the Communists that won back Poland and Czechoslovakia, and gained big concessions in Lithuania and elsewhere. Zingler would benefit from that. He'd also attract some votes because he's *not* Italian. The Italian bloc has declined to less than twenty percent of cardinals eligible to vote. If the cardinals did decide to stick to the fundamentalist line, then Zingler's their man."

"That'd be bad news for us?"

Bergantino nodded.

"Who else is in the frame?" asked Babakin as he refilled the glasses.

Bergantino was thoughtful. "The make-up of the con-

clave has changed dramatically since the Second Vatican
Council. Europeans have less than 50 percent of the votes
now. Apart from Italy, with twenty-three eligible cardinals,
only two other countries have significant numbers of representatives, the United States with eight and France with
six. But taking regional groupings as a whole, Latin America has twenty-four cardinals, Africa eighteen, and Asia fifteen. In the first couple of ballots, these newly emerging
powers will want to flex their muscles by voting for their
home candidates, rather like favorite son candidates in the
American primaries. Realistically, though, none of these
stands a chance of obtaining the two-thirds plus one votes
for election."

"So that's it?"

"No. I can well imagine most of the Latin American and
most of the United States votes swinging behind a European liberal after the first two ballots in order to block Zingler and Fasolo."

"Any obvious contenders?"

Bergantino nodded. "Demeure."

"Who?"

"Cardinal Bernard Demeure, President of the Pontifical Council for Christian Unity. French, and so that guarantees him five votes straight off. But I'd guess he'll show
well even in the first ballot. His work for Christian unity
means a lot of travel and so he's well-known—and respected—in many countries. He carries the liberal flag in
the Curia. While that's a thankless task inside the Vatican,
particularly at present, it makes him popular outside
Rome. Yes," Bergantino mused out loud, "I can imagine
the Americans—north and south—wouldn't feel threatened with Demeure in Saint Peter's chair. He has another
plus. Before he was brought to Rome, he was an abbot. It's
an odd thing, but cardinals, who spend most of their time
on administration, tend to think of abbots as holy men, and
that will stand Demeure in good stead among those who
are wavering. Silly things like that can tip the balance in a

conclave that looks to be dragging on with no obvious winner."

"Unstoppable?"

"By no means. Many think he's too radical."

Babakin laughed. "How can a cardinal be too radical?"

"For example, Demeure opened a hospice for AIDS victims established by his old monastery. That didn't go down well with the conservatives, who think that AIDS is God's punishment for homosexuality."

"I see." Babakin stroked his chin. "Has there been any suggestion . . ."

"Of course," said Bergantino, man of the world. "There always is about monasteries. A couple of dozen men confined together, youths coming in as novices expected to show unquestioning obedience to their superiors. The Italian press assume that all monasteries are hives of homosexuality and all abbots are queens. It's not true, of course, but it would be unnatural if some, shall we say 'deep friendships,' didn't develop in such circumstances."

"Has Demeure any 'deep friendships'?"

"Difficult to be certain. I'm told that many years ago the mother of a novice made a complaint about Demeure's influence on her son. Since he's been in Rome his private secretaries have all been distinguished by their striking good looks, but . . ." Bergantino shrugged, "that simply indicates his tendencies. It doesn't prove he indulges them."

"What's he like as a person?"

"See for yourself. He's leading the Catholic delegation to the biennial Catholic-Russian Orthodox Dialogue that begins in Leningrad a week tomorrow."

"I'm too busy. No other contenders?"

Bergantino shook his head.

"No chance of a surprise candidate, like Wojtyla in '78?"

Bergantino shook his head again. "They'll steer clear of surprises. I guarantee the next pope will come from one of the four names I've given you."

After Bergantino left, Babakin went to the Referentura at the end of the corridor. He pressed the buzzer to the right of the steel door, and a voice through the grille asked for his identification. He passed his red KGB identity card through a letterbox underneath the buzzer. A flap opened above the buzzer at head height. Babakin heard the sounds of keys turning, and the fifteen-centimeter-thick armor plated door, which could only be unlocked from the inside, opened. The armed guard was nervous. He'd never seen a KGB general at such close quarters. Babakin favored him with a smile.

Next to the cryptographic machines and the secret satellite transmitters was a steel safe. Babakin checked that week's number, which Protchenko had given him, and opened the combination lock. He looked among the shelves and found a plastic pouch with Lemesh's seal on it. He undid the seal and removed three notebooks from the pouch. He carried these to a table and sat down.

It took him less than an hour, skipping past notes on other agents but absorbing the aides-mémoire of contacts with one particular agent. He closed the books and leaned back in the chair.

It was time he had a meeting with Agent Judas.

Chapter ✚ Nine

RYAN DID NOT believe the KGB had an agent in the Apostolic Palace. Sadly, he concluded that it must be another CIA ploy. A series of events, however, which began to unfold less than three days after that uneaten lunch at Sabatini's, cast doubt on his disbelief.

A flurry of telephone calls to and from the private apartment throughout Sunday evening alerted him, but he was unprepared for the horror that greeted him on Monday morning.

Kasamir Hoffman, without comment, placed the morning's newspapers on his desk. The whole of *La Repubblica*'s front page was devoted to one story. Below a banner headline "VATICAN PREPARES TO EXCOMMUNICATE USA" and a subhead "Sensational Memo Leaked with Draft of Excommunication Ultimatum" were three photographs: Cardinal Zingler, the Pope, and Archbishop Brown. Ryan felt ill as he read the story.

The Catholic Church is poised on the brink of the greatest schism since legates of Pope Leo IX split Christendom in two by issuing a Bull of Excommunication against the Patriarch of Constantinople in 1054, thus dividing the Latin West from the Byzantine East.

The Pope is about to send a secret ultimatum to the Catholic bishops of the United States, telling them in effect to submit to the authority of the Holy See by Christmas or else he will excommunicate them. The draft of this ultimatum, together with a confidential memo from its author, Cardinal Johann Zingler, Prefect of the Vatican's Congregation for the Doctrine of the Faith, was leaked yesterday evening to ANSA, the Italian news agency. In the memo Cardinal Zingler described the American hierarchy as a "cancer in the body of the Church."

Vatican spokesman, 43-year-old American Father Robert Frawley, at first denied the existence of these documents. Frawley was then confronted with photocopies of the documents by *La Repubblica* at his apartment on the Via della Conciliazione. He later issued the following statement: "No document of the Holy See exists until it is issued with the authority of the Supreme Pontiff. The documents alleged to have been written by Cardinal Zingler have never been in the possession of the Holy Father. Consequently there is nothing on which the Holy See is able to comment."

The first three pages of this "non-existent" ultimatum addressed to Archbishop Joseph Brown, President of the National Conference of Catholic Bishops of the USA, review the clashes between Rome and the Church in America in recent years. They catalog the Vatican's warnings about pastoral letters issued by the National Conference on the immorality of nuclear weapons, the status of women in the Church, birth control, priestly celibacy, the recognition of different forms of sexuality, and other controversial matters. This section of the draft letter from the Pope concludes with "the deep distress with which we learnt that you had voted not to accept our request that all documents concerning faith or morals which you intend to publish be first submitted to the judgment of the Sacred Congregation for the Doctrine of the Faith."

The fourth page sets out the ultimatum. "Called by the inscrutable design of providence to the office of Universal Pastor of the Church, it is our unavoidable responsibility to affirm that there is only One God and One Truth, and that the Son of God founded One Church to protect and proclaim this One Truth. It follows that if any bishop or group of bishops arrogates that *magisterium* which Christ has vested in the Supreme Pastoral Office for the good and for the unity of the Universal Church, then that bishop or group of bishops has thereby cut himself or themselves off from full communion with the Universal Church.

"We beg of you, in the Name of Christ our Savior, to pray and reflect on the action you have taken. We ourselves pray that we shall receive from you, jointly or severally, the acceptance of our earlier request and your submission in humility to that *magisterium* which Christ instituted as the means of fulfilling his divine mission in the world.

"If we do not receive consent to our request by the Feast of the Nativity of Christ we shall have no alternative but to recognize that by such an act you have withdrawn from communion with the Universal Church, and we shall pray for your eventual reconciliation with the See of Peter."

Given the language of ecclesiastical diplomacy in which such documents are normally written, it is the bluntest possible warning to the American bishops that they face excommunication by Christmas. Any doubts about the uncompromising line taken by the Vatican are removed by the private memo which accompanied the draft Papal letter.

Your Holiness

Please find attached the draft for your letter responding to the refusal by the American bishops to accept the teaching authority of the Church.

A majority of the bishops in the United States have been in technical heresy for a number of years, permitting their priests to celebrate unauthorized forms of the mass, invalidating marriages without proper canonical authority, allowing ex-priests who marry to participate prominently in the mass, administering improperly to homosexuals, permitting absolution to be given to those who have no intention of renouncing artificial forms of birth control, allowing diocesan priests and members of religious orders to dress and behave in ways unbefitting their office, and so forth. It is little wonder that the effective secularization of the Church in the United States has led to a Godless society rooted in the values of materialism and consumerism.

I have little doubt that they will refuse to comply with the request. Whilst I am sure this will be of great sadness to your Holiness, on the positive side we shall be rid of a cancer that has been affecting the body of the Universal Church. May I suggest that our strategy should be to support those few bishops who cling to the authentic teaching of Christ, and to build anew the Church in the United States. We might ask Cardinal Ozoroski to sound out the Canadian Conference of Catholic Bishops as to what assistance they can offer bishops loyal to the Holy See.

I remain Your Holiness's most obedient servant,

Johann Cardinal Zingler

With two exceptions, the other papers were similar. The Vatican's own newspaper, *L'Osservatore Romano*, made

no mention whatsoever of the leaked documents, while
L'Unità included only a brief report on page 5.

"These documents . . . are they true?" Ryan asked.

Hoffman's jaw jutted out defiantly. "His Eminence
spent an hour on the telephone with the Holy Father last
night. The Church must rally round and support Cardinal
Zingler."

"Do we cancel this morning's audiences?"

Hoffman shrugged. "Fasolo's with the Holy Father
now."

Ten minutes later a grim-faced Cardinal Fasolo opened
the door from the Pope's private study and walked into the
private secretaries' office. "The morning audiences will
proceed as normal," he said, "but the Holy Father will see
Archbishop Korchan at one o'clock and Cardinal Zingler at
one fifteen. If any journalists do manage to get through to
this office, you must refer them to Father Frawley. I will
instruct him what to say until a statement is issued this afternoon. Centralino will route any calls from the hierarchy
in the United States through to my office."

Archbishop Korchan and Cardinal Zingler arrived together
just before one o'clock. Hoffman accompanied Korchan to
the private library on the mezzanine half a floor below to
await the Pope, who was concluding his audiences in the
State library on the second floor.

Zingler remained in the private secretaries' room. Just a
trace of the crimson bib below his white clerical collar
showed above the top button of his plain black cassock. A
simple brass pectoral cross and a ring on the third finger of
his right hand—given him personally by the Pope—were
the only other signs of his office. He slumped in the chair
by the corner, eyes dark and sunken.

Ryan felt completely inadequate. "I . . . I'm so sorry,
Eminence," he said.

"The first three pages of the draft were genuine," Zingler said, half to Ryan and half to himself.

"The rest were forgeries?"

Ryan was surprised by Zingler's wry smile. "They included words I did not commit to paper."

"Then we can expose . . ."

Zingler shook his head. This time the smile was a sad one. "I have my letter of resignation here." He tapped his breast. "For the Holy Father's sake I shall not let him refuse it."

After lunch Korchan came into the private secretaries' office. Normally he appeared cheerful, hinting at—or so it seemed to Ryan—the irreverence of an outsider without offending those Italian officials who took themselves too seriously. Now he was expressionless. "Here's the statement we intend issuing, James. If the Holy Father approves, will you please take it personally to Father Frawley at the Press Office."

Within ten minutes Ryan was leaving the Apostolic Palace by the Bronze Door and heading across Saint Peter's Square. The Pope hadn't even looked at the statement, but had waved it away as though he couldn't bear to read it.

Television camera crews were recording establishment shots: the usual pans across Saint Peter's Square and the basilica, and zooms up to the windows of the top floor of the Palace of Sixtus V from where—unknown to them—Ryan had just come. Reporters were rehearsing off camera, trying to inject drama into "Here in Saint Peter's Square," "Here in the heart of Christendom," and other stock intros. At the merest flash of crimson or purple they abandoned their scripts and chased after the luckless cleric.

It was worse at the press office—referred to by reporters of all languages as the *Sala Stampa,* as though that elevated them above mere news hacks. The arcade in front of the post-War stone office building at the top of the Via della Conciliazione, next to Pius XII Square, was like a scrum. Ryan pushed his way through the throng of unaccredited journalists only to be stopped at the glass door by a *vigilanza* who demanded to see his *tessera.* Ryan pro-

tested that he had come from the Vatican to see Father
Frawley, but he was not admitted without his pass. At last
he spotted Sister Francesca, who acted as receptionist.

Inside the entrance lobby some of the older accredited
correspondents affected an impression of indifference,
while taking care not to stray too far from the desk where
press releases were given out. Sister Francesca took Ryan
up three steps and turned to the right, the private side,
away from the long room with typewriters and telephones
which Vatican correspondents regarded as their territory.
Father Frawley's office was furnished like that of an American corporate executive.

Frawley affected that immediate, superficial intimacy
that Ryan found the least endearing of American traits.
"Make yourself at home, James. We should take time out
to get acquainted. Let's do that after we've cleared this particular hurdle."

Ryan handed him the brown envelope.

Frawley leaned back in his swiveling and reclining black
leather chair and read out loud.

> *"The Holy See denies the authenticity of documents
> purported to have been written by Cardinal Johann
> Zingler, Prefect of the Sacred Congregation for the
> Doctrine of the Faith, for transmission to the Church
> in the United States and which came into the posses-
> sion of the ANSA news agency by means which can
> only be described as devious, dishonest, and disrepu-
> table. The Holy See is pained that normally responsi-
> ble organs of the media should have reproduced such
> documents as though they reflected the thinking of
> the Holy See.*
>
> *"Cardinal Zingler, while denying that the docu-
> ments as distributed by ANSA were written by him,
> immediately offered his resignation to the Holy Fa-
> ther in order that the Holy Father be spared any fur-
> ther embarrassment. The Holy Father failed to
> persuade Cardinal Zingler to withdraw his resigna-
> tion. The Holy Father is deeply saddened by the event*

and the loss of one of his closest advisers, whom he describes as 'a theologian renowned for impeccable scholarship, a staunch defender of the inviolable truths of Christianity, and a beacon of light shining in a world gray with confusion.'

"The Secretary of State, Cardinal Domenico Fasolo, the Vatican's most senior cardinal, will fly to New York tomorrow with a personal message from the Holy Father assuring his brethren in the United States that any alleged ultimatum was a wholly unfounded speculation and that any differences between themselves and the See of Peter will be resolved in the spirit of fraternity in Christ cum Petro et sub Petro."

Frawley nodded. "That's neat, James, that's neat."

"Only the first three pages were authentic."

"Sure. But, true or false, we got to put daylight between Zingler and the Holy Father. I like the last five words. Most of these people outside won't understand, but the message won't be lost on the bishops Stateside." He buzzed his secretary, adjusted the time and date on a stamp, stamped the sheet, and handed it to his secretary. "Have Sister Francesca xerox two-fifty. Give our guys a half-hour start before feeding the unaccredited rabble outside. And have Rocco, Tommaso, Maria, Xavier, Kevin, Pierre, Robert, and Catherine in here in ten minutes for an off-the-record chat." He winked at Ryan.

"If there's nothing more, I'll be getting back," said Ryan.

"Okay. But you're welcome to stick around for the fun." Ryan left.

Walking across the Saint Damasus Courtyard, he heard an Aberdonian voice behind him. "Well now, James, what do you think of your first Vatican *terremoto?*"

"It's a personal tragedy for Cardinal Zingler," Ryan said to Monsignor Grimes.

"Indeed. But I'll tell you something. Many a Vatican apartment will be having a party tonight."

"Those documents were forged."

Grimes's tone was distinctly skeptical. "Is that so? It'll take more than your word to convince most people they weren't genuine."

They took the lift up to the Third Loggia.

"Well, James, take care. I take it you *do* have nothing to fear from Korchan's inquiry."

"What inquiry?"

"Don't you know? I'm surprised."

"Andrew, stop being mysterious. What inquiry?"

"Little birdies tell me that Archbishop Korchan has been appointed to find out who sent those documents to ANSA."

Most newspapers interpreted events that week as a Vatican climbdown. The only person to emerge with any credit was the peacemaker Cardinal Fasolo.

On Friday Archbishop Benedetti slipped into the private secretaries' office after Hoffman had left for a meeting at the Russicum. His face had a sly smile. "Look what I found in today's diplomatic bag from Washington." He dangled a white envelope, and dropped it into Ryan's lap. "I promise I won't tell Archbishop Korchan." Another conspiratorial smile and he was gone.

The envelope was addressed simply, "Personal to Father James Ryan, Apostolic Palace." Ryan tore it open. The notepaper was headed "Metropolitan Archdiocese of Chicago. From the Office of the Cardinal." Scrawled across the white paper were the words: *You're smarter than I gave you credit for.*

Chapter ✤ Ten

BABAKIN TURNED THE Volga into the side of the road in Komsomol Square. The square had been swept clear of snow, and the pavements trodden clear in front of the stations that dominated the square: along the north side, the neoclassical Leningrad Railway Station, the Komsomolskaya Metro Station boasting a six-columned portico, dome and spire, and the bizarre art nouveau Yaroslavl Railway Station; along the south side, the large red-brick Kazan Railway Station, modeled on building styles of Old Russia, with a tall Tartar tower over its gateway. Babakin had been through that gateway many times in the past to supervise the dispatch of prisoners to labor camps in the Urals. People still traveled from here to the Urals and western Siberia, but most of those who now milled outside the station were exotically garbed—fur-banded felt hats, and fur coats or colorfully beaded felt coats over wide trousers and felt boots for the men and bright trousers gathered at the ankles for women—Soviet Central Asians departing to or arriving from Kazakhstan, Uzbekistan, Tajikistan, Turkmenia, and Kirghizia.

Even with the station lights and the streetlamps in the

square Babakin needed to switch on the Volga's internal lamp to read the CIA map of Moscow. The American agency alleged that Soviet maps were published with deliberate inaccuracies in order to confuse Western spies. With characteristic paranoia the CIA never considered the obvious: the Soviet Union had no organization capable of producing accurate scalar street maps.

He found the address in the shadowy area behind the marshaling yards of Kazan Station. The early winter snow lay thick and white, but it could not dispel an all-pervading gloom. A woman with face make-up less subtle than that used by the clowns of the Moscow State Circus emerged from an alley and offered to warm Babakin inside her imitation rabbitskin coat. She matched Babakin's one-word expletive before disappearing back into the night.

Only thin strips of light escaped the heavy rough curtains which masked the windows in the building. Babakin opened the double doors and met the sight, sounds and stench of a beer hall. Through the blue-gray haze of tobacco smoke he saw men in working clothes standing round chest-high tables sordid with spilled beer and empty glasses. Skeletons of small fish, shells of shrimps and cockles, and cardboard tubes from *papyrosi* cigarettes littered the stone-flagged floor. The cacophony of half a dozen conversations and a dozen arguments wafted to him on the aroma of male sweat, oily fish, yeasty beer, and arid tobacco smoke.

A few heads turned toward him. The faces were unshaven, the expressions a mixture of curiosity, sullen indifference, suspicion, and fear.

He walked through the room toward a door on the far side. Two burly men rose to block his way. He flashed his red KGB identity card and brushed them aside. Three of the well-dressed men playing cards at the green baize table looked up as he entered the back room. He spoke to the fourth.

"Ivan Gorbatko, it will be to your advantage to take a

stroll with me. When you've finished your game, of course."

The jewelry on Gorbatko's fingers flashed in the light from the low, unshaded bulb as he placed one card face down on the table. Babakin estimated that the stacks of notes on the table totalled between five and ten thousand US dollars.

The two burly men had followed him into the room. One of them had his hand inside his right-hand jacket pocket.

"I should tell your friend he's not invited," said Babakin, "and that he's likely to shoot himself if he doesn't take his finger off the trigger."

Gorbatko looked up. His square Slav face, topped by wavy graying hair, was expressionless. He nodded to the two men, who left the room. The other three card players continued, but their hearts weren't in the game. Within two minutes Gorbatko had shown his hand and scooped up the stake. He added the winnings to his own funds and tidied the notes into a neat bundle which he put in the inside breast pocket of his jacket.

Slowly he removed his hand from inside his jacket. He dropped the bundle back on the table and stood up. He waved his hand toward the notes. "My apologies for the interruption, gentlemen."

He put on a bearskin overcoat and a fur hat, and followed Babakin out of the door. No one touched the money on the table until he had left the room.

Outside, Babakin looked at the short squat figure, from his handmade boots to his Barguzin hat. His heavy breathing misted in the cold night air. "Why do you come to a place like this?" Babakin asked.

"Because I like it. It's where my roots are. This is the real Russia, not the Arbat with its Westernized vulgarity."

Babakin nodded.

"Where do you suggest we stroll to, my friend?"

"To my car," replied Babakin.

"Do you take me for a fool?"

"I take you for neither fool nor coward. It's warmer in the car. It's also proofed against electronic eavesdropping." He handed Gorbatko the keys. "Examine it. Choose your own seat."

Gorbatko peered into the windows of Babakin's Volga and then glanced quickly up to detect moving shadows.

"They're your people," Babakin said. "Mine are not so clumsy."

Gorbatko opened the door to the driver's seat as if to enter, stopped, turned round, grinned, and walked round to the passenger door. Babakin shrugged and climbed into the driver's seat. He turned on the engine and the windscreen wipers, which would spoil any ordinary tape recording. "Happy?"

Gorbatko examined Babakin's face, cadaverous in the faint bluish light of the low-power mercury vapor street lamp. "What advantage can you offer me that's worth interrupting a game of cards for?"

"The advantage of not being arrested, convicted, and executed."

Gorbatko laughed. "Do you know who I am?"

"Ivan Vladimovich Gorbatko, aged fifty-seven."

"Don't make jokes with me, my friend. One telephone call and you're a dead man."

Babakin reached down slowly, picked up the telephone from its cradle between the two seats, and handed it to Gorbatko. "Go ahead."

Gorbatko heard the dialing tone. He'd seen two-way radios in militia and KGB cars, of course, but never a telephone. "What did you say your name was?" he asked, as he took the telephone from Babakin's hand.

"I didn't."

Gorbatko's voice was less confident now. "You know I have friends in high places. Very high places."

"Your friends would have to include the chairman of the KGB to make any difference to our discussion. Do I make myself clear?"

"How much do you want?"

"You supply heroin from Kazakhstan to a Mafia clan in Sicily." It was a statement, not a question.

"I don't take on business partners. How much money do you want?"

"I don't want money."

"A hundred thousand roubles."

"I said I don't want money."

"A hundred thousand US dollars."

"I want your friends in Sicily to pay for your next consignment with a gift instead of American dollars."

"What's the gift?"

"I want them to kill somebody in Italy."

Gorbatko's laugh was tinged with relief. "They'll do that for me as a favor, not instead of a payment."

Babakin stared at him. "I haven't told you who is to be killed."

Chapter ✦ Eleven

AN ARM GROPED out of the bedclothes. The hand failed to find the bedside light switch, but did locate the telephone on the bedside table and lifted the handset to stop the strident ringing.

"Eminence," said the telephone, "my apologies for disturbing you, but it's the Apostolic Palace. They say it's urgent."

"That's all right, Diego," Cardinal Davino said as his free hand continued hunting for the light switch, "put them through."

"Eminence," said another voice, "profound apologies for calling you at this time. Is your secretary still on the line?"

"Indeed I am," said Father Diego Marcuzi's voice.

"Then please put the phone down, Father. What I have to say is for His Eminence's ears only."

Davino managed to find the switch. It was eleven twenty-five.

"The Holy Father is gravely ill."

"Mother of God." From Davino's lips it was a prayer, not an oath. He was now fully awake.

"He has asked for you, Eminence. No one must know, you understand."

"Yes, yes," Davino said.

"There is a train at twenty-three fifty-five to Rome. A Vatican car will meet the train at Terminal Station and bring you straight to the Holy Father. May I suggest, Eminence, that with Central Station so near to you there is no need to use your driver. Just leave a note for Father Marcuzi to say that you may be away a couple of days and that you will telephone him tomorrow. The truth is, the Holy Father may not survive that long, but please mention nothing to Father Marcuzi. You understand, Eminence?"

"Yes, yes."

After the Archbishop of Florence put the telephone down he heard a discreet knock at the door.

"Enter."

"Is there anything I can do, Eminence?"

"Yes, Diego. Go back to bed. I may be away for a couple of days, but I'll telephone you tomorrow to say if Monsignor Zerbini needs to take high mass on Sunday."

"Shall I tell Aldo to bring the car round?"

"There's no need, Diego. Now you go back to bed."

Davino dressed as quickly as he could, praying silently at the same time. He was sensible enough to realize that a discreet journey to the Vatican meant simple black clerical dress, without the cardinal's crimson or the bishop's pectoral cross.

At twenty to midnight he left Archbishop's House on the Piazza San Giovanni, turning into Via Cerretani, away from his beloved Duomo. At the end of Cerretani he took the right fork and hurried past the small hotels that lined the Via Panzani. He was breathless as he began to cross the Piazza dell'Unita Italiana.

He didn't even see the black car that accelerated from the parking area. He did hear the squeal of tires as it swerved. He turned, and for a fraction of a second he was blinded by its headlights. Then the car slammed into him.

The car sped off into the Piazza della Stazione and disappeared into the streets behind the railway station.

Ryan heard that Cardinal Davino had been killed in an automobile accident. He attached no particular significance to the tragedy until he read Italy's Sunday newspapers. Most papers assumed it was a typical hit and run accident, probably by a drunken driver, but the more scurrilous asked what a cardinal of the Catholic Church was doing at midnight on Friday in the railway station area dressed only in a simple priest's clothes. One paper quoted Father Diego Marcuzi, his private secretary, as saying that the cardinal had received a telephone call from the Apostolic Palace at about half-past eleven that night, and then attacked this attempted "cover-up" by gleefully announcing that the Apostolic Palace denied that any telephone call had been made to Cardinal Davino at any time on Friday, still less at half-past eleven at night.

Ryan phoned Father Marcuzi. The distraught priest confirmed that he had indeed taken a telephone call from the Apostolic Palace, or at least someone saying he was calling from the Apostolic Palace.

Ryan no longer knew what to believe.

Chapter ✤ Twelve

THE MOZHAISK LABOR and Education Colony was one of two camps for criminals aged between fifteen and twenty years of age in the Moscow *oblast*. Babakin hoped it wasn't going to be another wild goose chase. He'd examined two unsuitable candidates that week, and time was running out.

When Babakin arrived at Mozhaisk, one hundred and ten kilometers west of the capital, snow lay thick on the ground outside the wooden perimeter wall. Two guards ushered him through the heavily padlocked door. The strip of land between the outer and the inner wooden walls was bare of snow. An electrified wire plus a barbed wire fence ran down the center of the freshly turned earth, parallel to the wooden walls. Every thirty meters red lettering on a noticeboard gave the familiar warning: *Forbidden Zone—Do Not Enter*.

The camp commander, Major Oleg Vasyutin, peered cautiously at Babakin from behind wire-framed spectacles. He didn't know whether he was about to be criticized for being too strict or for not being strict enough. Babakin put him at his ease.

"You only wish to interview one of my *rebyata*?" Vasyutin asked with relief. "Certainly, General. Tell me which one and I'll take you to his detachment."

"Plisetsky," said Babakin. "Sergei Ivanovich."

"Ah," the major sighed. He didn't like problems. "I'm afraid Plisetsky is in the isolator."

"Good," Babakin said. "It'll give me a chance to have a look before I talk to him."

Vasyutin led Babakin past six long, low buildings. Each held an *otryad,* or detachment, of between sixty and seventy inmates who slept in a single dormitory on narrow metal bunks arranged in two tiers. The system was meant to instil some group pride; it also provided a means of control. Like most Soviet penological theories it failed in the first but succeeded in the second objective.

Guards unlocked the two gates to the isolator cell. Vasyutin slid back the peephole cover and motioned Babakin to look.

Babakin saw a youth with a pretty face under a mass of blond curls. The new "humane" treatment insisted upon by the Supreme Soviet meant that juvenile criminals no longer had their heads shaved. Plisetsky was wearing scruffy black camp fatigues with his *otryad* number on his breast pocket. Babakin nodded and closed the cover.

"Tell me about him," Babakin said as they walked back to Vasyutin's office.

"He's a problem," Vasyutin said. "Eighteen years old. Born in Leningrad. Son of Nina Plisetskaya, who was a ballerina with the Kirov. His father walked out on them when the boy was only two. She doted on the boy, wanted him to be a dancer. She sent him to the Vaganova, but they 'released' him on the grounds that he lacked musicality. The real reason, I gather, was that he was a troublemaker. Plisetskaya moved to Moscow. She started teaching at the Bolshoi School, and arranged for Sergei to be admitted. He was also 'released' from there for the same reason. After that Plisetskaya abandoned hopes of a ballet career for her son, and she taught him French—she's half French, you know—so that he'd get a good job with foreign travel. He was expelled from school for buggering a younger boy. A year later he was convicted under Article 206: he'd seduced a queer and then robbed him. That's why he's here."

"Why the isolator?"

"He buggered a younger inmate."

Vasyutin hung his greatcoat on the peg next to his office door and waved Babakin to sit on one of the two armchairs in the room. "It's difficult to know what to do these days," he confessed. "You're never sure how many of your staff are *stukachi*. Anonymous letters have been sent to Supreme Soviet deputies accusing me of inhumane treatment."

Babakin nodded sympathetically. "How long has Plisetsky been in *shizo*?"

"Three days. But it's his second offense, so I put him on diet 9B. Now he's gone on hunger strike. Tell me, General, what would you advise?"

Babakin leaned back in his chair. A smile crossed his face. "The Supreme Soviet would not wish you to permit an inmate to harm himself, Major. Therefore I advise that you force feed him." He looked at his watch. "Say in fifteen minutes' time. And don't spare his feelings. Do I make myself clear?"

Vasyutin liked this KGB general. He reached for the telephone.

Babakin watched from behind the one-way observation window of the plain white interview room. A master-sergeant, holding Plisetsky firmly just above the elbow, steered him into the room. The pretty face was surly. Two guards, a duty officer, and Major Vasyutin followed them. Waiting in the room were a white-coated doctor and a nurse who held a deep dish of colorless liquid in one hand and a rubber tube in the other.

Vasyutin nodded. The doctor coughed and made a pronouncement. "Plisetsky, the regulations state that we must force feed inmates on hunger strike. I am asking if you will eat voluntarily."

The bright blue eyes blazed. "I'll not eat your shit!"

"Plisetsky," the doctor announced, "since you have repeated your refusal to eat voluntarily, we shall force feed you in order to preserve your life."

The master-sergeant and one of the guards pushed Plisetsky on to a chair. The second guard grabbed him from behind by his curls and pulled his head back. The doctor took the rubber tube and tried to force it through Plisetsky's clenched teeth. When that failed the doctor fetched a steel spatula from a table holding medical equipment. He attempted to force the spatula into Plisetsky's mouth while the nurse stood ready with a mouth-opener, a double steel plate with a screw to widen the distance between the plates. Plisetsky's foot lashed out and kicked the doctor in the groin.

"Right," said Vasyutin. "One orifice is as good as another. Use his favorite."

The master-sergeant and the two guards dragged Plisetsky, kicking and screaming, on to a cot and held him by his arms and legs face down while the duty officer pulled down his pants. The doctor took a delight in forcing in the life-giving liquid in the form of an enema.

When the last of the two liters had been pumped in, the doctor stepped back, but not quickly enough to avoid the stream of brown liquid that spurted out of Plisetsky's anus and splashed the doctor's white coat.

Vasyutin, worried lest he had gone too far, glanced nervously at the "mirror," and left the room.

Babakin nodded his satisfaction. "Leave him to wallow in his own mess for half an hour, then hose him down, give him new clothes, and bring him to your office."

"You have an important visitor from Moscow," Vasyutin said when the master-sergeant brought a cleaned-up Plisetsky to his office. Plisetsky still looked surly, but less confident than when Babakin had first seen him.

Babakin waved Vasyutin out of the room.

"*Comment ça va?*" Babakin asked.

"*Va te faire enculer. Salaud,*" the youth replied.

"You're fluent enough to be an interpreter," Babakin

said genially in Russian, "but language like that won't get you out of here."

"What will?"

"Your cooperation."

Plisetsky looked with interest at this important visitor who hadn't attempted to intimidate him. "How?" he asked.

Babakin put his fingers together reflectively. "It involves something that I imagine you'll enjoy. It's also very patriotic."

Plisetsky's wariness returned.

"It involves," said Babakin, "buggering for Mother Russia."

Plisetsky grinned. "Are you serious?"

"I take it you're not especially religious? You don't mind the odd act of sacrilege?"

Plisetsky gave a scornful snort.

"Good. Perform this task well, and I will find you employment buggering away to your heart's content, all paid for by a grateful State. Silk shirts, foreign clothes, anything else within reason you ask for." Babakin leaned forward, his eyes now cold. "Fuck it up and you're back on diet 9B, and I guarantee you'll never see another bare arse the rest of your life."

"When do I start?"

"This weekend. In Leningrad."

Chapter ✣ Thirteen

THE POPE'S LAST audience, with Cardinal Demeure, was overrunning. Hoffman had already cleared his desk and had gone through to chat with the Sisters in the kitchen. Ryan was tidying his own papers when Demeure knocked and walked into the private secretaries' office.

"How were the talks in Leningrad, Eminence?" Ryan asked.

"The talks?" Demeure seemed distracted. "May I sit down?"

"Of course, Eminence." Ryan showed him to the easy chair in the corner of the room. He was shocked by Demeure's appearance. Gone was the ascetic with the self-mocking sense of humor. A slack face emphasized the rubbery lips below the long nose; the eyes were bloodshot.

"No progress in the Catholic-Russian Orthodox Dialogue, I'm afraid," Demeure said to the carpet. "The Russian Orthodox side appeared divided. The atmosphere was . . . the tension made things difficult. Nobody knew how many of the Orthodox were clandestine Catholics, and whether they would show their hand. We didn't know, and it was clear that the Council for Religious Affairs people didn't know either." He stopped speaking.

"What was the result, Eminence?" Ryan prompted. "Did you deal with the Ukraine?"

"The Ukraine?" Demeure spoke as though reiterating a report in which he'd lost all interest. "Metropolitan Nikolei of Minsk repeated the standard line that the faithful of the Ukraine had voluntarily dissolved the Ukrainian Catholic Church in 1946 and had voted to return to the Russian Orthodox Church. He agreed that present-day Ukrainian Catholics should not be discriminated against, but said they had no legitimate claim to churches or property in the Ukraine, and that the seizure of Saint George's Cathedral was a grave setback to Orthodox-Catholic relations."

"Did anybody question that?" Ryan asked.

Demeure looked up. "James, will you do something for me?"

"Certainly, Eminence."

"Will you try to persuade the Holy Father to accept my resignation?"

"Eminence, I . . . I don't understand."

Demeure sighed. "I gave him my resignation this evening, but he refused it. He told me I must continue."

"But why . . . ?"

"He said it would give the wrong signal to the Russian Orthodox if I were to be replaced."

"No, no. I meant why do you want to resign?"

He covered his face with his hands. "If I stay on, it puts the Holy Father in . . . it makes him vulnerable." He raised his face from his hands. His eyes pleaded. "I must go back to a monastery, James. Better still, a hermitage, for the salvation of my own soul."

Chapter ✤ Fourteen

GENERAL BLAGOV'S EYES narrowed. "It's taken you long enough."

Babakin, the ankle of his left leg resting casually on his right knee, was relaxed in the chair on the other side of the KGB chairman's large desk. "I don't think three months is too long to ensure we get it right this time."

"When?"

"The eighth of December."

Blagov frowned. "You're not giving me much notice."

"How much notice do you need? You said you wanted it done before the end of the year. The eighth of December provides the best opportunity. You're fortunate I was able to complete the arrangements in time."

Blagov never liked to feel he was being bounced into anything, still less something as important as this. "What's so special about the eighth of December?"

Babakin smiled. "It's the Feast of the Immaculate Conception."

"What are you talking about?"

"The day when the Catholic Church celebrates the fact that, unique among humanity, the Mother of God was conceived free of the stain of original sin."

"Don't play games with me, Babakin. Cut out the smart talk and outline the plan." He took a pencil and opened his notepad.

Babakin was unruffled. "There is a certain poetic touch to the plan that I don't want you to miss. On the Feast of the Immaculate Conception the Pope is going to Siracusa in Sicily to pray at the statue of the Weeping Virgin."

Blagov looked up from his notebook.

"In 1953," Babakin continued, "a plaster statue of the Blessed Virgin Mary, modeled on her miraculous apparition at Fatima, began to weep tears. It continued to do so for three days. The Archbishop of Siracusa appointed a commission of experts to examine the phenomenon. They published a chemical analysis of the liquid that flowed from the eyes of this plaster statue and concluded that it was identical to human tears. Within three months the Church pronounced this to be an authentic miracle."

"I said I don't want nonsense," Blagov warned.

"We're coming to the poetic justice, of which I'm sure you will approve. You see, the reason this plaster image of the Virgin of Fatima was said to have wept was because the Pope had failed to carry out her request to dedicate Russia to her Immaculate Heart in union with all the world's bishops and thus save the world from Communism."

"What, precisely, is the plan?"

"When the Pope prays in front of the statue, it will once more weep tears. But this time they'll be tears of pure semtex, carrying His Holiness and a goodly few others straight to the arms of the Blessed Virgin in heaven."

Blagov frowned. "Won't the link with the Kremlin be obvious?"

Babakin shook his head. "Had you heard of the Weeping Statue?"

"Of course not."

"Few people outside southern Italy have. No, General, this will appear to be an exclusively Italian show. It will be carried out by a Mafia clan. The motive will be the Pope's condemnation of Mafia activities and his threat to excommunicate all *Mafiosi* and deny them Catholic funerals. That may not mean much to you, but in Sicily a Mafia godfather's funeral without the full Catholic works would be like a general's funeral without full military honors."

"How reliable are these people?"

Babakin reached down to his briefcase and put a copy of *Il Manifesto* on the desk. It showed a photograph of Cardinal Davino's body. "I tested out the system with a dry run, or should I say a wet run. They eliminated Cardinal Davino on my instructions."

Blagov peered at the photograph and at the Italian text he didn't understand. "Why this one?"

Babakin shrugged. "I wanted to see if they could kill a high-ranking churchman and cover their traces effectively. I didn't want to make any connections with the main target by using a member of the Roman Curia or somebody based in Sicily. Apart from those considerations, there was no particular significance attached to Davino."

Blagov nodded. "What's in it for them, apart from getting rid of somebody they don't like?"

"Two million US dollars in gold bullion. You'll need to sign this authorization for the State Bank to export the gold to a holding account at the Banque de Financement in Geneva. It'll be transferred to a designated numbered account as soon as the job is completed."

Blagov studied the authorization form. "It's a lot of money."

"I'm sure the Presidential Council will consider it a bargain if it stops the Pope's subversive activities in the Ukraine."

Blagov signed the form.

"Is there anybody else you wish me to brief, General?"

Blagov's eyes narrowed once more. "Who else knows about it?"

"Nobody. I made all the arrangements personally. I assumed you didn't want this one to go through the normal channels."

Blagov looked closely at the man he'd suspected of try-

ing to oust him. Perhaps his suspicions had been ill-
founded. His head nodded slowly. "You've done well, General Babakin. Very well." He leaned forward and stared at
Babakin. "No one else must know. I will carry out any necessary briefings as I see fit. You understand?"

"You're the boss. So it goes ahead on the eighth of December?"

For the first time Blagov smiled. Babakin was a man he
could work with. "On the Feast of the Immaculate Conception."

Chapter ✤ Fifteen

LUIGI BERGANTINO'S ALITALIA flight landed at Sheremetyevo-2, the most modern of the five Moscow airports used by the public.

A man in a full-length black leather coat met Bergantino off the plane, escorted him past passport control and customs, and led him to a black Volga waiting in an area cleared of snow outside the terminal building.

At the end of the airport approach road the Volga turned left on to the Leningradsky Highway, now grandly designated the M10 Motorway. Instead of continuing along Leningradsky, however, the car turned right at the first major junction on to the Motorway Ring.

"Are there problems on the road?" Bergantino asked his escort.

"It's fine," he replied.

Because of the disorienting white blanket of snow Bergantino was at first unsure where they were heading, but he was disconcerted to see the car pass the junction with the M1 from the west and then the junction with the M3 from Vnukovo-1 and the southwest.

Shortly after the junction with the M3 the car turned

left off the Motorway Ring and took a narrow snow-covered road into a dense snow-covered forest. A large sign was ominously cleared of snow: *Halt! No Trespassing! Water Conservation District.*

After two hundred meters they came to what appeared to be a militia post. The car stopped briefly and was waved on. After about another three hundred meters the road ended in a traffic circle, which led on either side to parking lots and straight ahead to a high chain-link fence topped by three strands of barbed wire. The car halted at a gate. The guardhouse next to the gate bore a bronze plaque inscribed in gold letters: *Scientific Research Center.* Bergantino's escort handed a buff-colored plastic card to a KGB guard in a fur hat, khaki greatcoat with blue flashes on the collar, and boots. The guard, who had a Kalashnikov slung over his shoulder, peered into the car to correlate the face with the photograph and then he examined the perforated codes on the card.

Bergantino was now worried. "Where are we going?" he asked.

"It's fine," his escort replied.

Bergantino's worries increased.

The car drove through the gate past snow-covered lawns and flower beds. Ahead loomed a seven-story aluminum and glass building shaped like a three-pointed star, with windows edged in blue stone. Bergantino had never seen a scientific research center with so many intricate communications aerials on its roof.

He followed the escort with the limited vocabulary through double glass doors into a large marble foyer. A sentry examined the escort's pass with even greater care than that shown at the gate. Bergantino gazed at the bust of Felix Dzerzhinsky. The flower beds outside may have been covered by frost and snow, but inside freshly cut flowers lay beneath the image of founder of the secret police.

The escort led Bergantino past a newsstand to a bank of elevators in the center of the building. Beyond lay a large cafeteria. Bergantino had lost his appetite.

They left the elevator at the second floor. The escort showed his buff-colored pass yet again to a receptionist behind a desk. Behind her was an armed KGB trooper. The receptionist telephoned. After five minutes' silent wait, an attractive, well-dressed woman came down one of the three corridors that led from the reception desk.

"Please follow me," she said.

Bergantino did so willingly; hers was the first smile he had seen since he had bid goodbye to the Alitalia stewardess.

She knocked at a door and, without waiting for a reply, opened it.

"Come in, Luigi. I trust you had a pleasant journey."

"It would have helped if my escort had told me where on earth I was going," Bergantino complained.

Babakin looked surprised. "You sent a signal that you wanted to see me urgently."

"I've never been here before."

"I keep an office at the Lubyanka, but all the First Chief Directorate, apart from the Twelfth Department, moved to Yasenevo some time ago. Coffee?"

Bergantino's pent-up recrimination poured out. "You promised me no violence! I made it clear that I wanted nothing to do with violence! You promised me!"

Babakin was impassive.

"Destroying Zingler's career was one thing—that was bad enough—but killing Davino . . ."

Babakin let the storm abate. "You must help me stop the killing, Luigi," he said quietly. "He's planning something much worse. You are the only one who can prevent it."

"What are you talking about? Who's he? The President? I don't believe you."

Babakin walked to the triple-glazed window and looked out over a blanket of snow, past a forest of snow-speckled pine trees, and beyond to the Lenin Hills on the skyline, from which rose the unmistakable skyscraper of Stalin's Moscow University, frilled like a wedding cake and topped by a tall spire. "The main reason you were brought here rather than the Lubyanka is that this is one of the few secure places we can talk." He turned round. "General Blagov is planning to assassinate the Pope."

"Then stop it!" Bergantino said.

Babakin gestured to two low black leather armchairs, and waited until Bergantino had sunk into one of them before he perched on the edge of his desk. "If it were an official KGB plan, or even if I had some proof, then I'd try," Babakin said. "Believe me, Luigi, I'd try. I'd go to the President. As I told you, he wants to negotiate with the Pope, not kill him. But I've no proof."

"Are you telling me that the head of the KGB is carrying out some . . . some private assassination scheme? I don't believe it. What's behind it? Who's backing him? If the target is outside the Soviet Union he'd have to involve the First Chief Directorate. You'd have to know."

Babakin remained calm. "All I know, Luigi, is that I passed on your assessment of the *papabili* to Blagov. I read about the Zingler leak. To be honest, I didn't attach any significance to it. You know better than I that Zingler's unpopular with the Romans, and I imagine there'd be at least a dozen who'd willingly leak a document like that to discredit him. But when I heard about Davino's death, I started making inquiries. Blagov denied any involvement. But if it wasn't me, then it must be him. He wasn't using any FCD agents; I'd know about that. I discovered that both the anti-drugs squad of the Second Chief Directorate and the Moscow Militia had been warned off a particular drugs baron. Nothing unusual about that, you may think, except that the order came direct from Blagov and this particular criminal earns most of his money by exporting heroin to a Mafia gang in Sicily. I had some people I could trust put their ears to the ground. One of them came back with a story he'd heard from somebody else. That somebody else had heard this drugs baron boast in the Cheryomushki Restaurant that associates of his had got rid of a cardinal in Italy, but that was peanuts to what they were going to do on the eighth of December on their home territory."

"My God," said Bergantino, on the edge of his seat. "That's less than a week away!"

Babakin held out his hands helplessly. "I can't take on the head of the KGB with only third-hand hearsay evidence to back me. It might not even be true."

"But if it is . . ."

"Luigi, I promised no violence. You've got to help me keep my promise."

"How?"

"Get hold of Ryan. Warn the Pope."

Bergantino sank back in the chair. "Comrade . . ."

"Yes?"

"I'm sorry I accused you of . . ."

"Don't worry, Luigi. We all suffer from strain from time to time."

Chapter ✦ Sixteen

THE VOICE AT the other end of the telephone was urgent. "What engagements has the Pope got the day after tomorrow?"

"The usual, I think," said Ryan. "But hold on a moment." He put down the telephone and reached for the diary. He picked up the telephone. "Luigi? I'm wrong. That's the day he's going to Sicily . . ."

"I must see you," Bergantino interrupted. "As soon as possible."

"The next couple of days are difficult . . ."

"It's a matter of life and death."

Ryan strode back into the Vatican through the Saint Anne Gate, hands in pockets, head down. The guilt he felt at having disbelieved Diana was fuelling his determination to protect the Holy Father at all costs. Luigi hadn't known of any Agent Judas in the Apostolic Palace, but what he had said convinced Ryan there was indeed a traitor in the Palace, and a plot to kill the Holy Father.

❖ ❖ ❖

After lunch Ryan went to the private chapel. He looked up at the suffering face of the Madonna and asked what he should do. The Pope wanted to go ahead with his visit to Siracusa. Hoffman had been adamant in supporting the Pope. No pope could be intimidated by an earthly power, he'd said. The Holy Father had promised the Archbishop and the good people of Siracusa that he would visit them. He had promised the Blessed Virgin that he would pray at her miraculous statue there. She would protect him. If the Holy Father did die that day, by whatever means, then it would be the will of God.

To Ryan it sounded like the "if God had wanted us to fly He would have given us wings" school of theology. He wondered if he would ever penetrate the Eastern mentality. The icon of the Mother of God to the right of the altar could never have been painted in the West. Only an Eastern . . . He stopped. Only an Eastern mind might persuade the Pope not to go to Siracusa. It had to be worth trying.

He left the chapel and hurried through the *salone* to the vestibule and out of the door to the Third Loggia. He went straight past the *uscieri* outside the Secretariat of State and through to Monsignor Botone's office.

"I must see His Excellency, immediately."

Botone's spoilt cherub face frowned even more. "It is usual, Father . . ."

Ryan ignored him, knocked on the door, and went into Archbishop Korchan's office.

Chapter ✤ Seventeen

KIRILLIN WAS WORRIED.

As Babakin had promised, Ukrainian Solidarity had agreed to postpone until the New Year negotiations on the return of all the churches and property seized in 1946. But at the Catholic-Russian Orthodox Dialogue in Leningrad, leaders of the Russian Orthodox Church had demanded that Saint George's Cathedral in Lvov occupied by Ukrainian Catholics, be handed back to them. That demand had provoked Ukrainians into illegally taking over more Russian Orthodox churches in the Ukraine. Matters were slipping outside his control.

And now General Blagov had walked into his office and announced that, as requested, he was about to remove the source of the Ukrainian problem.

Kirillin picked up the phone, dialed, and said, "It'll be fine by two o'clock."

Freshly fallen snow sprinkled the fir trees next to the Kremlin Wall and covered the lawns, flower beds, and paths in the Alexander Garden. It even clung to the Obelisk.

Babakin rubbed his gloved hands together. "It's too cold to stand around. And we're too noticeable. Let's walk."

Kirillin, swathed in fur hat and long fur-trimmed coat, didn't feel particularly noticeable. He followed Babakin along the path, underneath the bridge between the Trinity Tower Gate and the Kutafya Tower Gate, and out of the Garden's southern exit by the Borovitsky Tower.

They walked downhill, past the Water Pump Tower, to the Kremlin Embankment. Winter had set in early. Warmly clad men squatted on stools on top of the frozen river. Some were busy drilling holes through the ice, most were waiting for tugs on lines they held while smoking and chatting to their fellow fishermen. Behind, to his left, the trees were bare and no longer camouflaged the Kremlin Wall, bright rust against the white snow; above the wall the deep yellow and white Great Kremlin Palace was over-looked by the tall white Ivan the Great Bell Tower with its golden dome gleaming against a pale blue sky. Not for Kirillin the Europeanized elegance of the buildings that lined the Neva and the canals of Leningrad. Moscow was the only city in the world in which he felt at home, and especially so in winter when the snow brought out the magic of the colors with which Moscow painted its build-ings.

"It's time that place was closed," Babakin said. "It's an ecological eyesore."

Kirillin looked to his right, beyond the Great Stone Bridge that carried eight lanes of traffic above him be-tween Borovitsky Square and the southern side of the river. A thick cloud of steam rose and swirled like an infer-nal fog. The huge heated outdoor Moscow Swimming Pool had been built only after the foundations of Stalin's planned gigantic Palace of Soviets had collapsed—divine retribution, the religious claimed, for Stalin's demolition of the original building that occupied the site, the Cathedral of Christ the Redeemer.

The magic was broken. "What the devil's happening?" Kirillin demanded. "Blagov boasted this morning that he was removing the source of the Ukrainian problem. I asked him when, and all he'd say was the Feast of the Immaculate Conception."

"That's tomorrow," Babakin smiled. "I was planning to brief you."

Kirillin listened while Babakin detailed what response the President should make to the following day's events.

Chapter ✠ Eighteen

As the morning of the Feast of the Immaculate Conception drew to a close, Ryan found it impossible to concentrate on his work. His anxiety wasn't helped by Monsignor Botone's pompous summons, saying that Archbishop Korchan wished to interview him in connection with the leak of confidential documents to the ANSA news agency.

Archbishop Korchan was in full clerical dress and appeared grave. Botone, giving Ryan a look that a jailer might give a prisoner after handing him over to the executioner, closed the door behind him.

Korchan was seated at his desk, below the photograph of the Pope on the wall. "Have you ever given any confidential documents to an employee of ANSA, or to anyone in a position to pass them on to ANSA?" he asked.

"No, Excellency."

"I thought not," said Korchan, scribbling something in a file which he then closed. He stood up, removed his skullcap, shrugged off his cape, and drew yellow curtains across the tall window. "I did think you would want to see the news." He opened the sliding door of a walnut cabinet opposite the window to reveal a television set. "Please, James, sit down," he said, gesturing to two easy chairs.

Ryan watched the last few minutes of an Italian-dubbed episode of *Dallas* before a *Dallas*-type model beamed the delights of toothpaste. Korchan fingered his brass pectoral cross when the toothpaste dissolved into the title sequence and signature tune of the midday news.

It was the first item.

"An explosion rocks Sicily," the female newscaster announced.

The television cut to a scene of devastation. Ambulance men carried stretchers from rubble that had been an altar, while police and *carabinieri* vainly tried to keep back crowds of onlookers.

"Less than half an hour ago," the newscaster's voice continued over the picture, "an explosion in the Sicilian city of Siracusa killed two people and injured several others. It seems a much worse disaster was averted by the cancellation this morning of the Pope's visit because of a heavy cold. The explosion occurred at the shrine of the statue known as the Weeping Madonna of Siracusa at precisely the time the Pope was due to pray there.

"No warning had been given of a bomb, and so far no organization has claimed responsibility. Police forensic experts are now on the scene examining the debris . . ."

Korchan turned off the television set. "Well, James, it seems you were right to confide in me, and I was right to trust you."

Ryan was numb. Distress at the sight of the dead and injured was mixed with relief that the Holy Father's life had been saved. But it had been close. "How did you persuade him, Excellency?"

Korchan shrugged. "I talked in language he understands. Perhaps you had better go and tell him what has happened."

"Do you think it's connected with the leak of Cardinal Zingler's papers?"

Korchan shrugged again. "Who knows?"

* * *

Hoffman gave Ryan a strange look. "The Holy Father has a cold. He's retired to bed."

"Have you heard about the bomb . . . ?"

Hoffman nodded. "The Sisters heard it on the radio in the kitchen. They came to me straight away. While you were out, Signor Bergantino telephoned on the direct line. He wants you to phone him back."

"We owe the Pope's life to Signor Bergantino, Kasamir."

Hoffman's eyebrows lifted. "Do we?"

"It was he who told me . . ." Ryan left the sentence unfinished.

"It's all too neat, James. Be careful. Very careful."

"But Kasamir, the Holy Father was going . . ."

"Just be careful, James."

Ryan said, "I'm very grateful, Luigi."

Bergantino nodded. Neither of them was eating much of the *pollo al peperone* that Paolo served them in Rasella's, but Bergantino was drinking a lot. "I'm just relieved we found out in time. It could have been . . ." He filled up his glass yet again. "The President wants to settle this Ukrainian thing once and for all," he said. "Man to man with the Pope."

"How?" Ryan asked.

"It's simple. The President wants the Pope to come to Moscow. They'll solve the Ukrainian problem together. No Roman Curia or Central Committee getting in the way."

Ryan reached for his glass and sat back in his chair.

"Luigi," he said slowly, "I have to tell you that there are people in the Apostolic Palace, people close to the Holy Father, who are very suspicious about what has happened. They think it was all fixed."

"What do you mean? Fixed?"

"Strange things have been happening. Cardinal Zingler's career is destroyed, Cardinal Davino dies in curious circumstances . . ." Ryan didn't want to mention Cardinal

Demeure's wish to resign. "Some other odd events. Now, the Soviet President warns the Holy Father about an assassination attempt conducted by his own secret service, and then invites the Holy Father to Moscow."

Bergantino looked up to heaven. "Ecclesiastical principalities are exalted and maintained by God, and so only a rash and presumptuous man would take it upon himself to discuss them."

"Pardon?"

"Machiavelli, in *The Prince*. It's perfectly straightforward, James. Or at least as straightforward as these things ever are. This assassination attempt was made by certain elements within the KGB without the President's knowledge. If you don't believe me, watch tomorrow evening's news."

Supper was the usual soup and an apple. Korchan had wanted the Pope to stay in bed, but the Pope insisted on joining them to watch the television news as Ryan had suggested. He wasn't disappointed.

Once more it was the lead story.

"Tonight, sensational news from Moscow."

The film showed the Soviet President addressing a packed session of the Supreme Soviet. The Russian voice faded, to be replaced by the Italian interpreter's voice.

". . . I was furnished with evidence that the Chairman of the State Security Committee had personally authorized the assassination of a world leader whom I, and all peace-loving peoples in the Soviet Union, hold in the highest esteem for his unswerving commitment to peace and to the dignity of man, based on the spiritual values shared by all Europeans, both East and West. Such action is totally indefensible, and all the more so when we are struggling to emerge from a society based on the arbitrary use of power in order to build a society based on the rule of law. General Blagov has been dismissed from his post and is held under house arrest pending trial. I can assure this parliament

that, although the gold bullion that General Blagov transferred out of the country in order to finance this operation
may not be recoverable, I and the new Chairman of the
State Security Committee will ensure that legality is restored in the operations of our security service . . ."

The picture cut to a reporter huddled against the cold of
Moscow's night. Behind him, across the frozen river, the
floodlit Kremlin towers, palaces and cathedrals glowed like
fairy castles and, above, the internally-lit five-pointed stars
atop the tallest towers shone ruby red against the dark blue
night.

"Those were the scenes shown on Soviet television less
than an hour ago," the reporter said into his microphone.
"Moscow is buzzing with rumors about the identity of the
world leader who was the assassination target. Foreign Affairs spokesman Igor Churbanov has refused to amplify the
President's statement, but Western correspondents here
are convinced that it was the Pope. Only yesterday an explosion . . ."

Hoffman nodded. "Perhaps this is a Soviet leader who
can be trusted."

Chapter ❖ Nineteen

THE PENCIL BROKE in Kirillin's fingers. He hadn't even realized he had been playing with it. On his desk in front of him, *Pravda, Izvestia, Trud, Argumenty i Fakty,* and the rest all led with photographs of the disgraced General Blagov. Kirillin remembered the general's wife, a small, dumpy woman in a patterned frock who had accompanied Blagov to a reception in Saint George's Hall shortly after Blagov had been appointed KGB chairman.

His hand hesitated. Finally he picked up the green phone, dialed, and said, "It'll be fine by two o'clock."

"I doubt it," a voice replied. "The blizzard will last all day. I'll pop into your office in half an hour. There're a couple of things you ought to know."

Babakin was unaffected by the blizzard sweeping across Red Square. He'd come via the secret underground tunnel from the Lubyanka that connected with the warren of passages beneath the Kremlin.

"I've been thinking about Blagov . . ." Kirillin began.

"Spare your sympathies," Babakin interjected. He made himself comfortable in the seat on the other side of Kirillin's desk. "Don't ever forget that Blagov was conspiring

with members of the General Staff in a treasonable act
while the President was in the States. If you and I hadn't
headed Karavansky off at the pass, we'd now be in the middle of a civil war. Blagov would have been the one who
greeted the President off the plane. Don't imagine he
would have been at the airport to invite the President for
homemade soup at Kuntsevo. And," he added, "you would
now be scratching a line every day on the walls of a cell at
Lefortovo. That is, if you hadn't already been shot."

Kirillin shook his head. "We can't explain all that at his
trial."

"There won't be a trial."

"But you told me to advise the President that . . ."

Babakin shrugged. "Even my advice gets overtaken by
events. General Vladimir Blagov, late of the GRU and tem-
porarily of the KGB, was found this morning at his villa.
He'd been shot in the head from close range."

Kirillin put his head in his hands. "My God."

"Don't worry," Babakin said, "his service revolver was
on the desk next to his body. It's an open and shut case for
the investigator."

"But if he was under house arrest . . . ?"

"Either security was slack, or somebody must have
given him the opportunity of taking the honorable way out.
Will you ensure his widow is treated well?"

"Of course."

"Good." Babakin leaned back in his chair. "It'll be interesting to see," he mused, "how many members of the Government and the General Staff attend the burial." He
grinned. "You and I, however, will have the perfect excuse."

"I don't understand."

"The Pope's taken the bait. You and I are off to Rome to
agree arrangements for a papal visit."

Chapter ✤ Twenty

Luigi Bergantino brought his Fiat to a halt outside the partially shuttered steel gate. He wound down his window and spoke to one of the two armed *carabinieri,* who went inside a small gatehouse and made a telephone call.

Watching from the passenger seat, Ryan tried to hide his curiosity. The rear entrance to the Villa Abamelek was set in a high concrete wall augmented by gray steel panels and topped by green-painted stanchions that supported eight rows of barbed wire. Behind and above, densely planted tall trees provided further screening. The only sound he heard was the cawing of a crow. Across the narrow pavementless Via Aurelia Antica lay the Villa Doria Pamphili, the vast public park at the highest point of the Janiculum Hill, where Diana Lawrence used to run.

The gates swung back and the Fiat drove on through two solitary white Doric columns at the beginning of a narrow tarmac road lined with life-sized white marble toga-clad figures.

After passing through another shield of trees, Bergantino stopped the car outside a three-story neoclassical villa painted pastel pink with cream edging. All the windows on this side of the villa were shuttered. The open end of the portico facing the Doria was blocked off by a white-painted wooden barricade.

"They're fond of their privacy," said Ryan.

Bergantino smiled. "Discretion is a nicer word."

A broad-shouldered Russian, with elementary Italian, showed them to a large, pale green reception room. Life-sized busts and figurines of Roman nobility occupied niches in walls hung with paintings, mainly from the Renaissance period as far as Ryan could tell. It made him feel he had come to an art gallery rather than the discreet meeting place Bergantino had promised.

A youngish looking man, stocky, with ears sticking out from a friendly face, came into the room followed by an older, leaner man in an elegant gray suit. The top of the second man's head was completely bald, but it was his eyes that Ryan noticed most of all. Ryan had a vague impression that he'd seen that face somewhere before—just a momentary glance—but he couldn't think where.

"This is Father James Ryan," said Bergantino. "Father Ryan, permit me to introduce Dmitry Sergeyevich Kirillin, special assistant to the President of the Union of Soviet Socialist Republics, and Lev Stepanovich Babakin, who will be responsible for security on the visit."

Ryan shook hands, first with Kirillin and then with Babakin, whom he congratulated on his new appointment. Bergantino's profile in *L'Unità* of the acting Chairman of the State Security Committee had been encouraging: a man whose background was in the diplomatic service and foreign intelligence and who was therefore untainted by the brutality and suppression of freedom exercised by the domestic arm of the KGB, a man who was personally committed to a society based on human rights and the rule of law, and a man, moreover, whose mother was a devout Orthodox believer.

"A drink?" Kirillin asked in Italian. "It is traditional in our country."

Ryan took his glass of vodka.

"To the success of our meeting," Kirillin said and knocked back the drink.

After two more toasts the others looked at Ryan. "To the continued progress of religious liberty in the Soviet Union," Ryan said. Babakin laughed. They all drank.

"Have you ever been to the Soviet Union?" Babakin asked.

Ryan blushed. "I'd love to go to Russia. What a wonderful view you have."

Kirillin opened the French windows on to the north-facing terrace. The grounds of the villa dropped away, giving a direct line of sight down on to Saint Peter's Basilica and the Apostolic Palace. "Goodness," Ryan said, "if you had a powerful enough laser or something like that . . ."

Babakin laughed. "What a mind you have, Father Ryan. We're here to discuss peace."

"Indeed," Kirillin said. "With your permission, Father, Signor Bergantino will withdraw. I trust my Italian is adequate, but General Babakin is fluent should we need an interpreter."

Ryan hoped the four vodkas hadn't slowed his brain. This was the most important task he'd ever undertaken. In the Ukraine he'd simply been a messenger. Here he was entrusted with arranging the most momentous mission ever undertaken by the Pope—and potentially the most significant papal visit this century. He'd assured the Holy Father that the negotiating skills he'd learnt at Harvard equipped him for the task. The Holy Father had put his trust in him. Kasamir Hoffman had said the Mother of God would be on his side.

He sat down opposite the two Russians at a long oak table. His objectives and strategy were clear in his mind. "His Holiness would be happy to accept an invitation to visit the Soviet Union provided certain conditions are met."

The other two looked at each other. "Please continue," Kirillin said.

"His Holiness is first and foremost the spiritual leader of

the Catholic Church," Ryan stated, "and any visit he makes
to another country is first and foremost a pastoral visit to
his flock in that country. That means he would need to visit
the areas where members of the Catholic Church are most
numerous: Lithuania, Latvia, and the Ukraine."

Kirillin nodded genially. "That can be arranged."

"It is essential," Ryan continued, "that the faithful must
be able to prepare spiritually for the visit of their Supreme
Pastor. That situation now exists in Lithuania and in Latvia
but not, the Holy Father fears, in the Ukraine. It is not
enough for the Catholic Church in the Ukraine to be legal-
ized. There must exist the normal ecclesiastical structures
that enable bishops and priests to carry out their pastoral
work in full communion with the Holy See."

"I'm not a religious man, Father Ryan," Kirillin said.
"You must spell out in terms I understand what conditions
the Pope is proposing for his visit."

Ryan took a deep breath. "It means, Mr. Kirillin, that, as
elsewhere, the Holy See must be free to appoint bishops
for the local Church in the Ukraine . . ."

"As it does in the United States," Babakin amplified.

Ryan wasn't sure if Babakin was referring to the row
over the Vatican's nomination to the bishopric of Newark.
He decided to let it pass. "These bishops must be free to
run seminaries and to ordain priests, and to visit the Holy
See in order to maintain their contacts with the rest of the
Universal Church. The priests must be free to give instruction in the Catholic faith to those who wish it. And the
faithful must be free to use their churches for divine services."

"If these requirements were merely religious," Kirillin
said, "there'd be no problem. The President has made
clear that the process of *perestroika* leads to a society in
which freedom of conscience is guaranteed. But," his genial expression gave way to one of seriousness, "unfortu-
nately, religion and nationalism—nationalism of the most
destructive kind—have become entwined in the Ukraine.
The President is prepared to ensure that the State provides

the conditions necessary for believers of all kinds to practice faiths which genuinely promote peace and the love of fellow man."

"Which the Catholic Church does," Ryan said.

"Certainly we believe the Pope wishes this to be so."

"I think you should spell out, Mr. Kirillin, in terms I understand, what you are saying."

Babakin smiled. "Perhaps my Italian is a little more fluent. What Mr. Kirillin is saying is that religious freedom and secession from the Soviet Union are not the same things. One is pastoral, the other is political. The President would be dismayed if the Supreme Pastor of a Church committed to peace on earth were to condone secessionist nationalism that leads inevitably to bloodshed. That would only serve to reinforce criticisms of the Catholic Church made by reactionaries within the Soviet Union. On the contrary, we would expect the Pope to preach the Christian message of brotherly love."

"Are those your conditions?" Ryan asked.

"Let's not talk of conditions," Kirillin said. "But I hope you appreciate that the President has shown his good will toward the Pope. Not only did he prevent an assassination attempt by elements within the KGB, he risked a great deal by publicly exposing that attempt. He continues to risk a great deal by inviting the Pope to the Soviet Union and promising the Catholic Church its liberty. I hope the Pope wishes to reciprocate this good will."

It was time to exploit the other side's weakness. "The Pope can help the Soviet President solve his problems in the Ukraine," Ryan said.

"He *could* be helpful," Babakin said, "if he restrains certain extremists in the Ukrainian Catholic Church. But the Pope isn't essential to a solution. The security of the State will be maintained by whatever means are necessary."

"However," Kirillin said, "within the parameters of a peaceful Ukraine inside the Soviet Union, complete religious liberty is possible. That is the message we should like you to take back to the Pope."

"We haven't discussed the return of the Ukrainian Catholic churches seized in 1946 and given to the Orthodox," Ryan said.

"Ah," Babakin sighed. "We think this is essentially a Church matter, a dispute between the Orthodox and the Catholic Churches. Off the record, the President would like nothing better than to see the Orthodox Church rejoin the Catholic Church. That would solve all the problems in the Ukraine."

Ryan could scarcely believe his ears. He tried to disguise his excitement by nodding sagely. He was so stunned by the prospect of the Holy Father ending the 900-year schism between the Western and the Eastern Churches that he quite forgot to ask the new KGB chairman about Agent Judas.

Chapter ✤ Twenty-one

THE POPE WAS mad.

Cardinal Fasolo looked up from behind the piles of paper and the crucifix on his desk to the picture of the Pope on the wall opposite. The face smiled, but the eyes gleamed with absolute certainty. Peter, and even Christ himself in the Garden of Gethsemane, had been plagued by doubts, but not this Vicar of Christ. He possessed a monumental conviction indistinguishable from obstinacy. It was more than an unswerving faith, it was an obsession.

This Pope simply did not understand that the world consisted of various shades of gray, and that the Church's role was to shift the balance toward the white. For him there was only black and white. From Fasolo's first job in the Secretariat, when he was twenty-six years old, his life had been devoted to negotiating concessions here and there with Communist authorities so that, imperceptibly, the seeds of Catholicism could be planted in atheistic soil, be nurtured, and grow with roots deep enough to withstand the inevitable temporary setbacks. This painstaking work over decades was now reaping its rewards as he always knew it would. With the collapse of Communist power in eastern Europe, the Church was one of the few bodies capable of filling the ideological and organizational gap.

This lifetime's work was about to be torn asunder by a Pope who believed that Our Lady wanted, nay insisted, that he personally convert Russia.

The American ambassador to the Holy See had warned Antonio that the CIA had discovered the Soviets had a highly placed agent, codenamed Judas, in the Apostolic Palace. Antonio had been skeptical. Fasolo hadn't. He had experience of these people, and already suspected there might be a connection between Zingler's discrediting, Davino's death, and Demeure's intention to retire. He'd gone immediately to brief the Pope. But the Pope had brushed all aside with the news that he was going to Russia. In Moscow he would issue a public invitation to all Russian Orthodox bishops to join an ecumenical council of the Universal Church in order to consecrate Russia to the Immaculate Heart of Mary as requested by the Virgin of Fatima.

For one of the few times in his life, Fasolo had been speechless. This Pope had gone behind the back of the Secretary of State, bypassed all the proper channels, and had conducted secret negotiations with the Soviet Government. When Fasolo had recovered his composure, he had asked the Pope if it were possible that he was being used. Of course, the Pope had replied. He was being used by the Mother of God to unite the Eastern and the Western Churches so that, combined, they might withstand the final onslaught of the Antichrist that she had prophesied at Fatima.

There was no more to be said.

Not content with driving the Church in the United States toward severing its links with Rome—and also severing the financial assistance that saved the Vatican from bankruptcy—this Pope was about to inflict the ultimate humiliation on the Holy See: convening an ecumenical council that a majority of the world's bishops would ignore. Fasolo doubted that more than a handful of Orthodox bish-

ops would come to Rome. Certainly less than half the
Catholic Church's four thousand bishops would attend an
ecumenical council summoned without consultation in response to a story told in 1917 by a ten-year-old illiterate
peasant girl in Portugal. If this insane action wasn't
checked, the Catholic Church would disintegrate. The
Vatican would be reduced to a fundamentalist bankrupt
rump incapable of wielding any influence for good in the
world.

And he, a member of the Fasolo family, was powerless
to stop it.

That face continued to smile down at him. It smiled
from every room in the Vatican, from the lowliest cleaner's
to . . . to the Secretary of State's rooms. He stood up suddenly, knocking back his chair. He pressed his intercom.
"Giovanni, I'm going for a walk in the Vatican Gardens. I
don't know how long I'll be."

Hands in his overcoat pockets, the slight figure of Cardinal
Fasolo walked rapidly up the Slope of the Mint, steering
away from the Governor's Palace and continuing up the
Avenue of the Observatory toward the top of the Vatican
Hill. Out of breath from his exertions, he sat down on the
end of a bench and surveyed his world, the world con-
structed over centuries by Italian popes. From the original
thirteenth-century buildings of the Apostolic Palace commissioned by Nicholas III Gaetano of the Orsini family,
then enlarged by Nicholas V Parentucelli in the fifteenth
century, he knew who was responsible for every single
stone in the Palace. Similarly for the basilica that replaced
the Constantine Basilica, from the first stone laid by Julius
II della Rovere in 1506 to the enlarging of Michelangelo's
design by Paul V Borghese in order to emphasize the great-
ness of the Roman Catholic Church undeterred by the
Reformation. The Sistine Chapel named after its patron
Sixtus IV della Rovere . . .

"I didn't expect to find you, Eminence, at a Marian shrine."

Fasolo snapped out of his reverie. The large figure of Archbishop Korchan, also in black overcoat, loomed over him. He didn't know what Korchan was talking about until the latter stepped to one side. Behind him was the Lourdes Grotto. Built at a break in the wall of Leo IV, and guarded by railings painted Marian blue, a two-foot-high plaster Virgin looked down from a niche in a vulgar facsimile of the grotto at Lourdes.

"Your secretary said you'd gone for a walk in the gardens," Korchan explained.

Fasolo said nothing. He knew of Korchan's invitations to supper in the private apartment and his strolls with the Pope in the roof garden. Korchan had probably been involved in the Russian negotiations behind his back.

"The Holy Father told me of his plans for Russia, Eminence. I thought you should know straight away."

Fasolo nodded. "Thank you, Excellency. I know already."

Korchan sighed. He looked at the plaster Virgin. "It seems to me, Eminence, that private revelations should remain precisely that."

Fasolo looked closely at the *Sostituto*. In all the years he had known him, Fasolo had never heard the Ukrainian offer a personal opinion on a theological matter, still less one which, in this papal household, would be deemed near-heresy.

"Not even Fatima?" Fasolo probed.

Korchan shrugged his large shoulders. "I was taught that God's truths are revealed through Scripture and through the Church He founded, not through individuals, be they saints or merely children blessed with a vivid imagination."

Fasolo nodded.

"Eminence, this ecumenical council . . ."

"Yes?"

"May I sit down, Eminence?"

"Of course." Fasolo made room on the bench.

"I find this very difficult, Eminence. I have always tried to be loyal to the Holy Father . . . I hope I still am . . ." He turned toward Fasolo, as if to seek reassurance.

"Nobody doubts it, Excellency."

"Alexander, please."

Fasolo nodded. Their relationship had always been a formal one. It was his fault. He worked so hard that he had little time for socializing; the few he felt comfortable with were the friends he had made at the Pontifical Ecclesiastical Academy. He was aware people thought him aloof; the truth was that he was more at ease with documents than he was with people. But that was no excuse for never going out of his way to make this exile feel at home in Rome.

"The Holy Father tends to talk to me," Korchan continued. "I think it's because we're both Slavs, we can converse in his own language. I do try to let him know what the bishops think, Eminence, but . . . In recent times I do not think he listens. I wonder, Eminence, if the Holy Father is not well."

"A pope is never ill."

"But I'm sure the Holy Father . . ."

Fasolo smiled wryly. "An old Roman proverb, Alexander, says that the only sick pope is a dead one. Pius XII was seriously ill in 1954, John XXIII suffered agonies in his last months, Paul VI, bless him, was barely functioning in the last year of his pontificate. None of this was ever revealed during their lifetimes. It is not the Roman way."

"But it cannot be good, Eminence, if a sick pope has the power to summon an ecumenical council that will prove a disaster for the Church."

Fasolo shrugged. "There is nothing to prevent any pope from summoning an ecumenical council or making infallible declarations if he so wishes. The Church, in her wisdom, has decided that diocesan bishops and heads of Curial dicasteries must offer their resignations on their seventy-fifth birthday, and that no cardinal over eighty may vote in a conclave to elect a new pope. But eight out of ten popes in the last hundred and fifty years have lived beyond eighty, with no limit to their powers."

"Popes have resigned, Eminence."

Again that wry smile. "Most, Alexander, were forced to resign. Stephen VI, Romanus, John XIV, Benedict V. They were fortunate. Some of their contemporaries in the ninth and tenth centuries were killed rather than deposed. We live now in more civilized times."

"The Church has provided for resignation. Paragraph two of Canon 332 of the Code of Canon Law."

Fasolo leaned back. *"If it should happen that the Roman Pontiff resigns his office, it is required for validity that he makes his resignation freely and that it is duly manifested, but not that it be accepted by anyone."*

"But Eminence, if a pope is so incapacitated that he is unable to manifest his resignation . . . what would happen then?"

Fasolo thought. "I suppose," he said slowly, "that the Camerlengo might consider incapacitation a manifestation of resignation."

"And incapacitation can be mental as well as physical?"

Fasolo looked at the Ukrainian. "Why do you ask these questions, Alexander? Why do you refer to an obscure part of Canon Law?"

Korchan hung his head. "I confess, Eminence, it is because I myself have been asked these very questions in recent months."

"By whom?"

"I haven't mentioned anything to you, Eminence, out of loyalty to the Holy Father. I still find it difficult."

"You show a commendable loyalty, Alexander. But personal loyalty should not conflict with loyalty to Holy Mother Church."

"I know, Eminence."

"Then tell me who has asked these questions."

Korchan sighed. "My job means that I'm in constant touch with all the heads of dicasteries, whereas their meetings with you tend to be more formal. The bishops on their *ad limina* visits from dioceses all over the world pass through my office. They tend perhaps to talk more freely to me."

That was almost certainly true, Fasolo thought. People tended to be intimidated by his own intellect, if not his status, whereas Alexander Korchan was not renowned for a razor-sharp mind. But neither was he a prima donna or a gossip. His friendly face and his discretion—qualities that made him the ideal *Sostituto*—made him the perfect listener.

"You haven't answered my question, Alexander," Fasolo said.

Korchan stood up. He walked to the end of the tarmac and on to the lawn so that he could look down over the Governor's Palace, the Basilica of Saint Peter, the Apostolic Palace and, connected to it, the two long lines of buildings either side of the Belvedere Courtyard that housed part of the priceless Vatican Museum collection. Fasolo joined him.

"There is a deep and widespread concern about the Church, Eminence. And how much will be left for the next Successor of Saint Peter to inherit." He seemed to have made a decision. "Will you do me the honor of having supper with me, say tomorrow evening? I will unburden some of the load I have been carrying."

Chapter ✧ Twenty-two

FASOLO HAD OVER twenty-four hours to dwell on his conversation with Korchan in the Vatican Gardens. It was outrageous, of course, that the Pope no longer consulted the Secretary of State, the cardinal who was constitutionally the Pope's closest collaborator. Antonio Benedetti had also told him of the Curia's growing fears about the Pope's behavior, but Antonio owed his career to Fasolo's patronage and he had assumed that Antonio's views were colored by his loyalty and his friendship. Alexander Korchan, however, was different. He was widely regarded as the Pope's man, and to hear the same anxieties from him was a revelation. It confirmed that his own analysis was accurate and not jaundiced by *amour propre*. And it confirmed his conviction that he had a duty to prevent the destruction of the Church.

He walked along Foundation Road, which circled the rear of the basilica, until he came to the Piazza Santa Marta on the opposite side from the Apostolic Palace, where Alexander Korchan lived in the Palazzo San Carlo.

He had been here many times because the Palazzo housed the Pontifical Council for Social Communications, but he felt ashamed that he had never visited Alexander Korchan. The *usciere* pressed the button for the lift and told him that His Excellency's apartment was on the top floor.

The nun who opened the door looked young, but it was difficult to be sure because she was covered from head to toe in white veil and habit. Only her face showed. Her eyes were red, she sniffed, and after taking Fasolo's coat, she put a large handkerchief to her nose and hurried out.

"Eminence, welcome indeed to my home," Korchan said. "I apologize for Sister Olga," he whispered.

"Problems?" Fasolo asked as he followed Korchan along a passage and into a modest dining room.

Korchan closed the door behind them. He gritted his teeth, and his right fist smacked into his left palm. "The Vatican Health Service."

Fasolo had never seen the *Sostituto* display anger before.

"Look what they prescribed this afternoon for Sister Olga's depression!"

He took a brown pill bottle from the jacket pocket of his black clerical suit and banged it on the dining room table.

Fasolo picked it up. The label said Largactil. He shrugged and put it down again.

Korchan took back the bottle. "They may call it Largactil, but I know that it's Aminazin. I've had to tell Sister Olga that I will not have it in my house." He threw it into the wastepaper basket. "Drink, Eminence?"

"A small whiskey, please." Fasolo wondered if he should have asked for a large one.

Korchan poured out two whiskies, and handed one to Fasolo. "I apologize, Eminence. I should not show my anger. But it is very difficult if you've had the experience of Aminazin that I and many others have."

Fasolo sat down in one of the two armchairs in front of an electric fire. "When did you have experience of this drug, Alexander?" he asked.

Korchan, still standing, turned to the framed photographs on top of the drinks cabinet. The largest was a black and white portrait of Metropolitan Slipyj. He picked it up. "It was a long time ago, Eminence," he said quietly. "But memories like that can never be erased."

He sat down in the other armchair. His eyes stared vacantly into the three red bars of the electric fire. The quiet Ukrainian, who never spoke about himself, began to pour out his story. "I was twenty-four years old. I had been practicing as a clandestine priest for two years when the KGB caught me. They didn't give us tablets." He pulled back the sleeve of his jacket, undid his cufflinks, and pushed back his shirt to show the puncture marks. "They injected the Aminazin. Every day. I became like a cabbage. I couldn't remember anything. I couldn't think. All I could do was repeat what I was told to say." He gave a deep sigh. "That's the state I was reduced to at my trial. Like an automaton I repeated my confession. And, God forgive me, I repeated 'evidence' incriminating others—people I'd never heard of, or if I had, then I couldn't remember them."

"But it didn't have a permanent effect?" Fasolo inquired.

Korchan shook his head. "Once they'd drugged me into telling the courts what they wanted, they shipped me off to the camps. After the injections stopped, my memory began returning. Within a few months I was back to normal, if you can call living in a Soviet penal camp normal."

"You were sent to the same camp as Metropolitan Slipyj?"

"They sent me first to Labor Camp VL-315/30—once you've been to a camp you never forget any details—which is near Lvov. But they caught me leading prayers in the camp and punished me by sending me to Camp 1 in Mordovia, and that's where I met the Metropolitan. And also Mychaylo Antoniuk."

"The bishop who led the Lvov uprising?"

Korchan nodded. "Mychaylo was then a young priest like me, but much braver than I was. He might have been here instead of me. When Khrushchev eventually agreed to let Metropolitan Slipyj attend the Second Vatican Council, the Metropolitan had been almost eighteen years in the camps. His health was poor and he needed an assistant. It should have been Mychaylo, but he wanted to stay and help his countrymen. And so at the end of January 1963 Metropolitan Slipyj and I left the Soviet Union and arrived nearly two weeks later in Rome." He sighed again. "Metropolitan Slipyj died here in exile, and I . . . I'm still here."

Korchan's eyes refocused. "Eminence, please forgive me! I invite you here for supper and then bore you with the story of my life."

"No, no, Alexander. I'm interested. I'm flattered you feel you can confide in me."

Korchan stood up and refilled Fasolo's glass. "I'm not usually like this. I was upset by the sight of the Aminazin, and the idea that it was being prescribed for poor Sister Olga. I'll see if supper is ready."

Another nun, much older, brought the supper through: slices of a fatty sausage with brown bread, followed by borscht, and then cabbage leaves stuffed with minced meat and small dumplings filled with sugared sour cream. Fasolo was touched that they'd prepared a Ukrainian meal for him, though he actually preferred simple Italian cooking. The wine, at least, was Vatican Frascati, not some dubious Eastern wine nor the French wines that Antonio served.

They were still seated at the table, amid empty dishes and halfway through the second bottle of Frascati, when Korchan said, "It's not quite true to say, Eminence, that I didn't invite you here to unburden my problems. You see, I've been worried for some time about His Holiness. As I mentioned yesterday, I'm constantly asked by our own people in the Curia and by visiting bishops if the Pope intends to retire. He is a good pope, you know, Eminence. I want him to go down in history as a good pope, and not the pope who caused the break-up of the Church."

"You think that's possible, Alexander?"

Korchan looked into his glass. "I think it's probable,

Eminence, very probable, if he carries on. A papal visit
now to Moscow could reap huge rewards for the Church *if*
it's handled properly. But the Holy Father . . . he seems to
have only one thing on his mind. And the idea of summoning an ecumenical council to consecrate Russia to the Immaculate Heart of Mary . . ." He shook his head.

"I take it you've mentioned your fears to the Holy Father?"

Korchan nodded. "But he no longer seems to listen to
me."

"Does he listen to anyone?"

"Monsignor Hoffman. That's hardly surprising, of
course. Monsignor Hoffman spends more time with him
than anyone else. Breakfast, lunch, supper, and after supper—quite apart from office work and accompanying the
Holy Father at most engagements."

"Father Ryan?"

"Father Ryan was highly recommended by Cardinal
Harding. He's well educated and from a Western background. That's why I chose him as the junior private secretary, in the hope that he'd provide some counter to
Hoffman. But . . ." he shrugged. "Father Ryan is relatively
young and impressionable, and Hoffman's a strong personality."

Fasolo thought a little while. Then he said, "Tell me,
Alexander, what do you think a pope should do in Moscow?"

"I know what he should not do. But as for what he
should do, all I can tell you, Eminence, is that everybody
who has confided in me says that the pope they want to see
negotiating with the Russians is Papa Fasolo."

Fasolo tried to look surprised.

"And it's not just for negotiating with the Russians, Eminence. They say we desperately need a pope who can heal
the wounds and bring stability to the Church. They speak,
Eminence, of wanting you on Peter's throne."

Fasolo said nothing.

"Coffee, Eminence?"

"Please, Alexander."

"I won't be long. Sister Sonya is away visiting her sick father, and I've told Sister Maria to look after Sister Olga this evening."

"Let me help you clear the dishes, Alexander."

"Don't you dare, Eminence. My life would be made a misery by the good Sisters if they thought an archbishop was washing up in their kitchen. It would not be worth living if they thought I had let the Cardinal Secretary of State help me. The Sisters will clear away in the morning. Sister Maria did give me permission to make some coffee. It'll only take a few minutes."

As soon as Korchan had left the room, Fasolo looked toward the wastepaper basket. His heart began pounding. He wasn't committing himself to anything, he was simply giving himself an option. He'd have time to consider the options more thoroughly. But it would be foolish not to have all the options available.

He went to the wastepaper basket, removed the bottle of Largactil, put it in his pocket, and sat down at the table to await Korchan and the coffee.

Chapter ✣ Twenty-three

THE FOLLOWING EVENING Fasolo telephoned his sister.

"Domenico," she said. "How good to hear from you. Are you coming for Christmas?"

"I hope so, Francesca," he said. "Is Eduardo free?"

"I'll get him," she said.

Fasolo's cynical brother-in-law, a consultant at Faenza's main hospital, picked up the telephone. "Domenico, what an unexpected honor. How may an agnostic be of service?"

"It's a delicate matter," Fasolo said. "I would appreciate your professional advice, in the strictest confidence."

"It is a matter of profound regret," a weary voice said, "that my professional advice must always be given in confidence. It severely curtails my ability to gossip."

"Eduardo, try and be serious for a change. There have been some rumors about the Vatican Health Service and its drug prescriptions being—how shall I say?—less than rigorous."

"That's not so, Domenico."

"No?"

"No. They aren't rumors. They're facts. The Vatican Pharmacy operates entirely free of Italian drug restrictions. They get away with murder."

Fasolo held his breath.

"You never listen to me," his brother-in-law continued. "I keep telling you. Any fiddle the Vatican can get up to by using its sovereign state status it does. You should appoint me to run the Vatican Health Service. I'd soon sort them out."

Fasolo breathed deeply. "Eduardo. You aren't a practicing Catholic."

"Precisely. I'm far too honest for that. Now, you never make a vague inquiry without some purpose behind it. What in particular is worrying you?"

"Largactil."

"No problem."

"No?"

"No. I prescribe it for a range of ailments, from relieving hiccups to keeping terminal cancer patients drowsy. More usually, though, it's used for treating severe depression."

"No harmful side effects?"

"Not if the correct dose is administered. Why are you so interested in Largactil?"

"It's simply that one of the staff called it Aminazin and said it was dangerous."

"Aminazin? Perhaps they've got it mixed up with something else. I don't know. I'll look it up and phone you back. I take it Francesca has your direct number?"

Fasolo's brother-in-law phoned back within ten minutes.

"Domenico. Your member of staff was right. At least about the name. In Italy Largactil is the proprietary name for chlorpromazine hydrochloride. In other countries it may be called Chloractil, or Aminazin in the case of the USSR."

Fasolo took a deep breath and tried to remain calm even though his heart had begun pounding. "Is it always given in tablet form?"

"Not at all. It can be taken orally in the form of tablets,

powder, or syrup. It can also be administered by intramuscular or intravenous injection."

"What about the side effects? The staff member said it had been used by the KGB to turn people into cabbages. Is that possible?"

"Ah, that rings faint bells. I seem to remember some paper in a medical journal about the use of drugs by the KGB. I haven't got it to hand, but I do have the drugs directory in front of me now. Hold on, I'll check on the side effects . . . Your staff member's probably right, Domenico. Chlorpromazine hydrochloride has a depressant action on the central nervous system. We prescribe anything from between 25 to 50 milligrams three times a day. Higher doses are used for extreme psychotics. If you were to increase the dose even further, then you'd blunt the intellect, the emotions, and the memory. With a higher dose still, your patient would turn into a cabbage. Still more would be fatal."

"Fatal?"

"Sure. It would depress the central nervous system to such a degree that all the body's mechanisms would fail. There'd be a big drop in body temperature, and everything would just pack up. Come to think of it, it'd make an ideal poison. Unless you know specifically what you are looking for, and analyze samples from the urine and the stomach for chlorpromazine hydrochloride, you'd see no telltale signs and you'd assume death through natural causes."

"Surely you wouldn't put 'natural causes' on a death certificate? You'd have to do an autopsy?"

"Depends. If it were a young person with no clinical history of serious illness, then of course there'd be an autopsy. But if the patient had been suffering from a serious complaint, the doctor would assume that complaint was the cause of death. If it were an older man or woman, the doctor would almost certainly write 'cerebrovascular accident' on the death certificate, which would be true, except that it wouldn't be an accident."

"I don't understand."

"Cerebrovascular accident means a stroke in layman's language. And speaking of laymen, why is a prince of the Church so interested in Largactil?"

"One of the staff has been prescribed it. She's Russian, and she's convinced she'll turn into a cabbage if she takes the tablets because of what she's heard about the KGB."

"What dosage have those quacks at the Vatican Health Service prescribed?"

Fasolo looked at the bottle. "One tablet three times a day."

"Stick to being a cardinal, Domenico. You'll never make a doctor. What is the *dosage*? What does the label say about the strength of the tablets?"

He looked again. "Each tablet contains 50 mg, it says."

"For once those quacks have got it right."

"What, Eduardo, would be an unsafe dosage? The kind the KGB administer? And if this staff member accidentally took more tablets than she should, would the effects be reversible?"

"Domenico! Do you think the KGB publish the results of their deliberate overdosing? If I didn't know you better I'd think you were up to some mischief."

"I told you," Fasolo said sharply, "a young Russian nun is worried. I simply wanted to reassure her."

"Then tell her to switch out of the Vatican Health Service. But if one 50 mg tablet of Largactil three times a day is all she is worrying about, tell her she should have my problems. *Ciao*."

"Thank you, Eduardo."

Chapter ✢ Twenty-four

CARDINAL MORELLI HAD been Prefect of the Sacred Congregation for Bishops until the Pope had asked him to make way for the newly elevated Cardinal Stefanski, who could be relied upon to sift out any candidates whose records showed the slightest deviation from doctrinal orthodoxy. It was presented as promotion for Morelli, who was appointed Camerlengo of the Holy Roman Church. Morelli resented it, for the move was, in practice, retirement: the only work the Camerlengo does is to take over responsibility for administering the Church on the death of a pope and for summoning the conclave of cardinals to elect a new pope. In this period—known as the *sede vacante*—the Camerlengo forms a small group of cardinals to advise him. Usually this group consists of the Secretary of State, the dean of the Sacred College, and the senior cardinal deacon. All these offices were presently occupied by graduates of the Pontifical Ecclesiastical Academy. Fasolo was certain they would reach a unanimous view on recognizing the resignation *pro bono Ecclesiae* of this pope if he showed unmistakable signs of mental incapacitation.

It shouldn't be difficult. He saw the Pope every day at

half-past six in the Pope's private library, when the Pope had tea and he—to the Pope's incomprehension—had coffee. He usually arrived at the same time as one of the nuns who brought the tray of tea and coffee from the kitchen in the private apartment. He'd often take the tray from the nun and carry it through into the private library. The only question was the dose. If three tablets of 50 mg each was perfectly normal, and more was given to psychotics, say two or three times that, then he could begin with ten tablets in the tea pot, try that daily for a week, and if that had no effect, he could increase the dose.

Whatever the outcome of the election—though he found it hard to see any other viable *papabili*—he would be in a position to ensure that the former pope was well taken care of. In the early days, when relationships had been good, the Pope had often said he would far prefer to be in a monastery, where he could spend all his time reading, writing and praying, without the distractions of work suited to an administrator rather than a priest. It would be a kindness. Fasolo had seen four popes endure mental and physical torment as they struggled to withstand the burdens of the papacy in their later years. This pope would go down in history as a good pope, and spend his last days as he desired, in prayer and contemplation in a monastery, safely back in his home country. And the Church would be saved.

Fasolo began that evening.

Chapter ✣ Twenty-five

WHEN CARDINAL FASOLO returned to his office the following morning from a budget meeting of the Pontifical Commission for the Vatican City State, he saw a note on the desk from his secretary. Father Ryan had telephoned to say that the six-thirty audiences were canceled until after Christmas.

Fasolo's heart skipped a beat. Had the dose been too strong? He pressed the intercom. "Giovanni, did Father Ryan say that the Holy Father was unwell?"

"No, Eminence. I don't think the Pope is unwell. At twelve-fifteen he has an audience with the Archbishop of Siracusa. I believe they're discussing a replacement statue for the Weeping Madonna. That audience certainly hasn't been canceled."

Fasolo removed his finger from the intercom button. If anything confirmed the Pope's lunacy, this was it. How could a sane man believe that plaster statues weep tears? The head of the Catholic Church was devoting his time to reinforcing the superstitions of Sicilian peasants while cutting off even the barest contact with the Church's Secretary of State. It was madness.

He would have to find other ways of administering the Largactil tablets. Fewer opportunities meant that he'd need to give larger doses rather than the regular ten tablets daily that he'd planned. But that was a logistical problem. Nothing a man of his abilities couldn't solve. He sat down and began to work out how he could do it. When the tablets were ground to powder . . .

By mid-afternoon he was satisfied that he'd found three different ways of achieving his objective before the end of the year.

The intercom buzzed.

"Eminence, it's Father Ryan. Can you spare ten minutes?"

Fasolo put his notes away. "Certainly. Show him in, Giovanni."

Ryan appeared unsure of himself. "I'm sorry to disturb you, Eminence."

Fasolo nodded.

"There are two things I wanted to see you about, Eminence. I know this may seem far-fetched, but I was told by someone in a position to know—not somebody working in the Curia—that there is a traitor in the Apostolic Palace, an agent of the KGB. I did pass this information on to the Holy Father. I also told Archbishop Korchan, because he's investigating the leak of Cardinal Zingler's papers. I think that the leak and the death of Cardinal Davino and . . . and certain other incidents may be connected. I wanted to let you know, Eminence, because . . . because nobody seems to be doing anything about it in the excitement over the Holy Father's visit to the Soviet Union. I realize I may have been given deliberately misleading information—personally I don't think so—but I do think we need to investigate the allegation. The Holy Father may be in danger."

Fasolo was impassive. "And the second thing, Father?"

Ryan relaxed a little. "I wanted to explain why the Holy Father has canceled the six-thirty meetings."

"What is there to explain?" Fasolo asked stiffly.

"It wasn't something that could be left as a message with your secretary."

"No?"

"No, Eminence. You see, the Holy Father would like you to join him in prayer instead."

Fasolo was stunned. "Prayer?"

Ryan nodded. "There's only nine days to Christmas, and the Holy Father would like you to put aside the burdens of your office for a while and join him in a novena to help him prepare for Christ's nativity."

Fasolo tried to take it all in. Christmas was the time when it was impossible to find anyone to do urgently needed work, when one had an obligation to visit relatives, when . . .

"Eminence, the Holy Father is aware that, by accepting the offer to visit the Soviet Union, which came via unusual sources, he didn't consult you. He feels he has been arrogant and uncharitable in his eagerness to heal the schism between East and West. He wants your forgiveness. He would like you to say mass every evening for the next nine evenings in the private chapel and allow him to serve at your mass. Obviously I couldn't leave a message like that with your secretary."

When Ryan had gone, Fasolo covered his face with his hands and, for the first time that he could remember, he wept. His shoulders heaved convulsively while tears streamed down his face.

Pray? When had he last prayed? Not the routine mindless ritual but—what was it now?—the raising of the mind and heart to God.

How had it come to this?

Domenico, Cardinal Fasolo, Vatican Secretary of State, first servant of the Servant of Servants and the one most favored to be the next Vicar of Christ, was planning to turn the Pope into a vegetable, and risking an overdose that might kill him. Cripple, if not murder, the Pope.

For all the right reasons, of course. Everything he had done since he first entered the service of the Church had been for all the right reasons. There was probably no one more skilled in Washington, London, Paris, or Moscow at producing the most convincing of rationales to justify a policy, any policy—including the murder of a pope—if it was for the good of the Church.

He had always loved the Church. He had fallen in love with her the first time he had put on the small altar boy's cassock and had kneeled so close to the tabernacle, mysterious center of the parish church. His love had deepened as he had grown. With his family tradition of serving the papacy, it was inevitable that he would become a priest, inevitable that he would spend his life in the Vatican, mysterious center of the earthly Church. The Church was the Bride of Christ; he had loved no other. It was for her that he had been prepared to murder. What other motive could he possibly have?

The tears flowed again, uncontrollably.

The humility of this simplistic old man who occupied the throne of Peter had stripped away his own self-deception. What lay exposed was a pride rivalling that of Lucifer, the first and most brilliant of the angels who had wanted to be as great as God.

Only overwhelming pride could have convinced him it was essential that Domenico Fasolo occupy the throne of Peter at this critical point in history. Only overwhelming pride could have turned his outstanding abilities against the very God who had created him. Why else had he not bowed himself in prayer before God?

Everything was clear now, of course. Korchan, standing there on top of the Vatican Hill offering him the Church if only he would deny God. Korchan was the KGB agent. But it was he, Domenico Fasolo, who was the real Judas, the real Lucifer, whose pride blinded him to the obvious.

Once he had become pope, he would be in Korchan's power. Korchan knew, and doubtless had means of proving, that he had administered this drug to the Pope. As the next pope, Fasolo would be able to do nothing without Korchan's agreement. The pope would become a pawn of

Moscow as successive Russian Orthodox patriarchs had been. And if he refused to comply? Then Korchan would ensure that the evidence became known. Enough newspapers in Italy, Germany, and the USA would be eager to reveal how Cardinal Fasolo had drugged or murdered his predecessor in order to become pope. The moral authority of the Church of Christ would be shattered irreparably. The whole edifice would collapse. Domenico Fasolo would have achieved what Satan had desired for two thousand years: broken the rock upon which Christ had built his Church.

Fasolo tried to pray. He couldn't.

He couldn't say mass in an hour's time, say the words of consecration that turn the bread and wine into the Body and Blood of Christ, and then receive that Body and Blood of Christ into his soul, a soul so blackened by Lucifer's sin. Such sacrilege would drive yet another nail into Christ hanging on the cross.

Korchan was clever. Fasolo could prove neither that Korchan had supplied him with the Largactil tablets nor had persuaded him to administer them to the Pope. But Ryan was right. The Pope was in danger. He must warn the Pope. But how? The only person who was concerned about the threat was Ryan, and nobody took Ryan's allegations seriously.

Fasolo pressed the intercom. "Giovanni, you may go. There'll be no more work this evening."

Fasolo took out a clean sheet of his headed notepaper and wrote in his small neat handwriting. He put the letter next to the notes he had prepared, sealed the sheets in an envelope, and wrote on the envelope *Don James Ryan. Personale. Urgente.*

When he was certain Giovanni had left, he telephoned Ryan. "Father, I have some news about the Soviet agent you mentioned this afternoon. Will you come to my office in half an hour's time? Giovanni has left. I'm a little deaf, so there's no point in knocking. Walk straight in."

He felt calm now.

Chapter ✤ Twenty-six

RYAN DID KNOCK, but there was no reply.

He opened the door and froze. Cardinal Fasolo was slumped over his desk. His crimson skullcap had fallen off.

Ryan ran across the room. Fasolo's hand was cold. Deathly cold. It was unnatural. He had spoken to Ryan only half an hour ago.

Ryan gently lifted Fasolo's head from the desk. Rimless spectacles hung askew, detached from one ear. The eyes stared blankly, the mouth sagged open. The Cardinal Secretary of State was quite dead.

Ryan lowered the head back on to the desk, which was strangely cleared of all the usual mounds of papers and files. Only the black cross with the bronze Christ hanging from it, an empty glass, a brown pill bottle, and the red seal of the Holy See stood on the brightly polished walnut surface. The seal weighted down an envelope.

Ryan was about to put the envelope to one side when he saw the word *urgente*. He tore open the envelope and read the letter.

"Mother of God," he breathed.

Suicide was the unforgivable sin. The ultimate act of despair. The breaking of the commandment "thou shalt not kill" by an act that precludes the opportunity of repentance. And without repentance, the sinner denies himself God's forgiving grace. For all eternity.

But who knows what goes through the sinner's mind between the act of swallowing the tablets and the instant of death? What mortal can stand in judgment and put limits on the mercy of an Infinite God?

Ryan took Fasolo's cold right hand in his own, and placed his left hand on Fasolo's brow. "If you are still alive and capable of receiving the sacrament, I call upon God the Father of mercies who, through the death and resurrection of his Son, has reconciled the world to himself and sent the Holy Spirit among us for the forgiveness of sins; through the ministry of the Church may God grant you pardon and peace; and I absolve you from your sins in the name of the Father and of the Son and of the Holy Spirit. Amen."

He picked up the empty bottle of Largactil tablets and put it in his pocket, next to the envelope. Only then did he dial the Vatican Health Service.

Chapter ✣ Twenty-seven

RYAN WATCHED THE two brothers of the Order of Saint John of God place the body on a stretcher. Their white laboratory coats looked odd over the top of their black cassocks. They picked up the stretcher and, accompanied by Monsignor Giovanni Baldossi, Fasolo's secretary, and Dr. Garofalo, director of the Vatican Health Service, they carried the body through to the cardinal's bedroom. The Pope wanted to follow, but Hoffman gripped him just above the elbow and steered him out of the office. The Pope was unsteady on his feet.

Ryan turned to the only person left in the Secretary of State's office. He tried to control the rage burning inside as he said, "I'd like to speak to you."

"Certainly," said Archbishop Korchan. "Let's go to my office."

Korchan gestured for Ryan to sit in one of the two easy chairs in the *Sostituto's* office. He pressed the intercom. "Pietro, I don't want to be disturbed." He looked across to Ryan, who was seated upright on the edge of the chair. "Do you want a drink, James? You look as though you need one."

"No, thank you."

Korchan poured himself a whiskey, removed his skull-cap and cape, and sat down in the other easy chair. "Such a distressing event."

"Suicides always are," Ryan said through gritted teeth.

"I don't understand," Korchan said. "You heard Dr. Garofalo. His Eminence died of a stroke."

"Dr. Garofalo didn't see this." Ryan pulled the empty brown pill bottle from his pocket and thrust it toward Korchan. "It's yours, I believe."

Korchan took the Largactil bottle and frowned. "It's from the Vatican Pharmacy."

Ryan's face was white with anger. "Do you still pretend you know nothing about it?"

"James, what's wrong?"

"This is!" Ryan threw the opened envelope at Korchan.

Korchan took out the letter and the two sheets of notes. His brow furrowed as he read the letter. He glanced at Fasolo's notes.

"Well?" Ryan demanded.

Korchan gave a deep sigh. "I feel guilty."

"You admit it?"

"I admit that I didn't realize how much stress His Eminence was under. I should have recognized the signs. I should have done more to help."

"Is that all you have to say about the letter!"

Korchan pursed his lips. "It shows a very disturbed mind. Clearly His Eminence was not in possession of his faculties when he took the overdose. For that, at least, James, we can be thankful. He was not responsible for his actions, and so no sin was involved."

Ryan sank back in the chair. "I don't believe this. You sit there talking calmly about sin as though you weren't responsible for Cardinal Fasolo's death."

Korchan looked at the young priest. "Why do you think Cardinal Fasolo died, James?"

"Isn't it obvious from his letter?"

"What were my reasons for acting in the manner Cardinal Fasolo alleges?"

Ryan sat bolt upright. "Because you are Judas!"

"Judas?"

"The KGB agent I warned you about! The agent responsible for Cardinal Davino's death, Cardinal Zingler's resignation, and Cardinal Demeure's determination to retire because of something that happened to him in Leningrad."

Korchan put the tips of his fingers together. "Who else have you told about this, James?"

"About Judas, only you, Cardinal Fasolo and the Pope."

"Has the Pope seen this letter?"

Ryan shook his head. The Pope was feeling guilty about his lack of charity to Fasolo. He was going to make amends that evening. Fasolo's death was shock enough. If the Pope was told that Fasolo had first tried to kill him and then committed suicide . . .

"What do you propose to do, James? You can hardly issue a press statement. The scandal of the most powerful cardinal in the Catholic Church attempting to kill the Pope and then committing suicide would rock the Church to its foundations. Add that the Secretary of State's deputy is a KGB agent and . . ." He spread his hands wide.

Ryan didn't know. In his anger he'd acted impulsively to confront Korchan with his callous betrayal of the Holy Father. "Do you admit it? Aren't I right!" he burst out in frustration.

Korchan wilted under the ferocity of the attack. Then he nodded his head slowly. His voice was strangely altered, almost wistful. "You were right to come to me, James." For a few moments he said nothing; his thoughts seemed far away. "Did I ever tell you what happened to my parents?"

The question seemed addressed in part to Ryan and in part to some invisible angel standing in judgment at the far end of the room. Ryan hesitated. The urbane and confident archbishop seemed to have crumpled inside his cassock. "I don't ask you to understand, James. But I do ask you to grant me one kindness. Give me some time."

"Time for what?" Ryan demanded.

"To think, James, to think. To see how we can best deal with this situation. And, hopefully, to pray. For the salvation of my soul." Wearily he got to his feet, put the empty pill bottle, Fasolo's letter and notes into a safe in the wall, locked the safe, and handed Ryan the key. "I'm in your power, James. Grant me the favor I ask."

Ryan was uncertain. Even if he refused Korchan's request, what would he do? To whom would he go? The Pope, the Secretary of State, and the *Sostituto* were the only three people with authority to deal with a matter like this. Benedetti was in the United States, trying to mend relations. Ryan too needed time to think things through. And also to pray. He looked carefully at the *Sostituto*. Korchan was slumped back in his chair, eyes staring vacantly ahead, all pretense gone. He was a beaten man. "If I give you until tomorrow morning at nine, promise me you will do nothing foolish."

Korchan smiled sadly. "You are a good man, Father James Ryan, and a kind man. I promise that I will do nothing foolish."

Chapter ✣ Twenty-eight

RYAN DIDN'T SLEEP that night. He spent most of the time in prayer in the Pope's private chapel. By breakfast he knew what he must do.

At all costs he had to avoid a scandal. With the fate of the Church poised so precariously—in its relations with the Church in America and with the Russian Orthodox—public disclosure would be catastrophic. And he must avoid telling the Holy Father: if the shock didn't kill him, he would be left a broken man. Hoffman never kept anything from the Pope, and so he too must not be involved. It was down to James Ryan to prove he was a worthy assistant to the Holy Father.

Ryan's bargaining counter was to confront Korchan with the prospect of arrest by the Vatican security service and transfer to the Italian police for trial and sentence, like Mehmet Ali Agca after he'd tried to assassinate the Pope in 1981. Ryan would offer Korchan his freedom if he agreed to resign on the pretext of wanting to return to the Ukraine, and then slip quietly back to the Soviet Union.

When Botone ushered him through into the *Sostituto's* office, Korchan was at the door to meet him.

Before Ryan could begin his prepared speech, Korchan said, "James, I've decided it is important that you make a full and complete statement for the record of what you know. You can then say what you propose to do with me." He led Ryan into an adjoining conference room. "Signor Cagnetta here will be your witness. Have no fear, he is sworn to confidence." Korchan left and closed the door behind him.

Cagnetta looked at him with eyes magnified by the lenses of black horn-rimmed spectacles perched on a large Roman nose. He wore a dark blue suit with white shirt and striped club tie, like most senior members of the Vatican security service. "Pleased to meet you, Father. This is a distressing time for you, I'm sure."

He sat down on a sofa by the wall opposite the tall windows and patted the space next to him. "Do make yourself comfortable, Father." From a black briefcase he removed a tape recorder and placed it on the low coffee table in front of the sofa. "May I suggest, Father, that we record your statement. It will be a great help to ensure the accuracy of what you have to say."

Ryan, slightly bemused by the turn of events, nodded.

"Good." Cagnetta pushed the microphone toward him and switched on the tape recorder. "Statement made by Father James Ryan on the seventeenth of December in the presence of Giuseppe Cagnetta." He pressed the pause button and turned the microphone to face Ryan. "Do proceed, Father, to tell me in your own words what you believe to be the cause of Cardinal Fasolo's death." He released the pause button.

Ryan cleared his throat and began by stating that he had been told the KGB had a highly placed agent in the Apostolic Palace, and that he believed that agent was responsible for the leak of Cardinal Zingler's altered documents and probably also for Cardinal Davino's death and Cardinal Demeure's wish to retire.

"When did Cardinal Demeure make this wish known?" Cagnetta interjected.

"In private to the Holy Father, after he'd returned from Leningrad," Ryan said.

"But it hasn't been announced publicly?"

"No. I'm telling you this in confidence."

Ryan then related how he'd found Cardinal Fasolo's body, the empty pill bottle, and the letter addressed to him.

"Do you have this letter and the pill bottle?" Cagnetta asked.

"No," said Ryan. "They're in Archbishop Korchan's safe. I have the key."

"I'll need them to check the statement," Cagnetta said.

Ryan handed over the key.

"Please continue with why you believe Archbishop Korchan is involved," Cagnetta said, "and anything else you wish to add."

When Ryan had finished, Cagnetta switched off the tape recorder and smiled encouragingly. "It's good for you to get it all off your chest. You must feel relieved."

Ryan agreed. But what to do now?

"You must be thirsty after all that talking, Father. I'll get you a drink." He rang a bell and a young nun, covered from head to foot in white veil and habit, came in carrying a tray with a jug of water and a glass.

"I'll be back in a few minutes," Cagnetta said.

Ryan poured himself a drink while he waited.

He felt exhausted. It was, he supposed, a combination of lack of sleep the previous night and the relief of tension that had drained him. Time seemed to drag. He looked at the onyx clock on the marble mantelpiece. He was sure it must be half an hour since Signor Cagnetta had left.

Ten more minutes passed before Cagnetta returned. "His Excellency will see you now, Father."

Odd. He wondered if Korchan really was an archbishop, or if . . . He stood up. The lack of sleep had caught up with him. He walked slowly into Korchan's office.

Cagnetta had gone. Only Korchan was in the room, wearing his full ecclesiastical dress and sitting behind his

desk, below the portrait of the Pope. Ryan had expected
that at least one member of the Vatican security service
would be present.

"Do sit down, Father," Korchan said, indicating the
high-backed chair in front of his desk.

Korchan sighed. "Regrettably, the psychiatrist's report
confirms my worst fears . . ."

"Psychiatrist?"

"Signor Cagnetta is a psychiatrist."

"But I thought he was security service . . ."

Korchan put the tips of his fingers together. "Whoever
told you that, Father?"

"What the . . . ?" Ryan rose to his feet, unsteadily.

"Please be seated, Father," Korchan commanded.

Ryan sank back into the chair. Everything was happening far too quickly for him to take it all in. Korchan was
sitting across the desk from him, not a meter away, but his
body seemed to be at the other end of the room and his
voice came from the far side of the Apostolic Palace.

That distant voice was speaking. ". . . classic symptoms
of paranoia accompanied by delusions. We think it might
well have been caused by overwork and stress. I share the
Holy Father's great concern for your mental and spiritual
well-being. Accordingly we are sending you to a monastery
where you will receive . . ."

"The Holy Father! I demand to see the Holy Father!"
Ryan managed to say.

"Father Ryan. The Holy Father has been greatly distressed by the death of Cardinal Fasolo. If you love the
Holy Father as much as you protest, you will not wish to
add to his distress at this time. He is not a well man."

"Then I demand . . ."

"Father Ryan," Korchan interjected sharply. "When
you accepted the post of private secretary, you took an oath
of obedience to the Holy Father and to his lawful successors. Perhaps you need to be reminded of it." Korchan
handed Ryan the card that he had given him on his first day
inside the Apostolic Palace.

Ryan didn't need to reread the Latin words of the oath.

"It is the Holy Father's wish," Korchan continued, "that you convalesce in the Monastery of Our Lady of Sorrows. Here your mind will find the peace necessary for its recovery, and your soul will be afforded the opportunity of spiritual refreshment."

Ryan put down the card. He must fight now or all would be lost, but he was drained of energy, struggling like a swimmer in slow motion merely to keep afloat. He needed time, desperately needed time. Perhaps Kasamir . . . He took a deep breath and concentrated so that the words would come out properly. "I will go and clear my desk . . ."

"Your desk's been cleared, Father. All your personal belongings have been packed and are in the car waiting in the courtyard." Korchan stood up and walked round the desk. "Permit me to help you. The water contained a sedative and you seem a little unsteady on your feet."

Chapter ✤ Twenty-nine

RYAN RECALLED ONLY a few surrealistic impressions of that journey. The Courtyard of Saint Damasus. The stone-work which needed its ochre paint renewing. Above, the clock in the center of the Second Loggia which had shown ten past nine when he had first seen it, but whose time no longer made sense. The dark blue Fiat from the Vatican car pool. Weaving along once-strange now-familiar easily-forgotten narrow roads between high battlemented walls and through small courtyards. The striped blue, gold, and red of the Swiss guards at the Arch of the Bells. Behind, quickly, Michelangelo's dome, cut off by the looming Holy Office. The embankment. Should turn here into Tras-tevere, but instead cross the river, still green. Decaying Rome rushing back into the tranquility of the Old Appian Way, straight and true and lined with tombs. The Church of Quo Vadis, where Peter said to Christ—or was it Christ to Peter?—Where are you going? Suddenly speeding into the New Appian Way, the modern highway, the lurid or-ange buildings of the Capannelle racecourse, and cars flashing by in the opposite direction with mesmerizing reg-ularity. He closed his eyes.

When he opened them again all movement had ceased. Then the two large wooden gates swung open. The car restarted and drove slowly up the tree-lined drive, past a life-sized crucifix, until it came to a halt in a turning circle in front of a stone villa built next to an ancient church. An old monk, with thinning white hair and dressed in a gray habit, waited.

"Welcome to our monastery, Father," the monk said. "I'm Father Anselm, the abbot. While you are our guest, our home is your home."

Ryan opened his lips, but no words came. His mouth was parched. But at least things were happening at normal speed. He held out his hand and the abbot clasped it in both of his. Ryan felt the warmth of the abbot's welcome. The bright blue eyes set in the old man's lined face shone with an openness that disconcerted Ryan after his experiences that morning. Ryan knew he would never need to look behind this monk's words for any ulterior motive.

"Permit me to take your cases, Father."

Ryan coughed some saliva into his throat. "I wouldn't dream of it . . ."

"Oh, but you must. You seem a little unsteady on your feet. And anyway, I am enjoined by our Rule to treat each guest as though he were Christ Himself. At least on the first day," the abbot chuckled.

Ryan looked round. The dark blue Fiat with an SCV numberplate was already disappearing through the gates, which closed behind it, locking out the world of duplicity.

The abbot had picked up the two cheap brown suitcases that held all the worldly possessions of Father James Ryan, priest of the Archdiocese of Westminster and formerly private secretary to the Pope. Ryan followed his suitcases. Although the abbot appeared old, he carried the suitcases with an ease that showed familiarity with physical labor.

They walked through a hallway, along a stone-flagged corridor, up two flights of stone steps, and through a door to a modern extension. A narrow green carpet ran down the center of the wooden corridor. The abbot put down the suitcases and opened one of the doors that lined the corridor at regular intervals. He gestured for Ryan to precede him. The room reminded Ryan of one of the study bedrooms at his seminary: small cream room, narrow gray-blanketed bed, washbasin, single wardrobe with warped door that wouldn't close, table in front of window, one upright chair by table, one easy chair on thin red rug near bed, crucifix above bed, picture of the Blessed Virgin on one wall, and photograph of the Holy Father on another wall.

"While you are here, Father . . ."

"How long will I be here, Father Abbot?" Ryan croaked.

The abbot was sympathetic. "Until you are better."

Ryan filled the toothbrush glass with water from the washbasin tap and drank. "There's nothing wrong with me," he said.

The abbot sat down on the edge of the bed. "Perhaps I should have said, until you are fully recovered and are deemed able to take your place in the world once more."

"Who deems?"

The abbot gave a resigned smile. "The ecclesiastical authorities, I'm afraid."

"Do you know Archbishop Korchan?"

"Who?"

"The *Sostituto* at the Secretariat of State."

"I'm afraid we have no occasion to mix with all those important people at the Vatican, Father. You will find our little world here very simple, very different from Rome."

"May I ask who told you about me?"

The abbot sighed. "It was somebody from," he hesitated for an instant, "the Congregation for the Doctrine of the Faith. I think you understand."

Ryan understood better than the abbot. By arranging for that particular dicastery to take responsibility for him, Korchan had both distanced himself from the act and had branded him a potential heretic.

"Don't look so disheartened, my son," the abbot said

kindly. "I've been told all about the great services you rendered His Holiness and the great stresses under which you worked. A stress-related illness like yours is entirely understandable. One of the brethren, Father Thomas, is a qualified doctor and will give any medical help you need. But most of all, we hope you will find in our monastery the peace and isolation from the world that will nourish your soul."

Ryan turned the upright chair away from the desk so that it faced the abbot. He sat down. "Did you say 'isolation,' Father Abbot?"

Abbot Anselm looked unhappy. "I was intending to talk about this tomorrow, when you've had a meal and a good night's sleep, and you've seen at first hand what our little world has to offer."

"Tell me now, please, Father."

Abbot Anselm nodded. "We belong to the Cistercians of the Strict Observance. Our monastery is an enclosed one."

"But I'm not a monk. I haven't taken any vow of stability. A guest can leave any time."

"That is true. But while you are here, I have been asked to ensure that you observe our Rule, most particularly as it applies to contact with the outside world."

"No contact?"

"No contact of any kind, I'm afraid, Father. No visits, no letters, no telephones, no newspapers, no television, no radio."

Ryan put his head in his hands.

The abbot stood up and placed a hand gently on Ryan's shoulder. "This is no punishment, my son. Try it, I beg you."

Ryan looked up to that honest face.

"The brethren here relish their enclosure," the abbot said. "Only by detaching himself from the world is a person truly free to attach himself to God. Our life is not easy, but the rewards are infinitely worthwhile. In the end, what do the affairs of the world matter? They may occupy us for a

lifetime, but the affairs of the soul will occupy us for all
eternity."

"You mean I'm a prisoner here, Father Abbot?"

"No, my son. It is true that the gates to the outside are
locked, but that is to prevent unwarranted intrusion. Neither you nor any of the brethren are forced to stay here
against your will."

"But the monks have taken a vow."

"As you have, my son. When you were granted the privilege of serving His Holiness, you took a personal vow of
obedience to the Holy Father. It is the Holy Father's wish
that you spend some time with us."

"But . . ."

"No earthly power can hold you to that vow. You can
walk out of here tomorrow. But you, better than most,
know the consequences of such disobedience. It will be for
you to reconcile with your Maker."

Desperation crept into Ryan's voice. "But Father
Abbot, if I know something that is for the Pope's own good,
to save the Church falling into evil hands."

The abbot raised his hand in gentle admonition. "An
Augustinian monk, Martin Luther, knew better than the
Pope what was for the good of the Church. And who is to
say he was wrong to condemn the selling of indulgences
and the other corrupt practices? Yet was he right to forsake
his vows and lead countless souls away from the Church in
order to make his point? Would he not have been better to
work and pray for change from within the institution that
Christ created on earth? To pray and to petition the Successor of Saint Peter, while remaining obedient to the one
who inherits the authority that Christ himself gave to his
Vicar on earth?"

The abbot's eyes radiated compassion. "Believe me, my
son, when I say that obedience is the hardest vow of all. I
have never had any problems with my vows of poverty, of
chastity, or of stability. But obedience! When I know that I
am right!" He shook his head. "Yet Christ was 'obedient
even unto death on the cross.' That image of the obedient

Christ is the one that has helped me control my pride and bend my will to Christ and his Church on earth. I hope it helps you."

The abbot walked to the door. He turned to face Ryan. "We have supper after vespers at six o'clock. If you do make the decision to leave here, the key to the outside gate is in my office. I shall pray to God that you won't ask me for it."

Chapter ✥ Thirty

THE KREMLIN NUMBER One Polyclinic, housed in a five-story neoclassical building in Sivtsev Vrazhek Lane, was part of a system of clinics, hospitals, and sanatoriums administered by what was euphemistically called the Fourth Directorate, a department of the Ministry of Health run by the KGB.

Fourth Directorate facilities, which had equipment and drugs never seen in State clinics, were available only to one hundred thousand of the élite, and were graded according to the rank of patients entitled to use them. Above the Kremlin Number One Polyclinic was the Kremlin Special Polyclinic in Michurinsky Prospekt for members of the Presidential Council, the Party Presidium, and the Council of Ministers. Below were the Number Two and Number Three Polyclinics. Kirillin was privileged to have access to Number One, normally reserved for deputy ministers and members of the Central Committee.

Like the nearby Central Committee Hotel, the Kremlin Number One Polyclinic had no sign to indicate what it was. The Western élite who flaunted their wealth were vulgar; discretion was the rule of the Soviet class whose wealth was measured not by money but by access to privileged goods and services unavailable to ordinary citizens. The system had its rationalization. The country's leaders must be fit and healthy so that they were better able to do their jobs and thereby improve the lot of the masses. The rationalization had not, however, been subjected to the test of *glasnost*.

The doctor looked at the results of the morning's tests that completed Kirillin's six-monthly check-up. He peered over the top of his spectacles. "I suspect you've been less than frank in estimating the amount of alcohol you consume. You're basically healthy, if a little overweight and rather stressed. In your job you're susceptible to stress-related illnesses, and so you must minimize the factors that enhance stress and maximize the factors that reduce stress. In layman's language, you should cut down on alcohol and take up some exercise, like swimming or jogging." He glanced down at the file in front of him. "I notice you haven't had a break since you began your present job eight months ago." He coughed, and focused his eyes on the breast pocket of Kirillin's jacket. "I strongly urge you to take some rest; you'll find the recuperative effect extremely beneficial."

He coughed again. "In case you're not aware of what facilities your new job entitles you to, show your identity card to my secretary on the way out and she'll give you a list of the sanatoriums—I use the term loosely, of course—which you now qualify for." The doctor relaxed into a smile. "Speaking personally, at this time of the year I'd recommend Krasny Kamny. It has some spectacular views of the Caucasus Mountains, the air is healthy, and the rest house overlooks Narzan which . . ."

"I'm familiar with the delights of Narzan mineral water, doctor," Kirillin said drily. "If that's the end of the checkup, I won't detain you."

The clinic was only a couple of minutes' walk from his apartment, and he hadn't used the car. He walked back along Sivtzev Vrazhek Lane. The privileges system may be officially denied and its facilities masked, but you could hardly disguise the fact that some parts of Sivtzev Vrazhek Lane, in front of the modern, well-maintained apartment blocks like his own, were swept clear of snow, while other parts were slushy with trodden snow in front of shabby buildings housing families in multi-occupation.

Back in his apartment he looked up the paper he'd prepared for the President on dismantling the privileges system. It had been opposed, of course, by the *apparatchiks* who benefited from it, but if they didn't take the initiative in getting rid of the privileges system, the masses would take their lead from the East Germans.

Kirillin cut some bread and cheese for lunch. As for taking a holiday . . . He looked at the work he'd brought home the previous night and laughed to himself.

He did, however, have mineral water instead of beer. Then he called his driver.

Georgi said, "I've just heard that you've been called to an urgent meeting, sir," as he closed the passenger door of the Volga.

Kirillin frowned. He leaned forward but the glass partition separating the front seats from the passenger seats wouldn't budge. He knocked on the partition, but Georgi stared straight ahead at the road.

Instead of going toward the Kremlin, the Volga weaved through side roads until it picked up the Garden Ring Road and headed south to cross the Moscow River. Snow clung to the cables of the Krimsky suspension bridge. To his right, past the frozen river, the white expanse of Gorky Park: the giant Ferris wheels and the colorfully dressed skaters reminded Kirillin of those happy days when the four members of the Eclectic Music Appreciation Society abandoned rock 'n' roll records for the traditional delights of winter in Moscow.

He banged on the partition, but no response. The car was forced to stop in Oktyabrskaya Square, by the skyscraping Hotel Warsaw. Kirillin tried the handles of both passenger doors. Both were locked. With one forlorn glance back at the snow-covered bronze Lenin in the center of the square, Kirillin sank back in his seat as the Volga turned into Lenin Prospekt and headed out of the city.

Half an hour after leaving his apartment the Volga drove through a silver birch forest. The blanket of snow reflected the bright sun with a dazzling intensity. A few minutes later the car came to Vnukovo-2 Airport and drove through opened gates straight on to the apron.

Two men in full length black leather coats and fur hats stepped from the rear of the white twin turbo-prop Antonov-28 waiting on the apron. One opened the passenger door of the Volga.

"We apologize for the secrecy, comrade, but the plane's ready to take off."

Kirillin had no choice. As he followed them into the plane, he looked back. Georgi was staring fixedly ahead.

A calmness came over Kirillin during the flight. He didn't know where he was going—snow-covered forests and plains all looked the same from the air—and he felt no particular urge to find out. It was as though he had always been expecting something like this ever since he took on the job of special assistant and learnt just how vulnerable the President was and how powerful the forces ranged against him. The Army had most to lose by all the changes, and it had the perfect excuse of anarchy in the republics to justify a coup. He had done his best and—God knows—the President had done his best. He wondered if he'd ever see the President again. He suspected they would be taken to different places.

The Antonov-28 was not a particularly fast aircraft, but its big advantage was that it could take off and land on unpaved aerodromes and it needed only a one-and-a-half-kilometer runway. The plane descended to a frozen landing strip bulldozed out of a clearing in a forest. Once the bumping ceased and the plane came safely to a halt, Kirillin was tempted to thank the pilot for his skill. Perhaps not.

His mute companions led him through the opened hatch in the fuselage tail. Two white four-wheel-drive Lada

Nivas came out to meet them. Kirillin climbed in the first one, and it set off over the ruts of a snow-covered dirt road through the forest.

The drive didn't last long. The Niva stopped at a wooden gate in a high stone wall. Two troopers, muffled in fur hats and greatcoats and *valenki,* thick felt boots, swung back the gate. The Niva drove through a cleared area, then through a gate in a chain-link fence and down a bumpy road through birch trees until Kirillin saw ahead what looked like a large hunting lodge, with the ground floor built of stone and the first floor of timber. A dark ring round the stone chimney showed where the snow on the sloping roof had melted. Gray smoke curled up from the chimney.

Kirillin paused before entering the lodge. The sky was still a clear blue. The sun had grown and reddened and sunk below the top of the birches. The frost-hardened snow lying on the bare branches of the white-trunked trees glistened like rubies; the sculpted drifts on the ground glowed pink. In other circumstances it would be idyllic.

A log fire blazed in the stone hearth. The blend of traditional Russian and modern Finnish furniture was tasteful. Two black leather armchairs on stainless steel bases were facing the fire. One swiveled round.

"I'm glad you could make it," Babakin smiled.

Chapter ❖ Thirty-one

"I THOUGHT IT would be the Army," Kirillin said.

"The Army?" Babakin looked surprised. "As you once told me, the President believes that in a genuine socialist democracy the armed forces have no role beyond that of defending the country against external aggressors. Have some Pertsovka, it'll warm you up after the trip."

Kirillin ignored the glass of pepper-flavored vodka that Babakin poured and set down on the low, carved wooden table in front of the fire. "What have you done with the President?" he demanded.

"Done? I've done nothing."

"Then where is he?"

Babakin pushed back the cuff of his gray Italian suit and looked at his Rolex. "I guess he's still in the Kremlin. He usually is at this time. Do take your coat off and sit down, Dmitry Sergeyevich, you make me feel uncomfortable."

Kirillin remained standing. "Where's the arrest warrant?"

"Arrest? I don't understand."

"In case it's slipped your memory, General Babakin, the KGB no longer has the power to make an arrest. You must convince a procurator to issue a warrant."

"Whoever mentioned arrest? The President agreed with your doctor. You've been under stress and need a break in order to recuperate. I've put this rather splendid rest house at your disposal. It has its own *banya*, there's a cross-country ski course . . ."

"I demand to speak to the President!"

Babakin shrugged. "If you insist. But think twice before you do." He took a file from the briefcase beside his chair, pushed the Pertsovka bottle and Kirillin's glass to one side of the table, and spread out several large black and white photographs. "He's seen these."

Kirillin sat down in the other armchair in front of the fire in order to look through the photographs. The first set showed an unshaven Father Ryan dressed in workman's clothes outside Lvov Railway Station: with a woman; with Pavlo Stus and the same woman; and with Stus and the woman climbing into an old Zaporozhets. Enlargements identified Ryan. The second set showed the similarly dressed Ryan carrying a suitcase: outside a wooden church; and with the woman, Stus, Bishop Antoniuk and another man. The third set showed Kirillin with Stus in an hotel room. The fourth set showed Father Ryan, dressed in his clerical suit, with Kirillin. The fifth set showed Stus and Antoniuk outside Saint George's Cathedral in Lvov on the day of the Ukrainian uprising.

Kirillin was still wearing his overcoat and his hat. The fire was hot. Sweat formed on his brow and began running down his face. "The photographs of me . . . You know all about them. These meetings were your idea."

"I think you'd find that difficult to prove," Babakin said. "When we met I was carrying a little device made up by the Fourteenth Department that would ruin any tape recording of what either of us said. If you recorded our telephone conversations you'll find they consist of innocent exchanges about the weather." He smiled.

Kirillin's face flushed with anger. "You were with me when I met Ryan in Rome!"

Babakin poured himself a glass of Pertsovka, sat back in

his chair and rested his right ankle on his left knee. "How can you prove that photograph was taken in Rome when the evidence points otherwise?" he asked.

Kirillin turned the photograph over. On the other side, handwritten in the blank spaces in the KGB photo identification stamp, were a file number, the words "DMITRY SERGEYEVICH KIRILLIN," and "Kiev, 16 August."

"The sixteenth of August was a Sunday," Babakin said. "The President was at his villa on the Black Sea. No doubt you will claim you were at Zhukovka, but you won't find any witnesses. On the other hand, Ninth Directorate records show that you ordered a flight that morning to Kiev, returning the same evening. We can prove, incidentally, that Ryan was in the Ukraine on the sixteenth of August, and that the Council of Ukrainian Solidarity met in Kiev on the seventeenth of August."

Kirillin had never felt hatred for anyone before. As Kirillin watched Babakin drink up his Pertsovka, and calmly indicate that he should do likewise, he began to understand the difference between anger and hatred. A small voice in his mind told him not to let it take over: he must keep control of himself if he were to stand any chance of dealing with this man.

"All the photographs are corroborated by evidence the courts would find convincing," Babakin continued.

"I can explain all the photographs of me," Kirillin replied as calmly as he could. "Whatever 'evidence' you cook, the President will believe me." He removed his hat and coat but didn't touch the drink.

Babakin shrugged. "Possibly. Though when I talked with him, he seemed fully aware of all the consequences."

"Wait till I've spoken with him."

"Fortunately," said Babakin, "we now have a society based on the rule of law, and not on arbitrary decisions by Party chiefs. With this amount of evidence, and with national security at stake but with you protesting your innocence, *glasnost* would demand a public trial. And certainly, if you did contact the President, I'd have to consider it an attempt to pervert the course of justice. I'd be left with no option but to submit all the evidence to the Procurator-General, inform the Security Commission of the Supreme Soviet, and call a press conference so that justice is seen to be done. And yet," Babakin mused, "the President is aware of the problems that would create."

"If his special assistant were tried for treason?"

"Tried and found guilty under Article 64," Babakin corrected. "There is other evidence, of course."

"I'll take that risk," Kirillin said. "I know I'm innocent."

"You may be willing to entrust your fate to the hands of the Soviet courts. I'm not sure the President is. When Willy Brandt was at the height of his popularity as Federal German Chancellor, his private secretary was publicly accused of being an East German spy. Brandt was forced to resign. Our President is hardly at the height of his popularity. Do you think he could survive your trial for treason, Dmitry Sergeyevich?"

Kirillin slumped back in his chair.

"That would be a tragedy the nation would never recover from," Babakin said. "Understandably, the President was grateful of my offer to accommodate you here, in eminently civilized surroundings, for a period of voluntary interrogation."

So that was it. He wasn't to meet Blagov's fate of a bullet in the head. Babakin needed him alive in order to blackmail the President with the threat of a treason trial. "You plan to keep me here indefinitely?"

Babakin shook his head. "No, no. In another six months or so a scheme of mine will rescue the Soviet economy. I say mine, but I wouldn't be able to do it without the help of others."

"Without Judas's help?"

Babakin poured himself another drink. "Interesting man. We're exact contemporaries, you know. I first met him at a KGB training camp. The most striking thing about him was his hatred of the Catholic Church, and the Ukrainian Catholic Church in particular." Babakin settled back in his chair. "His parents were members of the Ivan Franko Peoples Guard, an underground Communist partisan group in Lvov during the German occupation. They were tortured and killed by the Nazis in front of him when he was only eight. He was told later that they had been betrayed by a Ukrainian Catholic priest who was collaborating with the Germans. It might even have been true. He was recruited by the MGB, as it then was, in 1953, just before Stalin died. He volunteered for any assignments specifically directed against the Ukrainian Catholic Church, so they gave him the cover of being a Catholic priest and told him to infiltrate the underground Church." Babakin smiled. "I'd been trained for the Orthodox priesthood, and since the Byzantine rituals of both Churches are very similar, I was seconded to help with his training." The smile widened. "Because the Ukrainian Catholic Church was so severely repressed, their own clandestine priests received very little training, and learnt hardly any theology. Alexander Korchan was probably one of the most highly trained priests to join their ranks. I say priest, I should say pretend-priest. Frankly, it was child's play to say that bishop so-and-so, who'd been killed the year before, had ordained you in secret. That's how it happened in those days, and nobody ever thought to question you. They were desperate for somebody capable of performing the mumbo jumbo and brave enough to do it."

He put another couple of logs on the fire and refilled his glass. Kirillin's glass was untouched.

"When Khrushchev came under international pressure to let the Ukrainian Metropolitan Slipyj attend the Second Vatican Council," Babakin continued, "we were presented with the ideal opportunity of sending Korchan with him as his assistant so we could find out from the inside what was going on. I didn't meet up with him again until my first Rome tour in '74, when I took over the network that included Korchan. After the Vatican Council he'd fed us stuff on the Ukrainian Catholic Church headquarters in Rome. It was good but, frankly, a man of his abilities and motivation had much more potential. I encouraged him to infiltrate the Vatican, become a sleeper, and we'd wake him when he was senior enough to be of real use."

Babakin appeared to relish the intrigue and duplicity. Kirillin wondered whether Babakin believed in socialism or the good of his country or indeed anything. Power was his fix; increasing his power was his sole motivation in life.

"I feel sorry for you," Kirillin said slowly. "You can never have a relationship with another human being. You despise everybody except yourself."

"Not at all," Babakin replied. "I like you. There's nothing personal in the arrangement, believe me. If there were, I wouldn't be prepared to release you after six months or so, when we've wrapped everything up."

"Release?"

"Sure. You stay here for about six months, officially under voluntary interrogation. You'll find you have every comfort, except the facility to contact people outside. When the time is ripe, I will conclude the evidence against you is not strong enough to warrant a trial, and you'll be released."

"I don't believe you."

"When have I ever lied to you, Dmitry Sergeyevich?"

Kirillin ignored the question and probed carefully. "What would I do then?"

"You could hardly resume your former post, of course. But I'm sure I can find you a good job, though clearly it would need to be away from Moscow, Leningrad and places like that."

"Siberia?"

"I had in mind the new factory that Fiat are building for us at Yelabuga. It'll be the most modern car plant in the country. It needs a top-class manager. You are. You're experienced in the field, and you speak Italian. It would be a terrific challenge. A prestigious post like that would naturally carry all the top privileges, provided you keep to your job and stay east of Yelabuga."

"And if I refuse?"

Babakin looked puzzled. "Why should you? Instead of keeping you locked up somewhere, I'm offering you the opportunity to make a really good life for yourself."

Kirillin gave a dry laugh. "You'll never let me leave here alive. You daren't risk it. I might just go and tell people that you have the President of the USSR in your pocket, and tell them how you did it. I might even tell the West."

Babakin shook his head. "I've calculated the risk. It's negligible. During the time we've worked together, I've come to respect you, Dmitry Sergeyevich. You're genuinely concerned for the good of your country. You believe the President is the only man capable of leading it out of the dark ages." His cold blue eyes seemed amused. "You wouldn't risk the public scandal that would force his resignation."

Kirillin knew he was right. The President was as much a prisoner of this . . . this megalomaniac as he was. But better he remain President than be forced to resign. Maybe he could find a way of removing this creature. "You're relying a great deal on my loyalty to the President, Babakin," he said.

Babakin smiled. "Not entirely. I must admit I've taken out a little insurance policy. I have a report from the Ninth Directorate stating that three hundred grams of cocaine have been found in your apartment. I also have a sworn statement from Ivan Gorbatko, a gangster, admitting that he has supplied you with drugs for dealing. If your personal loyalty to the President should ever waver, or should you fail to transfer that loyalty to his successor, these documents will be produced as proof that you were sacked for drugs offenses and, despite the President's foolish, not to say corrupt, generosity in not having you put on trial, you are bitter and twisted for having been dismissed." He smiled again. "Doubtless you would then be put on trial."

"You might control the propaganda machine here, but not in the West."

Babakin looked at his watch. "About now, a stupid man called Richardson, the CIA station chief in Rome, is becoming very excited. An intermediary is telling him that the Soviet President's special assistant wants to defect. Richardson's excitement will increase over the next few weeks when the intermediary feeds him information that establishes your worth, and begins negotiating the terms of your defection. Just when he's convinced he's about to pull the biggest fish since Gordievski, his opposite number in Moscow will enjoy his own personal triumph. One of his agents will supply him with these photographs of me." Babakin removed a second file from his briefcase. He handed Kirillin photographs of himself and Kirillin in deep conversation at the Obelisk of Great Revolutionary and Socialist Thinkers, at the Tomb of the Unknown Soldier, and in the Cathedral of the Assumption, plus photographs of each leaving the Sandunovsky Baths and the Central Committee shop in Granovsky Street.

"He'll be given other photographs of me, of course, but when the analysts at Langley link your face with Richardson's prize would-be defector, they'll instruct registry to search their files. Eventually they'll come up with 'Kirillin, Dmitry Sergeyevich, Assistant Commercial Attaché at the Soviet Embassy in Rome, 1981–3,' overlapping with my tour. As the ACA post is normally filled by a KGB officer, it will provide the confirmation the analysts are looking for. Your cover will be blown, at least, as far as they're concerned. Whichever Western country you go to, sooner or later their security service will contact the CIA, if only to trade your information. Then you'll be dead. Credibility-wise, at least."

Kirillin stared at the burning embers of the fire. "You've had this all planned out, haven't you? Every single detail."

Babakin laughed. "Nothing ever goes entirely to plan. If it did, Fasolo would be sitting on Saint Peter's throne instead of feeding the worms."

Kirillin looked up. For the first time that evening hope showed in his eyes. "Your plan went wrong?"

Babakin stood up and put on his cashmere overcoat. "A chess grandmaster with a rigid game plan will never beat another grandmaster who's quick enough to adapt his strategy to unforeseen circumstances. That distinguishes the world champion from the others."

"What does that mean?"

"It means, my dear Dmitry Sergeyevich, that I've adapted the strategy to produce an even better endgame."

"You might as well tell me, I know everything else."

Babakin put on his Barguzin sable hat. "That would spoil the fun."

FINALE

DMITRY SERGEYEVICH KIRILLIN was a prisoner in a gilded cage. The hunting lodge provided every luxury he might want. Ivan and Dagmara Sedov, a couple in their late fifties, gave him breakfast in his double bedroom which overlooked a lake at the rear. For lunch and dinner he sat in splendid isolation at an oak dining table that could seat twenty, while the Sedovs served him meals worthy of a Central Committee member. Ivan, with his deadpan face and eyes that had seen everything and registered nothing, suggested which French wines he might choose for each dish. Between meals he wandered through to the billiard room where one of the guards offered him a game. The attraction of the gymnasium in the basement was not the weights and the jogging machine but the fitness trainer. Tatiana was in her twenties, had a supple body and a coquettish smile, and suggested she massage away his tension after a sauna in the room next to the gym. The sauna was the most luxurious he had ever seen, made of kiln-dried solid pine logs imported from Finland instead of the usual Russian paneling. Tatiana gave him imported fluffy towels and the hint of a more intimate massage whenever he felt the need. A covered walkway led from the rear of the main building to a low single-story structure of glass and metal housing a twenty-five-meter swimming pool. Beyond the pool the gardens sloped down to the frozen lake, and beyond the lake a forest stretched so far that the perimeter chain-link fence plus outer stone wall was lost to view. Major Oleg Steltsov, commander of the guard detachment, advised that he might find it helpful if one of his men acted as a guide whenever he intended to walk or ski.

While every luxury was available, the one thing that Kirillin deemed a necessity was denied him. The Sedovs, Major Steltsov and the guards, and even the obliging Tatiana smiled and said that his peace and quiet would be disturbed by contact with the outside world. No newspapers, no television, no radio, no telephone. The gilded cage was secure and soundproofed.

The frustration of not knowing what was happening to the President and to the country was a mental torture that threatened to unbalance him. His first instinct was to reach for the bottle, but the readiness with which Ivan Sedov proffered a range of spirits, and the knowing look on Dagmara's face, flashed a warning light in his brain. This was what Babakin wanted.

He channelled his hatred of Babakin into a determination to defeat him by any means. That meant he had to be fit and mentally alert, ready to adapt his strategy, as Babakin had boasted of his own, to any circumstances. He began by turning his enforced rest to his advantage.

The doctor was right, even if he had reported to the KGB before his patient. Kirillin cut out alcohol and drew up a program to get himself in mental and physical shape. Major Steltsov, he learned, was an accomplished chess player. Their games after dinner each day sharpened his mind and built up a relationship with Steltsov. Before breakfast he swam and before lunch he used the gym. In the afternoons he took whatever exercise he could. Before dinner he relaxed in the sauna and then let Tatiana employ her expertise in massage. She showed him ways of making love that he'd never even fantasized about. He hoped she enjoyed the sessions as much as he did, but she learned nothing from him to report back to Babakin.

In those first few weeks he often went cross-country skiing with his guards. Steltsov even let him go hunting with them. Dressed in white hoods and white smocks, the four of them moved silently through the snow. They always let him have first shot. He knew that two guards had their rifles ready to swing round and cover him, but that didn't matter. He wanted to improve his shooting, not kill a lowly KGB officer. He visualised Babakin's smiling face on every silver fox, wild boar, otter, or muskrat they sighted.

Winter melted into spring, and spring greened the hunting lodge gardens and the forest. The lilac bushes outside the verandah bloomed white and purple, and the breeze wafted their fragrances to him as he sipped his morning coffee. Physically he had never been in better shape, but as spring was overtaken by the heat and humidity of summer a worry grew in his mind. Babakin had talked of six months. Perhaps he was imagining it, but the guards seemed unsettled. Major Steltsov became edgy and taciturn.

One Monday morning in August, as Kirillin was drying himself after his morning swim, Major Steltsov entered the pool extension. "There will be an announcement at eight, comrade. You're to hear it."

Kirillin's heart beat rapidly. His face flushed. He grabbed his towelling robe and followed Major Steltsov up the covered walkway to the main part of the house. In the living room the Sedovs, Tatiana, and most of the guards sat looking at a transistor radio on the coffee table. From the radio came the sounds of a cellist playing Bach. Bach faded and an announcer began to read the statement that had been placed before him. Mesmerized, Kirillin listened to the unreal words, the first he'd heard from the world beyond the hunting lodge:

> In a dark and critical hour for our country and for our peoples, a mortal danger hangs over our great homeland. It is high time to tell the people the truth: unless we take urgent and resolute measures to stabilize the economy, we shall inevitably face, in the very near future, famine and a new turn of the spiral of impoverishment, from which it is but a single step to mass manifestations of spontaneous discontent with

devastating consequences. Millions of people are demanding the adoption of measures against the octopus of crime and scandalous immorality. The deepening destabilization of the political and economic situation in the Soviet Union is undermining our position in the world. The pride and honor of the Soviet person must be fully restored. The State Committee for the State of Emergency in the USSR is fully aware of the depth of the crisis afflicting our country. It takes upon itself responsibility for the fate of the Motherland and is fully determined to adopt the most serious measures to lead the state and society out of the crisis as quickly as possible.

Kirillin gripped the top of the leather armchair he was standing behind. "What's happened to the President?"

"He's at his dacha in the Crimea," said Major Steltsov.

"He's an idiot for going on holiday," smirked the youngest of the guards.

Steltsov's glare silenced the guard.

"Is he . . . has he been harmed?" Kirillin asked.

"They say he's not well," said Steltsov. "He's not able to carry out the functions of President."

Dagmara Sedov's expression was far more eloquent than any words she might have spoken.

Kirillin slumped in an armchair and put his head in his hands. Was this what Babakin had meant by a solution to our problems "after six months or so"? Was the President being held incommunicado, like himself, or had Babakin taken measures to ensure that he was physically or mentally incapacitated? Was he still alive? Of one thing he was certain: Babakin was behind it. He looked at Major Steltsov.

"We must obey the authorities," said Steltsov in answer to Kirillin's unspoken question. "I think it's better if you stay in your room the rest of today."

Tatiana led him to his room and asked if he wanted a bottle of vodka. He had never been more tempted. He stood in front of the window. It was the middle of August, yet the clouds were black and the heavens were weeping copious tears. In the rain-lashed lake he saw Babakin's smiling face. He kept his resolution.

By Wednesday his resolve was weakening rapidly. He had eaten nothing and had drunk only mineral water from unopened bottles. He wanted to believe that the Sedovs hadn't doctored the meals and the tea they brought him, but he wasn't taking any chances. They couldn't, however, put drugs in a sealed bottle of vodka.

When he heard a knock, he opened the door, but it wasn't the Sedovs with yet another tray of food he daren't touch.

"Comrade," said Major Steltsov, "the State of Emergency Committee has resigned. The President is to be reinstated."

Was this a trick?

Steltsov looked at the suspicious eyes staring from an unshaven face. He smiled sheepishly. "Please. Come down for supper. You can hear it on the radio."

Kirillin punched the air. The President had outmaneuvred them! He would soon be free!

For Father James Ryan at the Monastery of Our Lady of Sorrows, the days merged into weeks and the weeks merged into the timelessness of the Trappist life.

After struggling with his oath of obedience, he decided finally to heed the advice of the abbot and follow the example of Christ, "obedient even unto death on the cross." Once he had made that decision, he committed himself wholeheartedly to it. The abbot granted his request to become an oblate. He moved out of the guests' wing into a similar room in the monks' quarters, wore the gray workday habit of the Trappists, and lived their life short of taking their solemn vows.

His day began at 3:15 A.M. when a bell woke the monks. After a quick wash in cold water he put on his habit and sandals, and joined the other gray shadows moving silently along the stone-flagged corridor and down the stone steps into the twelfth-century abbey church for vigils, the first office of the day.

The Cistercian plainness of the church attracted him. No statues or pictures of the Madonna or saints lined its walls; a large crucifix hanging over the altar provided the only visual aid for contemplation.

He liked vigils best of all the offices. In winter the flickering of the red sanctuary lamp and the glow of the low-powered bulbs spaced along the walls fought a battle with the shadows of the night. He stood with the twelve monks in the old mahogany choir stalls that faced each other across the aisle, and merged his voice with theirs in the unaccompanied plainchant of psalms celebrating the goodness of God and the defeat of His enemies, just as monks had done here uninterruptedly for eight hundred years—despite antipopes, schisms, and Reformation. When he returned for the office of lauds after two hours' spiritual reading, the shadows were banished and the church flooded with God's pure light.

By the few words they spoke, by their expressions, by their gestures, by their offers of help, and by the way they celebrated mass and the holy offices, the monks radiated a simple joy in Christ that Ryan had found lacking in the Vatican. And in the abbot he found a man worthy of the title Father.

He adjusted readily to the spartan meals, and threw himself into the physical labor that occupied a third of the monks' day. Most of the monks were old, and he felt that he could make a real contribution to the community by taking on the heaviest work. In winter he painted and maintained the inside of the buildings, in spring he dug the ground for the planting of the crops that were the community's main source of income, and when summer came he helped harvest the early crops and painted the outside of the buildings.

The monastic discipline provided a framework for his life, creating a self-sufficient world with its own values and

sense of time. Hours, weeks, and months had no meaning:
the year was divided into agricultural seasons that coincided with the divisions of the liturgical calendar, and each
day was divided by seven holy offices that separated periods of private contemplation, silent communal meals, and
physical labor. For Ryan it was the Christian life of the gospels, the simple life the apostles had followed before the
Church was adopted by the Roman Empire and acquired
the worst characteristics of an imperial court.

As the abbot had predicted, the affairs of the outside
world assumed a different perspective: they had no significance in the mind of one whose whole being was focused
on the Absolute and the Infinite. Sometimes his mind
drifted back to Katie, or Sister Iryna, or Diana, but he was
only human and he prayed that he not be distracted by
such thoughts. No other images disconcerted him. It was
as though a whole part of his former life were blanked out
from his memory. He did read some of the books the abbot
suggested—works on contemplation by John of the Cross,
Theresa of Avila, and others—but most of his spiritual
reading time was devoted to the Bible.

While reading a passage from the Book of Revelation
after vigils one cool summer morning, he heard a knock at
the door.

The abbot entered. "James, forgive my disturbing you,
but I wanted to prepare you for an announcement I shall
make at mass this morning. I shall ask the brethren to give
thanks that good has triumphed and the suffering peoples
of the East have been rescued from evil."

Ryan looked up, perplexed.

The abbot sat on Ryan's bed, rested each arm in the opposite wide sleeve of his habit, and said, "Earlier this week
a coup took place in the Soviet Union. The Soviet President was deposed and evil men from the Communist
Party, the KGB, and the Army took over."

Ryan reached for the Bible.

"But," said the abbot, "the people rose up against them.

The rightful government has been restored and the Communist Party has been outlawed."

When the abbot had left, Ryan didn't move. The outside world was breaching a dam in his mind and threatening to engulf him. He opened his missal to prepare for mass. Today was the Feast of the Immaculate Heart of Mary. It was the feast day instituted by Pope Pius XII to fulfill a request made by the Mother of God at Fatima. It was the feast day on which the faithful of Ukraine had reclaimed St. George's Cathedral in Lvov. And now it was the feast day on which the Russian people had risen up against evil. He sank to his knees. The Mother of God had defeated Communism, just as she had promised at Fatima! Tears of joy rolled down his face.

Kirillin's joy lasted a week.

In that week Major Steltsov took care to be as accommodating as possible, even letting him see copies of *Izvestia*. It seemed that Steltsov, too, expected his imminent release. It was surely only a matter of time, once the President had dealt with the urgent matters arising from the attempted coup.

But no word came from Moscow.

The copies of *Izvestia* dried up. Major Steltsov apologized: his orders hadn't changed. As the leaves of the birch trees yellowed and fell floating to the ground, and the frosts of morning and evening deepened and spread chilling fingers to touch at midday, Kirillin's spirits sank. At least before the attempted coup he knew precisely what game he was playing, but now nothing was certain. Nuances of behavior unsettled him. Steltsov stopped addressing him as "comrade." Tatiana said nothing, but gripped him tightly. Ivan Sedov was no longer a rock of imperturbability, his eyes darted from Steltsov to Kirillin as though he, too, were looking for a sign. Steltsov, however, was steadfast in his refusal to answer the one question that Kirillin asked daily: "Do you still take your orders from Babakin?"

"You know how it is, Dmitry Sergeyevich," he would shrug, "I receive my orders from my superior officer."

One day, as the bleak December weather threatened to extinguish the last vestiges of hope in Kirillin's breast, Steltsov came to his room. "Dmitry Sergeyevich, the President has resigned. The Soviet Union is no more."

Kirillin's mouth opened, but no words came forth. "But . . ." he finally stuttered.

"We are now subordinate to the President of Russia," Steltsov said. "I hope orders for your release will come soon."

Kirillin's concern for the President was overtaken by hope. That night he sat at his desk and began the first of several drafts of a letter to the Russian President. But as he wrote, a disturbing thought gnawed away at his mind. In those copies of *Izvestia* that Steltsov had let him see, the list of putschists had not included the name Lev Stepanovich Babakin.

Ryan's joy knew no bounds. His faith was reaffirmed. He asked the abbot if he might join the community. The abbot embraced him, but counseled that he should pray and reflect before formally applying to take monastic vows.

Ryan redoubled his work, his prayers, and his spiritual reading through Advent. On Christmas Day the community assembled in the abbey church to concelebrate mass. In his sermon the abbot said that their prayers in preparation for one of the greatest feast days in the Christian calendar, commemorating the day on which God became man in order to redeem the world from sin, had been rewarded. He had just received special tidings of great joy: the atheistic Soviet Union was no more; this very day the hammer and sickle had been lowered and the flag of Holy Russia had been raised above the Kremlin.

For Ryan it was a sign from God. He knew what he must do. After the Nativity mass the community went to the refectory for a special dinner, one of the three days in the year (Easter Sunday and the Feast of Saint Benedict were the other two) when the abbot served them wine. Ryan left his wine untouched. His mind was focused on the interview he sought with the abbot.

The bright blue eyes in the old man's lined face twinkled. "I know why you have asked to see me, my son. You wish to join our community."

Ryan smiled at the wisdom of this man he called Father, sitting behind the small desk in his study that was simply the room next to his bedroom, as austere as Ryan's room except for the clutter of papers and the old steel filing cabinet and the crude bookshelves that lined the walls.

"But," cautioned the abbot, "before you ask, let me say that until now you have had little choice. That situation may soon change." His face creased into a smile. "I have a Christmas present for you. I've been so pleased with your progress here that the authorities have finally agreed to let you receive communications from the world outside. You understand that this is the first step to their agreeing to your release from this period of contemplation and prayer."

Ryan frowned.

The abbot rose, opened the filing cabinet, and took out a file. From the file he removed an unopened letter and handed it to Ryan.

Ryan looked at the blue envelope. The postage stamps were strange, neither Italian nor English. He looked more closely. They were Polish. He slit open the envelope and saw the printed address: *ul Cysterow 15, 80-330 Gdansk-Oliwa, Polska,* and below it, written in misspelt Italian:

> My dear James
>
> I was very sorry to hear of your illness and your sudden departure from our little home in the Apostolic Palace. I wanted to visit you, but I was told this would not be helpful until you recover.
>
> Now I am told that you are much better and I am asking if I can visit you. We have much to celebrate!

Thanks to the Virgin of Fatima, and your brave mission, Ukraine is at last free and independent, and—praise be to her Immaculate Heart!—the First Beast of the Apocalypse, Godless Communism, has been defeated.

I don't know when a visit will be possible. Two weeks after your departure I was told that I was to be made Bishop of Gdansk. I didn't want to leave the Holy Father, but he said that he was determined to reward me for my services. When I protested that I wanted no reward, he said that sending me to Gdansk would be the clearest sign of his personal support for a people who are experiencing very difficult times. What choice do we have? With our vow of obedience, none at all. My only consolation is that the Holy Father is in the capable hands of Archbishop Korchan.

Till we meet again, I shall pray for you as I hope you pray for me.

+ Kasamir Hoffman

Ryan stared blankly at the letter.

"James," said the abbot, "before you finally decide to take our solemn vows, I think we should first obtain your release from here. After you've spent a few months in the world outside, if you still wish to join our little community we shall know that the decision is one of your own free will and we shall be overjoyed to receive you."

Ryan barely heard the abbot's voice. The last sentence of Kasamir Hoffman's letter—about the Pope being in the capable hands of Archbishop Korchan—had wormed its way into his mind and would not stay still.

Kirillin never received an answer to the letters he wrote to the President of Russia. At first he asked, then he pleaded, but Major Steltsov simply repeated that he had received no communications from the President's office, nor any change of orders. He hinted that he was happy he still had a secure job, and urged Kirillin to count his blessings: he was living a life that was the envy of most people in Russia. Kirillin, however, wasn't sure how much longer he could bear this isolation, however luxurious. He craved news, and particularly he craved news about Babakin.

One Monday morning he heard an unexpected knock at his door. He tensed. Tatiana sneaked in. He relaxed. She had been on weekend leave and he'd missed her.

"Has Mitya been a good boy while I've been away?" she pouted.

"What choice do I have?" he sighed.

"If Mitya has been a good boy, then he can have a present," she said as she teased off her coat and turned her back to him. "Help me off with my dress."

Sex at this time of day was an unexpected bonus. Her short dress clung to each hand-sized buttock. He reached for the zipper, pulled it down, and saw a copy of *Izvestia* behind her bra strap.

"I said Mitya could have a present."

He pulled the newspaper out from behind the strap and saw a photograph of Babakin on the front page. Kirillin's shaking fingers tried to hold the paper still while he read the main news story, headlined NEW SECURITY CHIEF APPOINTED.

> The President has appointed Lev Stepanovich Babakin to head the National Security Council, a body he has established to coordinate the work of the armed forces, the Interior Ministry, and the Security Ministry.
>
> The President has been attacked repeatedly for his failure to combat lawlessness and organized crime in the cities, armed nationalist gangs operating in the Russian Federation's autonomous republics of Chechen-Ingushetia, Tatarstan, and Yakutia, and the persecution of ethnic Russians living in the former Soviet republics. The Council is the President's response to mounting criticisms of a lack of decisive leadership: it will be answerable neither to parliament nor to government. Although the Council is

under the President's nominal control, the man vested with personal authority to ensure that all government ministries obey its decrees is Lev Babakin.

Babakin seems ideally suited for the job. He was born in 1935 in Vladivostok to parents who were devout Orthodox believers. He spent most of his career in the diplomatic and foreign intelligence services, and is thus untainted by the brutality and suppression of freedom exercised by the domestic arm of the KGB. Nothing was heard of him at the time of the abortive coup of August 1991, but Babakin later emerged as one of the key figures in the KGB leadership who supported democratic change. It is believed he was personally responsible for transforming the KGB into the Ministry of Security and opening it up to public scrutiny.

In a rare interview he explained his philosophy to *Izvestia*. "The era of repression and lawlessness by the security services is over. The only people who need fear us are criminal elements whose activities threaten the well-being of the Russian people." He identified three classes of criminals who were targets for the security services: first, corrupt government officials who live off the backs of honest citizens; second, perpetrators of organized crime, most especially those dealing in drugs, who threaten the moral health of the nation; and third, armed gangs who masquerade as nationalists and seek to bring Russia to her knees.

Recently a special anti-drugs squad was involved in a shootout with a notorious drugs gang whose leader, Ivan Gorbatko, was killed in the exchange of gunfire. Babakin said he regretted not being able to bring the criminal Gorbatko to trial, but he wasted no tears on the removal of a cancer from the Russian people.

While public attention has been centered on the battle between the young radical economic reformers in the government and the more conservative representatives of the armed forces, the military-industrial complex, and state-owned enterprises, Babakin has quietly been consolidating his power base. With the armed services now effectively answerable to his National Security Council, Lev Babakin has emerged as the second most powerful man in Russia.

Kirillin took the glass that Tatiana handed him. He was never seen sober from that day on.

Ryan tried hard, but he failed to recapture the serenity he had experienced at the monastery prior to reading Hoffman's letter. Now he prayed with particular fervency for the Holy Father. On Sunday afternoons, the monks' half day of recreation, he prayed in his room.

On one such Sunday afternoon the abbot knocked and entered. "James, it troubles me that you no longer go for walks in the grounds on a beautiful day like this."

"I'm fine, Father," Ryan said.

"I do hope so. To cheer you up, I've had an English-language magazine sent here from Rome." The abbot smiled encouragingly. "It contains an article that I know is close to your heart."

The abbot placed a copy of *Time* magazine on Ryan's table. "It's a week out of date, I'm afraid, but if you feel it will help you prepare for rejoining the world outside I shall have the magazine sent here regularly."

It was fully fifteen minutes after the abbot had left before Ryan opened the magazine. He found the story on page 4, headed POPE'S TRIUMPHANT JOURNEY. Slowly he began to read.

On Wednesday the Pope began his historic five-day visit to the former Soviet Union, for over seventy years the world's most virulently anti-Christian state, when the Alitalia plane bearing the papal insignia of the crossed keys of Saint Peter touched down at Vilnius Airport in Lithuania.

The Pope was greeted by the Lithuanian President in a welcome normally reserved for the head of state of a major world power. Crowds lining the route from the airport to the center of the Lithuanian capital were never less than ten deep, cheering and waving yellow-and-white papal flags. The Pope, sitting in an open-topped white jeep, blessed the faithful of this Baltic republic, 80 percent of whose 3.6 million people are Catholic.

At least a quarter of a million packed the historic square below the old Gedimas Castle in the center of Vilnius, singing hymns and waving the yellow, green, and red flags of independent Lithuania alongside papal flags. It took the popemobile ten minutes to cross the square to Vilnius Cathedral, reconsecrated by the Church in 1989 after forty years' use by the Communist authorities as an art gallery.

On a temporary altar erected in front of the six pillars of the cathedral's classical portico, the Pope concelebrated mass with Lithuania's cardinal and six diocesan bishops, and spoke of the Christian heritage that united all the peoples of Europe.

The following day he celebrated mass in the Latvian capital of Riga, and spent half a day at the seminary there, exhorting the students to remain faithful to the authentic teaching of the Church.

But even this rapturous welcome in the Baltic republics could not have prepared him for the sight that met his eyes on Friday in the western Ukrainian city of Lviv, heartland of a Ukrainian Byzantine Rite Catholic Church banned for forty-four years. The Pope's jeep was showered with so many flowers on its journey from the airport that several times his private secretary had to offload the tulips and daffodils to prevent the Pope from being submerged.

The authorities estimated the crowds, which packed the surrounding streets as well as Ivan Franko Park where the Pope held an open air mass, to be more than half a million. As the Pope stood at the microphone to give his homily, broadcast live on television, he was visibly moved by the sight of so many people of all generations carrying icons and banners and candles and placards with religious slogans like "God Bless Our Pope," "Faith of Our Fathers" and "True to Rome till Death!" mixed with overtly nationalist ones reading "Church and Nation Are One" and "Only a Catholic Ukraine is a Free Ukraine."

Speaking in Ukrainian, the Pope developed his theme of the previous two days. He exhorted Ukrainians to see themselves first as Christians and second as Europeans. He said their faith had been steeled by the fire of persecution and was strong enough to rise above ancient enmities and embrace in a spirit of reconciliation and Christian charity other Christians who, by historical accident, had been separated from them. They now had a unique opportunity, not to separate themselves from other branches of the Slav people, but to work for the re-Christianization of all the descendants of Saint Vladimir's kingdom.

To reinforce his message, his first stop in the Ukrainian capital of Kiev was a visit to the Ukrainian Orthodox Patriarch Konstantin, who has been a strong opponent of the Ukrainian Catholic Church.

The Pope showed signs of fatigue during his trip and had to be helped several times by the Vatican Pro-Secretary of State, Archbishop Korchan. On Friday night he rested at a former Communist Party villa in the *Lipki* district of Kiev. He completes his trip with two days in Moscow, the schedule for which has been shrouded in mystery. The only comment made by Vatican spokesman Father Frawley was, "You ain't seen nothing yet!"

Ryan looked at the date on the cover of the magazine. The Pope's visit had ended in Moscow a week ago.

Ryan found the week's wait for the next copy of *Time* almost too much to bear.

He withdrew even more into his shell. He attended the

seven holy offices each day, but excused himself from work and from most meals. He fasted and, instead of seeing to the abbey farm or the repairs, he studied the Bible and tried to pray. But his prayers were sterile: he was asking God to intercede in an event that had already taken place. The sheer futility of such prayer depressed him; he was no longer praying in the proper sense of the word, merely mouthing words stripped of efficacy. It was as though Christ on the cross were crying out in reproach: However much you try and pray, you're too late. He didn't feel able to take communion on Sunday—how can you invite Christ into a temple of despair?

The abbot came into his room after lunch. "Are you feeling all right, James?"

He nodded.

"You weren't at lunch again today."

"I'm fasting, Father." His eyes were fixed on the brightly colored roll of magazine in the abbot's hand.

"Are you sure you wish to read this, James?"

He nodded. "Yes, Father."

"In which case, may I sit with you? I have some catching up to do with *L'Osservatore Romano.*"

It was a transparent excuse, but Ryan didn't care. His eyes were staring at the front cover of *Time.* It showed a photograph of Korchan, in crimson cassock, kneeling before the Pope in a packed cathedral. The headline announced: POPE CAPS RUSSIAN VISIT WITH HISTORIC UNITY GESTURE.

With a chilling presentiment Ryan read the lead story.

> In a ceremony unprecedented in the annals of the Roman Catholic Church, the Pope last Sunday bestowed a cardinal's hat on Archbishop Alexander Korchan, the Ukrainian-born Vatican prelate, in the Russian Orthodox Cathedral of the Assumption within the walls of the Kremlin.
>
> No one is more aware of the power of symbolism among the Slav peoples than this Pope. The full

meaning and implications of this act are only now being analyzed in the West.

This is not the first time a pope has created a cardinal outside a consistory in the Vatican, but it is the first time a pope has performed such a ceremony in a non-Catholic cathedral in a country which, until recently, was officially atheist.

The colorful fifteenth-century Assumption Cathedral is the largest and most historic of the Kremlin cathedrals. It was here that Grand Princes and Czars were crowned and Patriarchs were enthroned, and where important proclamations of state were made, including the deed of reunification of Ukraine with Russia in 1654.

Rows of chairs had been brought in to seat the distinguished guests. On the right-hand side, behind the Patriarch's throne, were arrayed religious leaders, who included the Holy Synod of the Russian Orthodox Church plus Ukrainian Orthodox Patriarch Konstantin, Catholicos Torkom of All the Armenians, and Catholicos Ilia III of All Georgia, together with the Catholic prelates Patriarch Chuprynka of the Ukrainian Catholic Church, Cardinal Tamkevicius of Lithuania, and Cardinal Cakuls of Latvia.

On the Cathedral's left, behind the throne of the Czaritsa, ranged the secular guests of honor, who included the six Catholic heads of government of the European Community together with Pierre Dubac, President of the European Commission, who comes from a long-established Catholic family. More remarkably, the front row was occupied by leading members of the Russian government, many of whom had been, until recently, committed Communists. Seated next to the President was the man who is now seen as the second most powerful man in Russia, security supremo Lev Babakin, who smiled benignly as Archbishop Korchan received the highest honor a pope can bestow on a member of the Catholic Church.

The Pope, looking frail and reading from a prepared text, stressed his theme of the unity of Europe, both spiritual and political. The momentous political changes begun in Eastern Europe in 1989, which had led to the downfall of atheistic Communism, had been due, he said, to a re-emergence of spiritual forces which were "the heritage of the common European home that stretches from the Atlantic to the Urals." The danger to world peace came no longer from a conflict between Western and Eastern Europe, but from a conflict between rich and poor. This conflict was being exacerbated by a rise in secularist materialism among the rich. It was here that the deep spirituality of the Slav peoples had a "vital contribution to play in Europe in combating this selfish, divisive, Godless philosophy that is the work of the Devil and his agents." Only by uniting could the Eastern and Western Churches combat this pernicious evil, and spread the gospel message of brotherly love and the sharing of God-given natural resources. Only by uniting in a confederation of equal, sovereign states could the eastern and western halves of Europe achieve stability and show the world that the way to save the planet was through cooperation and not conflict.

He regretted that he was not yet able to celebrate mass together with his Russian Orthodox brethren. But, he added, the day was drawing close when all Russians, while retaining their distinctive rites and rituals, would reestablish communion with the See of Peter, first of the Apostles. When that glorious day dawned the Russian Patriarch would concelebrate a mass with his compatriot, Cardinal Korchan, to rededicate his country to the Immaculate Heart of the Blessed Virgin Mary in communion with all the world's bishops, thereby guaranteeing peace in the world as promised by Our Lady at Fatima. This, truly, he said, would be a fitting celebration of a thousand years of Christianity in Russia.

RUSSIA TO JOIN EC?

It is only on occasions like state funerals that so many heads of government gather together informally. In a sense this is a funeral, the burial of enmity between Eastern and Western Europe. And, as at state funerals, these European leaders will certainly have taken the opportunity for informal discussions.

It is believed that a formal application by Russia for associate membership of the European Community will be made in the near future. Sources close to Pierre Dubac indicate that, in the current climate of pan-European cooperation, the application will be favorably received. Such a step, which will involve the reduction of many barriers to the interchange of trade and technology, is likely to lead to full membership. If this did happen, Russia would be the largest state in what looks set to develop into a United States of Europe.

NEXT POPE?

It is taken for granted in Vatican circles that the Pope will appoint the newly created cardinal, Alexander Korchan, as his Secretary of State. Archbishop Korchan has been Acting Secretary of State since the sudden death of Cardinal Fasolo, tipped by many as a future pope.

When details of Sunday's unprecedented ceremony were released in Rome, rumors became rife in this city which thrives on rumor. Opinion is hardening here that the Pope, who has appeared frail in recent months, will retire once he is confident that Cardinal Korchan is elected his successor. Certainly Sunday's ceremony leaves no doubt whom the Pope sees as his heir and, with the deaths of Cardinals Fasolo and Davino, coupled with the retirements of Cardinals Zingler and Demeure, it is difficult to see any other strong candidates for Saint Peter's throne.

The Russian Orthodox Patriarch Ioann is also expected to retire soon, which would pave the way for his successor to bring the 60-million-strong Russian Orthodox Church into communion with the Catholic Church, presenting the intriguing possibility that the new Russian Patriarch will accept the supremacy of a Ukrainian-born pope, Alexander Korchan.

If events took this course, as appears increasingly possible, Pope Korchan would lead an almost billion-strong Church that would not only dominate Europe "from the Atlantic to the Urals," but would also be a major force in Central and Southern America and be the largest Church in the USA.

Father James Ryan let the magazine slip from his hands. He dropped to his knees, held his arms out wide like the crucified Christ, and let forth an unearthly cry of anguish.

The abbot looked on in horror. "James, James, what's the matter?"

"After the thousand years are over, Satan shall be let loose from his prison, and he will go out to deceive the nations scattered over the whole world," Ryan wailed.

The noise brought a novice to the door.

"Bring Father Thomas, quickly," the abbot ordered.

"James," the abbot soothed, "you're safe here. Tell me what's troubling you."

Ryan looked up with unseeing eyes. His voice possessed a dreadful certainty. *"The day cannot come before the final rebellion takes place, when wickedness will be revealed in human form, the man doomed to destruction. He is the ad-*

*versary who raises himself up against every so-called god
or object of worship, and even enthrones himself in God's
temple, claiming to be God."*

Father Thomas arrived with his medical bag. He looked
at Ryan and then at the abbot.

"Oh dear," the abbot whispered. "The authorities did
warn me that he might suffer a relapse. Rome is right, as
always."

JOHN HANDS is a writer, lecturer and consultant. *Perestroika Christi* is his first novel. His researches took him to Rome, the Ukraine and Russia. His articles on the Vatican and the Soviet Union have been published in national weekly newspapers and magazines. John Hands lives in London and is now working on a new novel.

MORE THAN FRIENDS
Barbara Delinsky
The Maxwells and the Popes are two families whose lives are interwoven like the threads of a beautiful, yet ultimately delicate, tapestry. When their idyllic lives are unexpectedly shattered by one event, their faith in each other — and in themselves — is put to the supreme test.

"Intriguing women's fiction." — *Publishers Weekly*

CITY OF GOLD
Len Deighton
Amid the turmoil of World War II, Rommel's forces in Egypt relentlessly advance across the Sahara aided by ready access to Allied intelligence. Sent to Cairo on special assignment, Captain Bert Cutler's mission is formidable: whatever the risk, whatever the cost, he must catch Rommel's spy.

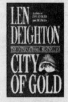

"Wonderful." — *Seattle Times/Post-Intelligencer*

DEATH PENALTY
William J. Coughlin
Former hot-shot attorney Charley Sloan gets a chance to resurrect his career with the case of a lifetime — an extortion scam that implicates his life-long mentor, a respected judge.

Battling against inner demons and corrupt associates, Sloan's quest for the truth climaxes in one dramatic showdown of justice.

"Superb!"
— *The Detroit News*